WRITTEN ON THE DARK

GUY GAVRIEL KAY

Ace
New York

ACE

Published by Berkley

An imprint of Penguin Random House LLC

1745 Broadway, New York, NY 10019

penguinrandomhouse.com

Excerpt from "October" from *Poems 1962–2012* by Louise Glück copyright © 2012 by Louise Glück. Reprinted by permission of Farrar, Straus and Giroux. All Rights Reserved.

"Voices" from *C. P. Cavafy: Collected Poems* by C. P. Cavafy, translated by Daniel Mendelsohn, translation copyright © 2009 by Daniel Mendelsohn. Used by permission of Alfred A. Knopf, an imprint of the Knopf Doubleday Publishing Group, a division of Penguin Random House LLC. All rights reserved.

Map copyright © 2025 by Martin Springett

Book design by Lisa Jager

Typeset by Daniella Zanchetta

Interior images: horse and rider © Dariusz Kopestynski /
Adobe Stock, ornaments © Rawpixel.com / Adobe Stock

Cover design by Lisa Jager

Cover images: village © ac productions, bridge © craig fordham, horse © WorldWideImages, all Getty Images; moon © Daria, clouds © evannovostro, ornaments © Rawpixel.com, all Adobe Stock

Library of Congress Cataloging-in-Publication Data

Names: Kay, Guy Gavriel, author.
Title: Written on the dark / Guy Gavriel Kay.
Description: New York : Ace, 2025.
Identifiers: LCCN 2025006004 (print) | LCCN 2025006005 (ebook) |
ISBN 9780593953983 (hardcover) | ISBN 9780593954027 (ebook)
Subjects: LCGFT: Fantasy fiction. | Novels.
Classification: LCC PR9199.3.K39 W75 2025 (print) | LCC PR9199.3.K39 (ebook) |
DDC 813/.54--dc23/eng/20250211
LC record available at https://lccn.loc.gov/2025006004
LC ebook record available at https://lccn.loc.gov/2025006005

Printed in the United States of America
1st Printing

The authorized representative in the EU for product safety and compliance is
Penguin Random House Ireland, Morrison Chambers, 32 Nassau Street,
Dublin D02 YH68, Ireland, https://eu-contact.penguin.ie.

For Laura, Sam, Matthew

With very great love, and an enduring awareness
that what I write, what I can shape in these stories,
is because of them, because it is for them.

Imagined voices, and beloved, too,
of those who died, or of those who are
lost unto us like the dead.

Sometimes in our dreams they speak to us;
sometimes in its thought the mind will hear them.

And with their sound for a moment there return
sounds from the first poetry of our life—
like music, in the night, far off, that fades away.

—CONSTANTINE CAVAFY
Translated by Daniel Mendelsohn

What will you do,
when it is your turn in the field
with the god?

—LOUISE GLÜCK

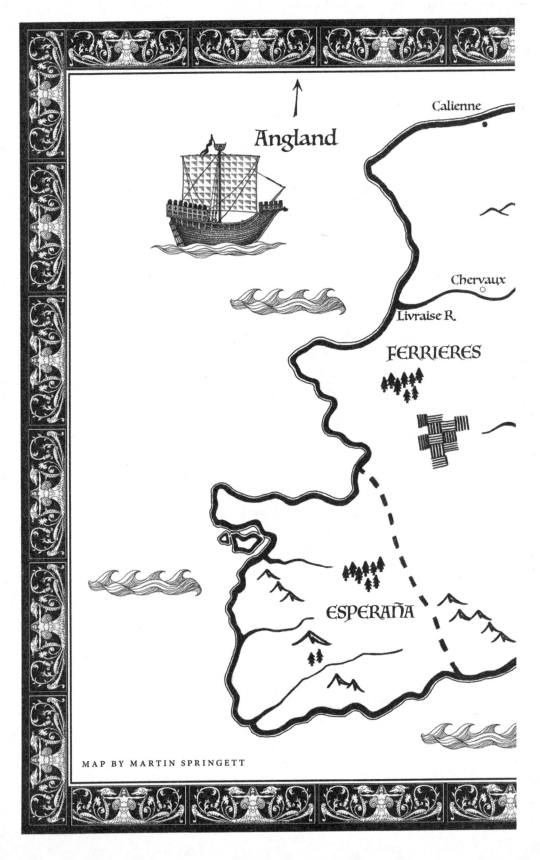

Calienne

Angland

Chervaux

Livraise R.

FERRIERES

ESPERAÑA

MAP BY MARTIN SPRINGETT

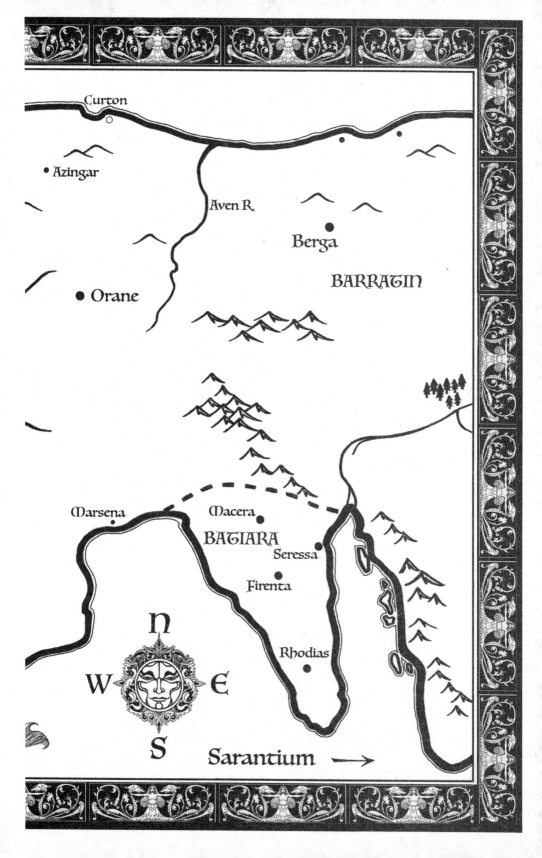

CHARACTERS

(a partial list)

Thierry Villar, a poet of Orane
Adelie, his mother
Ambroise Villar, a cleric, his adoptive father
Silvy Gautier, his friend, in The Lamb Tavern
Eudes, owner and proprietor of The Lamb
Anni, employed at The Lamb
Jolis de Charette, once a lover of Thierry

King Roch of Ferrieres, "the mad King"
Bianca di Rizzetto, his queen, from Batiara
Girald, their young son, the royal heir
Rollin, Duke de Montereau, the king's brother and principal
    adviser, acting as regent when King Roch is unwell
Bettina, his wife
Duke de Barille ⎫
                ⎬ the king's uncles and advisers
Duke de Regnault ⎭
Laurent ("the Bold"), Duke de Barratin, a royal cousin,
    also an adviser
Arnoul and Guiart, his sons
Count Burkard van Aribert, Barratin's principal adviser

⚜

Robbin de Vaux, the king's provost in Orane
Medor Colle, his senior serjeant
Gauvard Colle, Medor's uncle, acquainted with the half-world
Aubrey, another senior serjeant
Claquin Guiene, one of Montereau's private guards
Corbez Barthelmy, once a soldier
Lambert Maar, a thief

⚜

Marina di Seressa, also a poet, living near the Livraise River,
　　often at the court
Clare, her mother
Alaina d'Arceval, her neighbour in the countryside

⚜

Le Futrier, proprietor of The Fife Tavern
Fermin Lessieur, a (bad) poet there
Branco Merlant, proprietor of The Needle Tavern

⚜

Denis Cassin, a lawyer and academic at the university
Hutin Peyre, high cleric of Orane
Vicomte Fermin de Mardol, an aristocrat

❧

Jeanette, a young woman from the village of Broché
Peire and Eran, her brothers
Lysbet Guerin, a young woman from the hamlet of Cassaude

❧

Bascot de Thunier, a minor lord near the Livraise River
Mercier, high cleric of Aurage, residing nearby
Rogier, an innkeeper in a village by the Livraise

❧

High Patriarch Tessio, in Rhodias
High cleric Viotti di Virenza, also in Rhodias
Claus van Leyland, an artist from Barratin, working in Rhodias

❧

King Hardan V of the Anglcyn, at war with Ferrieres

PART I

CHAPTER I

The deepest part of the night in the most savage winter of the coldest year anyone could remember.

So he thought, hearing the middle-of-night bells that meant he needed to get up—to go outside, right now. Into the city. Into the ice, in the blackness.

He didn't want to. Why would anyone in their right mind want to? Were there enough coins to steal to make it worth going out into the streets now?

Evidently, yes. Because they were going to try. Not so many coins but . . . enough?

He was lying alone in Silvy's bed. Silvy had gone upstairs to Anni and Eudes's room, carrying the candle. He had no light here. She had let him stay in her room, however. She knew why he'd wanted to sleep away from his mother's house tonight. She didn't ask questions, didn't force him not to answer, or lie. Silvy was his most trusted friend, possibly his only trusted friend (he didn't want to think too much about that, just now). They'd agreed some time ago not to bed each other. Probably wise. Most of the time he thought so. It protected the friendship.

He'd already been awake when the night's third bells sounded from the sanctuaries. He'd counted them. He tended to awaken too early when he had a thing to do, a place to go in the dark, or at dawn. A lifelong fear of being late, oversleeping. He didn't sleep well, in any case. Often lay in bed (at home, in a tavern bed with a girl) work-ing up a poem. Lines in the dark. He was a man who shaped lines in the dark. He'd rise and light a candle at the embers of a fire to scribble by. That defined him, he thought. It would do as well as anything else to define him.

He was still young, of course. He might grow into something dif-ferent, someone different. You weren't the same through the whole of your life, were you? Not marked by one thing. If you lived long enough to change, of course.

Thierry Villar didn't expect to live a long life. In this city, in this time, it was a reasonable way to feel. So he thought, anyway. Perhaps he might be modestly famous before he died? Not just known in a few taverns here in Orane. Known, and sometimes hated. His verses could be harsh, and he named names. Sometimes names of people who were, well, famous. And not happy with what he wrote about them. He took chances that way. Didn't you do that for your art? For some reason the thought amused him, even though nothing was really amusing in this cold.

His poems, their mockery, drew raucous laughter in the taverns and had earned him drinking and dicing companions. And sometimes the company of women afterwards. Worthwhile, accordingly. He was young enough to judge things that way.

It really was time to get out of bed. He had some distance to cover, after curfew, through streets where the ice lay in places as a coating over manure and refuse.

But it *was* smart to have established his presence over at The Mule earlier this evening and then to sleep here tonight. Eudes had served him two cups of wine downstairs and Thierry had played dice for a bit, low stakes. He had no money to lose. Eudes would remember, would say as much: *"Thierry Villar? Yes, was here drinking with some students, why?"*

It was Jad-cursed cold outside. It was cold *inside*. It could make a man mad, or kill him. People died in a winter like this. There were wolves in the city. They slipped through the walls, crossed the frozen river, roamed the darkness, starving, bold. You didn't want to encounter starving wolves in the night.

The god was supposed to battle demons on behalf of mortal men and women in the black cold beneath the world now. That was probably a lot like this, Villar thought. Heresy! His mother and stepfather were deeply pious. He was . . . less so. He didn't know what his father had been like. Had been too young when Rochon Larraigne had died of a fall and mother and child had come to Orane the way so many did, desperate for food and shelter. Seeking a way to survive while poverty stalked the world.

They'd been lucky. Protected by the god, his mother would say. Had said. He had an education, a life of some security ahead if he wanted it. And yet here he was, about to dress and go outside to rob a holy place. Folly and need. Someone might say greed, but he'd stay with *need*, thank you. When you gambled at dice or cards and lost to certain people, you really did need to pay them back. And he'd long ago spent what money he'd ever had on a woman. The wrong woman entirely.

He was halfway dressed already, lying in bed. Ridiculous, but necessary. He pushed aside the three blankets Silvy had (Jad bless her forever) and pulled on and belted his trousers over leggings. The trousers were stiff, half-frozen. Of course. He swore. A second pair of socks over the ones he already wore, then a second ice-cold woollen shirt over his tunic. He pulled on his boots with difficulty, swearing at them, too, at himself, at the Jad-cursed world.

Not at the city, mind you. He loved Orane too much.

"I hate how much I love this city," he'd even said to Silvy once. Said it to others too, but she was the one who'd told him it was an odd thought, and asked him why. It was the way she was. She asked questions.

They'd been in the tavern downstairs, he remembered. He'd just recited a new poem, received coins and drinks for it. And laughter. He chased laughter, Villar thought. Always had. Needed it.

In the inns and taverns he was quick with his words, was known (feared) for it. But that time he'd thought for a bit before answering her. "Because if you love something too much, you can be destroyed if you lose it," he'd said, eventually.

She'd left it at that. She knew Jolis de Charette, too. Of course she did. Had even warned him about her. Silvy had an annoying habit of being right about things.

No time for that thought, either, just now. He needed money. He needed to do a thing tonight.

Villar found his cloth cap on a post at the end of the bed. Pulled over his ears, it made him look like an outlaw. One of the Jacquards, with their secret language and safe houses dotting the countryside, with door-knock sequences you needed to know to be admitted, not killed, and then coded phrases to speak. He even knew some of those, from a late-night conversation with a man who'd had too much to drink once.

He didn't know the countryside at all. He didn't like the country-side. He was a city person. This city. Which he loved. Too much.

It was holy for him, really, for all the violence and danger within it. For all that he hadn't been born here. Orane was what he knew of the world, really.

Holy for him. He laughed at himself. He was about to take part in the robbery of a genuinely holy place. The cloth cap of an outlaw suited.

Moving cautiously in the utterly black room, trying to stay quiet, he retrieved his patched-up coat, pulled it on. Dark outside, dark in here. Dark in his heart? Not really, Thierry Villar thought. He just had needs. And perhaps one of those, beyond the fact of poverty and a dangerous debt, was for adventures such as this, with people such as the ones he was headed out to meet.

Of course calling it an *adventure* was to avoid certain questions. Silvy, if she'd been here and listening to him, if he'd been speaking aloud, which he might have been doing if she'd been here, might have said as much.

But she was upstairs. With Anni and Eudes. Warm in a wide bed.

He swore again. Opened the door and went out. Closed it softly behind him. Went down the stairs.

⚜

The tavern called The Lamb was, predictably, known for its mutton, when it could be obtained. There was a large door at the front, with the signboard over it. It would not reopen for some hours yet.

Robbin de Vaux, the king's provost in Orane—the mad king's provost—sat astride his horse, shivering. They heard the last of the three bells ring and fade away. They'd been waiting for some time, but he expected a door to open now.

Not the main door. The small, half-hidden one, recessed, to the side, that led to stairs and the private rooms The Lamb rented by the year, the month, or the hour sometimes.

The hooves of their horses had cracked the ice of the roadway as they stamped in the cold. The smell of the street came to de Vaux. People threw their refuse from upper-floor windows. Frozen dung and piss from pots and everything else one could hurl from a window. It was not one of the best neighbourhoods of Orane's south bank, though hardly the worst.

There were no moons right now. That would have been planned, by the small-scale thieves and by the possibly much more important men whose reported deed had driven him from his bed tonight.

De Vaux had had years of war against the invading Anglcyn, or fighting outlaw bands, rebels against the crown, or disbanded soldiers who chose a different, unlawful life. He had known hardship, cold nights, savagery, wounds, fear.

He was more frightened right now than he could ever remember being.

And he could not have entirely explained why he had asked certain questions of his senior serjeant and come here to The Lamb, after being summoned to view a dead body on the other side of the river. An . . . identified dead body. A named one.

Was it instinct? Something else?

There was an extremely good chance that, come morning, when word of this death got out—he could only hold it back for so long—

the city and much of the country would explode into violence. Possibly civil war. Depending.

Depending on a thing he *really* didn't want to think about.

A sound. Soft, but he'd been listening for it. The small door opened. Precisely when he'd thought it might. A minor pleasure, of a sort, to have anticipated so well. A man, a shadow in blackness, stepped out.

"Torches," de Vaux said quietly, and three were lit behind him from a single carried flame.

Villar knew he had a reputation for swearing. Invective worth remembering, and reusing with laughter. He didn't mind that, though he knew that some of his own most quoted phrases he himself had taken from others, if modified sometimes. He *was* a poet, after all, he worked hard on his words.

Right now, standing outside The Lamb, he was shocked speechless when torches flared and he saw mounted men. Men waiting for him. Which last he knew because the one at the front said, calmly, "You can run, or go back inside, but we know you are here, and why, Villar, and we also know where your mother and stepfather live. And . . . Lambert Maar has already talked."

They knew these things? They knew his name? And he, in turn, knew this voice. It shocked him even more. He cleared his throat, his mind whirling in helpless circles. He managed to say, "Lambert Maar, my lord?"

"Don't bother trying, Thierry," said Robbin de Vaux, his majesty's provost, astride a horse in a vicious night, here waiting for him. For him? It made no sense! "He really has talked. Was careless in a tavern, someone reported it. I had him picked up. He's a careless man, isn't he?"

Fucking, fucking, *fucking* Lambert! Villar would have liked to have profanity equal to this moment.

He cleared his throat. "He is, yes. I've met the man. But you are not careless by reputation, my lord, and I have no idea why the royal provost himself would be here waiting for me at this hour, for something so . . . small?"

It was worth trying. What else did he have?

"Robbing a sanctuary of the god isn't *so* small, but we'll leave that for the moment, it is a fair observation." The provost's voice, which he'd heard many times, including at the gallows before an execution, was deep, memorable.

It was also, Villar realized, strained, tight, tense right now. Villar had no idea why. He had no idea about *any* of this. There were at least half a dozen horsemen behind the provost. Probably more, the three torches didn't cast their light very far.

"I have robbed nothing, done nothing," he said. He tried to sound confident. He failed. Why was there a fraying in the other man's voice? And why was he *here*?

"You will doubtless wish to know why I am here," said de Vaux.

His reputation was complex. Fair, usually, but a hard man, and too clever by half for the underworld of Orane. Two decades of warfare, mostly in the north but not only, before taking up his position here five years ago. Owned a large city home, had a large annual salary. It was an easier life than battling all over the country for the king and royal council, especially if you were no longer young.

"Of course I want to know," said Villar, looking up at the big man lit by torches.

He realized he was shivering. So many stars overhead on a clear night, like gems above the streets and houses, above the myriad stupidities of mortal men and women, with sunrise a long way off, still.

"I want to know that, and also," he added, taking a chance, but he was like that, "why you sound uneasy right now."

A silence. Too long a silence.

He'd had a good enough life, on the whole, Thierry Villar thought. Aside from too much poverty, and Jolis de Charette, curse her. People liked his verses, were amused when they were meant to be. And women liked him, too.

He heard laughter now, short, bitter, but laughter. Only from the one man, the provost himself. The others, however many were behind de Vaux, remained silent. They'd kill him at a word, Villar knew, perhaps take pleasure in it. Or not. Just another thief killed in a city they tried to control for the mad king.

"I sound uneasy because I am," de Vaux said. "It has to do with the reason I'm here."

Thierry said nothing. But something like hope began, like a stringed instrument plucked, inside him. At least a chance, from that answer, that he might not be on his way to a cell in the Châtelet to be tortured into a confession, and then taken to be hanged on Gallows Hill. He thought of his mother weeping for him there. Curse Lambert Maar forever, he thought—loose-lipped, sober and drunk. Stupid at all times.

"There is a horse for you," the provost of Orane said. "Mount up. Someone will help you. I'll explain as we ride. You're right, of course, I'm not out in this night with ten men to arrest a poet about to do something stupid."

Ten. And the provost knew he was a poet.

"I don't ride with any great—"

"I said someone would help you. You have two choices, Thierry Villar. You come with me, or we arrest you now and you are taken for interrogation. I like your stepfather, he's an honest cleric, a better man than you deserve, but he won't save you once you are with the questioners. Nor will your mother's pleas."

Bastard, thought Thierry. Had to mention his mother?

"I say these things," said de Vaux, "to make matters clear for you, and because I have little time. I need to know some things before sunrise."

Thierry blinked. There felt to be frost forming on his eyelids. An image for a poem? "And you expect *me* to know these things?"

"I do not, no. But I do need a clever man who is known in the taverns. Mount up, Villar. I won't offer again."

A clever retort came to his lips. He didn't speak it. You didn't have to say every witty thing you thought.

Also, they were not arresting him yet. And he was . . . Jad curse it, he was curious now. A vice, the key to his life and to his writing: curiosity. His life? A short life so far. He'd prefer it not end just yet. *I would like*, he thought, *to see spring again and be warm.*

"Someone lift me up, then," he said, "and in the god's name I hope the horse is gentle."

Silvy was a restless sleeper and thought she heard a jingling sound outside. Then she heard the bells, and then that same sound again after the third one.

She got out of bed and crossed to the window, two pairs of heavy stockings on her feet. Stood there and looked down. Eudes, who was good with tools, had contrived a way to hinge the shutters on this third floor so a part could be folded back on either side. There was no light, no one could see her, the watcher, the witness. Behind her, Anni and Eudes slept, Anni snoring softly, as she usually did. The cold was appalling, but she knew the bed would be warm went she went back.

There were horsemen in the street. She saw them when Thierry came out and torches were lit. She was very afraid then, and there was nothing at all she could do. She was so angry with him. Nothing to do about that, either. Should she have told him not to go? Would it have done any good at all? Did he ever listen?

Maybe sometimes. Once or twice.

Words were being exchanged below. From the way he stood, she knew Thierry was frightened. He'd be thinking of running; he'd know there was no way he could. He stood where he was and spoke to the men on horses. To one of them.

Then, after more words, Silvy at her window saw him mount up, with assistance, on a horse. It was entirely unexpected. She'd never seen him on a horse. She'd never been on one either. Had dreams of riding sometimes, galloping on a vast plain under both moons, going nowhere that she knew in the world, but going there very fast.

She watched the riders disappear up the street towards the river. A dozen or so men, three torches, her friend inexplicably among them. She wondered if she'd ever see him again. She didn't know who these men were. They had evidently been waiting for him at this impossible hour, for no reason she could even imagine.

Then the street was empty again, and black. Nothing to see. You could almost imagine you had dreamed the whole encounter.

Anger and fear wouldn't shelter you from this cold. Silvy went back to the bed, which was indeed warm with two bodies. She didn't sleep, was tangled too much in questions. At some point Anni woke in the dark, turned to her, and they made love quietly, carefully, so as not to wake Eudes, who would have to rise soon enough to open The Lamb, sweep it, start the fires. It didn't ease Silvy very much, the lovemaking, but Anni rolled over happily after and fell back asleep.

They were both friends of hers, for years now. Anni liked to push, to define. "Am I your closest friend?" she'd asked, more than once.

"Anni, I don't think that way. Really."

"Is Eudes? Is Thierry? It's Thierry, isn't it?"

"Anni. Stop."

Anni usually stopped. She was very sweet.

Silvy lay awake. She thought about the men and women who had been her lovers, how it was easier in the life she lived to be with a woman, be with Anni, really. She thought about the time she'd had to seek help, from a woman with rooms by the river, to deal with being with child—a child she couldn't possibly have. She thought about that often. The woman had been gentler than Silvy had expected, even kind. It had gone well, but Silvy had wept for days. Not regret. Sorrow. They weren't the same thing.

She had no idea what was happening outside tonight, with Thierry. She wished, even though she knew it was embedded heresy, that she had more of her mother's gift of the sight.

She slept, eventually. When she woke again, dawn was breaking on what would prove a dramatic and terrible day.

⚜

The winter would not last forever, even if it felt that way at times. Winters never did. And this frigid savagery was not a marker of how soon or late spring would arrive, with the ice in the river melting, buds on the trees of Orane, rainfall, flowers springing up, shops and their wares spilling into the streets again.

The city was harder to love in the dead of winter, easier when spring came. Very easy, in fact. It was a glory of the world, Orane. Fewer people than it had held before the worst years of the plague—which was why there were places with young trees and open meadows within the walls. But it was growing again. The sounds of construction would begin all over at first light, even in the cold: shops and homes being built—in some neighbourhoods they were the same thing. But also new sanctuaries and great, tall city mansions for the wealthy who needed to be in Orane because the mad king's court was still here.

Not everyone alive in that winter night, and the following day when chaos erupted, would live to see the flowers return, or the warmth of summer, or enjoy the fruits of the harvest that followed. But that is always so. Men and women live with a heart-deep uncertainty every morning when they wake. It is why they go to war, why they write poems, fall in and out of love, plan thefts on dark nights, or try to forestall them. Why they pray. Or refuse to pray.

It is the uncertainty that shapes and defines our lives. The tears of the world, a longing for joy. Or even just safety. Just that.

Joy. Safety. They can be present for us, more often are not.

CHAPTER II

Claquin Guiene had never planned to become any lord's guardsman, in Orane or anywhere else. He owed his current position to his "Uncle" Ruppe, his mother's very special friend, as she'd described him to her son when Claquin was quite young and his father still alive.

He'd had vivid dreams of killing his so-called uncle once he was old enough to understand a little of the world, including the sounds that sometimes came from the other room of the farmhouse when his father was working in their field.

Then his father died of an injury in that field (fell, cracked his head on a rock he ought to have cleared away before), and it had to be admitted that Ruppe Hanse took steps to ensure a future for the young man, no longer a boy, who was now, evidently, his charge.

The officer paid to keep the peace in their market village said he knew someone who knew someone, and Claquin was sent away from home. To Orane, on his own (which was terrifying), with a letter of introduction. He couldn't read, but Hanse read it out to him, and he was told what man he had to find inside the city's walls.

A little over a week later he walked through the southern gates of the king's city, the mad king's overwhelming city. He was given directions to where he was to go. No one had robbed or murdered him on the road to Orane, things he'd pretty much expected would happen, and no one did so now.

At a château larger than any house he'd ever even seen in his life, Claquin was admitted to the guards' quarters. He showed a man his letter, then answered a few questions briskly asked by the very large, bald, thickly bearded captain their village serjeant knew (he could use a stave in a fight, yes; not a sword, no, was very willing to learn; no, he didn't know he spoke with a peasant's accent, was very sorry about that).

He was hired provisionally as a manservant to the guards of the duke they served in their red-and-blue livery. The enormously power-ful duke. Brother to the king. A name even ignorant, unlettered Claquin Guiene from the countryside had heard.

Five years ago that had been. He was capable with a blade now, and was an actual guardsman, not their servant. Had lost most of his country accent, too. It had taken hard years, head down, doing what he was ordered, but he had a decent life now: a bed, food and drink morning and night, his horse in the stable with all the others. Even a plump, soft girl from the northern coast, with her own accent, who was recognized as his by the other guards.

You needed to be discreet, watch the example of your captains, stay out of trouble, but there were ways for a guardsman to make a little money in Orane. He owed his "uncle" a great deal, in truth. He said that in a letter he dictated and sent home. No reply came, so he never knew if they got it. He didn't send another.

Matters of politics and war were not his concern, he didn't under-stand them, but life here was good, Claquin had often thought, even in a vicious winter.

Until tonight. Until this dreadful night.

Thierry had no idea what he was supposed to do with a horse, but he could stay on one, it seemed. The horse was indeed gentle and they weren't moving quickly in the darkness. The horse was also warm, which was good. The provost reined his own big mount and it fell into stride beside Thierry's.

"And so, why do you need me? What is this?" Villar spoke first. He tended to, if he was honest with himself.

"Hush," said Robbin de Vaux. "You aren't in a tavern. Learn to wait."

"Why?" he asked. He reacted this way when he felt out of his depth.

"Holy Jad," said the provost. "Do you really want to be sent to the Châtelet?"

He didn't, really.

"Would you do that? Because I ask questions?"

"The order to take you there," de Vaux said bluntly, "was given, right after your friend Lambert talked."

"Not my friend!" Thierry said quickly, but he swore silently again.

"Does it matter?"

Thierry cleared his throat. The cold made that painful. He felt more frost forming on his eyelashes and short beard. He said nothing, for once.

They rode through streets leading to the river. He knew them all, these streets, even though most people were at ease only in their own neighbourhood. He knew his city very well, even in the night. He could see the Great Sanctuary on its island, ahead of them. The majestic dome of it a massive presence. Some grumbled that it was too big, too dominant. Thierry loved it. Grace and power, both. Could the men who made sanctuaries like this be named holy? It rose up like a blessing as they drew nearer.

A blessing. Strange word for him to think of. He would die loving this city, he thought suddenly, whenever that came to pass.

The provost, in turn, now cleared his throat. It made Thierry more nervous, that *this* man was on edge.

"There's been a murder," said Robbin de Vaux.

There were murders in Orane just about every night, Thierry thought, but was wise enough to stay silent. The king's provost was out in the dark with a dozen or so serjeants. This wasn't a tavern stabbing over dice or cards, over a girl, or by a girl.

He waited. He became aware his heart had begun beating rapidly again. The horses stepped carefully on the ice, or in the mud.

"We're going to need to investigate quickly, and I do require someone who can talk to people in the taverns and shops as soon as they open, without drawing attention. At the market stalls, too. Even before sunrise, if you can get into places. They won't speak readily with any of us."

"Or with me," Thierry said quickly, "if I'm known to be with you, my lord."

De Vaux nodded. "Yes. You'll come with me now, see what we can see by torchlight, then go off on your own before morning."

"The body is . . . in the street?"

"Three bodies. Only one matters. You'll go to your usual places after. Just be curious, seek out what people are saying, thinking. The way you always are, no? The whole city will be doing the same, after sunrise. You'll come find me—at home, not the Châtelet—at midday. I imagine you know how to move about without being seen or followed."

"Unless someone is waiting outside my door with serjeants."

A grunt. Acknowledgement more than amusement. They rode without speaking again. The clop and jingle of the horses. Eventually Thierry really couldn't wait anymore.

"Who is it, then?" he asked.

And this time the provost answered him.

Thierry found himself gripping the reins of his horse very tightly. He realized he'd made a sound, somewhere between a gasp and a cry.

He looked up at the hard, cold, brilliant stars. They had not the least interest at all, he'd always felt, in the doings of men down here, whatever some faiths might wish to believe. The stars? They were too dazzling, he thought, to ever care. Too glittering and remote.

"It is murder for certain?" he managed.

"His head is almost severed, I am told. And one leg. And a hand cut off. Half a dozen wounds in the chest and back. Someone desired him extremely dead."

"Dear Jad defend us all," Thierry Villar said.

"Ah. Well. Have to do it ourselves this time, I think," the other man said. "If we can. If we even can, with this, and what might now follow."

The Duke de Montereau's hacked-apart body had been covered by someone, for decency.

It lay in the Street of the Linenmakers, a good neighbourhood, up from the river on the other side, across the Old Bridge, where all the shops were closed, of course, their lights doused. The linenmakers had long since left the street, the name remained.

The duke, the king's brother, had, it appeared, been attacked in the night—by some eight or ten men. They had emerged in a rush from the stable gate of a house as he rode back towards the bridge with a small escort. So they were told.

Two of his guards also lay dead, their own swords beside them. One had a gaping axe wound in his skull, it had carved his face almost in half.

These two weren't covered, Thierry thought, when he was able to frame thoughts again. Just guardsmen, after all.

Rollin de Montereau, however, was—or had been, alive—the most important man in Ferrieres. Governing it, pretty much, while King Roch was entangled in a furious darkness of the mind. Montereau had also been named, formally, guardian to Girald, the prince and heir.

He had also been, if you believed the rumours, the queen's lover.

And her own elegant house lay just ahead, at the top of this street, for the days and nights when she wished to be away from the intrigues of the palace. For whatever varied reasons. One would be able to see it, Thierry thought, when sunrise came. He looked up that way in the dark, and in fact he did see it. There were lights in windows.

The provost noticed him doing that. "She's in residence tonight, yes."

Thierry said nothing. Didn't even nod his head. This was dangerous beyond words.

What am I doing here? he thought. Well, he was perhaps saving himself from a death on Gallows Hill. That was an answer.

A good one, really.

A serjeant dismounted at the provost's nod. He pulled the heavy, bloodstained cloth back from the duke's body. By torchlight Thierry looked at the ruin of a beautiful man.

He had seen dead men before. He always carried a knife, had stabbed people himself. Once, memorably, with consequences. But this came near to making him throw up what he'd eaten and drunk at dinner.

"You've looked in that house?" the provost asked, gesturing towards the still-open stable gate nearby.

One of the duke's surviving guards confirmed it. He looked stricken, lost, terrified. All appropriate, as far as Thierry was concerned.

"Nothing to see?"

"Not much, my lord provost," the man said. A voice barely above a whisper. "Signs of occupation. Neighbours say a large party moved in two days ago."

"Two days? Descriptions?"

"We haven't had a chance to talk properly to anyone yet, my lord. We also thought we should . . ." He trailed off.

"You thought to leave it for us. Very well. Your name?"

"Guiene, my lord. Claquin Guiene."

"And you survived because?"

"Four of us have, my lord. The assassins did . . . what they did . . . very quickly. Then they fled, my lord."

"Which way?"

Guiene pointed up the street, away from the river, towards where the queen's house lay. "They turned east at Goldsmiths Lane and three of us pursued."

"They were horsed?"

"Yes, my lord."

"Livery?"

"I couldn't tell, my lord. It was . . . it is very dark. It happened so fast. And very . . ."

"And very violently. Yes. You stayed here?"

"To guard the bodies, my lord."

"You commanded this night guard of the duke?"

"I did. I . . . do." Guiene could hardly speak.

"Very well. You will give my serjeants your most precise description of what you saw, what happened. Is there a house here we can use?"

"The same one they did?"

"No. I'll want a closer look at that in the morning. No one is to go inside now."

"We can get the people on the other side to open their shopfront for us."

"Good." De Vaux turned to the serjeant behind him. "Do it, Medor. Wake them if they are asleep. I doubt anyone is. We'll need to talk to them all."

"My lord," said the well-built man named Medor, "Aubrey found this, up the street." Medor was one of those holding a torch. Another serjeant held out a metal object, with sharp spikes protruding.

The provost stared at it. Then nodded. "Wait for light, then look for more. They'll signal a direction. Aubrey, have the city gates on this side of the river closed. Ask the guards there if anyone went through on horseback already. Medor, this street is also to be closed off, below us towards the river, and all the way to the end above."

The queen's house was at the end. Thierry wondered if she was awake. If the provost was going to wake her. Or let the morning and tidings of horror do that.

"Villar," the provost said. "Nearest tavern? The Mule?"

"No, my lord. Two or three are nearer."

"You are known in them?"

"I am, lord." He was known in a significant number of the city's taverns.

"Very well. We will investigate here, talk to people in these houses, begin gathering facts. You are to do what I told you. In and out of taverns, now if you can, then through the morning. Talking at shop-fronts, inside them. Use the curiosity everyone will have. Hear what is being said. Be clever, Villar. I need you to be clever."

Thierry said, "That caltrop they found, the spikes. So they expected pursuit, threw them to defeat it."

"I do know that, Villar."

"And taking a large house on this street for so many men and horses? Means considerable resources. That they might serve someone who—"

"Stop! I know. Wiser, perhaps, not to speak yet, Villar. Do what I need you to do. Find me at midday. Go."

Thierry looked at him. Then he dismounted cautiously, did it without help, and walked away, back towards the river. As he went, he saw that the blue moon had risen, a crescent. The Kindath—there were a number of them throughout Orane, they were not sequestered as in some cities—worshipped the two moons. Saw divinity in their phases and movements. A heresy against Jad, of course.

He'd had a Kindath lover once, a few years back. Dark-haired, dark-eyed, very clever. She'd been one of those who claimed to be able to read futures with cards. She'd never done his, not that he knew, at any rate. He hadn't wanted to know.

Still didn't.

Robbin de Vaux watched the poet go off.

He was remembering a winter campaign from his early years in the army, defending north towards the sea, against the Anglcyn and their treacherous allies among those who should have been loyal to the crown.

It had been more of a raid than a full campaign. It had been led by the constable of Ferrieres, however, and in the dead of winter, and in darkness, too, like this.

De Vaux missed the constable more than he could ever say. Would ever say. He loved his children, he respected and admired his wife, and he was properly grateful to his parents, but Jean Montel had been the enduring love of his life, right up to the older man's death. You couldn't say things like that. People wouldn't understand how soldiers could feel about their commander.

They had approached the Château de Curton on the coast towards day's end, waited at a distance, out of sight, then advanced after darkfall, in swirling snow. Curton was an Anglcyn bastion now on the soil of Ferrieres, taken years before. There were too many of those. But Curton had a harbour on a coastline with few of them, and so it mattered more.

They took it because the constable, Jad shield him forever in light, had arranged for a man within to unbolt the main gate for them when darkness came.

They were, to put it bluntly, not expected. Not in winter, at night, in snow. That never happened.

It was war against a hated, occupying foe, with traitors to Ferrieres among them inside the fortress walls. The constable's force wreaked a slaughter that night among the enemy soldiers, among known allies of the Anglcyn—and then within the populace that had permitted them.

That last was not truly fair or just, and they knew it. *Permitting* was not the point for citizens dealing with occupying soldiers. But warnings and messages needed to be sent in war. Ferrieres had a larger population than its enemy across the channel but was terribly divided, with a vain, rivalrous, glory-seeking aristocracy, each lord leading his own force while hating the others more than the Anglcyn, it often seemed. They had been losing this long war. Surrendering cities and territory. Not yet to the point of destruction, but . . . not so far away from it.

Retaking the castle, town, and harbour of Curton had been a memorable moment. Had indeed sent a message. And he'd been there, young Robbin de Vaux, commanding a cohort, killing in the name of the king, wielding a sword behind his constable. In the name of Jad, too, although both sides claimed to have the god's favour, of course.

He had been promoted, honoured, rewarded. Owed so much, really, to that night and to the constable. All, really. And he carried, to this day, right to this frigid night in Orane, a memory of riding through snowfall towards a castle on the coast. A pivot in his life. The moment when fortune's wheel had begun to carry him upwards.

Tonight the wheel might bring him down, he thought. He might be dead within days.

There were more lights in the queen's home now, he saw. He'd been to her city palace a few times, for functions. Dances. He didn't dance by choice, but he did of necessity. His wife had taught him how.

Lights didn't mean the queen was awake in the middle of the night, but they did suggest that she was. Robbin de Vaux felt a rare uncertainty. He had trained uncertainty out of himself in most circumstances. Not this one, however. Not sitting astride his horse over a ruined body. This body.

The constable used to say, before a battle, "Now we are for chaos and old night."

It was night now under the stars and the blue moon rising—though the city and country did not yet know the chaos that might be coming.

He wished he were home and in bed. A foolish wish but a real one.

He abruptly changed his mind about something. Ordered Medor and four men to go up the street immediately, with torches, but on foot to protect the horses, to see if they could find more of the caltrops. Aubrey had already ridden for the gates with another serjeant. A mistake. Their horses could be lamed if they trod on a spike; caltrops were vicious things. But he had needed the gates barred. And word if someone had gone out already. They'd have been muffled and cloaked for a certainty, he thought. Identification would be unlikely.

It was peacetime now. Spring might change that, but people were permitted in and out of Orane. The danger outside the walls was wild animals this winter, and wolves didn't need gates. No one sensible would be going out in the dead of night, of course. Or no one not fleeing pursuit.

He had stopped the small poet from speaking any name as to who might have done this. Couldn't stop himself from thinking one. It terrified him. But really, if you weren't afraid now you were a fool, and he'd never been that. Besides, he reminded himself, they didn't know anything yet. The slain duke lying here had made many enemies over the years. Husbands of his lovers, among them. This might be that. He . . . he wanted it to be that.

He had watched Thierry Villar walk, gingerly on the ice, back towards the river and then, harder to see beyond the torchlight, east along a laneway. Several taverns would be that way. Villar could hope to gain admittance, even in the dark, long after curfew. Some sort of knock or spoken word, maybe. The provost realized he liked the man, wasn't sure why. You trusted your instincts.

It had been purest instinct, married to chance, that had led him to stop outside The Lamb on the way here and wait for Villar to come out with the third bells of the night. A poet-scholar, trained in philosophy and law, they'd told him. De Vaux supposed if you were going to be a thief, it might be of use to know the law.

The information as to where he was sleeping tonight had been good, and the timing was right. You used accidents like that. In warfare, and in these duties you had taken on when the constable had died and you'd decided it was time to bring your wife and family to the city. Change how you lived. Closer to the court, for the boys. Work towards shaping a future for them.

The information he'd gotten earlier about a planned theft at a sanctuary attached to the university had come before the vastly more eventful tidings of an assassination. So he'd been awake when word of this murder came.

He didn't know Villar, only of him. Had actually read a few of the man's verses—when someone brought a copy of one poem to him, demanding he arrest the poet for blasphemy. There were many who disliked this Thierry Villar, it had emerged then. Some with rank.

De Vaux had found the poem (and others he'd ordered brought to him) amusing and harmless, unless you were the one being pilloried in rhyme, which was not his affair. He knew Villar's stepfather slightly. Ambroise Villar was a cleric of middling rank. Associated with a small sanctuary near the one to be robbed tonight. If Lambert Maar was to be believed.

Not especially pious of the cleric's adopted son, Robbin de Vaux had thought. Had the thieves gone through with it, or even not, they could hang for this night's plot—he hadn't lied to Villar. There were the usual tangles of clerical law versus civil law, battles of jurisdiction, but he'd negotiated those before.

He'd decided to proceed differently with this man. Clever men could be useful as well as troublesome. And he knew he'd need access to whatever the citizens of Orane might know, or have heard. Or hear now. Most of it would be nonsense, it always was, but he'd judge that, and also have a chance to assess the small poet with his small beard and the cleric's tonsure he wore as a university graduate.

Of course if civil war broke out this would move far beyond such things. And there could be other killings in or around the palace. Even tonight. He made the sign of the sun disk to avert the evil of that possibility.

Had another thought, though. He called over a serjeant and sent him back to the Châtelet. He ordered fifty men posted on guard outside the royal palace, and he wanted the king's guard put on notice of danger, with more information to come. It might unsettle people, but it needed to be done. He considered doing the same for the other senior dukes and their guards, but decided not to. They were careful men, generally.

A door opened just along the street. A woman stepped out. She clasped her hands in front of her and offered an awkward obeisance. "We have a fire we can light, my lord, if you want to be inside," she said. "It is a bitter night."

The kindness of ordinary people, even amid their own sorrows and hardship, Robbin de Vaux thought. Not for the first time.

He wondered if she knew who he was, or was just reacting to the horses and perhaps orders overheard. She'd be aware of the dead man. The dead men.

De Vaux did want to be indoors, of course he did. Couldn't. He declined with thanks, asked for a hot drink if at all possible for his serjeants. And more torches, if she had them. Said he would pay, of course. She nodded, curtsied again, went back inside. Little warmth in there from one fire, but some warmth, he thought, and no wind. He couldn't feel his nose. There was ice in his beard when he brushed at it with a gloved hand.

De Vaux dismounted, ordered the cloth over the duke to be pulled back again. He was a man who had been at war. Seeing death did not undo him. This death might. He ordered a torch to be brought nearer, and confirmed: right-handed blows to sever the head at the neck. Almost sever. Which was worse, in a way, but the embalmers at court would be skilled. There were things they could do before the burial rites.

Terrible, to already be thinking of that.

Looking at the leg he saw that the blow there had been wielded by a left-handed man. Small, possibly useful information. Or not.

The woman came out again carrying two unlit torches, a boy with her bearing two more. De Vaux had a man give her a silver coin (too much, but . . .). He had a serjeant light the four torches.

"We'll bring ale, my lord," she said. "It is warming over the fire."

He nodded. Heard a sound. Aubrey, riding back.

"Horses all right?" de Vaux asked.

Aubrey nodded. "Jad's mercy. We picked up a few more caltrops."

"Which direction?"

"East, as reported, my lord. Along Goldsmiths Lane to where it meets South Gate Road."

"And they went out?"

Aubrey hesitated. "No, my lord. There were caltrops on South Gate Road, but on the way back towards the river. Not to the gate and out."

De Vaux felt fear renew itself. Refused to let it show. He knew—everyone knew—who lived in the great palace on South Gate Road, halfway back towards the river.

"Did you . . . did you look for fresh tracks? Cracks in the ice from horses?"

Aubrey hesitated again. "No, lord, we turned back when we saw they went that way. Came to . . . tell you."

Prudent. The assassins had gone *away* from the gate. Not out of the city. And Aubrey would not have wanted to ride up to that palace in the night without instructions. He was a capable man.

"Well done," said de Vaux. He thought about giving those instructions—to ride up, ask questions there—but decided to wait. It would have to be him doing that, in any case. If it happened.

He ordered the duke's body covered again, had the severed hand brought under the canvas covering. Such an ugly death.

The king's brother was—had been—famed as a collector of artworks: books of hours showing life through the seasons, portraits and religious paintings, golden sun disks, even mosaics in the style of the Ancients, assembled at his palace by the Livraise River a few days to the west, and at his home here in the city. He was also the man tasked with keeping Ferrieres safe, guarding the queen and the young prince during these intervals when the king was mad. There had been a document signed by the king. At a time when he wasn't mad.

Thinking of the queen, and about guarding her, de Vaux looked that way again. More lights, now in the upper windows at the top of the road. People were stirring there, in the middle of a winter night. She'd be awake. He decided he would not, could not wait on this. There were things he needed to know. He gave orders, sent someone to the Châtelet for more men to come this way. He mounted up and headed the short distance to her home.

"He is dead, isn't he," said the queen of Ferrieres.

Not a question. Bianca di Rizzetto was in a deep-purple night robe, elegant even now. No jewellery, her still-golden hair down. She had a fur-lined cloak over the robe against the cold, even with fires lit. She was known for her perfumes, was not wearing a scent now. She'd have been asleep.

She was from Batiara to the south, from the wealthy water-shaped city of Seressa, and accordingly was not greatly loved here in Ferrieres. An old story with queens and princesses. They were needed for alliances and money; they were seldom popular among the people in the country they came to. The dead man's wife was also from Batiara, in fact. A different city-state. There was money down there, and Ferrieres at war always needed money.

What could he say to this woman?

He knelt on the marble of the entrance hallway. It seemed proper. She had come down the wide stairs to meet him. Its own sign.

"He is, highness," the provost said, simply. "It is a sorrow for me to say it, and a sorrow for Ferrieres." *And for you*, he thought, but did not, could not, say.

"Are we in danger here now?" A proper question. He could not read her expression. She was good at hiding her thoughts. A necessary skill at court.

But . . . *we?*

"The prince is with you?" de Vaux asked, chilled.

"He is, provost. I like to bring him out of the palace at times. If we cannot go riding we can at least leave that terrible place."

His anxiety only grew. The heir to the throne was here? Barely guarded?

"It might be wisest to return now, your grace. Until we—"

"Until we know who did this and what it is. I agree. Will you send for an escort?"

"I already have, your grace. They will be on their way."

"We will wait for sunrise, then go back in our carriage with your escort, provost. You will remove the body from the road?"

"I will." She'd already been told where the killing had happened. He wanted to ask about that, but did not.

He did have duties, however.

"Can you . . . are you able to tell me if the duke visited with you and . . . and the prince here?"

She nodded; she was utterly unreadable to him. "Why else would he have been in this street after dark? He came, we three played at cards. Girald went to bed, the duke and I were served our dinner, and he left."

"When, please?"

"After dinner. I did not track the hour, provost. It is not a thing I do." She spoke with a Batiaran accent still, if a slight one.

"And he showed no signs of distress or apprehension?"

"The duke?" She raised an eyebrow. "He never did that."

Which was true, de Vaux thought. The Duke de Montereau was not a soldier by nature, though he'd been to war, but he was a worldly man. And why would he have been apprehensive, riding from a pleasant evening to what became his death?

"He was going back to his own palace?"

"I assumed as much, but he might also have been riding to a mistress or a friend."

She was extremely clever. Wise to remember that.

She dismissed him—a word, a gesture. Had shown no hint of emotion or any disquiet, other than being awake and meeting him downstairs in the middle of the night. Almost too controlled, he thought.

She would wait for the serjeants, she repeated, and for daylight.

He had a task. To find who had done this.

It might kill him, Robbin de Vaux thought, back out in the night under a blue crescent moon. He wondered, briefly, how the small poet was faring. A possibly useful man. But his more immediate concern was with where the last caltrops had been found. Not towards the city gate. The other direction. The message that sent.

He was probably going to have to go there in the morning, he thought. He really didn't want to. He had ambitions for his children, a life he was building for himself, for them. He didn't think of himself as old yet, or ready to cross to the god.

But who controlled that, in life? Who could imagine they did so, after the plague years and so much war?

In some ways warfare had been easier, Robbin de Vaux thought. A bitter enough notion. He rode back towards the bodies in the street.

It was later said, a tale told, among many that sprang up, that the dogs of Orane had barked for much of that night, after the assassination.

CHAPTER III

There was a thin line of faint light under the heavy oak door of The Needle, the nearest tavern to where the dead men lay. The street still had many clothing shops and tailors; the name suited, Thierry thought. Curfew meant they were not allowed to unlock the door, but really, what night watchman or serjeant would be out enforcing that in this cold?

He did the four-three-two-one-four knock and a moment later the door was opened slightly, enough for him to turn sideways and go in. It was closed behind him, quickly.

This was a tavern he hadn't been in for some time: a small but important matter of a poem mocking the proprietor a year ago. He had suggested the tavern's name matched the tavernkeeper's sexual apparatus.

Said tavernkeeper now stood staring at him. Coldly.

"Come to apologize?" Branco Merlant asked. He had not, it seemed, forgotten the earlier matter. Unsurprising, really. A burly Esperañan, in Orane for many years. Had probably changed his name at some point, Thierry thought. Still had an accent, a strong voice. Strong man, too. Carried a long knife.

Villar thought about it. "It was a good poem. It was funny. I write that way about many people, you know that. But I'm sorry if I offended you. I can't undo a poem—too many people know it by now—but I undertake never to recite it in here."

Branco sniffed and glared. Then shrugged. A well-known poet frequenting a tavern was actually good for business and they both knew it. Also, a year was a long time. Lives were short, everyone knew that, too.

"What are you doing outside?" he asked.

"I was headed out on some . . . affair. But it is too damned cold, Branco. I saw your light. I could use wine and the fire."

"Have money?" An expected question. A fair one.

"I have money." He did, a little. Should have gotten some from the provost, Villar realized. He added, "I have questions, too. Why in Jad's name are all those serjeants out and about?"

"Aha! That why your affair had to be called off?" A voice from by the fire. There were half a dozen people in The Needle, nursing drinks in the middle of the night.

"A girl or a theft, Villar?" someone else called.

Thierry grinned, didn't bother answering. Not a good question to answer.

He looked back at Branco Merlant, who sniffed again and said, "Someone's been killed. Someone important, it seems."

"No idea who?"

A hesitation. "A rumour it's the Duke de Montereau."

"*What?*"

It wasn't difficult to sound shocked. He was still shocked, in truth.

"Couple of people came in and went out, said as much."

"Who would dare to do that? Who would *want* to do that?"

Branco Merlant, tavernkeeper, allowed himself a small smile. "Not many, for the first question. Quite a few husbands, for the second, word is."

There was laughter from across the room.

Branco led Thierry to the bar, poured wine into a battered cup, waited pointedly. Thierry fished out a coin, and waited, in turn, for his change. The other man gave him his wine. No coin back.

It was terrible wine. Watery and sour, both, which was hard to achieve. A reason, he remembered, that he hadn't been unhappy avoiding The Needle.

"Have to be a powerful husband, then," he said.

"Well, not as if Montereau slept with whores in a tavern," someone else said from the fire. "And his own wife lives mostly outside Orane, they say."

A second man added, "And if you can bed the queen of Ferr—"

"*Hush with that! Not in my tavern!*" Branco Merlant snapped. "Or you're outside on your ass on the ice and frozen shit! Hear me, you slack-brained fucker?"

The man so emphatically addressed fell silent. They all did. Thierry thought of Lambert Maar, who had spoken too freely in a tavern about a robbery being planned. Which had led to his being here.

The things that could shape your life . . .

He sipped his wine, kept from grimacing because Branco was watching him. He said, "There's really no idea who did this?"

The tavernkeeper snorted again, a habit of his. "As if someone will come into The Needle and tell us?"

"True enough. We'll know more in the morning, I imagine."

"Maybe," said the man behind the bar. "Not always for the likes of us to know anything."

Which was also true. Thierry said as much.

"Someone over that way said there was a tall man in a red cloak among the assassins," said the talkative one from by the fire. "Maybe leading them."

He was excited by the murder, you could see it. People were like that, Thierry thought. As long as it stayed just a story and didn't shake up their own lives. People needed stories, he thought. They lived for them. But this was the sort of thing the provost would want to know. Odds were, de Vaux would hear it directly from whoever *someone* was, by now or come morning.

He finished his glass. Straight face again. "Thanks for the warmth, and for forgiving me," he said. "I need to get to my bed. Probably we all should. Out after curfew on this night . . . ?"

"Indeed," said Merlant, wryly. "You look like the sort of man who'd kill a duke."

"Really! Tall and with a red cloak?"

The tavernkeeper grinned.

He walked Thierry to the door, opened it, looked out, then stepped back with a nod. "You're welcome here," he said. "Just be careful with your verses."

"Can't be," Thierry said seriously. "They're no good if I am."

He stepped out, wincing as the wind hit him. Heard the oak door close. He wasn't going to his bed, or Silvy's. He was supposed to keep moving through the city, asking questions, listening.

I am a spy for the provost of Orane, he thought. Then, *And the Duke de Montereau has been murdered.*

King's brother. A world-shaking event. Jad of the sun was under the world right now, the liturgy taught, defending his children. Some of them, maybe.

The blue moon crescent was up in the sky now. Spirit moon. He continued east, walking away from bed and Silvy's wonderful blankets. He glimpsed an animal ahead, big one. He hoped—could only hope—it was a dog, not a wolf. He didn't really feel he was destined to die eaten by a wolf, but who could know? His father had died of a fall in the barn.

Death was always in life. His primary poem sequence, his best-known work, was an ongoing series of bequests he purported to make to various people. Some he knew, some were just celebrated, or notorious. Villar was known to be impoverished, he had nothing to bestow—which was a good part of what made the poems funny. He had bequeathed Branco Merlant a strap-on device such as women used with each other in lovemaking—to make up, he'd written, for the tavernkeeper's own diminutive needle.

It had been a very successful improvisation, he remembered. Enormous laughter that night. Had gotten him thrown out of The Needle. And the poem had been greeted with delight elsewhere, every time he recited it. A measure of achievement for a tavern poet. Not like being printed and sold, or read aloud at some nobleman's court to aristocratic acclaim, but this was his world. You took what it gave you.

—

He went into three other taverns before sunrise. He was well known in two, not so much in the third. In that third he learned that the man in the red robe was said to be tonsured like a cleric or university graduate. But having a tonsure only took a barber, or a friend skilled with a razor. You could do it for yourself if need be, if you wanted a disguise of sorts. It didn't mean that much. Villar had one himself, courtesy of his degree in law from the university, home of his wildest years—assuming those weren't still to come.

Speculation in all three taverns still centred on Montereau's women. Mostly wives of other men of stature, it was confidently said by people who would know nothing about it at all. Knowing nothing, in Thierry's experience, did little to slow rumours.

Enraged, humiliated husbands could kill you, of course. That much was true. Someone told the story—Villar had heard it before—that the duke had commissioned portraits of the women who'd taken him to their beds, or come to his. He allegedly had those hanging in a locked room in his city palace. What the duke's wife thought of this Villar didn't know. How could you know?

Maybe *she* had had him killed.

Unlikely. Even for a woman from Batiara. If he was dead, she lost all significance here. Maybe, he thought, she wanted to go home. That was unlikely, too.

There was a feeling of agitation and unease everywhere he went as morning approached.

Few had loved the Duke de Montereau, that was known, well before tonight. The taxes he'd been levying on the flow of goods into Orane, and a new house tax in the city last spring, had ensured as much. He wasn't the king, only the king's brother, but the king was too often incapable and Ferrieres endangered because of it.

But not loving someone powerful didn't mean you couldn't feel fearful and uncertain when he was murdered. Some might celebrate it, but they were unlikely to proclaim that right now. Not yet. Too much was unknown, and the king was again mad this winter. He might emerge, as he did at intervals, and be . . . himself for a time, but governance would become an issue now, and behind *that* lay the possibility of civil war, while they were still at war with the Anglcyn.

It wasn't a good night in Orane. And the day would be worse, Villar thought, when people woke up and learned of this.

It was also still stupidly cold.

At sunrise, as the shops began to open, he did the logical thing and went to get a haircut.

Barbershops were even better than taverns for chatter. He doubled back and went to one not far from the street where the duke had been killed. He avoided the site of the murder. Did see, glancing over and down the street as he passed, that there were still serjeants there. The provost had said he wanted to enter the house the assassins had leased, as soon as there was enough light to see by.

Would a jealous husband arrange so *many* killers, ahead of time, at such cost, and risk?

It almost amused him, how he was beginning to think the way the provost probably was, trying to work this through. There was an excitement in this. He didn't want to think too much about that yet. Some hours ago he had been headed out in the night to rob a strongbox in a sanctuary because he needed money to pay a gambling debt.

Two barbers, two men in the chairs, two more waiting, several just lingering, as happened. Thierry leaned against a wall, spoke a little to be friendly, mostly listened. He didn't mind the wait for a chair. There was a morning fire, Jad be thanked, and people were talking.

He learned things, while reminding himself that none of this was more than men sharing what they'd heard—or claimed to have heard. Only men here, no women. He liked the presence of women, was vulnerable to them. One had almost gotten him killed. He was thinking a great deal about death just now, it seemed.

Unsurprising.

It appeared that one of the two barbers had been sleeping in the shop, not at home. A small room, the fire kept it a little warmer.

The shop was probably closer to his last tavern of the night than his home, too, Thierry thought. The barber said he had heard noises in the night (said it often, as men came and went and the sun rose). He'd taken a lantern to the window at the front—just as a dozen (or ten? or fifteen?) horsemen came clattering by in the darkness.

"We're the night watch!" one had screamed at him. "Put out your light or we'll kill you!"

As if. As if the night watch in Orane did that. Said that. *Screamed* that, the barber declared. As if they even had horses. Then, after they'd raced by, riding east, he'd boldly stepped outside—and found a caltrop in the street! Almost stepped on it! Could have lost a foot, he exclaimed. He pointed to the caltrop on a shelf beside his chair.

"Lucky indeed that you didn't!" Villar said. "Jad was guarding you! Did you see what they were wearing?"

"Too dark, they went too fast. But . . ."

The man paused, he clearly liked having an audience.

"But?" Villar asked, obligingly.

"But I don't think they were wearing livery. Even if they were serving nobility."

"Who else would assassinate a duke with so many men?" the man he was shaving said.

"Keep still," the barber murmured, his blade at the other's neck. "But yes, who else indeed, my friends? And keeping their identity secret! Pretending to be the watch!" He paused, lifted the blade, said portentously, "These may be dark days for Orane!"

Villar made a mental note that the provost needed to talk to this man. And any others along the street who might have been awakened by horsemen passing, perhaps seen more.

He had his hair trimmed around his tonsure and let the barber neaten his beard. Declined the scent the man wanted to apply. Didn't learn anything more that seemed to matter. The caltrop on its shelf told a tale, he thought. And the absence of livery, if it was a true thing, was worth relaying. He reminded himself, paying, to get money from the provost.

He went back east along the street after, lingering at shopfronts. The city was feverish with talk, people out and about despite the cold. The sun helped, a little. He was extremely tired, Thierry realized. Hardly a surprise. He was tempted to go to Silvy's, after all, and sleep, but didn't. He did go back across the river. He'd had an idea. He'd go to a sanctuary. Not the one they'd been planning to rob (that would have been a bit much, really) but another one close to it.

He really needed to sleep for a bit.

Adelie Villar was unsurprised to find Thierry asleep in his room when she came back from the morning rites across the way. She'd stayed standing at the back of the sanctuary, as she always did, unless it was a memorial or thanksgiving day for herself.

Ambroise was always telling her to come forward, sit or kneel with those gathered, make the sign of the sun disk among them—but she had chosen her place.

She remained after everyone else left. She tidied up, readying their small sanctuary for the evening rites. There had been nine people this morning. The usual six, and three others present for whatever reasons had brought them to Jad that day.

Ambroise never counted, never cared, had often said he'd lead the rites for a single person if need be. That was . . . fine. But donations from a single person—or nine—wouldn't keep this sanctuary going. Adelie cared, and she counted.

Ambroise Villar was gentle, wise, deeply pious, truly generous. Adelie and her son knew how generous. He had given them both his name. He was a man the god surely loved. And he was also, sometimes, painfully innocent about how the world worked. Mostly concerning money. He wanted her to put in fresh, tall candles for evening rites every day. She didn't. Good, clean-burning candles were expensive. She knew that. He didn't.

Adelie took care of the budgets—for the sanctuary, for Ambroise's rooms attached to it, and for her own little house—out of the wages he paid her, plus an allowance for expenses. She was frugal. It was necessary. She worried their sanctuary might be shut down and sold off by the city's high patriarch in his Great Sanctuary on the island. Ambroise was widely respected for his holiness, but . . . in Orane this winter, times were very hard. Two sanctuaries had already been closed and sold off, even as new ones were rising in better neighbourhoods.

She lit Thierry's bedroom fire with a taper from downstairs, made sure it was drawing. From by the bed she looked down at him sleeping and smiled a mother's smile. He'd had his hair cut and beard trimmed. She liked this look. He was neater, more distinguished, less of a . . . tavern man. Even with the tonsure, he looked very young, which he was. She left him to sleep.

He came home often, still. To eat, sleep, talk to her, and to Ambroise. She didn't ask where he slept on other nights. There had been a woman a year ago, the de Charette daughter. A class well above them, and not a good person, Adelie had been told.

Ambroise had had to work very hard to keep Thierry from the Châtelet that time, when the woman had caused so much trouble. Thierry had been stabbed, and had stabbed the other man! It was hard for her to even imagine. She didn't want to, really. Thierry's was not a virtuous life, she knew that much. Boys grew into men, had companions who were not always decent people, but men could change, too. She prayed, and held to her hopes.

Downstairs, she looked again at the note he'd left her. It asked her to wake him before midday because he had to meet someone. She was proud of being able to read. Between Ambroise and young Thierry (her quick, clever boy) she'd learned. Not something she could do when she'd arrived here with a small child, having buried a husband in their village. She had come to Orane as a last hope, to a distant relative of her husband's. More than twenty years ago now.

She knew they were both proud of her, about her reading. They called her clever, but she also knew that pride was frowned upon. She *was* proud of her son, however, for all his faults and transgressions. She prayed the god to forgive him, and her. Heartache and joy, children.

Some people believed Jad had had a mortal son who died because of pride. Falling from the sky. Heladikos. It was a heresy, of course.

She took up her knitting in her chair beside the fire. The two cats, grey and gold, slept next to her on the hearth. It was an unusual morning for Thierry to be sleeping late, she thought, with chaos engulfing the city.

The Duke de Montereau was dead, people were saying. The poor king's brother, murdered? Adelie could scarcely believe it. Didn't want to. What she wanted was a quiet, safe life, as much as that was ever possible. Simple pleasures. Shelter and food and prayer, perhaps some music? Ambroise staying healthy, the sanctuary doing well enough to continue. Then sheltered in light with the god when her days and nights were done.

Her son the poet? For him she wanted joy.

His mother woke him gently before the midday bells. He smiled up at her, roused himself quickly. He had tasks and a place to be.

He allowed her to feed him first, kissed her at the door. Asked, before leaving, "What did you hear this morning? In sanctuary?"

"Nothing. You know I stay at the back."

He made a face. "And you know you need not?"

She made the same wry face. "You too? I am happier at the back, you both know it. It feels my proper place."

"I don't think you're right, and neither does Ambroise. And if he and I agree, can we be wrong?"

His mother laughed. He loved her laugh. "All the time," Adelie said. "Go say hello. He'll be very happy to see you."

He nodded, kissed her again, went out and across the little street that separated their house from the sanctuary. Ambroise Villar opened to his knock and, after a surprised moment, hugged him fiercely. He was a tall, gaunt man, with a habit of stooping, as if leaning in to listen more closely to whomever he was with, give them his fullest attention. He had pale-blue eyes. Innocent eyes. He was fierce in his faith and in his love for a few people, Thierry and his mother foremost among them.

Thierry knew he didn't deserve this degree of love. And he also knew it had saved his life when he'd been wounded by Jolis's new lover, and had stabbed him back, in a rage. The problem had been that the new lover, Rasse de Barille, had been a cousin of the duke of that same name, and a tavern poet didn't stab a relative (however distant) of the king's uncle. Not without consequences. He would have appealed for a clerical trial, not civic, but he hadn't had any great hope that would save him.

Instead, Ambroise Villar, respected cleric of a small sanctuary near the university, had gone to the Duke de Barille's elegant mansion and been admitted. No one ever knew what was said there.

Rasse de Barille survived. Thierry Villar was ordered to leave Orane for six months, and to pray for Jad's forgiveness. No further punishment. He had been wise enough not to ask what punishment de Barille received. Thierry bore a scar on his left side now. Could call it a trophy if you were that sort of man.

And Jolis? The fight only added to her lustre and allure. Two men knifing each other for love of her? Thrilling, really, in certain circles. A beautiful woman, sharp and cold, ice in her heart like another knife. A woman of the winter. He'd written those things in a poem when he'd returned to the city. Hadn't named her, having learned a slight measure of caution, but everyone knew. Everyone knew.

He'd expected her to send someone to attack him for that verse, for some would-be next lover to do it for her esteem. Hadn't happened, yet. Rasse had been discarded already, he'd learned. Hadn't lasted long. Only a distant cousin of power, after all. Jolis aspired to more.

Ambroise Villar led him—limping a little this morning on the bad knee—into his simple room: a bed on one wall, a small table, two stools, papers, some books (books were expensive). One fireplace, not large enough, and an altar with a sun disk. Gold-plated only, the disk, but not tarnished. His mother worked hard to keep it bright.

Thierry would have loved to have enough money to buy him a new one. If the planned theft last night had happened . . .

That was an awkward line of thought.

He asked his necessary question, and his adoptive father answered. No one this morning had known anything about the assassination, though rumours were all about. Everyone in the sanctuary had been terrified of what might happen next. Thierry asked about a very tall cleric, one who had been seen wearing a red robe, apparently, when Montereau was killed.

"He was among the assassins? A cleric?"

"Or pretending to be one."

"No order in Orane wears red robes."

"I know. Might have been just a winter garment."

"Or a traveller from away. Very distinctive," said Ambroise Villar, "if you want to be unknown." He was, Thierry never really forgot it, a quick, clever man. Not as innocent as his eyes suggested.

"I thought about that. Maybe he did want to be known. Maybe he'll never wear it again and people will search in the wrong direction."

"Are people searching?"

"The provost is, yes."

"And you are?"

Too clever sometimes, Thierry thought. He smiled, though. "He asked me to make inquiries this morning, in the taverns and shops."

"And at a barber's, I see. Why you, Thierry?"

So he did have to lie, after all. "Said I owed him, for last year."

"That's untrue! It was Barille, the duke. It had nothing to do with the provost."

Another smile. "I should have argued with him?"

Ambroise laughed. "Fair." He looked down at Thierry a long moment. "You'll be careful?"

"I always try." He hesitated. "Don't tell anyone about this?"

"Bad in the circles in which you move? To be linked to the provost?"

"Quite bad, yes."

"You trust Robbin de Vaux?"

To his own surprise Thierry answered, "I think I do."

He hugged the lean cleric who'd saved and made their lives. Ambroise Villar was so tall, he made Thierry feel almost a child again. Not, in truth, a bad feeling with this man.

"You really need to eat more," he said. He knew his mother was always saying it. "Especially in a winter like this."

Ambroise shrugged, predictably.

Thierry kissed the other man and went out again into the bright bitterness. He was expected at the provost's.

He walked quickly through midday streets, oblivious, as we almost always are, as he approached a defining moment of his life.

Looking back we can sometimes see this, but can rarely look ahead with any clarity at all. As to the future, we have guesses, hopes, plans, apprehensions. Or perhaps, for some, there is no time for any of these, caught up as they are in the hard, endlessly demanding task of living, of staying alive.

Yes. I truly didn't know. We so seldom know.

CHAPTER IV

It was a little past midday, in fact, but the provost noted that the poet arrived at a time that could fairly be called prompt in all the circumstances. He hadn't been specific about the hour, and Villar had been—he assumed—traversing the city.

That turned out to be correct. He had the man escorted to the ground-floor workroom in his home and had the two serjeants awaiting orders in there go out, leaving them alone. He didn't know what Villar would tell him, and the fewer people who knew what they were hunting the better. Even among his own men.

For one thing, he had already decided this was not an assassination ordered by the jealous husband of one of the Duke de Montereau's lovers.

He dearly wished it had been. Easier in every possible way, if so.

Villar removed the scarf he'd wrapped around his face. He'd kept it on until they were alone. De Vaux understood. The poet could be marked for life, and not usefully in his own circles, if known to be assisting the provost. He was doing it under duress. Extreme duress, really.

De Vaux felt no distress about this. You couldn't let yourself be affected by an unexpected liking for a tavern poet. He'd have been acting properly had he sent Thierry Villar to the Châtelet for questioning last night, and Villar knew it. Questioning in the Châtelet could kill a man, even before he made it to the gallows.

"What do you have?" he asked.

He gestured to the flask of wine and the glasses on his desk. The poet shook his head, surprisingly. He did take the chair he was offered.

He spoke well, and precisely. Not a surprise, really. He had two degrees from the university and made his living (such as it was) with words.

He had been to several taverns. He reported about a barbershop, suggested talking to the barber, who had seen mounted men race by in the dark. They had claimed to be the night watch. He had heard about a tall, hooded man in a red cloak. So had de Vaux, by then.

Villar continued, finished. He added, "I will guess you already know most of what I learned." The rumour of the tall man had been in two of the inns he'd visited in the night. He said, almost against his will, "Do you have a name for him?"

They did.

"Corbez Barthelmy. A soldier from wars north and southwest. Tonsured, it appears, but we think it is a deception."

"And?"

And. That *and* was the terrible problem. The provost poured himself a glass of wine. Offered it again. Again the other declined. "I was drinking bad wine through the night for you, my lord," he said.

"This isn't bad wine," de Vaux said. He almost smiled.

"Even so. If it doesn't offend, I think I am better off sober now. I will drink to celebrate if I have discharged my debt to you."

Again the provost didn't smile. Still didn't answer the one-word question, either. Then, after thought, he did.

"He has been reported to be of a party I'd rather he not belong to, honestly."

Villar had been red-cheeked and red-eared with cold when he came in. He grew paler now. The poet had, de Vaux realized, been thinking along the same lines, even without what the provost knew. So he would understand, and fear.

Sounds from outside: serjeants making the floor creak. He heard the voice of his youngest son from down the hallway, towards the stairs to the family quarters.

"Perhaps," said Thierry Villar quietly, "you will not tell me about that party? Who he is aligned with?"

Robbin de Vaux shook his head. "Have to, Villar. There is another thing I need done, and you are the only person I can think of who can do it without arousing suspicion."

"Suspicion?" said the poet, still in a small voice.

Not a time to feel guilt or regret, the provost told himself again. He had a task.

"I need you," he said, keeping his voice level, calm, authoritative, "to go to the city palace of the Duke de Barratin. This afternoon. Time matters in this."

A silence. Then, "I had really, really hoped you would not say anything like that, my lord. Do you wish me dead?"

"You are of no use to me dead," said de Vaux briskly.

Thierry Villar shook his head. "But I am no danger to that man if I'm dead. And I become a warning to you, my lord."

Disturbingly correct. Both things.

"I wouldn't take the warning," the provost said.

"Oh!" said Villar. "That makes everything all right, then!"

Clever. Amusing. Useful.

De Vaux said, "You haven't even asked why you are the only person I can send."

"Not the first thing on my mind, my lord. But do tell me."

"His Grace, the Duke de Barratin, has a house guest," said Robbin de Vaux. "A poet, as it happens. A work has evidently been commissioned."

"He's here? This poet? Travelled to the city in this weather?"

The provost enjoyed surprising people. Probably a weakness.

"She," he said. "And yes, she did."

Of course he knew of Marina di Seressa, Thierry thought, outside in the cold again, scarf back over his face. How could someone who shaped words for a (precarious) living not know her name?

In the provost's house he had been given better clothing than he'd been wearing, a warmer coat, and, finally, money to spend. Also to reimburse him for bad wine and a haircut. How fortuitous, he thought wryly: he'd had his hair and beard trimmed, would make a *good* impression!

He had said one more thing in the provost's room.

"If this is . . . correct, will the court even want you to reveal it? Force a resolution?"

De Vaux had stared at him. "Half of them will," he said, finally.

"Which is—?"

"Which is the difficulty, yes. But that is not my decision to make, Villar. It really is not."

Walking the streets again now, sun shining, careful on the ice, Thierry was edgy, unhappy, afraid. Also, being honest, still perversely excited.

Not by the court-world poet he was going to see, if he could, though he would be happy to meet her, take her measure, but by this wildly unexpected proximity to power, to great events, however terrible.

It wasn't a world he had ever expected to know. Jolis de Charette had been the closest he'd come, he supposed: born into a wealthy, ambitious family, though not noble. Her marriage was meant to achieve that last, of course. But in the meantime she'd enjoyed sampling tavern life: rogues and mild danger. Even, for a time, bedding a small, clever poet she'd found there and taken for her amusement. For what had turned out to be just her amusement. Silvy had warned Thierry, too.

Hadn't worked out all that well for him, had it? Six months' exile from his city, and limited to that only because of Ambroise Villar's intense, immediate intervention, and because Rasse de Barille had been good enough not to die of his wound. Otherwise, Thierry would have hanged.

But this, today, was significantly loftier ground, both the woman he was going to meet and the city palace where she was. Loftier ground? This was a jagged mountain. And you died on mountains in winter.

Pushing the image a bit, Villar thought wryly. Thoughts, as well as writings, needed revisions. Also, he could have said no. The provost had a hold on him, but he'd made it clear *this* request was only that. Could be refused. Its own warning, that opportunity to decline. De Vaux knew what he was asking.

Because they both thought now, both feared, that the immensely wealthy and powerful, the ferociously volatile duke of the vast Barratin lands to the north and east—larger than Ferrieres by many measures, even if nominally part of it—might have ordered the assassination of his cousin last night.

Thierry had a sudden, vivid image in his mind again, in bright daylight, of the dead man under torches and a blue moon. The two guards lying beside him, too. Destined to be forgotten, he thought. Such figures always were.

Before leaving, he had said again to the provost, the two of them still alone, on either side of the desk in the other man's handsome room, "You'd probably be safer to leave this alone, no?"

"I am quite certain I would be," said Robbin de Vaux.

"Dog with a bone?" Thierry asked.

But after a pause the other man shook his head. "Provost of Orane. And the king's brother was murdered last night."

Had to respect that, Thierry thought.

He walked through streets and lanes he knew only slightly. The river was behind him. This was a wealthier part of Orane. Larger homes, most with guards in front, he saw. The streets were quiet here.

He was headed, as instructed, towards the very grand mansion near which caltrops had been seen by de Vaux's serjeants last night. A mistake, that had been, Thierry thought, too clear a trail. But men overwhelmed by the enormity of what they'd just done, fleeing real or imagined pursuit in the night, could make mistakes.

A cold, westering sun. Still a bright winter's afternoon, few clouds. He had been offered a page as an escort, but a tavern poet would never have such a companion, and he'd declined. This needed to be an impulsive visit. Presumptuous, absolutely, but not beyond reason or possibility, if Thierry had recently learned (as he had!) that Marina di Seressa was in Orane and staying with Barratin.

It was delicate, of course, choosing today, with word of murder racing through the city like a runaway horse, to pay some sort of collegial visit—at that palace—but it wasn't something that could be deferred, and it *was* where she was staying, wasn't it?

The provost was right. Speed mattered. There would be a funeral procession, de Vaux had said. They'd give the widow and children time to come to the city—more winter travel—from the Montereau estate in the west.

He found himself briefly hoping that Marina di Seressa, who had come to Ferrieres as a child when her father became a doctor and astrologer to the royal court, might not be at the Barratin palace just now, or choose to receive an unexpected visitor on such a day as this one was.

He took a left turn, then another, and there it was. There were guards here, as well, on the street in the cold. Of course there were. Half a dozen. Tall men, all of them, hard-faced. There was a stone tower looming above high stone walls. Men up there, too, he saw, with crossbows.

He named himself to the man who stopped him. He asked to see the steward. This was, after discussion, permitted.

He had written a note for the woman. After being escorted through a spacious courtyard to an inner door, Villar was ordered to wait in a marble-floored entranceway, amid statues from ancient times and recent tapestries, while the black-clad, disdainful steward went within, carrying his letter.

The man came back after an interval, his manner now distinctly more courteous. He even nodded his head at Thierry. Closest he'd get to a bow? Villar was led up a wide staircase with recesses for sculpted busts, also very old.

The lady, he was told, was at home and would be pleased to see him.

Fortune's wheel did what it did, regardless of your hopes, prayers, cleverest planning. Jad *could* help the virtuous, the clerics taught, but they also tended to admit it was never a certainty.

She was waiting in a good-sized sitting room, standing by a built-up fire, holding his note. She wore a day-gown of burgundy silk, with a black knitted cap and a black shawl for warmth. Also for mourning the duke? That was possible.

He bowed. He actually knew how to do that properly. Jolis had taught him.

Marina di Seressa waited until the steward took Villar's borrowed coat, laid it down on a chest by the door, and went out.

She smiled, a small, ironic smile. She was older than him, perhaps by ten years? She gestured with the note, said, "The poet Thierry Villar most humbly beseeches the great honour of my presence? I'd not have expected such a tone from Orane's most astringent tavern poet."

Astringent. Thierry blinked. "I was brought up to be courteous. I fail, often. Not always, my lady. It seemed . . . proper." He took a chance. "What should I have written? That I wished to see if your beauty was as great as repute had it, matching the renown of your writings?"

Her smile deepened, a wide mouth. She said, "Do not flatter. I resist it. I have never been beautiful, or called so by anyone sincere. My writings have found some favour, Jad be thanked. We might have starved otherwise, or lived only by way of charity."

Unexpected, again, such directness. She was tall, quite thin, expressive features, large, lively brown eyes. She was more attractive than she was admitting, or claiming. Her dark-brown hair was pulled back and pinned beneath and behind the cap.

Her husband and her father had both died some years ago, within months of each other, he knew (it was well known). Another of the plague years that had afflicted them all. She'd been left with her mother and two small children and a need to find a way to survive.

She hadn't gone back to her family in Batiara. She'd become a writer, instead, with patrons at the royal court and in the palaces of several dukes. She moved from one nobleman's castle or city home to another, or worked at her own late husband's estate west of Orane, north of the Livraise.

She'd written commissioned poems about legendary figures (linking them to her patron of the moment, of course), guides to proper behaviour at court, and a satire on how not to treat women, among other things. He'd read most of her work, when he could obtain it. The university had copies. He'd liked the satire supporting women. Respected, didn't love her courtly poems. Not his preferred style. He thought they were humourless. But he also knew she was using chivalry, the courtesies embedded, as a *corrective* to the violence of their world. As if to teach those reading her that they could be better? Because life was so seldom beautiful?

She added, changing her manner, "I'd have expected better than flattery from the man who wrote the bequest poem to Jolis de Charette offering her a renewable maidenhead. Instead, here is another pallid courtier come to call. You disappoint, sir!"

She wasn't humourless.

And she knew—somehow—not only who he was, but *that* poem, of all of them. He was unsettled.

He said, stumbling a little, "I am hardly a courtier. And had truly not thought you'd know of me, my lady. We move in very different worlds. Mine is wine-fuelled or sodden, in loud rooms with rough wood floors, or even bare earth in some taverns nearer the walls. Yours is . . . scented with perfumes and compliments, with quiet music in the background."

That smile again. She deployed it, he thought, in different ways. None of this was as he'd expected.

"That was clever," she said. "Better."

"You are surprised?" he heard himself say. "Expect cleverness only from those well-bred?"

Her expression changed again. "You are offended. I am sorry. No, it was only appreciation. I have read some of your verses, as I said. I am not surprised to find wit." She gestured. "There is wine on that table. There is only good wine in this household. Please pour for us?"

He walked over, did so. Reminded himself why he was here, and that bristling would achieve nothing good. He approached her with two goblets. Silver, he noted, quite heavy. This palace, the wealth of the man who owned it. When he neared her he became aware of perfume. Sandalwood in it. Almost amusing, given what he'd just said.

She accepted her wine. Then after a moment she recited, very clearly:

And for the endlessly changeable lady of uncharted shallows,
Who has nothing but what she wants and only what she wants,
How could I not bestow an enchanted purse between her legs
(Blessed by holy Jad!)?
One that opens easily when she wishes it to,
For whomever she wishes, and when,
And for howsoever many times, and men,
Then seals itself magically shut again,
Against her wedding day?

Marina di Seressa laughed. "That is, I should tell you, widely recited by the women at court. One did so recently with . . . well, gestures. It was very amusing. You are hardly unknown, Thierry Villar. And not a few have said they'd wish for such a purse."

Thierry felt himself flush. "It is a tavern verse, my lady. Not for the likes of—"

"Of well-bred women? You jest, sir! I have written to assert the freedoms women should have, and that includes a privilege not to be empty-headed. And *that* includes laughing at a genuinely funny image, however bawdy it might be. Do you disagree?" She sipped from her wine.

"I . . . would not dare," Thierry said, and discovered that he meant it. "But I also did think I was presuming, in coming to visit, that you would not know me."

"A clever man can become widely known, I think."

"I had not known I was known," he tried.

She wrinkled her nose. "Perhaps not your wittiest offering?"

"Perhaps not. Am I allowed to be surprised, and somewhat off my footing?"

She nodded, serious again suddenly. She was like that, he realized. "We are all off our footing today. Why are you here, Thierry Villar?"

And with that, a sudden awareness again of how much danger

might lie before him in this room. Bracing and frightening. He had no idea where her allegiance lay. She was living here now, wasn't she?

He said, carefully, "I had learned that you were in Orane, and in this palace. I wished to pay my respects. I did so now because I imagined the coming days might see you with tasks at court."

He had prepared this with de Vaux. It was plausible. Best they could do. He took a small sip of the wine. It really was exceptional.

"For a funeral? And mourning rituals? Yes. I have no formal position, but the queen has asked for me, you're right."

The queen has asked for me.

And here he was, alone in a room with her. Still near enough to catch that scent.

She added, "Pay your respects, you say. And also request another poet's assistance?"

He blinked again, shook his head firmly. "Not at all. In no way. To be honest, my lady, in the world in which I live, and for which I write and recite my verses, I don't believe you could assist me at all." He seemed to have regained his voice now. He had a good speaking voice, when not daunted.

"And if you wished to be known in . . . a different world?"

"It has never occurred to me, my lady. You have seen what I write." He meant that, too.

She put a finger to her lips, looking thoughtful. "Jolis de Charette is cold, it is said."

He hesitated. It remained difficult for him to speak of her, more than a year after. "She . . . calculates, my lady."

"Women have often needed to do that, to survive."

He knew her history. "My lady, of course. But she does it . . . for amusement. Playing with lives?"

"Ah. Not the same, then?"

"No," he said. "Not really the same." He didn't add that she was very beautiful, Jolis.

A sound, from the hallway.

The door behind him opened. No knock. He saw her eyes widen briefly, then she smiled. Thierry turned.

The immensely powerful man standing just inside the room was not loved or admired as much as his father had been, though he had been named "the Bold" for his courage (some said recklessness) in battle years ago. He was not tall, was solidly built, very fit, black hair still, a soldier's wide stance. A long, narrow face with a long, narrow nose, dark eyes under heavy brows. A watchful look. He was dressed entirely in black. He was undeniably striking, undeniably angry now, and perhaps afraid.

Had also, very possibly, ordered the murder of his cousin the Duke de Montereau, the king's brother, the acting ruler of Ferrieres. Thierry did not feel prepared for this.

"I do not recall your arranging to receive guests in my home at a time such as this, my lady," said Laurent de Barratin, staring at the woman coldly with those suspicious eyes. "The city is unsafe. I have no idea who this man is."

He didn't even look at Thierry. He was glaring at the woman in the burgundy gown and black shawl.

And she surprised Thierry again.

"Good afternoon, my lord duke," she said, her voice calm, but almost as cold as his. "I was unaware I needed your permission to receive other poets in these rooms you have been kind enough to offer me. My apologies. Clearly I am not as welcome here as I believed myself to be. I shall relieve you of the duty of hosting me. The queen has asked for my presence. Indeed she asked for it a week ago, with a view to my writing something for her—just as you did, in fact. She has now requested I attend on her again, in light of current circumstances."

The Duke de Barratin suddenly looked, Thierry thought, as if he'd been slapped. His face slowly reddened. He closed and opened his hands, twice. Anger, and something else now, even more. The duke drew a long breath, as if to find self-control. There was a silence. Thierry felt genuinely afraid, but also oddly detached, fascinated, as if all of this were happening at a distance, and to someone else. A performance, puppets on a stage in a marketplace.

It wasn't, though. He was here, and could be killed. He was nothing. The duke might be the most powerful man in Ferrieres now. The woman, he thought, was astonishing. It helped, he also thought, to move among power, be familiar with it.

And have the queen of Ferrieres wanting her company.

He himself had no protection that meant anything at all. He kept quiet. Hadn't been addressed or even acknowledged.

Barratin said, more calmly, "My lady, a very great lord has been foully murdered. Orane is a dangerous place right now. And I *do not know this man in my house.*"

With seemingly effortless poise Marina di Seressa said, "Ah. I see. You are afraid. Understandable. Let me assist. My lord duke, permit me to present Thierry Villar, one of the best-regarded poets in the city. His name is known in every tavern in Orane, I dare say."

Thierry received the force of the duke's hard gaze for the first time.

He bowed. "My lord, it is an honour to be in your presence. I would not have offended you for anything in Jad's world."

Which last was entirely true.

The duke nodded, a registering of words spoken, of his existence. To be forgotten in moments, Thierry thought. Hoped.

"I do not know your writing," he said.

"I would never dream you might, my lord. I write for the people of Orane, not the powers of the realm." His voice, Thierry thought, was acceptably level.

"We were just discussing one of his more recent poems," said the woman, her own tone shading back towards cordial, as if to guide the three of them there.

Dear Jad, let her not recite it again, Thierry thought. It was a prayer, really.

"I see," said the duke.

He looked Thierry up and down again. Too much registering, Thierry thought. He really didn't want to be remembered by this man.

"And he was kind enough to express admiration for some of my own writings," Marina di Seressa added brightly.

"I should hope so," said the man Thierry was here to investigate for murder, if he could. "Everyone knows your worth."

She smiled. "Not everyone," she demurred. "But thank you, gracious lord. Again, I am sorry to have distressed you. I will make arrangements to leave at first light."

"Please! Do not. That would very much grieve me," said Barratin. "You are as welcome as you have always been. I spoke far too bluntly, in my concern for you and . . . for my household. You will stay, my lady?"

Her turn to nod. A forgiving smile. "Happily!" she said. "After I do my duty to the queen."

Barratin turned back to Thierry. "Messire . . . Villardin, is it? Please accept my apologies. These are sad, difficult times."

Thierry bowed again. It was generously spoken, even with the mangled name. Dukes did not apologize to tavern poets.

And because of that apology, looking back, he would decide that it was in that moment that he knew with certainty that Laurent de Barratin had ordered the Duke de Montereau's death in the street the night before.

Too conciliatory a tone, suddenly. Too *much* fear behind it, underlying it. And it wasn't a fear of being assassinated himself by someone pursuing the nobility of Ferrieres in the city. Not that. Thierry had a swift, sure sense of a truth. Nothing reasoned through yet, but it arrived with a terrible immediacy. He felt sick.

And then, after the duke withdrew with another nod, to both of them this time, and closed the door behind him, there was more.

Marina di Seressa waited a moment—as if to be certain no one was listening on the other side of the heavy door, he thought—then said, quietly, but with great force, "I really want to leave. I think I will, after the funeral. I do not wish to remain in this house."

She looked at him, waiting. It was, he realized, an invitation to ask. He almost didn't want to.

"Why?" he said. "Why do you not want to be here?"

Last night he'd been headed out to rob a sanctuary strongbox with three men from his own world. One had gotten drunk in a tavern and talked too much. And now . . .

Her expression was strange, he thought. A kind of tenderness? She said, quietly, "Thierry Villar, you didn't come here to meet me and talk of poetry. You need to be extremely careful in doing what you are doing."

"With you?" he tried.

Only a flicker of a smile. She shook her head. "Clever, but no. Because of the man who just came in."

She knew, he realized. He opened his mouth, closed it. Had no idea what to say. She held his gaze another moment, then turned and took an object hidden behind a pair of silver candlesticks on the mantelpiece behind her.

She came forward with it. "I'd conceal this when you leave, were I you."

It was a caltrop.

She handed it to him. Along with, he thought, everything it meant.

Again he could find no words.

She said, "I saw it just to the side of the door this morning when I went to sanctuary services up the street. I also heard horsemen arrive here late at night. And then leave before sunrise. Reckless, with the horses, to do that, if they'd strewn these on the road. If you are here doing what I think you are, you will know what this object means. And those horsemen. Do not ask me to say it aloud, please."

Thierry cleared his throat. His heart was pounding again. "Why?" he managed. "Why are you . . . ?"

She said, "This could throw Ferrieres into chaos, at a time when there are enemies who want that, and can use it. But there was a vicious murder last night of someone who mattered greatly. Rollin de Montereau was a man of many facets, but he was good to me at a time when I needed that. If what they are saying about how he died is true . . . I do not want it unpunished."

"Whatever the consequences?"

"Others," she said, "will have to decide those."

Thierry said, "I saw the body, my lady. It is true, what is being said."

She nodded. Was staring at him now.

He was holding the caltrop carefully. The spikes were sharp. He added, "Punishment may mean war here, not just chaos, if . . ."

"If this object I found means what it likely does. And that is revealed. Yes. Others, as I said, will have to make those decisions."

It was difficult to believe he was having this conversation. It was very nearly impossible.

"Was . . ." He paused again. So *many* chasms in front of him, he thought. "Was one of the riders a tall man in a red cloak?"

"I didn't see them," Marina di Seressa replied. "I was in bed. Only heard the horses. And then shouting."

"And they . . . they came inside? Here?"

She nodded again.

"And went out again while it was still dark?"

Another nod.

Thierry sighed. "To be honest, my lady, I'd be happier discussing poetry with you."

This time she laughed. A vivid, appealing, unexpected sound. "And I, Thierry Villar. Perhaps we will. Would you take me to one of your taverns?"

He was genuinely startled. "Would you come to one?"

She said, "I wouldn't have asked if I would decline to go."

He made a face. "You would not be the first well-born lady who wanted to taste that life."

Her expression grew serious, another of her quick changes. "I think you will find I am not very much like Jolis de Charette."

His turn to nod. "I am quite sure that is so, my lady. I . . . would be honoured to escort you of an evening, should you choose. When— if—life in Orane allows."

"Good. I will not be staying here. How can I get a message to you?"

He gave his adoptive father's name, and that of Ambroise's small sanctuary. He was aware of recklessness, but also of a steadily thrumming excitement underneath.

He watched her walk to a low chest and open it. She took out a scarf in green and gold, and a small cloth bag. She came to him, reclaimed the caltrop, wrapped it in the scarf, laid it in the bag. "Will your coat's pocket hold this? I don't think it matters if the bag is seen, but better it isn't."

He reclaimed the coat, put it on, took the bag. He felt it bumping against his leg in the inner pocket, sharp and hard, even wrapped.

"I should survive this," he said.

"Don't speak lightly," she said. "And . . . walk quickly, wherever you are going."

"He knows my name," Thierry said. "He can find me."

She smiled. "He *almost* knows your name, Villardin."

His turn to laugh.

He went out. At the top of the wide stairs a guard met him and escorted him down past others. Laurent de Barratin had his house very well defended just now. Thierry was eyed coldly by every man he passed, and then again by those in the street before the palace. He didn't see the duke again.

Walking back west, he registered two things. It seemed to be warmer. He wondered. He hoped. They had to hope, but it was likely just a brief easing as the wind died down.

Also, it was growing dark now. Light draining from the wintry sky, his city gaining shadows. He loved it this way, too. The street he was walking was very quiet. Shops closed or closing on either side. *I am,* Thierry realized, *carrying evidence against a murderer.*

And then years of training at the university came back and he realized . . . he really wasn't. Only something that could get *him* killed. A tavern poet had a caltrop in his pocket. Said he'd gotten it inside the palace of the Duke de Barratin. That it had been found on the street in front. A shocking accusation! And it proved what, in any case? He might have found it anywhere in Orane! Could he summon Marina di Seressa to support him? Throw her into this cauldron too?

No. It was wisest to discard the accursed object right now.

He didn't do that.

A lifelong stubbornness for which he still didn't know, even as a grown man, the origins. He was also angry, he realized. Not a prudent thing, but it was there.

Also there, he realized a little later, hearing sounds behind him in the quiet street, were footsteps. He glanced back quickly. Two men. Maybe a third. Hard to tell. Not too close yet, but close enough. "Walk quickly," she had said. He did quicken his pace. So, alas, did the crunching boots on the ice behind him, as twilight in Orane shaded towards darkness and Jad's winter sun went down.

CHAPTER V

By late morning the provost had learned more details about the tall man in the red, hooded cloak.

De Vaux was having all information brought to him at his home. A more private place to work. The man, Barthelmy, was reportedly hostile to the Duke de Montereau, in ways that suggested the likelihood of his committing a murder.

Rather too suggestively, Robbin de Vaux thought.

It fit, and it didn't fit at all, if you took a few moments to think. Even exhausted now, late in the afternoon, with a city and court in panicked turmoil, he was clear-headed enough to manage that.

Someone was very possibly *guiding* him to Corbez Barthelmy as leader of the killers. The enraged husband of a young, pretty wife the duke had seduced—and had then commissioned a portrait of, allegedly unclothed, for his notorious private collection. In which collection someone else was reported to have recognized her, and—evidently?— told someone who had then informed the hot-tempered, cuckolded military officer, Barthelmy.

Someone and someone and someone.

Except . . . except the seduction, if real (which was certainly possible, knowing Montereau), was said to have been years ago. Also, last night's assassination had been meticulously and expensively planned. Down to arranging to lease a good-sized house with stables before the killing. Down to caltrops obtained and strewn behind assassins fleeing on horseback. Down to provisioning those men and horses for some time before an opportunity might arise for them to kill.

Corbez Barthelmy, no longer even in the army, had nowhere near the resources for such preparations. The provost had satisfied himself of that.

Nor, de Vaux had decided, after reading the reports brought to him, had Barthelmy the intelligence for it. A soldier, respectable rank, less respectable end to his career. Gambling and debts. An old, tired story.

In and out of Orane for some years now, doing . . . various things. Not all, it seemed, legal. But if he was going to kill the king's brother in a long-delayed vengeance all these years later, it would have been done alone, and impulsively.

Still, the tall man was experienced enough, and fierce enough, and in need enough to have been assigned a series of tasks as tests, and then an assassination, for a fee. He would have planned none of this, and been paid out of someone else's pocket.

It would have had to be, de Vaux thought, a handsome fee. Barthelmy's own grievance against the duke, if it was real, was what would have made him more likely to agree. The passage of years was still a difficulty. Money, the provost thought. Enough money offered could bridge those years.

And he wouldn't have known he had been chosen to be a sacrifice if—when?—someone needed to be identified, and captured. Barthelmy wasn't clever enough for that.

And no one who'd worked with him, or paid him, could be tied in any way to the man who seemed to be at the heart of this plot. Of that, the provost was certain.

They might not even capture Barthelmy. It was likely the man had left Orane by now, probably with most of the others from last night. De Vaux had a good idea where they were likely to have ridden in the darkness once they were outside the walls. City gates could be closed and guarded, but there were always ways in and out of a large city if you knew it well enough, and had resources.

De Vaux was very uncertain the tall soldier—or any of his men—would be allowed to live. Screens and deceptions *could* be penetrated, after all. Torture was always available to the provost and the court. Why take a chance, even if you had hidden yourself behind other men? The assassins were insignificant, but their survival could become a weakness, if he was correct about who had hired them.

De Vaux still hoped to be wrong. The poet had asked him, before walking out, if he thought the court would even *want* a powerful figure named. "Half," he had answered. Which was truth, as he understood this court. What he was *not* certain about was if he—or Ferrieres—could survive if he proved it. And revealed it.

He'd been ferociously busy all day, serjeants hurrying in and out bearing reports, then sent forth again to find or generate others. The fire was kept high, warming the room.

Justice, the provost of Orane kept thinking through a challenging day, was not always obvious. You could pursue it dutifully and lead a country to ruin. Or you could consider terrible consequences and . . . leave this alone?

The assassins were unknown, he could easily report. Had likely fled in the night. He might lose his position, almost certainly would, since someone would need to be blamed, but . . .

But they had a king who was frequently mad, locked away in the palace, held down at times, shouting and biting, so that he could be decently cleaned and groomed. They had enemies across the channel north, bitter rivalries within. And the king's brother and regent was the man de Vaux had seen lying hacked and dead last night. The ripples of this went out into a wide, dangerous world.

Because it was the dead man's principal rival at court, a figure in some ways even more powerful, who de Vaux believed had ordered him slain.

You really didn't want to make an enemy of the Duke de Barratin, he thought. Or level accusations you could not prove. You'd open the gates to so much violence it didn't bear thinking on. You'd likely die, too. Hanged as a traitor.

But did that mean you looked away? That you told yourself this was too fraught, too perilous? That there were too many powerful pieces on the game board to treat last night as a straightforward murder to be solved?

Straightforward? One could laugh.

What *was* his proper task, though? Where did he owe allegiance in this moment? Country? King? City? Holy Jad of the Sun? Some idea of justice? His own family?

And what if these pointed in different directions? To different decisions?

He had done things in his years at war he could not be proud of, things he tried to forget, but he had never been a coward, and had never stood down from his duty as he saw it.

Was he to do that now? Stand down? Was it true, as soldiers at campfires or old men in taverns declared, trying to sound wiser than they were, that *there's a first time for everything*?

He needed more evidence, the provost thought. But Laurent de Barratin was far too intelligent, and would have had time to plan carefully if this really was of his devising. The provost had sent his newest, impulsively chosen man, the young poet he liked, to the duke's palace in the hope he might—

De Vaux arrested his own thought. He swore.

He had, he realized, forgotten to do something. There were reasons, excuses. There often were for errors. But someone could die because of this one.

He summoned Medor from the corridor. Gave him orders. The serjeant went out. It was probably too late, the provost thought. The sun was low already. Jad headed down beneath the world. If something was meant to happen, well, it had probably happened already.

He swore again under his breath, then offered a brief prayer, making the sign of the sun disk. Only men who went to sea, Robbin de Vaux often thought, prayed more frequently than soldiers.

The streets were too quiet. It wasn't safe. Thierry thought about it briefly, then broke into a run. He was far enough back west now, knew this part of Orane well, could possibly shake these men off in twilight lanes, if he didn't slip on the ice. He'd have to elude them, he realized. Because it became clear, when they began running too, that he *was* being followed.

He cut to his left at the second crossing he came to. He fumbled in his coat, still running, grabbed the caltrop in its bag, and threw it away. Kept the scarf. He wouldn't want to have it found and identified as belonging to the woman who'd given it to him.

He did note where the object landed. Then swore because one of the spikes had cut his finger. *A battle wound!* he thought. How amusing. If it was such, he had been injured running from the field.

Well, what else was he supposed to do? He skidded right at the next small street, almost falling, then left again at the first laneway. A tavern he knew lay ahead. There might be—there *might* be—safety in a crowd. And there'd be people in The Fife now, surely?

There were. He could hear the noise. Thierry stopped running at the door, under the signboard, drew several deep breaths. Didn't want to burst inside and draw attention to himself. He wasn't sure where his pursuers were now. He did have a good idea who they were.

He opened the door, walked into the tavern.

Heard a loud voice, almost immediately—no quiet entry today, it seemed. "In the name of the god's drowned son!" cried Fermin Lessieur. "It's Thierry Villar, come to grace our poor corner of Orane."

Fermin was a bad poet, and a fool. The latter because, in part, he was prone to saying heretical things. He thought it made him a bold, dangerous man. There were people who didn't like him, and who might happily report heresies to the clerics. Believing Jad had a son who'd drowned in his father's chariot of the sun was a sacrilege. Could get you burned, not just hanged.

Also, poor corner of Orane? The Fife was one of the most respectable taverns in the city. Solid wooden floor and tables. Chairs, not just stools and benches. High ceiling, decently reliable wine and ale, three fireplaces. Better quality of whore, too. Thierry doubted the proprietor would appreciate his resident poet's remark. This was actually, he thought, the sort of place he could take Marina di Seressa, if she was serious about coming to a tavern. If he lived to do so.

He wouldn't bring her here, though, he thought. He'd take her farther west, maybe back across the river, to his own parts of Orane. The Lamb. Where he'd been sleeping in his friend Silvy's bed last night before he woke in the darkness and went out and everything changed.

Not just for him. Though he *was* now being pursued by men who probably wanted to kill him. That was hard to imagine. What cause could anyone have?

Except, he did more or less know. If their employer had ordered the assassination last night, then he'd not want anyone looking into it. He'd be sending a message to whoever had sent Thierry. Even a dead tavern poet was a message today.

Laurent de Barratin probably did know who had sent him, Thierry thought.

He crossed to the bar, greeted Le Futrier, the burly proprietor (no one knew his given name), begged a clean cloth to wrap his cut, and ordered a glass of Barratin wine—because doing so appealed to his sense of irony. Expensive, but the provost had given him money. Spend some before dying?

He turned around, rested his elbows on the bar. Lessieur looked as if he was considering coming over. Thierry hoped he wouldn't. He said hello to one of the girls he knew, smilingly declined an immediate invitation, and kept his eyes on the door. He had a knife in his belt, but it really wouldn't help if they attacked him. His better hope was the crowd here. The Barratin guards wouldn't want to make this public, would they?

He was surprisingly calm.

Then the door did open again and they came in, and he was . . . less calm. Three of them, after all. He watched them search the room. He wasn't hiding. They saw him soon enough. Thierry knew what he had to do.

"Look!" he shouted. "Le Futrier, you are honoured. These three are guards of the Duke de Barratin! I just saw them at his home!"

Gave them pause, being identified from the start. He saw them exchange glances. Big men with swords. They had all been big men back at the duke's home.

"The fuck you were doing there?" Le Futrier asked, genuinely startled.

"Visiting Marina di Seressa," Thierry replied matter-of-factly, as if it were the most obvious thing in all Jad's world. He raised his voice again. "She's staying with the duke just now. Might leave him to be with the queen, though, for the ceremony and the funeral. I saw the duke, too. All in black for mourning, he was. Wasn't happy to see me, alas. A stranger. Maybe worried for his family?"

His words carried through The Fife's ground floor. The room went remarkably quiet. People could read tension, and three large, armed men in the entranceway carried weight. Especially today. Why he'd mentioned the funeral.

Someone else pushed on the door, two men trying to enter.

Le Futrier was no fool, and no coward. "Gentlemen," he called to the three guardsmen, "come in or go out, you are blocking my trade! I have good wine and comely women here, should you wish."

"And poetry!" Thierry cried, on impulse. "Should everyone wish!" He wanted it widely known that he was here, and who he was. If he disappeared . . .

There was, gratifyingly, a quick murmur of approval. He had a thought.

"Fermin! Fermin Lessieur, give us a verse!"

A grumbling mutter from the man next to him at the bar and a quick laugh from the pretty woman beyond that one. Thierry was not alone in his view of Lessieur, it seemed.

Lessieur's view of himself was otherwise. He came over with alacrity. Didn't, as the tavern phrase went, need to be invited to bed twice. Thierry smiled at him. "You go first, my friend," he said.

Lessieur offered a return smile. He had good teeth, give the man that. He placed his left foot forward, like a stage performer, and promptly launched his voice into the quiet of the room.

When drinking in a tavern I approve
I am not always seeking love!
But if a comely whore summons me upstairs
I'll fuck her soundly and yield my cares!
Back down to the bar, another glass of wine . . .
I offer this as proof life can be fine!

Thierry was at pains not to wince. He put his own wine down and applauded politely with some of the other patrons.

"Save us, Thierry Villar!" someone cried—amusingly, if not courteously.

Thierry shook his head in self-deprecation. Stayed where he was, elbows casually on the bar. He stared for a moment at the three big guardsmen in black before he began. They had moved a little his way from the door. Because of that someone was able to enter. Someone he knew. Accordingly, he changed what he had planned to recite. Switched to something improvised. You needed to know how to do that in a tavern. React to the moment. He tucked new words into his well-known series of mock bestowals. Funerary bequests from a famously impoverished poet, offering his last, sardonic gifts.

He lifted a hand. He was watching the man he knew. A slight

nod from there. He nodded back, immensely relieved, though not calm yet. Violence, he thought, was embedded in this moment.

He spoke: his recital voice, clear, not hurrying, but not any kind of formal declaiming, either. That didn't work in a place like this.

> For the black-clad guards of a nobleman
> What can a poet offer from his meagre hoard
> Of objects gathered in a tavern life
> With only a tavern's room and board?
> These are trained men, armed, know how to kill.
> Do they do it for pleasure, for the blood-soaked thrill,
> Not just out of duty, ordered to use their skill?
> If so, in Jad's merciful name, I offer them a night
> In the Châtelet for questioning, as is surely right.
> And from there? A cart to bear them through Orane,
> With fruits and stones hurled at will,
> To meet their destiny on Gallows Hill!

A tense silence, then real applause. As much for his recklessness, Thierry suspected, as for the verse. They'd realize it was improvised. And they'd also know what a provocation it was. Lessieur, he saw, looked genuinely frightened. Had moved down the bar a few steps, to the other side of the man and the woman, to achieve some distance from Thierry and those words.

The applause subsided. An expectant ripple of talk and whispers followed. Thierry glanced briefly back at Le Futrier, who also looked afraid now, his eyes boring into Thierry's.

"*Fuck you!*" said one of the guardsmen. Not loudly, but everyone heard. "Someone wants to speak with you, so you're coming with us, you with the big mouth on you."

"How dare you! I believe," said Thierry Villar, "that I have a very ordinary-sized mouth. No one has ever offered me such an insult in all my days!"

Laughter. Nervous laughter. Lessieur was halfway along the bar now, Thierry noted.

"Trust me," said the same guardsman, "you'll deal with worse soon enough."

"I'm sure you'd enjoy that," said Thierry. "But I just visited the handsome palace of the Duke de Barratin. It would be a presumption to turn around and go right back."

Naming their employer again. If those in The Fife heard it, most of Orane would know tonight.

"You going to make us bring you, or you going to come calmly?"

"I'm afraid I'm not going to come at all. I think it more likely *you* have a journey ahead of you now."

Reckless again, but he *had* recognized the man who had come in alone.

And, by Jad's very great mercy to one of his poor children, that man—Medor, Robbin de Vaux's principal serjeant—took two steps back towards the door, opened it, and gestured outside.

Five armed men came through and took up positions beside him and across from him, on the other side of the duke's guards. People crowded quickly back from the door, even more so than they already had. Medor wasn't wearing the provost's livery. These serjeants were.

"I think," Medor said in a deep, clear voice, "that instead of your proposal to the poet, we'll need you to come with us, to explain what you are doing here, threatening a citizen of Orane. Given the times, I'm afraid we have no choice. He mentioned the Châtelet in his verse just now. Prophetic words."

Thierry blessed him silently. Did the same for the provost.

"You know you can't take us," the leader of the guards said.

"Really?" Medor asked. "Tell me why."

"Because you know who we are."

"A matter of indifference, or a *reason* to take you. Not sure which, yet. Why we need to talk. Are you, ah, what was the phrase you used . . .

going to make us bring you, or are you going to come calmly?"

Jad's blood, Thierry thought. The captain of the serjeants was impressive.

"We are not," the leader of the duke's guardsmen said, "going anywhere with you."

At which point one of the other guards made a mistake. It was so easy, Thierry thought later, to make mistakes in life.

The man drew his blade. Or tried to. It cleared the scabbard, just, before he was killed from behind by a serjeant's efficient sword thrust.

Someone screamed. Then a number of people did. A general push even farther away from the door. People crowding against the walls now. Murder was not unknown in taverns; this was different.

Medor and the other serjeants had their swords out. Six of them, around the remaining two of the duke's guards. The third guard lay on the wooden floor. There ensued a stillness: as cold and deadly as the winter was, Thierry thought.

Medor said, mildly, "Is this poet worth dying for?"

The leader of the guards was a brave man. "Is taking me to the Châtelet worth it, for you?"

Medor smiled thinly. "Well, now it is," he said. "More than before. A foolish threat, whatever your name is. The Duke de Barratin is unlikely to intervene before you are properly questioned tonight. After? Well, who can know the future?"

Properly questioned, Thierry thought. Also, the duke's name spoken yet again. The greatest mistake, he thought, might not have been his guardsman's. It might have been Barratin's own, sending them. On the other hand, it was wisest to remember that the world in which they lived, in Orane, Ferrieres, beyond, was shaped and ruled by power, and the Duke de Barratin had as much of it as anyone, perhaps more than anyone.

I don't know why that guardsman's death stayed in my memory so vividly. Why that one? How do we control what we remember?

I had seen death before, including violent death, and I would see more, after. I had, to my sorrow, almost killed someone myself, in that knife fight over Jolis de Charette, Jad curse her. She had not deserved to be the object of such a fight. Which was part of my sorrow. The larger part being I'd had to leave Orane for months.

So, looking back, there's no obvious reason the death of a guardsman in a tavern should have remained so vividly with me, given other events of that terrible time.

But that man in The Fife, late that day, not long after sundown, stayed as sharp in my mind as a master's painted portrait of a noblewoman or lord. A man alive. A man no longer living.

I saw him in my mind at times, for years, usually when I was falling asleep, or trying to.

Moments that never leave us. Randomly? I don't think it is that, but it might be.

The leader and the remaining guard were taken into custody by the serjeants, their swords removed from them, and the daggers they carried. The death of a man had served notice that the provost's men were serious and unintimidated. Whether that was wise was yet to be determined.

Events were moving swiftly, Thierry thought. Death sped things up.

Medor looked across the room at him. "You, too, Thierry Villar. You're coming for questioning."

"What?" Thierry exclaimed. "What did I do?"

But he knew what Medor was after. He was realizing, moment by moment, how clever this man was.

"They wanted to take you with them by force. We'll need to hear your story. Come. I'm not inclined to linger here."

"Not even for another poem?" Thierry managed.

No response. Stony face.

The other serjeants hustled the Barratin guardsmen out the door. Medor waited for him. Thierry crossed the room.

"*He did nothing wrong!*" cried Fermin Lessieur. Which was, Thierry thought, unexpectedly brave. People could surprise you. The head of the serjeants ignored the poet. Thierry turned and gave him a nod of thanks.

At the door, Medor turned back to Le Futrier behind the bar. He gestured to the dead man. "Take him to the home of the Duke de Barratin," he said.

"No," said Le Futrier, bluntly. "Sorry, serjeant, but no. This is your doing, you deal with him."

"Then send to the duke's people and have him picked up."

"Again, no, I am not intervening here. And don't leave him in my tavern, either. Bad for business."

Medor hesitated. Then nodded. "Very well. Move him to your stable. Have a boy keep watch on the body. Can you do that much? I'll have a cart sent."

Le Futrier looked at him. Another capable man, Thierry thought. "Thank you," he said. "I can."

Medor gestured to Thierry. They went out. Full darkness now. Stars, blue moon.

"You may have saved my life," he said quietly to the serjeant.

"Possible," said Medor.

"The Châtelet?" he asked, after a moment.

"No. He's still at home."

"A short detour first? I want to pick up something. For de Vaux."

"He's the provost to you, Villar."

"Of course," said Thierry. But he watched Medor collect a torch from one of the serjeants. He spoke instructions. Likely concerning the dead man. It looked as if a dozen men had come for Thierry. Jad bless them all, he thought again.

They waited until the duke's guards, hands bound now, were taken away, then the two of them walked back the way Thierry had come. Two turns—he'd been running, then—and a short way farther along. He'd thrown the caltrop beside the closed-up shopfront of a silversmith. Found it readily enough. He collected it again, wrapped it in the scarf Marina di Seressa had given him, then put it in her small satchel. He placed both back in the pocket of his coat. The serjeant watched, asked no questions.

"It proves little," Thierry volunteered, "but this was found outside Barratin's home at sunrise this morning."

"Can anyone swear to that?"

"Perhaps. I'll tell the story at the provost's house."

"Do you think they wanted to kill you? Because of that?"

"They didn't know I had it. They might have just been ordered to follow me?"

"Where were you going?"

"Coming back to report. But when I walked faster and then started running, they did too. And in the tavern . . ."

Medor nodded. "Barratin wouldn't have cared if they killed you. You aren't important."

"My mother loves me," Thierry protested.

He saw a brief smile, quickly suppressed.

The serjeant looked up past the flare of the torch he carried. "It's warmer," he said. "Can you feel it?"

Thierry nodded. "With Jad's grace, maybe it is not just one evening's—"

Medor shook his head. "There will be those who say, if it does turn milder now, that it is happening because the evil Duke de Montereau is dead. Jad sending a sign. Watch for it."

Thierry blinked. He hadn't thought of that at all.

"The provost is lucky to have you," he said.

Medor stared at him, a tall man, broad-shouldered, bearded, dark-haired. "The provost is the best man I've ever known in my life," the serjeant said. "Let's go."

They walked together in the night. The blue moon, rising above the city, was behind them. But every moment of the rest of their lives, long or short, brightly lit or dark-ensnared, lay ahead of them.

—

I also remember that walk very well, oddly. We passed through almost empty streets.

Sometimes we retain the quiet moments that come in the midst of chaos, or after it. The city, my city, in the night. Our lives, written on the dark.

CHAPTER VI

Thierry never came back to The Lamb that day and Silvy never heard from him. No messenger, no note sent. She knew how to read, had been taught by her brother before he died. He'd had some schooling, girls didn't. What she knew of letters and numbers she knew from him. Missed him every day. When she prayed in a sanctuary it was usually for his soul. (Their mother had never prayed. Not to Jad, in any event.)

Word of what had happened on the other side of the river had reached them early in the morning. Fear came with it. She'd have been angry with Thierry, but she didn't know what had happened to him, and that was at the heart of her fear. Was he in the Châtelet? Couldn't very well send a message from there. She was pretty sure now that it had been the provost who'd put him on a horse and taken him away in the night. She didn't know why. Had no idea why.

The Lamb was crowded from mid-morning. The girls had few customers through the day, however. Everyone wanted to talk, and listen. Mostly talk. Sharing rumours. Sometimes rumours they had loudly started themselves. People who were afraid, Silvy thought, weren't usually thoughtful.

She tried to be, but this was a terrifying thing.

She was busy with ale and wine all day, tried to listen to what was being said, then realized that most of it really was shaped of ignorance.

It was just noise. Why would *they* know, here, what this was about—who had killed Montereau?

She and Anni found a moment in the hallway leading upstairs, but neither had much to say. What was there to say?

Didn't stop people from speaking, mind you. Many words.

She thought about sending a message to Thierry's mother (she knew where she lived, and the small sanctuary beside it) asking if she'd heard anything about him, but she didn't. Would do nothing but frighten her. Silvy didn't want to do that.

Late in the day people coming into The Lamb began commenting that it felt less cold today than before. Someone, then someone else, suggested perhaps Jad was sending a sign, responding to the death of the tax-imposing tyrant who had ruled them just because he was the brother of the king.

Slept with the queen, too, someone said sourly. Eudes heard that, stepped out from behind the bar and right to him. Ordered the man to muzzle himself, or leave, or be thrown out. Eudes, massive, normally so placid, was a defender of almost all women. Also, those were dangerous words.

Darkness approached. Someone said, as the evening crowd grew, and grew louder, that there might be violence now, in Orane and across the country. Armies in two camps. At least two, someone else said, trying to sound wise. It was impossible to say if they would be safe, he added.

Silvy had never believed the world was safe.

She thought, as she had at times ever since her mother died, of going to Batiara, to her cousins. She had family who had settled there centuries ago, near some town on the eastern coast. Varena, it was named. She'd never met them, knew almost nothing about them, but her mother had always said they might be a place to go, in need.

She could learn another language readily enough, Silvy supposed. She was clever, wasn't she? Everyone said so. She was young, could start anew somewhere else. People did that all the time.

But really . . . where was *safety* to be found? Was Batiara safe? Not if you believed the stories told. She had friends here, a roof, a bed (sometimes shared with women or men, sometimes pleasingly). She had a life.

It entered her mind unexpectedly that she was missing Thierry's voice right now, amid all this loud, stupid talk. He might be sardonic but he wouldn't be stupid.

Of *course* she was missing him, was the next, quick thought. He was her friend!

Later that night, when she finally fell into bed (her own bed), she listened to the wind for a while, then the bells. It *did* feel as if it was warmer. She had no idea what to make of that. Decided there was nothing to make of it. Slept, eventually.

Medor Colle performed an intricate sequence of knocks at the door. Thierry was good at remembering such things, mostly without even trying, and he did so now. Had an idea of where they were in the city, but no notion why they were at this house.

Nothing of this situation was remotely familiar to him. He was still acutely aware the Barratin guards might easily have killed him. It was strange to be aware of that, think about it. Someone had written that life was an island of light between darkness and darkness. Unless Jad granted you greater light when you died.

Medor said, while they waited, "If you prefer not to be known, best say nothing. May be wisest in any case."

"I will be as silent as all the bodies in all the burial places of Orane," Thierry promised. Medor made a face.

They heard a bolt being drawn back, then a second one. The door was opened.

Later, he would try to remember his first impression of Gauvard Colle. But though the person who opened to them—himself, not a servant—carried a lamp, and there were others hanging on the hallway wall behind . . . Thierry couldn't. There was an odd kind of blurring, a shifting, lack of clarity. As if his eyes were looking through rain, or tears.

Once inside a handsome home, and seated in a large, well-furnished room with a going fire, he saw more clearly, as if the figure who'd opened the door had somehow taken pains to *be* obscured until confident of who had come.

"Medor!" he had said at the doorway. "Nephew! And a companion I don't know." A light, quick, precise voice.

"Can be trusted, Gauvard," Medor said. "I'll vouch."

A nod. "Come in then. Kiss me, first."

Medor bent and saluted Gauvard on one cheek, then walked past. Thierry followed him. He glanced back, saw the person named Gauvard bolting the door. They waited, were led into the large room. Medor was clearly familiar with this house. Thierry had no idea what they were here to do. They sat down, Gauvard nearest the fire. Medor didn't take off his coat, so Thierry didn't. He was aware of the caltrop, sharp in his pocket, against his leg.

Something else, though. Gauvard was a man's name but there was an element of uncertainty now that he saw their host more clearly. Soft features and hands. Slender fingers, a slender frame, though tall. Grey hair worn long under a blue or maybe a black cap. A loose tunic, fur vest over it. This might be a woman, Thierry thought.

And with that, he realized where they were, who this was.

Someone known, even notorious, by reputation if not, to him, by name . . . before now. He kept silent. He had said he would, and really didn't know what he'd want to say.

But Medor's uncle (his *uncle?*) was looking at him now. A measuring gaze. Then an amused smile. "Hello, Thierry Villar," he said.

"How do you know who I am?" He spoke because he'd been addressed. He was uneasy, and intensely curious, alert. There was a scent in the room, incense burning on two braziers, one by the fire, one across from it. He saw flowers, yellow and red and bright blue. How were there fresh flowers in the midst of this winter?

Gauvard Colle shrugged. "Not much use to those who pay me for help if I can't at least know your name."

"How, though? And help with what?"

Gauvard ignored the first question. "You have never spoken with someone with access to the half-world? Consulted as to love, perhaps?"

"No. But I've been with people who have done that. You're . . . different."

A giggle. "How flattering!"

Was it possible, Thierry thought, that this person was also slightly mad?

They both looked at Medor.

Gauvard said, "You want to know who murdered the Duke de Montereau. I know."

A silence.

Medor said, calmly enough, "You know who did it, or that I came to ask?"

"The second thing, clever nephew."

Medor said, "I need to know who has asked you about it today, and who might have asked for guidance in a matter such as this, in the last weeks."

Another unsettling giggle. "Clever," repeated Gauvard. "But you know I can't answer. Would destroy my trade if people didn't believe they could trust me. *You* wouldn't even come back, and I should miss seeing you so much. Besides which, you and the provost already know who killed the duke."

Flat, confident, assured. If there was madness here, Thierry thought, changing his mind, it was of a very particular sort. *He has seen too much* was the phrase that came suddenly to him.

Gauvard glanced at him quickly, as if he'd heard the thought aloud.

"*Two* clever boys," he said. "How exciting."

It wasn't. It was frightening.

Gauvard gestured, and a cat Thierry hadn't seen came from by the fire and jumped up on his lap, circled, and settled.

"I understand," Medor said, "but I still hope you can help us. This is important, and you've known me all my life."

"I held you as a newborn babe in my arms!" Gauvard's tone changed. "Doesn't matter as to those two questions. You know it." No hint of amusement now. "And yes, of course this is important. The provost will have choices to make."

"Are they his to make?" Medor asked.

Gauvard hesitated for the first time. "That's a good question. I wouldn't want danger to come to him. Or to you, nephew. Or even to this little poet who has amused me with his writing."

Thierry blinked. He said, "I have spoken with fortune tellers, astrologers, chiromancers. I've seen people go into a trance and emerge with what they say are words from the dead. I have not known anyone like you." He asked again, "How did you know me?"

"More flattery!" Gauvard cried. "I do like this boy, nephew!"

But he still didn't answer, and Thierry realized he wasn't going to. He also realized he kept thinking *he* and . . . he wasn't certain. Medor had called him uncle, Thierry decided he would be guided by that.

People spoke of the half-world, and those with access to it. Most, he'd decided long ago, were charlatans, preying on men and women with losses, needs, fears. This one . . . he wasn't sure. The uncertainty kept coming back.

"*Are* we in danger?" Medor asked. "If we investigate?"

Again Gauvard hesitated. "I think you are, yes. There are very high levels of power engaged here. The . . . rules change with that?" He looked at Medor with what Thierry thought might be affection. Their host stroked the cat. "You know what you believe by now, but you want to be able to prove it?"

Medor nodded. "Yes. Uncle, is the man in the red cloak dead?"

Laughter rippled. "He should be! But I don't know that."

"They left Orane last night?"

Gauvard's expression became disdainful. "Are you a child looking for adults to tell you things? I don't know."

"Not a child. Trying to help the provost do the right thing. I expect more from you than mockery."

"Always a mistake," Gauvard said, almost sullenly this time. Medor's uncle tossed his head, pushed a hand through his hair, then smiled at each of them. He left his gaze on Thierry. He pointed a finger at him.

"You do not always need to know answers. And you do not always need to tell everything, either."

Thierry felt exposed, raw. He cleared his throat. "That's hard for me."

Gauvard looked at him, one hand gentling the cat. "Why would it be easy?"

He gestured, dismissing them. The cat jumped down, went back by the fire.

"De Vaux will have a choice to make," Gauvard repeated at the door, letting them out into the night. "I am happy it isn't mine."

"You would step away from this?" Medor said. A note of accusation.

"Yes! I would! I may be old, but I'd like to grow older still. I have things yet to discover," said his uncle. "I believe your provost might feel the same. Good night. Be careful in the streets."

He closed the door. Thierry heard him bolting it.

Gauvard had suggested they depart through a back way to an alley, unseen. Medor had declined. It was, Thierry thought, likely not in the nature of serjeants to hide in the city. They walked, briskly, but not hurrying.

"I have questions," Thierry said.

"Of course you do," Medor said sourly. He was looking up and down the icy, unlit roadway as they walked. They were alone, or appeared to be. Carried no torch now. Probably should have asked for one, Thierry thought.

"This is a man? A woman? You said *uncle*."

"He says it is better for his business to present himself as a man. It is . . . complex."

"I'm sure it is. He really held you as a babe?"

A few steps in silence. "He's related, on my father's side. He was rejected by the family young. Made his own life after that. In Orane, and elsewhere for a time. I don't think it was easy. Gauvard is . . . different, as you saw. I only learned of his existence from my older brother some years ago. Was curious, sought him out."

"Why?"

"Told you. I was curious. You ask many questions, Villar."

"Says the man who just said he was curious. Questions are *good*," Thierry exclaimed. "How else do we learn things?"

"Not my task in life to help you do that. Unless you decide you want to become a serjeant. There I could help, might even be ordered to. You could do worse. I told you, de Vaux is the best man I know. You could change your life, Villar."

Thierry's turn to walk in silence. He heard an animal behind them. A dog, he hoped. He said, "I don't want to change my life."

Medor glanced over at him. "Poetry? Dice and cards and drink? Different beds every night?"

"Those, and freedom."

"And poverty? The need to rob a sanctuary?"

Thierry winced. "That was a stupid thing."

"Very. Why?"

"So many questions, Medor Colle."

The other man laughed again, that quiet laugh, almost unwilling, as if his own amusement surprised him.

Thierry said, "Gambling debt, as you seem to have already guessed. Unpleasant men. Threats were made."

"I see. You'll likely be paid for your assistance, if that helps."

"Oh, it does," Thierry said feelingly. "Depending on how much. The provost uses you to consult your . . . uncle?"

Another silence. The stars above were fiercely bright now with only the thin blue moon riding. Scattered clouds. The night was hard and clear, but not as cold. A change in the air. Orane at night. The mysteries of it. Shadows and domes.

"Yes, he does," said Medor. "He uses astrologers and others. Most military leaders do. I told him about Gauvard. He knew of him."

Thierry took a chance. "It helped you rise among the serjeants? A useful connection to the half-world?"

Medor sighed. "I'm sure it did. I was never a soldier. Grew up here, entered the provost's ranks young, running errands at the beginning, grooming horses. Usually they prefer military men. Not always, but . . ."

"So this was good for you. And did he really hold you as an infant?"

Medor shook his head. "He likes to say he did."

"He didn't tell us anything just now, did he?"

Medor stopped in the street. "Now you've disappointed me, Villar. Think back. What he said. Think carefully."

Thierry, stung, tried to do so as the other man looked down at him, waiting.

It didn't take long.

Chagrined, he said, "High levels of power involved. Dangerous choices to be made. He . . . said what you and the provost have been thinking? And he didn't know if the man in the red cloak was dead."

"Well," Medor said, "that's better. Maybe you can learn things after all. He told us a great deal, in his way. Also . . . I saw you looking. The flowers were from the queen."

"*What?* How? How does she have fresh . . . ?"

"There's a room in the palace, I'm told, kept extremely warm with fires, piles of earth, gardeners attending. The queen likes flowers. Even in winter."

"So if flowers were in Gauvard's house . . ."

"She likely sent for him today, yes. With a gift, before or after. So she's also trying to learn what happened last night."

"And he'll have told her . . . ?"

"I have no idea," Medor said. "I'll just report it to the provost."

"Who has choices to make."

"Choices which could get him, and me, and even you killed, yes."

Which gave a man pause.

"I'm just a poet," he said.

"Not right now you aren't."

"Do you . . . do you really think they'd have killed me? If you hadn't come?"

"If the provost hadn't sent us, you mean?" Another animal heard, also behind them. Or the same one? "Likely, yes," Medor Colle said. "No reason not to, the way the world is. Safer for him to have it done."

Thierry had time to draw and let out a breath, then they were attacked.

Gauvard hadn't intended to say what he'd said to the two men as they left. He'd been distracted by their youth, probably. Pretty boys. He remembered being pretty once. But they were true, the words he'd spoken at the door: he did feel old, but he wasn't ready to surrender what life might yet offer before he crossed over to whatever would follow.

There was a paradox here (he liked paradoxes): he'd told the appealing poet that he shouldn't look in his work or life for certainty, or share everything he knew. But here he was, walking back to his sitting room and his fire, wanting to gain more from life in what others called Jad's world. The mysteries of it. He smiled, with no one there to see it.

Well, his cat. Who jumped up on his lap again, as he subsided into his usual cushioned chair.

They really had been pretty men, he thought. The poet, Villar, was the sort who'd have tormented his reveries when he was younger. Quick-witted, alert, a smooth, softly bearded face, probably sweeter without the beard. It had been years, he thought, since that actual torment had occurred within him because of a man or a woman.

Lovemaking, given how he was made, had always been complex, requiring a special kind of partner. He'd travelled in search of those (among other things), years ago. All the way to Sarantium, where rumour had it that people such as he were known and accepted in some quarters, not fiercely rejected by family or so-called friends. And the rumours had proven blessedly true, for once.

He'd stayed for years in the wonder of that city. Diminished from its splendour a thousand years before, but still glorious. There was something about the ruins everywhere, how they made you feel walking through, or past. The thoughts they shaped. Fallen statues, monuments from long ago, inscriptions to long-dead charioteers. He had even seen the fabled night fires dancing once, moving in darkness ahead of him along an empty street very late, then gone. Gone. He would remember that as long as he remembered anything, he thought.

He was also remembering now the small house he'd leased not far from the ruins of the Hippodrome, vivid, wondrous pleasures taken there.

And kindness found for a time.

You could live, Gauvard thought, on the memories of love, physical and otherwise. He was doing so, wasn't he? Right now, by the fire, with a cat? He had come home because he'd known he could do well here, shape a proper livelihood, which had been challenging in the east. Still, to this day, he didn't know if it had been the right thing to do. Lives were built on such decisions, and regrets sometimes.

A sharp nudge in his mind. A prodding from the half-world. He lived with those, too. Always had, from first awareness as a child.

Some danger in the street for his nephew and the poet. He could sense it, but not *do* anything about it. Then a moment later he grasped more clearly what this was and he settled back, stroked the cat more easily. Thought about what he wanted his cook to prepare for dinner.

He was quite sure Medor was equal to this, even in darkness. Couldn't send him a warning in any case. There were limits to what the half-world allowed him.

Be grateful for what it did allow: his reminder to himself, every day. He looked at the queen's flowers, yellow, red, and that rich blue.

Another inward nudge. Not about a thing to be done but a new awareness. A thing to remember. Might be useful one day. Or not. You did not control the half-world. It allowed you, at times, glimpses.

He decided he felt more like a woman tonight. He called his housekeeper to tell the cook what he wanted to eat and then bring down an evening robe the queen had given him in thanks for counsel some years ago. It was eastern silk of the very finest kind, a colour between burgundy and red, fur-trimmed in white at collar and wrists.

He adored it. One of the pleasures life could still offer. Like two handsome men coming to call, one of them the nephew who did not know he was going to inherit everything Gauvard had. He liked surprising. He'd be dead for this one, of course, but who knew—who could possibly know?—he might be able to watch, see, smile when Medor learned what he'd done.

He didn't intend to just die and drift away. Might happen, but it wasn't his plan.

"You have a knife?" Medor asked briskly, over the animal sounds.

"Yes, but I'm not very—"

"Do what you can, if you need to," the other man said, and turned, drawing his sword.

In the event, nothing was needed of Thierry at all. He stood there, gripping his knife, peering into the night. There were no lights where they were. One house up the street still had a lantern lit, you could see it faintly through closed shutters. It wasn't even late, he thought.

He saw blurred shapes moving fast. And then Medor.

It was over with shocking speed. His eyes had adjusted just enough for him to see two wolves lying in the street.

He watched the serjeant walk over to one of them, carefully, and put his sword into it again. He was trying to come to terms with what he'd just seen.

Medor came back to him. "Did either of them reach you? Bitten or scratched?"

"No. Nothing close to me."

The fear, the great fear, was the disease from an infected animal's bite, for which there was no cure and of which you died in agony. Lyssava, the physicians called it.

He sought refuge in trying to be clever. Cleared his throat. "I thought you said you were never a soldier."

"Never was," Medor said calmly. "But there's very often violence in the city, as you know. And we train. All the time. You learn. You're all right?"

"As I said, neither came close. Just the two of them?"

"Seems so. I'll have someone come with a wagon. Can't leave dead wolves in the street for other animals. But I don't think they were diseased, just hungry."

Thierry drew another deep breath. "Indeed," he said, for lack of any other response that came to him just then. He was still gripping his knife, he realized. He sheathed it. "More violence than I'm accustomed to," he said.

Medor Colle looked at him, tilted his head to one side. "You've done well enough," he said. "Let's go. We'll report. De Vaux will give us food and drink. Aren't you hungry?"

"I suppose I am," Thierry said.

"He has a good cook," Medor said. "Come."

Thierry couldn't be sure, but thought he saw the other man smile. They walked on. One moon, winter stars. The life you chose, or were given.

Later that night, by way of a boy defying curfew for a coin, Thierry sent word to Silvy at The Lamb that he was all right. Only that. Nothing more. Not where he'd been all day, or where he was now.

It was, Silvy thought, when the last patron left and the tavern was clean again and she finally fell into bed, enough for the moment. She dreamed of punching him: on the nose, on the chest, high up between his legs, really hard. It was satisfying.

CHAPTER VII

The two pre-eminent dukes of Ferrieres, the king's surviving uncles, were men of great sophistication, although neither was particularly engaged by the business of the state and its survival.

The murder of their nephew had shaken both to the core, and also induced feelings of dismay that *they* now appeared tasked with addressing it. They did not share this latter feeling with anyone, of course.

The Duke de Barille had firmly intended to spend what years Jad saw fit to leave him engaged in commissioning and acquiring and enjoying works of art. Dealing with something as savage as an assassination had not been in his plans.

Accordingly, along with the Duke de Regnault, his brother, he eyed inimically the provost of Orane—and a number of his serjeants—in their path on the roadway to the palace the day after their nephew's funeral. They wanted to mourn, and be left in what could pass for peace in such a time, after necessary discussions as to the governance of Ferrieres now.

It was not to be.

The provost was in black, as were they. In a world replete with colours, the black stood out—as it was meant to, of course.

Neither duke noted, since they had no possible reason to, a small man, also dressed in black, among the serjeants behind Robbin de Vaux. Someone paying attention would have observed that the small man looked as unhappy as the dukes did, but in his case it appeared to be a result of his horse being restive at the moment. One of the serjeants reached over, took the horse by the bridle, and calmed it. The two dukes didn't see that either, of course.

What they did see—heard it first, in fact—was the queen's carriage behind them, also approaching the palace, from her own home in the city. They looked back. An accident of timing, everyone arriving at once. Her driver pulled to a halt behind the dukes and the provost. Queen Bianca leaned out of a rolled-down window into the morning cold of Orane, a dyed-black marten-fur hat on her head.

The dukes turned their horses, bowed to her. This public encounter was *deeply* unusual. Of course it was. It also meant that she'd hear whatever they now heard from the provost.

Robbin de Vaux's face had been grimly serious, waiting for them. It tended to be, the Duke de Barille thought. Old soldier, de Vaux. He wore a helmet not a hat. The man would be better suited to be sculpted than painted, the duke thought. Hard, powerful features. An idle reflection, given the moment. He was prone to such. He lived in a fierce pursuit of beauty, in a world that resisted that.

The queen spoke first. She said, her voice carrying to the crowd that had gathered in the cold beside the road, "Provost, are you here to offer us tidings and conclusions?"

De Vaux bowed. "I am, your grace."

"Not here, then," she said briskly. "In the palace. Uncles, I *will* be present for this. Begin nothing at all until I join you."

The Duke de Regnault wished to say he would prefer to begin nothing at all! He greatly desired to be home just now, warm, with one or two of the young women to whom he felt indebted for what remained of his vigour and joy in life. Along with wine.

He didn't share this thought either. There had been a murder. Of one of them. The king's brother. They might all be in danger now, if you thought about it.

"Shouldn't Barratin be here?" he asked suddenly. It had just occurred to him.

"He should, my lord," said the provost calmly.

De Vaux always appeared so unruffled, Regnault thought.

"Then why . . . ?" asked Barille, bewildered.

"He is no longer in Orane," the provost said.

If you had been looking at the queen of Orane just then, you might have seen a look of bitterest satisfaction on her elegant, imperious features.

"*What?*" said the Duke de Barille. "He was with us at the funeral! He helped carry the casket!"

"Yes," said Queen Bianca. "He did, didn't he? Only yesterday." You could almost taste poison in her voice. "No more words! Inside the palace, my lords. The smaller stateroom upstairs. Make way in the road for my carriage, if you'd all be so kind."

Kindness, Thierry Villar thought, astride a horse again, unhappily, was not a word you'd associate with the manner of the queen of Orane then. Or with any of what was happening.

The funeral procession from the palace to the Great Sanctuary on its island in the river had been a difficult affair. The roads were lined, six or seven deep, by the people of Orane. As their nobility processed past, the mightiest of the realm carrying the bier of the Duke de Montereau, there were tears, and cries of grief and fear. But also, unmistakably, shouts of denunciation of the dead man. He had been greedy, came some cries. Corrupt. Cruel. Forsaking the god.

So many sins! The crowd was too thick, Thierry Villar remembered thinking, for anyone to be identified. Or they'd not have been shouting.

The weather was warmer.

His own presence among the serjeants, walking (Jad be praised!) not riding, remained a matter of disquiet and anxiety to him. De Vaux was not, evidently, releasing him back to his own life yet.

Among those ahead of them, well ahead, had been the Duke de Barratin. Thierry had seen his face as the procession assembled in the palace courtyard. He remembered it, of course. He was not about to forget it.

It was stricken with visible grief, that hard, hawk-like face, tears running down into the dark, neatly barbered beard.

"He left in the night?" Queen Bianca asked in the room where they'd assembled.

It was more of a statement, Thierry thought. He was bemused, and frightened, to find himself here, but de Vaux had insisted. Because Thierry was a lawyer, he'd said—and had refused to accept any disclaimers as to that. Thierry had training, yes, had studied the Codex and Digest of Valerius of Sarantium and other ancient texts. He had graduated, had his diploma somewhere (his mother's house, she'd know where), but had never done anything with law at all. He had tried to avoid encountering the law, instead! Surely there were proper advocates the provost could summon.

But . . . no. Robbin de Vaux, for reasons of his own, which he did not deign to share, wanted Thierry Villar with him.

The provost had also given Thierry a substantial sum of money (very substantial for a tavern poet) two nights ago, after he and Medor had returned and reported.

The next morning, early, before they'd walked in the funeral procession and ceremony, Thierry had sent a necessary portion of that to a necessary destination: a man who might now not proceed to break various of his limbs, or kill him outright for debt.

To say it was a relief was to understate.

"Yes, your grace," de Vaux now said, answering the queen. "He left at nightfall, after the funeral service and burial."

"You know this because you had people watching his house?"

She was sharp, attentive, alert. The women of Batiara seemed to be like that, Thierry thought.

The king? The king remained as he had been all winter. Not here with them, not here for his people in any way. He hadn't been at the funeral.

"Yes, your grace, we did," said the provost now.

"And why did you do that?" The Duke de Barille. Asking almost reluctantly. As if sensing where this might be going and not liking it at all: the ways in which it might impinge upon his serene, orderly life. But also not able to let this pass, glumly aware of duty emerging, as from mist, unwelcome. The distaste on his face.

"Because we had previously taken and were still interrogating two of his guards in the Châtelet, my lord duke."

"And you did *that* why?" Regnault now. He didn't look detached anymore either.

"Because they, and a third guard, had attempted to capture and very likely kill a man I had asked to assist me in this matter. My serjeants were able to prevent this and take the two for questioning. The third was killed. The Duke de Barratin will have learned of this."

"What man of yours?" asked the queen. Her voice was cold, very precise.

"He is with us here, your grace. Still assisting me. A citizen of Orane . . . an advocate, among other things."

Thierry, so identified, stepped into view from behind tall serjeants and managed a bow. His heart was pounding. That never used to happen to him, he thought. Lately it seemed to be occurring all the time! But this was . . . this was the queen! The court!

"*Ah.*" A woman's voice. "Thierry Villar! I know him. A fellow poet and my newest friend!"

Queen Bianca turned. "You know this person?" Voice still icy, commanding.

"Happily so, your grace," said Marina di Seressa.

He had noticed her, of course, as soon as she'd walked in, one of three women and two clerics accompanying the queen. She had told him she had been summoned. She had responded. Hard to imagine how not. And she was *attesting* to his identity. Here. To royalty.

Who was he, that she would do that? He knew, after a fashion, why the provost had kept him close: he had done what he'd been asked to do, at risk. De Vaux was a soldier, would value and honour that.

Proper value and honour, Thierry had felt like saying the night before, would have meant letting him go back to The Lamb to drink and eat among friends, then go upstairs with a girl. Free of debt.

Not, evidently, how this was to unfold. The cards had been laid out otherwise.

"And did these two guards . . . did they share information with you, provost?" It was Regnault. Taking the lead here, Thierry thought. Reluctantly?

De Vaux nodded his head. "They did, my lord duke." He turned to the queen. "Your grace."

"And this information . . . ?" asked Queen Bianca.

"Led me to go myself and ask to be received by the Duke de Barratin at his palace."

"And were you received?" The queen, Thierry thought, was looking very much on edge. Again, unsurprisingly.

"I was not, your grace. He sent word with his steward saying he was not free to receive me. But there was . . . a letter."

"A letter? You have it?" Regnault again. The Duke de Barille was silent now.

"I do," said the provost simply.

"Read it," commanded the queen of Ferrieres.

De Vaux hesitated for the first time. Medor Colle stepped forward and handed him a document.

De Vaux cleared his throat. "It is brief," he said. "It reads, 'I concede I have done certain things that might appear to be wrongful, but they were done only for the good of Ferrieres and in the name of Jad. I rest easy in my conscience. I will send advocates to plead my case before the court, but you must also know I am not without the resources or the will to uphold the justice of my cause, in any and all ways that might be required.'"

"That last," said the queen, breaking the taut stillness that followed this, "is treason. He threatens war."

"He does it carefully," said the Duke de Regnault. "Not . . . in so many words." But his voice was . . . his voice was *pale*, Thierry thought.

"What? Are you *afraid* of him, my lord?" the queen demanded.

"I am afraid of civil war, your grace. We have enemies without. We cannot afford to be fighting within. I believe . . . I am certain . . . that you know this."

"Barratin has his own court at Berga and revenues and ports, and an army at least as large as any we could put into the field. He also has followers here in Orane." It was Barille, regaining his voice. "We cannot be reckless."

The queen was white-faced with fury, Thierry saw. "Reckless?" she snapped. "It is *reckless* to respond to a confession of murder? The murder of the king's brother? The guardian of the prince? The governing steward of Ferrieres? Really, my lords? *Really?*"

"Indeed, power and justice can sit uneasily together, your grace." Barille might have been a man who preferred the world of art to that of the court, but he was no fool, Thierry was realizing.

"And you, provost of Orane? What say you?"

De Vaux kept his voice level. "Majesty, I am neither of the court nor of the army anymore. My task is peace and justice in this city. I was charged by my office with finding who murdered the Duke de Montereau, and to report this here. I have now done so. If there is war, with anyone at all, my sword and my life are at the service of Ferrieres, to death. Decisions beyond that are for others to make."

"Understood," said the queen. "But I am asking for your *view*, as an adviser to the court."

De Vaux looked, again, deeply uneasy. He cleared his throat. He said, "We have confessions from those in the Châtelet and—"

"Were they among the killers of the duke?" Regnault again.

"No, my lord. But they saw them being assembled, and they saw them return to the Barratin palace that night, then leave the city before sunrise."

"They *saw* them leave the city?" Regnault was being very precise.

De Vaux said, "Thank you, my lord. No. They saw them leave the duke's palace. My serjeants confirmed with the guards at the wall that ten or twelve armed men rode out."

"They *let* them do that?" demanded the queen. Poison in her voice again, Thierry thought.

"Two men were struck down trying to stop them, your grace," de Vaux said quietly. "They are dead."

There was a silence.

The Duke de Barille said, as if against his will, "You have those statements and we have . . . this letter. There is no attempt being made to hide this. He will seek to justify it, he says."

"By savagely maligning a murdered lord," said Queen Bianca. "Is that how this is to happen? Because Barratin has an army in the east? Provost, I am still waiting for your counsel."

De Vaux was pale now, Thierry saw. He felt faint himself. What was he *doing* here? The provost said, "A large army is a very great thing, your grace, in the times in which we live. The king of the Anglcyn may be across the channel north, but he has forces on our land, and fortresses here he occupies, and his informers are everywhere in Ferrieres. He will know all of this very soon."

"So Laurent de Barratin succeeds?" said Queen Bianca bitterly. "He wins a battle for power by killing Rollin like a dog in the street? Is that where Ferrieres is now? Is it what we are?"

No one spoke. No one seemed about to speak, to answer a terrible question.

Thierry Villar cleared his throat softly. The provost heard. Looked over his shoulder, his brow knitted. Later Thierry would decide it might have been fear on *his* behalf. But de Vaux said, "Yes, counsellor?"

Counsellor?

In his mind, Thierry named himself a fool, attaching every imprecation he could conjure. Aloud, he said, from a step behind the provost (as if for shelter), "Your grace, my lords, the letter spoke of advocates, and pleading his cause. There is . . . there is an opportunity in this."

"And what will any of that matter?" the queen said scornfully.

"It might, majesty," said Marina de Seressa.

Queen Bianca turned to her. Thierry began to breathe again. He hadn't been, he realized.

"Tell me why," said the queen. Not to him. To the other poet.

With composure, Marina di Seressa said, "His admissions and the provost's allegations will be spoken aloud at that time. They will be recorded, and eventually shared. Whatever explanations the Duke de Barratin offers, his words and actions become written down. That may matter."

"Marina, he will buy the best advocates in Orane," said the queen.

"Even so, your grace. They can be opposed. I believe Messire Villar might be right."

Thierry hadn't actually said this, he wanted to protest, he had merely reminded everyone that a hearing had been proposed, but . . . this *had* been his thought, yes. If a great deal less precise. He looked at Marina di Seressa. She didn't smile, but she briefly met his gaze, then turned back to the queen, as was proper and necessary.

The hearing in the matter of the assassination of Duke Rollin de Montereau took place three days later in the great hall of the royal palace in Orane. No one wanted this affair to linger, fester. It was too dangerous. One way or another, a response was required.

Again Thierry was present, still in black, as was the provost. Again he did not know why de Vaux wanted him here. Was it a considered plan? An instinct? He had asked, twice, to be dismissed to go back home, or to The Lamb, and his life. He had been refused, though courteously. Perhaps a little less so the second time.

De Vaux was under great strain and Thierry knew it. It was entirely possible, depending on how this hearing went, that the provost could be arrested himself, charged with overreaching, offering a gross indignity to a powerful lord. Treachery to Orane, even.

There had been a mob and a fire at the home of the Duke de Barratin two nights before.

Word of the duke's flight from the city, and his admission that he'd had the king's brother slain, had run through Orane about as quickly as one might expect. People had gathered before the Barratin walls and courtyard, and had broken through the gates as darkness fell.

A terrible thing. There was widespread destruction and looting, until the provost's serjeants and royal guards broke it up and then men acted, with difficulty, to quench the flames.

A considerable number of citizens were arrested and taken to the Châtelet. Thirty-two, three women among them, would later be hanged on Gallows Hill, the most at a single time in memory.

So the provost had defended the Barratin palace, but he had earlier precipitated the duke's flight with his guards and some of his household, leaving that palace exposed to what happened. De Vaux could be assailed whichever way the impending hearing went.

He might be permitted, Thierry thought, to be a little short-tempered with a poet pleading to leave his service.

Thierry had actually ridden out with the serjeants when word of the fire and looting had come. Hadn't *done* anything, just stayed on his nervous mount, with some effort, amid the screaming and smoke. He had been looking at the people of his city. So many here, and so enraged—or perhaps just caught up in the illusion of rage. The fraternity of it. The theatre. City life was often theatre. But not usually this violent.

The mob hated Laurent de Barratin in that moment, but they might love him another day—as soon as tomorrow. Mobs could be like that.

The smoke had hidden the stars, he remembered. Someone, as he watched, threw a stone in their direction, and then another. One of the serjeants was struck on the head by that second one. The man rocked in his saddle but didn't fall. There was blood, Thierry saw. Medor Colle saw it too, glanced quickly at the crowd over that way.

"The big one in the green coat, front row," Thierry said, before he realized what he was doing. He looked at Medor, swallowed hard.

"I didn't hear that," the senior serjeant said after a moment. "And you didn't tell me." Another beat amid the shouting and smoke, the flames from the house. Medor added, leaning closer, "You aren't one of us, Villar, you have your own world. These people are part of that. I know I suggested you come with us, but be careful you know what you want."

But he didn't know! Even now, today, in the great hall of the palace—a room he'd never thought to see in his life—he didn't know.

The main doors opened. A court herald first. His staff pounded the floor, shaping silence. The queen walked in, followed by her entourage, including the high cleric of Ferrieres and the dukes. Marina di Seressa was with her again. Someone might say that she—and he— had steered court and country to this moment.

That was a terrifying thought.

Bianca di Rizzetto seated herself on one of the two thrones. The second was empty. The king was not here. Much might have been different in Ferrieres and the world if the king had been present. This moment would not be upon them had he been well, Thierry thought. He might come back to them, for an interval, as he did when the madness receded from him, but it hadn't yet, this time. It was almost certain, de Vaux had said, that King Roch had no idea his brother was dead. He glanced at the provost. Robbin de Vaux was standing ramrod straight, facing the thrones.

There was a dais to the left of those. A stone lectern had been placed there. Three tonsured men in judicial robes sat on a long stone bench behind it, near a fire. Thierry knew them all, from his time at the university. Two had been retained by the duke-uncles of the dead man and the king. One was here to speak for Laurent de Barratin, who had acknowledged murder. And fled. That third man he remembered quite well, the best teacher he'd had, even if he hadn't cared for his studies very much.

He stared at Denis Cassin. Poise and intelligence could be frightening, deployed in a cause. He wondered how much Cassin was being paid. A great deal, for certain. He was, Thierry thought, at some risk here, too. Everyone was!

Certain documents and findings, including the letter from Barratin and the confessions of the two men from the Châtelet, were read out. This was the making of a record, as much as anything. After checking with the clerics writing it down, the court chamberlain, a stout, bald man, nodded his head at the dais.

Cassin was all that Thierry remembered. Smooth, eloquent, drily astringent.

"The queen and the court will remember, of course," he was now saying, having begun with principles of law precisely set forth, including those of the Emperor Valerius, naturally, "how Aristimedes defended Rhodias of the Ancients and the lands it ruled from the unbridled ambitions of one we do not name, by custom, but who wished to be a tyrant over a thousand years ago. Aristimedes took the hard, harsh steps that ended a deceitful man's life, and thereby saved glorious Rhodias. The would-be usurper was . . . well, he was a man who craved wealth, and was known to lust for the wives of others in the circles of power. There is even a tale he had his mistresses painted in frescoes on a wall in a private chamber, for his private enjoyment."

There was, Thierry knew, no such tale at all.

And then, predictable as rain under springtime clouds, Denis Cassin used that falsified image to begin describing the slain Duke de Montereau as a dire and desperate threat to Ferrieres: a vicious, greedy, self-absorbed hunter of wealth, chasing down the hard-earned coins of honest citizens for his own vainglorious goals.

The queen, who might have been one of those mistresses, listened, stony-faced. Her poise was impressive, but if you looked closely, you could read fury in her body language, including the hands with which she gripped the arms of her throne.

Cassin went on, with a slight, sorrowful shake of his head. "I now turn, of necessity, to the matter of dark magics employed against Jad's anointed, our beloved King Roch, by the demonic Duke de Montereau, and his wife from Batiara, from the city of Macera, where such evil arts are known to—"

"*No!*" said the queen of Ferrieres.

She had risen to her feet.

"Counsellor, you have great licence here, defending a nobleman. But not this slander. Not this. If you persist, your role as counsel will not protect you. Be advised!"

Cassin stopped as if he had collided with a wall. He smoothed his gown with a nervous hand. He coughed, lowered his head.

"Yes, your grace," he said quietly, when he was able to look up again.

That exchange would be in the record, too, Thierry thought. It really would have been wiser for Cassin to bear in mind that the queen was from Batiara as well. She didn't like—it was widely reported—Bettina de Montereau, the slain duke's wife, now his widow, but she would not, she *had* not stayed silent for this double slander.

Cassin was too experienced to be undone by this, but he did lose some of his force, Thierry thought, if not his eloquence.

You would have said it was too lengthy, his speech, except he spoke so well, with light and learned allusions, flattering those who listened, three clerics independently recording his words, to check their writing against each other's later. He had a habit of laying one finger along the side of his face when he was pausing for a particular effect. Thierry remembered it.

He drew a breath. This had nothing to do with him now. The dukes had two advocates to counter and rebut what Cassin was devising: an image of Laurent de Barratin as a heroic protector of Ferrieres, both the court and the humble citizenry, against a power-mad nobleman chasing his brother's throne, a threat to every man's purse, and to every woman at court, married or otherwise.

And perhaps a magic-user, accursed of Jad?

Cassin had paused again. Now he drew himself up and spread his legs wider. A signal he had come to an end, that people ought to pay even more rapt attention to the words he vouchsafed them from the dais.

"And so, your grace, lords and ladies of this noble court, clerics of piety and renown, I say to you now, with holy Jad as my witness, that rather than falsely accusing the Duke de Barratin of treachery, as *some* here have done"—he looked directly at the provost—"we ought to be extending our grateful appreciation that he stepped forward bravely to protect us all from terrible danger. And that he has a considerable force to bring to bear upon . . . ah, on behalf of . . . our beloved Ferrieres, in darkly challenging times. Times," he added, soberly, judiciously, "are always challenging, but perhaps never more so than now."

GUY GAVRIEL KAY

He nodded once, to show he was done. He bowed to the queen, seemingly oblivious to the icy gaze she visited upon him, and withdrew to his seat on the bench behind the dais. There was a ripple in the great hall. Thierry judged it one of approval. He knew audiences. In some ways they were all the same.

"Jad rot the soul he doesn't have!" Medor muttered beside him.

Thierry looked at him. Medor was staring at where Denis Cassin was settling himself like a hen upon eggs. The advocate gestured and was brought a cup of wine. He took a sip. Didn't smile, but looked as if he was close to doing that.

"He's speaking from power to power," Thierry said softly. He saw de Vaux, in the row ahead of them, tilt his head back to listen. "He did what he was hired to do, what we could have expected him to do. Did it well. Now we see the other two, how they balance this."

Except, for reasons that became increasingly, painfully clear, that did not happen.

It ought to have been anticipated, really, the provost said afterwards. The two senior dukes, neither young, neither a war leader, neither known for political ambition—or courage—had evidently come to a pragmatic understanding. They might, de Vaux had added, even have prided themselves on acting for the good of Ferrieres. Avoiding a civil war, with the Anglcyn hovering, poised to invade.

They might, he added again, have been correct.

Only one of the dukes' two advocates spoke in reply to Denis Cassin. If you could call it a reply. He began by applauding Cassin's learned invoking of Aristimedes. He then spoke, at some length, of the need to be aware of the examples of the past as guides to proper conduct in the present day. Historical knowledge, he suggested, was always of value. He actually turned then and bowed to Cassin, who rose and returned the bow.

It was all very cordial. Theatre.

The only thing the speaker said—the closest he got to directly addressing Cassin and the man for whom he'd spoken—was to suggest that each case of violence needed to be considered on its own merits, as legal precedents all agreed.

Killing an enemy in wartime was not murder, for example, he said. But killing a man for his purse was. He carefully cited a case for each proposition. He said the court would need to decide to which pole of these two the present matter (he used that word) fell more closely. He noted, with limited relevance, that no money had been stolen in this affair. He closed by lamenting that the king was indisposed and unable to lend his great wisdom to their task today.

He sat down.

The other advocate for the two dukes nodded his head soberly. Patted his colleague on the shoulder. Did not rise to add anything. At all.

The queen stared at them. She turned and looked back at her husband's two uncles, the protectors now of Ferrieres and the prince, her child. The king's child. The men who had chosen these advocates. Thierry could not see her face then. He did see the dukes shift in their seats. It allowed him a guess as to her expression. Her rage.

He felt it rising within himself. For no good reason concerning his own life, concerning young Thierry Villar, tavern poet.

He met the gaze of Marina di Seressa among the women behind the queen. He saw her eyes narrow. She shook her head quickly, emphatically, but by then he was already on his feet, and so quite visible in that hall, among that company.

He leaned forward, said quietly to the provost, "Have I permission to speak for you? Lacking that, I have no standing here at all."

Robbin de Vaux turned to look at him. And after what felt a long moment said, "You do. Let me speak first."

"Are we fools?" Thierry asked.

"Very likely," said the provost of Orane.

De Vaux rose to his feet. A big man, distinguished-looking. Not among the higher nobility, but with a lineage, and of importance in this room given his history and his office. He bowed to the queen, to the nobles behind her, to the high cleric. Then he bowed one more time, to the empty throne of the king of Ferrieres.

He said, after waiting for Queen Bianca to acknowledge him, "Your grace, I claim no eloquence at all. I am a soldier and an official of the court, defending Orane from danger as best I can. I was called in the middle of the night to investigate a terrible murder. I seek leave to have an advocate speak on behalf of the provost's office, with no aspersions cast on either of the fine men who have just spoken. Will you grant it?"

Eloquent enough, Thierry thought.

So, evidently, did the queen. "I do grant leave. Your advocate may speak. I will hope," she added, "he does so cogently." Which was telling, really.

De Vaux turned and nodded to Thierry, who found himself, as in a fever dream, approaching the dais and the stone lectern. He glanced at Denis Cassin as he approached. Cassin looked . . . furious. He'd thought this was over, clearly.

Good, thought Thierry Villar. He also thought, *Fuck you.* He kept his face expressionless. He turned his back on the three advocates and looked at the queen of Ferrieres, clad in black, mourning.

He drew a breath. "Your grace, my lords, I stand before you with diffidence—and with anger." That last word because of what he saw in the queen. He wanted her to hear it.

She nodded, his reward. He wondered how the two dukes were regarding him. He didn't glance their way, or at Marina di Seressa. There was only one person who mattered right now, along with the clerics, scribbling everything down. He looked briefly at the lectern to gather himself. He was pleased to see his hands were steady. He hoped his voice would be.

His fury was real. It astonished him.

He said, "I remember Messire Cassin from my days at the university. I studied the law with him. I had—and have—nothing but respect for his skill as an advocate. Alas, today, I have an equal disdain for his betrayal of Ferrieres."

"*What!*" cried Cassin from behind him.

Thierry heard him stand. "Your majesty, I must—"

"Messire, you have had a goodly interval to make your case. Be seated and let someone else make theirs." Queen Bianca was not, Thierry thought, mincing words. "I still do not really know the provost's advocate . . ." she said. "Marina?"

Thierry saw Marina di Seressa lean forward then and whisper to the queen. He saw the woman on the throne raise her eyebrows. "Ah. Yes. I remember now. We have heard tell of you, Thierry Villar . . . in other contexts. We await your submission to us. Continue."

"I am honoured beyond words," Thierry said. "I will add, lest my old teacher feel singled out, that I am equally disappointed in the advocate who spoke after my old instructor Cassin. There may be reasons why he took so much time to say nothing . . . but he said nothing. Among other things I will note that what happened in the street that night was not a *matter*. It was a murder. An assassination."

If, Thierry thought, he was going to be killed today, or hanged on Gallows Hill soon, he'd do so leaving words that might be remembered. He had said before there needed to be a record. There would be. He'd have preferred his own last words be poetry, and perhaps to have had a chance to say some goodbyes. Maybe that would be allowed? But standing there, hands gripping the cold stone of the lectern, he did not expect to live past nightfall, or even through the hours left of Jad's pale sun shining on a winter's day.

He cleared his throat, more for attention than anything else, though he was aware from the quality of the silence that he had the attention of the room. He really did know audiences. This was just another one of those, he told himself again.

He said, "It is always pleasing to hear a learned advocate make reference to the Ancients. It shows that such knowledge is not dead in these times. But, as to Aristimedes, please, *please* let us remember that he also had an army, and allies, and could have caused a civil war for control of Rhodias."

He paused. Let no one here miss the point of this for today, he thought, as to the Duke de Barratin and *his* threatened forces. He even turned and looked back at Denis Cassin, for greater emphasis. The advocate's face had accomplished a shade one might have called white-green.

Thierry turned back. He said, "He did not summon an army, Aristimedes, nor did he flee the city. He yielded his person and his sword, submitted himself to justice, admitted the nature of the crime he'd done, the murder, and vowed by the gods the Ancients worshipped to accept the verdict of Rhodias and the judgment of history. He was tried, convicted, and executed."

He paused. "*This* is why we honour him! When the past is twisted, as it has just been, before the noble people of this court and pious servants of Jad, when it is falsely presented, as it has been today by a man I once respected, then the judgment of those who come after—that is us, here, today!—cannot be fairly rendered. Whether concerning the Ancients, or as to a savage killing in our own time, with a noble lord dismembered in the street, his head almost severed by a coward's axe."

He was used to improvising before listeners. It was a good thing, he supposed.

He had a thought, and was speaking it before he could weigh it. He did that all the time, but this was not a tavern poem, or a conversation with a girl in her bed.

He said, "Your grace, what happened, what brings us here today, was not a regrettable incident within a family, was not . . . *something unfortunate*. It was murder. Brutal and ambitious. Forgive me for reminding everyone here, but the Duke de Montereau was butchered in the street by a cousin who hated him, and wanted his powers. And so, too, were two of the victim's aides. Innocent men, doing only their duty. Let us, today, not forget them, either, but commend them to Jad's light and our justice."

They *would* likely be forgotten, Thierry thought. But he himself was far more akin to those two than to anyone he was addressing. Let the tavern poet, at the very least, mention them.

He added, "Let us also remember some other things that the distinguished advocates have not mentioned. First, as you heard at the outset, the Duke de Barratin *confessed* to ordering this murder. The provost of Orane is not alleging things yet to be proven. Two of the Barratin guards also confessed, offering details, including the choosing of a leader for this butchery, the hiring of horses, and of the house whence they burst forth in a black night to hack Rollin de Montereau down in the frozen muck of the street." He spread his arms wide. "There is no uncertainty here, your grace, members of the court. There is none! There are confessions."

He paused. "And then there is a cowardly man's flight from Orane, from his crime, from this court. *This* is the person who will now seek to be protector of the prince? Guardian of Ferrieres until the king comes again to lead us? He is most of the way to his own lands by now! He will hide behind his city and castle walls and winter's distances, while an advocate, paid extremely well for his skills, tries to disguise what has happened."

He didn't want to end on Cassin. He needed some—

He had it.

He said, "I am at an end now, and I appeal to your grace for mercy if I have overstepped in my attempt to serve Ferrieres. Here is my last word. Powerful men often believe justice has little to do with them. That they live above it, outside it. Maybe it is true. Maybe it is! But perhaps it is not so now, here, for one reason: an equally powerful man was slain. And we know, we all know—it is taught by our holy clerics—that the dead cannot find rest, or shelter and light with Jad, when they have been murdered and those who did it are permitted to walk away free, to ride away free, to flourish in their power. A slain lord cries out to us. Will we not listen to him, in the god's name?"

He stopped there. He bowed again. But not, this time, to the three men behind him. He was, he realized, still enraged. Fury was not done with him. A strange feeling, the way it could rule you. His hands were shaking now, he saw. He put them behind his back, walking again to his place behind the provost. He'd look like a contemplative advocate, he thought, bitterly.

There were whispers everywhere. A hum, a buzz, a steady throb of noise in the chamber. He tried to ignore it, to slow his racing heart. Robbin de Vaux turned in his seat again. He said, softly, "I wasn't certain why I kept you with me, Thierry Villar. Something of an impulse. It was for this, I now realize."

Thierry said, as quietly, finding it difficult to speak now, "See that some of my poems are published, if you can."

Of all people to ask, he thought. It should have been amusing. It didn't feel so. He looked at Marina di Seressa across the open space, behind the queen. Saw that she had one hand over her mouth, and that she was crying. He didn't understand that. His thoughts weren't especially clear at the moment.

De Vaux offered a bitter chuckle. "I'm likely to be hanged beside you, Villar. I've lived a decently long life."

"I haven't," said Thierry.

De Vaux looked at him.

"You should leave the city," said Medor. "Both of you."

"No," said the provost.

"No," said Thierry Villar.

Acting with unusual speed, the royal council of Ferrieres, coordinating with the high cleric of Orane, came to a decision that could only be described as judicious. It satisfied no one, really, which is often the mark of careful proceeding in a challenging, dangerous matter.

The Duke de Barratin was exiled from the city and the court for a year. If he chose to ignore that, to bring an army and return, well, that *would* mean war—by his choice, his exposed ambition. Everyone would know it.

On the other hand, he was offered amnesty if he did one additional thing. Barratin was instructed, on pain of expulsion from the rites of Jad, and his immortal soul being lost to eternal darkness, to make a pilgrimage to Rhodias. There to seek audience and kneel before the

High Patriarch, offer contrition, and beg forgiveness and absolution for his crime.

Immortal souls mattered, to everyone. And the High Patriarch, and even his appointed senior clerics in different countries, had real power concerning those.

Eternity was a long time. Darkness was darkness.

That night, the same sort of mob that had tried to burn down the home of the Duke de Barratin, including many of the same people, went to the equally handsome city palace of the murdered Duke de Montereau.

The elegant speech of Denis Cassin, abetted by a number of strategically placed people to relay the essence of it quickly through Orane, had its desired effect. Mobs were threats to the powerful—or tools to be used.

The serjeants and the court guards, and the guards of the slain duke were, however, ready. No damage was done, although there was considerable violence in the square outside the gates and courtyard of the home. Some in the crowd were killed. More arrests were made. There were executions of the common folk again. Seventeen of them this time.

Gallows Hill's birds of prey were busy in those days.

PART II

CHAPTER VIII

The winter passed. Slowly, but the days did grow longer, the sun warmer, a gift. There were one day . . . and then the next, and again the next . . . songbirds in gardens. The god does not forget his children, clerics preached, even if they suffer. Time carries us, plays with us.

The ice melted in the rivers, dangerously in places, with flooding. Gifts can carry other things.

Some streets in Orane—and elsewhere, of course—were deeply under water, waist-high in places. You waded along them, or stayed away. Some houses near the river were ruined, people rendered homeless. Two of the city's bridges were destroyed that spring by great, broken-off ice floes driven into them by the current. Gardens all through Ferrieres were drowned. The Great Sanctuary on its island in the river flooded. That had happened before.

Still, it was better than the killing cold. It was. And there was no plague that spring, either, by the god's grace. People prayed. When the Great Sanctuary was dry enough, there was a ceremony of thanksgiving there. It was thronged with people.

Orane slowly regained its vitality, reclaimed a celebrated beauty. Leaves began to appear on trees. Trade picked up for everyone, from basket-makers to jewellers, wine-sellers to prostitutes. Happier people spent more money in taverns. Food for the markets came in through the gates or along the river. There was noise all day again, and music in the streets. Beggars also did better: people in good humour were more generous.

Yes, there were corpses rotting on Gallows Hill, mostly from the two riots after the Duke de Montereau's assassination. But there were always corpses there. You didn't have to look. Unless you were entering Orane from out that way. Or you wanted to see a hanging—or rob someone who'd gone there to watch a person swing and die.

Or unless, perhaps, someone you'd loved was hanging there.

In *The Dance of Death*, the great fresco on the wall of the sanctuary nearest the city's largest cemetery, those dancing hand in hand with skeletal, scythe-bearing Death were shown doing so in springtime. A message: the world might flourish again, flowers and leaves return, but men and women could still be cut down, old or young—summoned to the god's light, or the dark.

Thierry had actually begun making plans, deeply unhappy, to leave the city after the hearing before the court. The provost had made it extremely clear: if the Duke de Barratin was displeased with you, to say your life might be in danger was to put it very mildly.

Except the royal council had then exiled Barratin for a year, demanding a pilgrimage of contrition to Rhodias. And Barratin had accepted the terms, with a right to return, after.

A return, in his case, very possibly meant coming back to absolute power, depending on the king's health, and . . . other factors. Or it meant war. But there was time to watch and wait now. The duke's people here would be closely observed, and he had his enemies.

Intense, and sometimes violent disagreements had emerged in the city and elsewhere between factions. Those supporting Laurent de Barratin, and those allying with the slain duke's family, which had vowed vengeance on Montereau's assassin.

Ferrieres, violently divided? How very startling, Thierry Villar thought.

But he didn't want to leave Orane, and he didn't. He wasn't rushing away—to somewhere, no idea where—in flight from imagined revenge for words he'd spoken at a lectern one day.

He said as much to de Vaux in the provost's study. The older man replied, calm as ever, "I am not in a position to give you orders. Only counsel."

"Ah. And your counsel is that I should huddle by a farmhouse fire or in some hamlet, away from everything and everyone I know? Read poems to the cow before milking it?"

De Vaux actually smiled at that. "Do you even know how to milk a cow?"

Thierry acknowledged he did not.

"I'll assign you a guard here, then. No, *not* in my livery," the provost added quickly as Thierry opened his mouth to protest. "Villar, you are still a witness to matters that may come up again, and I'd prefer to keep you alive, on the whole. Where do you plan to sleep?"

He hadn't thought it through. "Where I have been? My mother's house or The Lamb. One or the other, mostly. You can't have men watching me all day and night!"

"They do so for me," the provost said mildly. "And my family now."

"I am not a serjeant. I am not . . . anything!" Thierry said.

They compromised. A guard, no livery, keeping a discreet distance, with Thierry's acknowledgement that greater distance meant less effectiveness.

It came to be understood in the taverns that Thierry Villar was aligned with the Montereau faction and they had someone keeping an eye on him. It was plausible. People knew by then that he had spoken up at court. He was a trained lawyer, after all. He didn't discuss the subject.

One morning, Marina di Seressa sent him a note, reminding him of something. That evening she came to The Lamb, in a small carriage from the palace, through the muddy streets.

He had promised, more or less, to entertain her in a tavern. From Silvy's face he could see she was . . . displeased. He introduced them, with trepidation. Marina wore a deep-blue robe with a crimson overtunic and elegant black boots, her hair artfully dressed. He recognized her scent. Little jewellery. She was too intelligent to wear it here, he thought. Even if she'd never been in a city tavern.

Silvy looked her up and down, then turned to Thierry. "The last time an aristocrat came to see the common folk here it did not turn out well for you, if memory serves."

She wasn't one to hide her thoughts.

Marina looked at her and smiled. "I'm not Jolis de Charette, and she's not an aristocrat."

"I see. Forgive me for not knowing the precise rankings of wealthy people, my lady."

"I'm not wealthy, either. My family and I live on the patronage of the wealthy. Precariously. I write poetry to survive." She smiled again. "I think I like you. You would probably like me, if you gave us both a chance."

Silvy just stared, then walked away.

Thierry bought wine for his guest, introduced her to some of the poets in the tavern, and to Eudes, who was courteous and inscrutable, as always. Later, a few of the other poets recited their work, and Thierry accepted a call to do so. It was what he did. What he was. No politically volatile poems, even if he'd already written one mocking Denis Cassin.

What he was, he thought, included not being a complete fool.

Marina drank two cups of wine at a table near the bar, sitting among the other poets. She declined, smiling, to recite.

"I am only a visitor tonight," she said, "happy among you all."

She left early, still smiling, that wide mouth. Thierry watched her go. She turned in the doorway, gave him a nod. He felt uncertain what more had been expected of him. She was young still, brilliant, not beautiful, but arrestingly appealing. And brave, he thought.

Silvy was still angry. He wasn't entirely sure why.

Weeks passed. It had become full spring, suddenly, almost overnight, not just the promise of it.

And then someone tried to knife him in the dark, as he was coming back to The Lamb from a tavern on the other side of the river, and things changed.

He'd heard footsteps in a quiet street, well after curfew, and was seized by a memory of the day he'd been to Barratin's home and was pursued at sundown, and fled. They'd chased him into The Fife. A man had died.

He changed direction now, started walking faster, then running towards the provost's house. Again, a memory. He had lived this before. He was supposed to have a guard! The guard he had argued against. It was quite possible the man had gone to sleep by now. It was late this time. There was only so much the provost could do for a man who didn't even want protection.

He saw someone leaving another inn up ahead. The White Hart. He grabbed a coin from his purse as he moved. "Wait!" he said to the man in the street. "Take this, run with it. It's yours, just *run*!"

The man did exactly that. Simply running through the street for a silver coin was a gift! You didn't ask questions.

Thierry ducked into the shadows by The White Hart's doorway. Same sort of second entrance The Lamb had, to the side. The footsteps behind him, also running, drew nearer. They'd follow the other man now. He hoped.

They did. Thierry had his knife out by then. The figure—just one man—appeared in the street in front of him. Thierry stepped forward and stabbed him in the ribs, and in the back.

A cry. The man fell to the street, lit by the white moon and a glow from within the tavern. A dropped sword clattered. The body didn't move. Didn't appear to be breathing. Thierry turned him over with his boot.

Knew him.

More running steps. "Villar!" he heard. "What have you done?"

His guard. His belated guard.

"Where were you?" he shouted, trembling.

"Fuck off," the serjeant said. "Is he dead?"

"I think so. I know him!"

"What? Jad's blood. Out of here now! Let's go!"

They ran.

The guards at the provost's house knew them. At the serjeant's direction men went out to claim and take away whoever had been sent to kill him.

Whoever. He knew him. He knew him. He knew him.

Jad curse the day and the dark night.

"Rasse de Barille? Again? Really, Villar?" said Robbin de Vaux, when he'd been awakened and had come down to his study.

"Yes, really."

The man he'd stabbed and almost killed in that stupid, stupid street fight over Jolis. It seemed so long ago. It wasn't.

"You really didn't like him, I see." The provost was outrageously calm.

"He was chasing me! I had no idea why! Or who he was!"

"He'd joined the Barratin party. We had word. Thought to curry favour killing you, I suspect. A fool, but ambitious. He picked his side."

Lamps had been lit in the room, by then. "Time for you to leave," said de Vaux, behind his desk now. "Villar, we clearly cannot guard you properly, not in the life you want to live. Go away for a time, stay in contact, see what happens. People do that! It is better than dying."

"Maybe," Thierry said.

But he did. He did leave. And what followed was what followed.

⚜

It would be untrue to say Gauvard Colle never left his house. There were clients with enough power and money to summon him, and they'd send a carriage. One time it was a litter, sent by the queen: poles held by four men as they carried him through the streets of Orane. He'd enjoyed that. Memories of the east, in fact. She had likely done it with intent, since they'd talked of his time in Sarantium more than once. A remarkable woman, in his view, Queen Bianca, and he didn't think that of many women, or men.

He was judgmental and knew it. Didn't cultivate friends, found most people tedious, unnecessary. He had two or three colleagues he'd invite over, or visit. Hired a coach and horses for occasions when he dressed with care and went calling. Seldom in winter, of course. He was happier then by his fire, with books and good wine. Any sane person would be, was his view. Not infrequently visitors would knock at his door by appointment. One did need to have clients, charge them his substantial fees. Nothing was cheap in Orane, especially in winter. He certainly wasn't.

All of which is to say that on the morning, springtime warming the city, that Gauvard Colle ventured forth in a small carriage to make three calls it was noteworthy to the neighbours, and also somewhat so to himself.

He'd had one of his visions in the night.

It had been alarmingly specific. He didn't feel right about delaying a response, even if this had nothing to do with him at all. He was a selfish person but not a bad one, or so he always told himself. And if the half-world sent a message, he listened to it.

He. Today he was male in his thoughts. It changed, but he always was so for the world outside. Safer that way.

He named his first destination to the coach driver and was pleased the man knew it. He wouldn't have been able to offer more than vague directions. Once they arrived, he dismounted, with assistance, gratified to see the street had been swept in front of the doors.

He was wearing lined, stylish boots he liked.

It was pleasingly warm inside this tavern, The Lamb. Three fires, and very clean. The owner, Gauvard decided, took pride in his inn. He liked that. Not crowded just then. The first-light people had gone to work—or elsewhere—and the midday-meal arrivals were not yet present, though he saw servers busy behind a long counter preparing cheese and meats in anticipation. A perfectly agreeable place, he thought, if you liked taverns.

He addressed a slim, neat woman going quickly by. "A word?"

She paused, glanced at him. And then looked more carefully. Facial expressions were always interesting when people looked at him. He was very well dressed that morning, as it happened, for his next stop of the day.

"Yes?" she said, noncommittally.

"I am looking for any friend of Thierry Villar here," he said. "The poet," he added helpfully. And then, "It is important."

⚜

The two women—and she was one of them—made, Silvy thought, genuinely strange companions. Amusing, if you were in that sort of mood. She wasn't. She was still uncertain why she was doing this. Why anyone had thought *she* could be useful. Yes, the soothsayer, the seer, whatever he called himself, that unsettlingly ambiguous visitor to The Lamb, had been precise about what he'd seen—in a vision, he said—and what needed to happen now. But even so . . .

"And would you also be going on this journey?" she'd asked, back in the tavern.

He'd laughed, so loudly Eudes had looked over from behind the bar.

"Don't," the very well-dressed man had said, "be ridiculous."

"But you think *I* should?"

He'd turned serious. "I wouldn't be here otherwise."

"And who are you?"

It was by way of confirming, mostly. She'd known him before he named himself, just from the look of him. Gauvard Colle was a name wrapped in mystery in Orane's twilit world, which included the taverns. His services were used by the court, too, so . . . not exclusively twilit. He wasn't exclusively male or female, either, was the word people shared quietly. Silvy didn't care about that. All kinds made up the world, in her experience.

She did care about what he'd told her.

It was why she now found herself, two days later, in a large carriage travelling west on a rutted, bone-shaking road with Marina di Seressa, two serving women crowded in with them. Decisions had been made at speed.

The servants were here to assist the lady, of course. A well-born woman did not travel without attendants. Having only two was a deprivation of sorts, probably, Silvy thought.

But also, in a deeply uncertain time, they had eight guards on horseback escorting them. Four from the provost, and four had been added by the queen when Gauvard had gone on from the Châtelet to the palace to inform her concerning this matter of the poet.

Silvy had been with him in both places, overwhelmed, trying hard not to show it. In the palace—the palace!—she had fumbled through a curtsy. She had no idea how to do a proper one. Why would she know? She'd felt like dropping to her knees, looking at the queen.

Marina di Seressa had been summoned. She'd entered, performed a flawless salute to the queen. Looked quizzically at Silvy, and raised her eyebrows on seeing Gauvard Colle. She knew him, Silvy registered. He repeated for her what he'd just said.

It seemed that the queen felt a measure of gratitude to Thierry. She decided to heed the seer's words. It appeared she knew Colle very well. It was all astonishing, Silvy thought. And happening so fast! She watched, listened. She stopped trembling at some point.

Marina di Seressa also agreed to go west. It was unclear why, or why she was wanted, or how much choice she'd had once the queen asked her to do so. Had to do with representing the crown, making the court a presence in whatever would come.

Silvy had needed to go back and talk to Eudes. Which she did.

On the road the first day she learned that the other woman's family home (her husband's family) lay near to where Thierry had evidently gone. Marina di Seressa said she had urged him to go in that direction when he'd had to leave Orane, and had suggested where he might stay for a time. But was he there, or somewhere else against his will, now? Whichever was true, he was in danger, if Gauvard Colle's visions could be trusted.

They were acting as if that was so. Throwing their own lives into chaos, and not just the chaos of a carriage on bad roads. Gauvard's nephew, one of the senior serjeants, was among those escorting them. A horse, Silvy thought, would have been easier. She loved horses. Had never ridden one. Just had those dreams of doing so. An escape? Freedom?

There was no such thing as freedom, she still tended to think, especially for a woman.

"Why are you doing this?" Marina di Seressa asked her abruptly.

Second day, sun emerging after morning rain, clouds skittering. Silvy had been looking out the window. She still didn't know what she thought of this woman. She didn't like the well-born sort who dropped into a tavern for idle amusement—a taste of danger—and then retreated to their silks and soft beds.

Silvy had wanted to ask her that same question, earlier. Had felt too cautious. Now the tall, poised woman sitting opposite in the carriage had done it first. Before that, they'd talked of nothing more consequential than the state of the roads, and the weather, which was mild. Fully springtime now.

She hesitated. She ought to have had an answer ready, she thought. The other woman added, casually, "Is he a lover of yours?"

If you worked in a tavern in Orane—were actually a part-owner of one, if only to a small degree—you weren't easily discomfited by such questions. That helped.

Silvy looked at the other woman. "And you are entitled to ask this, why?"

Marina di Seressa smiled. Also, Silvy thought, not easily made uncomfortable. "I'm trying to understand what we are doing. Why Gauvard summoned you. I truly don't care who your lovers are."

"You know him? Gauvard Colle?" Silvy parried.

The poet smiled again; she had a wide mouth, good teeth. She recognized the parry, Silvy thought.

"Only by name and reputation. The queen has summoned him a few times, I understand. Never when I've been with her."

"You usually aren't?"

"No," said Marina di Seressa simply. And waited.

Hers was a known story. She wasn't really wealthy, people said. She'd said as much herself, in their brief exchange in The Lamb, when Silvy had been irritated by her. Her husband had died young, left her with a country estate to maintain, a family to support, a good reputation—and not enough money. Silvy didn't know why there hadn't been money. Perhaps he'd been bad with it, or a gambler. But Marina di Seressa had become perhaps the best-known writer in Ferrieres. Thierry had told her that. She'd been asking about poets, she remembered.

She sighed. "Villar is my friend. Not my lover."

"Why not?" the other woman asked. "He's an appealing man."

Direct, this one was, Silvy thought. That sort of confidence could come with status.

"I suppose he is," Silvy said. "It's easier as friends."

"You dislike men?"

"I do not."

"You dislike risks?"

Silvy shrugged.

"We've nothing but time right now, you know," said Marina di Seressa.

One of the ladies-in-waiting was sleeping, snoring quietly. The other was awake, looked bored. It *was* boring on the road. Unless someone clever was probing you. For amusement?

She didn't like it. "Have you bedded him?" she asked.

Laughter again. "Hardly. We've had two meetings. One in your tavern. I've read his poems."

"Well, that would excite him."

They laughed together this time. The attendant still awake looked over at them, and then away again, as was proper.

"I was also present when he spoke against the Duke de Barratin at court. In a way it was my doing. I vouched for him to the queen."

"Why?" It felt better to be asking the questions.

"Someone needed to. And I'd already realized he was clever. And I knew he had his degree in law. He'd also stood up already, which took courage. Is he brave, your friend Thierry?"

"I've never thought about it, to be honest." It *was* honest, she hadn't. "Are you?"

"Same answer, my lady. And you?"

"I've not thought so. I've just done whatever I needed to do, the tasks that fell to me."

"Same answer again, then, here."

The other woman smiled. "As many women do."

"Most?" said Silvy.

"Most," agreed Marina di Seressa. A brief smile.

Thierry was increasingly certain he was going to die here, in the fetid castle dungeon of an arrogant toad of a puffed-up provincial high cleric. And it was his own Jad-cursed fault. Didn't make anything easier, admitting that.

The odour here, he also admitted, was, by now, in good part his own smell, after a month, more or less (he'd lost count of the days). That awareness improved nothing. They had left him his boots. No change of clothing. Nothing to wash with. Of course not. There was one grimy, barred window, very high up. At ground level, he assumed. It admitted the merest hint of daylight, allowed him to know when it *was* day.

He stomped rats when he could. It was difficult in the night's blackness, but he'd gotten quite good at tracking their movements by sound, treating it as a challenge. He had killed quite a few. Then the others ate the dead ones. He would hear the crunching of small bones in the blackness.

A lyric poem in that, Villar thought bitterly. He was ill by now, coughing.

His folly had taken place in the other castle, the first one, de Thunier's.

Minor nobleman, fatuous, thought himself a poet. Had been very happy to receive Thierry after his flight from Orane. He'd carried a recommendation letter from Marina di Seressa, after all.

She had given him instructions before he'd left Orane, as to which he had missed the urgency. Or he'd not be here, coughing in darkness.

"De Thunier is vain," she'd said, in a sitting room in the palace. She had discovered he was leaving, he wasn't certain how. Probably the provost. "If you flatter him, he'll let you stay as long as you like, give you a chamber in which to sleep and write. It is a good place to be, I think. I've not been, but he is said to have a superb cook, and his gardens will be lovely now. Keep your patience and your wits and you can wait there until it is safe to return."

All she'd said had been true! But his patience had been . . . wanting. Also his wits, the wits he prided himself upon.

In the cold, damp blackness of his cell, Thierry coughed and shivered and blamed everything on how lost he felt outside of Orane, in the countryside. Uprooted. Adrift. Unbalanced. Ought to have been prepared for these things. It had happened before, when he was exiled while delicate matters associated with his stabbing of Rasse de Barille had been worked through.

His *first* stabbing of Rasse de Barille.

It still disturbed him that he'd killed a man. With cause, but even so. He'd . . . killed a man. And the provost and his serjeants had covered it up. Made him think about how often that sort of thing happened.

He'd gone south that time before, for want of a better idea, towards the village where he'd been born, hating every moment. Tilled fields?

Oxen and horses pulling ploughs? Hawks circling overhead? Shepherds fucking their sheep? Milkmaids carrying pails? All extravagantly overpraised, in his view. He'd take Orane's river and bridges and taverns. The bustle of the streets, day and night. The markets. The noise. The street performers. The Great Sanctuary's dome gleaming in a morning sun. He'd take those any time. Always.

He'd travelled west this time, on Marina's counsel.

But he had been even more off balance. Irritated and saddened by being away. The need to be, with a killing behind him, and an attempt on his own life. The vastness of the countryside dismayed him.

Then he'd arrived at de Thunier's château . . . and the pompous idiocy of Bascot de Thunier had dismayed him even more! A petty lord who thought he was a great one, and a writer. A poet who *read* his day's work aloud to those trapped at his table at night after the evening meal. Every Jad-cursed night. The meals were excellent, as promised, the poetry . . . execrable.

Thierry had said nothing—may the god give him credit for that when he died! For *weeks* he'd nodded agreeably, murmured a new, benign vacuousness each evening. Until forced to be honest by de Thunier one night. Or, being accurate, was pushed that way by an extremely direct question. He could have lied. He hadn't *had* to say what he'd said. Which had been, undeniably, direct in turn. Silencing a dining hall.

"My lord," he'd said, "you are a generous, gracious host. Everything the lady Marina said you would be, and more." The small, plump country aristocrat at the table's head beamed at him. "But my lord, it would be better for yourself, and for the world, if you concentrated your . . . inner forces on hunting. On collecting art. On patronage. On the affairs of our difficult times, the wars which might now come. On finding pleasing bed partners! My lord, there is neither skill nor insight in your writing. No talent for phrase, or for thought. There is nothing. Words are not of value just for being . . . words! My most earnest, well-intended counsel, my lord, is to consider a different avenue for yourself."

There were no words of remonstration at the table that night. De Thunier was, if nothing else, well brought up, and Thierry was his guest.

It was the next morning that the castle steward suggested, politely enough, that perhaps Villar might wish to carry on with his travels. Enjoy more of the countryside and the season. Grace a different château with his presence.

Thierry, of course, acceded. No choice, really. And his own doing. He even agreed to carry a letter west for de Thunier, to the high cleric of this district in his own château at Aurage a little farther west. Indeed, added the steward, it could well be a place Thierry might linger, given his own clerical status by way of the university in great Orane.

Linger. He was lingering. In a dungeon. It would have been amusing, except it wasn't, at all. It was likely to kill him.

He hadn't been careless this time. He'd steamed the letter open at an inn on the road. Its contents were innocuous, unimportant. A request from de Thunier for another cleric to be sent to serve him and his peasants, as there were "tasks enough for two of them here."

He'd made a point of covering his opening of the letter by dropping it in the mud as he'd continued west, even though he'd been taught some time ago how to invisibly open letters. Two days later, he arrived at the small, well-appointed château of the high cleric of Aurage, along this road near the Livraise River. He'd prepared an apology for the mud stains.

No chance to offer it. He was seized by guards as soon as he entered the courtyard. Not greeted. Seized. Then hustled into the yellow-robed presence of another tiny man with intensely blue eyes and wispy blond hair around his tonsure. Two men flanked Thierry, standing very close. Neither was tiny. They each gripped one of his arms.

The high cleric of Aurage stared at him from a dais. He smiled. It was not a good smile, Thierry remembered thinking. The man said, "For our amusement, have you anything to say before we commit you to a dungeon?" It was not a good voice, either; reedy was a fair word. And he pompously deployed a *we* far beyond his status.

Thierry kept his temper. It had not been a moment for anger or demands. Also, he really ought to have considered that de Thunier might have sent another message by a faster horseman. And almost every horseman was faster than Thierry Villar.

"May I ask why, my lord cleric?" he'd said calmly. A flicker of the blue eyes, he remembered (he had relived this conversation endlessly in the dark), as if the other man had wanted rage. As an excuse?

"Why would we feel any obligation to answer that?" the cleric on his throne said. There was a sun disk on the wall behind him.

"Simple courtesy? To someone unaware of any offence done to you, or the god."

"And yet we have good evidence of offence you have given," the cleric—his name was Mercier—said. His voice was genuinely irritating.

"Evidence? Offence? Then invoke a clerical trial, offering that evidence, as is proper for someone tonsured as I am," Thierry said. But he knew by then exactly what had happened, and what was happening.

"Perhaps," said Mercier, the high cleric of Aurage. "In good time. Perhaps. I'd be your judge, of course." He smiled again.

Time to play, Thierry thought.

He said, "Given that I recently acted as advocate for the provost of Orane before the queen of Ferrieres and the dukes of the court in the matter of the death of the Duke de Montereau, I would expect no delay at all, my lord. People of considerable importance will know where I am. I have sent word back, as I journey, at their request. Indeed, I venture to say, these are people of vastly greater importance than your local friend de Thunier."

Perhaps a bit much to not give a nobleman his title, but he was feeling rage by then.

He went on, "Events of great importance are about to unfold in Ferrieres. I have already acted in these matters for the court, speaking to and addressed by the queen. I expect to do so again."

That last was a lie, but this man could not know that. He hoped so, at any rate.

He added, "If Bascot de Thunier was aggrieved in his pride as a poet, is that really a cause to which you want to be attached right now, with what I have told you? And given that you can ascertain the truth of my words for yourself? His fate, for this affront to a friend and trusted servant of the crown, need not be yours—unless you choose to make it so."

A mistake, he would decide in the damp blackness, some uncertain time after.

The high cleric of Aurage did indeed look less sure of himself, but he wasn't going to be cowed by a nondescript, mud-spattered tavern poet. And he'd have, Thierry guessed, a long relationship with de Thunier.

After a pause in which he could almost be *heard* weighing his options, the high cleric said, "We will indeed send to learn the truth of this. It may"—and he smiled again—"take time. The roads, as you'll know by now, are not of the best in spring. In the meantime, you will remain here. And not as a guest."

"You *are* attaching yourself to the wrong man," Thierry said. "A mistake. I'm afraid it will cost you, whatever happens to me."

But by then he was being hurried out of the room by the two guards. They took evident pleasure in pulling him along a hallway, then down slippery, winding stairs to one of several dungeons, banging his shoulder and a knee on the wall, then unlocking a door and throwing him inside.

Where he remained.

CHAPTER IX

Silvy was grateful for blessedly uneventful nights at inns north of the river, along the road. They were guarded, of course, men in the hallways outside—serjeants or the queen's guards, alternating.

Medor Colle, leading their party, sent riders ahead late each day to arrange for food and lodging. Two each time. One man alone on this road was vulnerable, even if trained and armed. There were Jacquards—the notorious fraternity of outlaws—here in the valley of the Livraise River. Along with other random brigands, hungry and angry and reckless.

They paused outside a sanctuary one morning so those who wanted to could go inside for the rites. Silvy didn't. Had a sun disk her grandmother had given her. She did value that, even if she never used it. Family, memories. She knew some of their ancestors had been pagan, going back to their origins in Varena. She remembered her mother telling her she could always go there, at need. She remembered her mother's visions, not common, but present in their lives. Maybe . . . maybe why she'd been so receptive to Gauvard Colle's summons? Hard to know. Your family history went with you, she thought, wherever you travelled in life. Hers wasn't especially dark, but it was hers, and the half-world hovered at the edges.

Four women in a room each night. They had a very large bed once, Marina invited her servants to join the two of them. Silvy thought it generous, but she didn't know the norms of a court. She slept with

Anni and Eudes often, didn't she? It seemed that the one who snored in the carriage also did so at night.

It was Marina who knew this countryside, and who told Medor when to send his men ahead to arrange for food and rest. Her own home was hereabouts, north and west. That was, Silvy assumed, why Gauvard (and the queen) had asked her to be part of this rescue. If it was a rescue. If it could happen. Her anxieties were considerable, she was realizing.

They came to the château of Bascot de Thunier late the fourth morning. It lay on the north side of the road. The lord was out hunting, they were told after they pulled the carriage up at the end of a short drive. Silvy was regretting knowing nothing about him. She'd had time to ask questions, just didn't have . . . the habit of doing so.

"We'll attend him in his reception room, then," said Marina di Seressa to the steward, her tone brisk. "Food and drink, please." It really did help in life to have that kind of confidence, Silvy thought. And experience.

They were ushered into a good-sized room on the main floor. Medor came in with them, without asking. This might not be a cordial encounter, Silvy realized. He had confidence too, she thought. A different sort.

Marina's ladies were also with them, of course. Food came quickly. Silvy had a sip of wine, then put her cup down. She was very tense, kept squeezing and opening her hands, a lifelong habit. She looked at the others. They were an unwashed, road-weary party in this reception chamber.

Marina seemed to read her expression. "I don't mind him seeing us travel-stained. This isn't a social call. Villar won't be here now, I suspect, from what Gauvard said, but we need to know where he went, and in what circumstances."

There was time to ask now, Silvy thought. "Who is he? This man."

Marina di Seressa smiled thinly. "De Thunier? He's nothing. His grandfather was a military leader who fought for Ferrieres with honour and died in this long war. I forget where, or I never knew. The family was elevated by that to rank, given this house and the lands around it. It made them decently well off. Then this one's father was an adviser to the king's father. He'd have hunted with him around here. Bascot I have met twice. He imagines himself to be like the Duke de Barille—a figure of taste and discernment. But he has little of either, really, and he is not clever, or a poet."

"You don't like him?"

Marina looked at her a moment before answering. "Now I don't. Before this, I had scarcely given him a thought in my life, other than to suggest Thierry might stop here when he left Orane."

"What? *You* suggested it?"

Marina winced. "He needed to go somewhere," she said defensively. "I told him to flatter."

"Did you? I see! Not his strength," Silvy said. "He's a tavern poet, not a courtier, remember?" There were other things she thought of saying, but didn't. Anger in her again now, possibly unfair. She reclaimed her wine, took another small sip.

De Thunier came home in the early afternoon. He made them wait while he changed. A small, fair-haired, fair-skinned man with an impeccably groomed beard entered, dressed in green velvet. Two armed men came with him, also in velvet, a paler shade of green. He was vain, Silvy decided.

"My lady di Seressa! I am honoured beyond words to have such a distinguished writer in my home! I hope you will stay as my guest for some time!"

Marina let a pause register. Then said, "The last poet who stayed as your guest appears to have been sent from here into mortal danger. I will not stay, no. You will answer some questions, however, my lord. And quickly."

Bascot de Thunier blinked. And flushed. The fair skin showed it vividly.

Marina took three steps forward and slapped him, hard, on the cheek.

Silvy gasped, almost dropped her wine. One of the attendants clutched the back of a chair to stay upright. Medor dropped a hand to his sword, Silvy saw. He was watching de Thunier's guards.

"You should know," Marina went on, her voice like ice on rivers in winter now, "that I was under instructions from the queen of Ferrieres to do that on her behalf. I will happily do it again in my own name."

Bascot de Thunier appeared to be having difficulty with his breathing. Unsurprising, really.

"I have no idea what you . . . *What in Jad's name* . . . ?" he managed.

"None of this deserves the name of the god," Marina said. She'd shown no signs of this steel in the carriage. Silvy was stunned. She'd slapped the man! She wouldn't have minded a chair to hold on to herself.

Marina snapped her fingers at one of her attendants and the woman hurried forward with an envelope, almost stumbling. Marina claimed it and extended it to de Thunier. The hand he took it with was trembling, Silvy saw.

Marina di Seressa said, "You are directed to present yourself at court as soon as you can travel to Orane. I am instructed to say that you stand at the foot of the gallows, my lord. I'd not linger on the journey east."

"What . . . what am I thought to have done?" exclaimed de Thunier.

Silvy could see the red mark of the slap on his left cheek. There was a cut, as well. Marina wore a large ring on her right hand. She had removed her travelling gloves; Silvy hadn't noticed.

"The court has been reliably informed that you sent our friend Thierry Villar from here with intent to cause him harm. Or death. Either of these things will have you ascending the scaffold—and forfeiting your family's château and title."

"*Harm?* My lady, I sent him onward with a note commending him to the attentions of the high cleric of Aurage!"

"And did you also send a separate letter there by way of a courier, my lord?"

Her voice was quiet, but lethal. And they now knew where Thierry was. It was why they'd stopped here. Gauvard had been unclear on some things, precise about others—such as a letter that had been sent, a courier. Somehow he'd known. The way his visions were, he'd said. You could not demand clarity of the half-world, he'd also said.

Silvy knew that, actually.

She was still reacting to that slap, the *sound* of it. She hadn't been there when Marina di Seressa had been given that instruction. Suddenly, she wondered if it really had come from the queen.

She was so far out of her depth.

"We will not linger, de Thunier," repeated Marina. No title, Silvy realized. "Nor, if you are wise, will you. I mean that very seriously. And you'd best hope Messire Villar is safe and well. There are loyal allies of the crown who would enjoy this château, and use it and the power it offers to serve the court, not endanger a man the queen values. You need to make it extremely clear that your heartfelt desire is *only* to please Queen Bianca. And the king, of course, may Jad defend him from all enemies."

"That . . . that tavern poet has the favour of her grace?" Words uttered as if from the edge of a chasm . . . or the foot of the gallows.

"He very much does," said Marina di Seressa calmly. "As high cleric Mercier is about to discover. Also," she added, "if we come to learn you have sent another messenger to him today, after we leave, a warning, you will not be permitted to defend your actions before you are sent to Gallows Hill in Orane. Am I understood?"

De Thunier could manage only a spasmodic nod. The colour of his face had changed again; it was unique in Silvy's experience now. Or maybe not: it was akin to that of a man about to violently vomit forth whatever food and drink he'd had through a tavern evening. It was, she had to admit, pleasing to see.

A thought came to her. She spoke before she could stop herself.

"Was he critical of your poetry, perhaps?" she asked.

His mouth fell open. Marina's eyes narrowed.

Later she would wonder why she'd said it, how she had formed the question, and knew the answer to it, even though the man did not reply. But Thierry was more passionate about writing than anything else in the god's created world. If he was to have offended here, risking a place of refuge . . .

She looked at Marina, who nodded.

They turned and left.

She had been anxious before. She was afraid now.

Back in the carriage, on the same road west. They were in the country of hunting lodges for members of the court, scattered along the course of the Livraise. They could see the river at times on their left as they rolled and bumped along. One château and then another. This was a playground for the wealthy. Gardens and forests and the river, a landscape made for pleasure.

Another night in an inn, two rooms free for the women this time. It was easier. Marina di Seressa seemed disinclined to talk about what had happened earlier. Silvy didn't press her. The poet was scented and slender, kept to her side of the bed.

One more day, another night. It had been possible to keep going, arrive at Aurage in the dark, but Medor had refused. "This is not safe country," he repeated.

And then, in the early afternoon of the next day he pulled his horse alongside the carriage and gestured the driver to a halt.

"That's an ambush place ahead," he said. "I've a bad feeling."

Bascot de Thunier had not been able to get his breathing under control after the Jad-cursed woman left. He was sprawled in a chair in the room where she had . . . she had slapped him! He was perspiring. Wiped at his forehead with a sleeve. He could see his death approaching, a ghastly skeleton.

He did do one thing. He ignored the instruction to send no message west. He *had* to do that! He knew what was being done to the trivial, presumptuous poet he'd sent to Aurage. Punishment and a likely death—but not at his hands, not in his château. The high cleric owed him favours. Many of them.

Perhaps, *perhaps*, if Jad was kind, the poet was not yet dead. Mercier would have sent word, surely, if he was. Surely?

He summoned his most trusted guard (though could he trust anyone now, after today?) and made the man wait by him in his study, with its pleasing view overlooking the woods and the pond he'd had dredged and stocked with fish.

He wrote a letter. Swiftly.

I pray for both of us to holy Jad that the accursed poet is alive. Release him, if so, clean him up, send him from you—with money. As much as you can manage! Frame an apology as best you can. The queen is a patron of this man! Her people are headed your way now on his behalf! How could we have known? I am ordered to Orane, to present myself. I was threatened with Gallows Hill. You will be too! Do what I have said. Immediately! Destroy this letter.

—de Thunier

The guard was instructed to ride to Aurage through the night. Speed was utterly of the essence, de Thunier said. His man was also to ensure he was not seen by anyone in or escorting the women's carriage when he overtook it! The guard's own life depended on it, he said.

A trained man on a good horse could go much faster than a carriage. De Thunier was relying on that, with all the prayers he could think of.

⚜

Guards came for him again in his dungeon.

Thierry knew it was day, he could see the faint presence of sunlight in the high, small window of his cell. He was still alive. Weak, gaunt, rat-bitten, and coughing. But not dead, by the god's mercy.

It could make someone into a pious man, Thierry Villar thought, depending on what happened next.

What happened next was his departure from Aurage.

First there was a hot bath in a warm room, two women washing his body and hair, trimming and cleaning his fingernails, carefully picking the lice from him.

Then there was a barber for his hair and matted, tangled beard. And then came a doctor, attending to his bites and injuries. And then the same two women again, helping him into better clothing than he'd arrived in, by far. After, food at a table in a different chamber, simple food, in small portions, on the physician's instructions. They had very nearly starved him in his cell, his body needed time, the man said. Thierry took a sip of the offered wine and felt it rush to his head. He didn't drink any more.

He realized he was weeping at one point. Tried to make himself stop. It took some effort. He looked at his hands, his fingers. They didn't even seem like his own. His eyesight was not good. He hoped it would recover. The light, even just candles in a curtained room, felt very bright.

He wondered if Mercier of Aurage, a cleric, a holy man, had broken him in the blackness underground. It was possible.

They sent him away that same day.

No time to recover. His absence, Thierry realized, was urgently required from here. Was someone coming? Likely so. His horse was waiting in the courtyard. They'd fed the horse. Better than him. He was given food in a leather bag they attached to the saddle. He was given a sum in coins, and a startlingly large amount by way of a letter of credit.

"It is too dangerous for you to carry an amount like this," the steward said sententiously. "This is safer. Also, know that if you lose the letter, the amount will still be waiting for you at the clerical registry in Orane. It has been determined that your proper chastisement was . . . somewhat exceeded. This is by way of the high cleric's well-known generosity."

And *that* was his apology, Thierry thought.

"Very generous," he said. "Extreme piety in the service of Jad."

It seemed he was already a little more like himself.

"If I don't even need the letter, why give it to me?" he asked. Pointless question, really. The steward didn't answer. The man tried to remain expressionless, didn't quite manage it. He looked nervous. Made Thierry feel better.

He never saw the high cleric. Mercier of Aurage did not appear, to express regret, to bluster, to demand Thierry make peace with the god for his sins. But something had happened if *this* was happening.

He had said, the day he arrived, the day he was imprisoned here, that people would find out where he was and the cleric would pay a price. Bascot de Thunier, too, if Jad was just. You didn't throw people in a dungeon for disliking your poetry.

He would say that now, to anyone who would listen.

Although, in truth, in the world as they had it, if you were powerful enough you *could* do this: a dungeon, or just killing someone of no rank or stature. But it seemed these two men were not powerful enough. They'd thought they were. Thierry wondered who had found him. He didn't ask the steward. It was unlikely the man knew. He was edging towards the doorway to the courtyard now, gesturing to Thierry. They badly wanted him gone.

So he left. Took a deep breath outside. Then another. He coughed. That was still there. He accepted help getting into the saddle. He'd learned how to do it by now but he was extremely weak. The horse didn't seem unhappy to see him, but he really didn't know horses.

It was a cloudy morning, blessedly so. His eyes were extremely sensitive. He needed them to start working better. This might be a countryside where the nobility of Ferrieres amused itself, but it was also a place of villages and farms—and of outlaws. Outlaws were everywhere in turbulent times, but notoriously so along the banks of the Livraise. He remembered learning that in Orane. Long ago, it seemed. Everything seemed long ago. He needed to find an inn, rest for a day, or more. *More* felt like a good idea.

He had no plan, no idea what to do. No least hint of what was happening in Orane, where he wanted to be. Or even how much time had passed. He should have asked, he thought. It was warmer. Leaves were on the trees, and there were flowers.

He saw that his hand was trembling, holding the reins. He drew another slow breath when he reached the road at the end of the gravel drive. He might have been broken, yes, it was possible, but he decided he was not going to be. Not by these men.

He turned back east, the way he'd come. Not to Orane; it was much too far, many days away. But he had passed a village before arriving at this Jad-cursed château, and he now had coins. Courtesy of the so-generous high cleric of Aurage. He'd stay at an inn. Try to recover, to become . . . himself again.

He decided he might even find a sanctuary and pray. Give thanks. His mother would want him to do that, he thought. He was alive, in the open air. Under clouds, but with the god's sun behind them, and it was springtime.

The village was farther than he remembered, or he was even weaker than he knew. It was a difficult ride, even on a level road on a pleasant day, with the bright slash of the river to the south. He was genuinely afraid of outlaws here. Too many stories told. He didn't have much, but he had a horse, and he was alone. An easy target for brigands, or a party of the Jacquards themselves—who were known to be hereabouts, because wealthy people were. They could kill him for his horse.

He found proof of them when he finally reached the village.

It shaped a plan or, better put, a semblance of a thought in a tired mind. Good or bad thinking, he didn't know. But he'd seen the discreet marker—two vertical lines scratched and a diagonal crossing them, higher on the right—on a tree near the first houses here. Then on another, other side of the road. If the first had been missed, he thought.

And then a third, beside the door of the village inn, which was called The Harvest. It wasn't easy to see: high up, mostly hidden by an oak tree branch in the courtyard. But he'd been looking for it by then. People who saw this would be looking, he thought. He paused, checking for a memory, to see if he still had it. He thought he did.

If the words hadn't changed. He handed the horse to a young stable hand with orders to feed and water it. Offered a coin.

It occurred to him that the young man was probably his own age. He felt old. Wondered if he always would now. If a passage in your life, an interlude, could make a forever demarcation. *Before this, I was still young. Now . . .*

He said it to himself again: *They have not broken me.* He entered The Harvest.

A village inn by the main road through the Livraise Valley would be for travellers as much as for people living around here, he knew. But the markings he'd seen identified it as serving a third group. He remembered being a student, encountering that man who knew (claimed to know) Jacquard signs and passwords. Thierry Villar had thought this was the most interesting thing imaginable. He'd had a romantic image of outlaws in the countryside (even if he hated the countryside).

He'd been young, ignorant. Only excuse, really. But he'd made a point of memorizing the things the man had told him in a tavern in exchange for many cups of wine through a long night.

The person behind the counter in The Harvest was not your usual innkeeper. Very tall, big-chested, huge hands. A scar on one cheek, and a cold glance where a welcoming one might have been expected for someone entering to spend money.

Might just be country reserve. Or not. Thierry was a little too well dressed for the road, courtesy of the steward at Aurage. He wondered, briefly, if that had been deliberate. Have the Jacquards deal with him, prevent any story being told? No blame to them?

He was too tired to follow that thought through, but it was there.

He walked up to the bar. The inn's main room was smaller than most he knew in Orane. They'd have beds for guests upstairs. A bed was what he needed. Right now. There were four men in the room. Not as formidable as the one behind the bar, but none looked like someone you'd like to encounter in the dark. One of them seemed drunk already, at midday. He eyed Thierry. You could call his expression hungry.

The innkeeper came over. "Wine? A meal?"

Thierry said, "I'm not sure what I need. A room if you have one."

"Can do that. For how long."

"Two nights?"

"Can do that, too." He contrived a friendlier grimace. "Which way are you going?"

"Not sure of that, either," Thierry said. And then he pushed on. "I've just been released from the dungeon at Aurage. I need time to recover, and sort through many things."

He had the other man's attention.

"And why was that? You tried to rob the fucker?"

Blunt word. "He'd never have released me if it was that. No, he locked me up as a favour for Bascot de Thunier."

"Oh?" said the very large innkeeper. "Another fucker. You have important enemies. What did you do?"

Thierry managed a weak smile. "I insulted de Thunier's poetry. Apparently that's enough, around here."

He had decided, especially after seeing the men in the room, that if he was to survive, he needed to be direct. Mostly. They had released him from a dungeon into danger.

"Poetry?" the big man said. He seemed taken aback. It was almost amusing.

"De Thunier writes it, thinks he's gifted. I'm Thierry Villar of Orane, and I write and speak my poems in taverns throughout the city. I know what's good work and what isn't."

"And you told a lord that?" An element of respect now, possibly.

"After too many nights of hearing his, and having him demand approval."

The innkeeper whistled. "And you were with de Thunier because . . . ?"

"*Because* he was a poet, and I was told he was someone I could stay with while it wasn't safe for me in Orane."

Thick black eyebrows were raised. "Why that? What'd you do in Orane, Thierry Villar?"

Time for the first untruth. "I was part of a planned theft, from a sanctuary. One of us drank too much the day of. Then talked too much, like the Jad-cursed fool he is. Or was. Probably hanged by now. The serjeants got word. Made him talk in the Châtelet. They were hunting the rest of us down. I got a warning just in time, left in the dark."

He paused. And leaped. As if from a high cliff into deep water, it felt.

"Heladikos did not die," he said quietly.

He could be killed right now, he thought, if the phrase was wrong.

The black eyebrows levelled. The benign inquiries ended. The innkeeper stared at him for what seemed a long time. Then said, slowly, also quietly, "What happened to the god's son?"

Thierry felt so much relief. Tried not to show it. "Fishermen saved him. Carried him ashore."

"And where is he now?"

"No man knows. He might he a fisherman, a farmer, a noble lord somewhere in the world." So far, all were words given him by a man in Orane years ago. But he was what he was, Thierry Villar, and he added, "Or a poet, I like to think."

A frozen moment, like ice on the rivers in the winter now past. Then the big, scarred man behind the counter burst into laughter. He reached over, poured Thierry wine in a dented tin cup, still laughing.

"I'd best go easy," Thierry said. "I really am not well. Need sleep in a decent bed."

"Decent enough upstairs," the man said. "You want a girl?"

"Not now," Thierry said fervently. "I'm sure they are lovely."

The innkeeper made a face. "Not especially, but they serve for what's needed." He paused. "You became one of us in Orane?"

"I did. But I've never been outside the city before."

Another lie, not an important one, he thought.

"Born there?"

"Came as a child. Managed to survive, in the ways one uses to survive."

The innkeeper nodded. "Old story."

Not for the first time, Thierry gave thanks that he seemed to be able to tell stories . . . appeal to people. Even here, he thought. A gift. Could keep you alive sometimes.

The man said, "I'm Rogier. I'll give you a key. Third room on the right upstairs. Best bed here, and you'll have it to yourself. We can talk after. I'll want to know more about Mercier of Aurage."

"Can we kill him?" Thierry asked.

He hadn't intended to ask that, but it was an intense desire suddenly.

"Talk later, I said. You look like death is at your elbow, waiting to pull you into his dance. Go upstairs." He handed Thierry a heavy key, pointed to the stairway.

He never did go upstairs. Life intervened. Our intentions matter, and they don't.

Which is why he found himself one of eighteen men hiding at the edge of a forest, north side of the road, a short distance east of the village.

He was exhausted, weak, light-headed. And deeply afraid. He knew who was coming now but had no good idea what to do. Awareness of danger was in him like a thrumming. Probably part of the light-headedness, he thought.

Someone had given him a stave as a weapon. It had been useful to lean on as they walked, off the road, moving through the trees. He struggled to keep up on uneven ground.

Rogier had had a place he'd wanted them to get to. Thierry wasn't sure how so many Jacquards had materialized at the edge of the village so quickly, but they had. And then moved quietly, quickly, in a disciplined single file through the trees.

And now they were here, hidden, watching the road, which was quite close.

A man had burst through the door of The Harvest, made his way straight to the bar. He'd glanced at Thierry, waited for Rogier's nod, and said, low and fast, "Gaspard and I saw a carriage coming west. Good-sized, well-made. Might be a woman's. Crest of a red flower in a gold circle on the door? I don't know that one. They have horsemen guarding. I think six? Maybe eight."

Red flower in a gold circle. The man reporting didn't know it. Thierry Villar did. Everything had suddenly become even more complex, and he was not thinking at all clearly.

Rogier's brows had knit together, a thick, straight black line, as he thought. Then, "Very well. Let's go. We'll weigh things when we see them coming. Guards mean money." He glanced at Thierry. "You going upstairs? Or want to be part of this?"

"Eight men on horses?" Thierry said.

"Maybe," the man who'd entered said. "Maybe not. We moved off before they got close, wanted to get here first."

"We'll look," Rogier said. "You want to be a part of this, poet?" he repeated.

"I'll come," Thierry said. He coughed. "I'm tired and hurting, not dying."

He hoped. He also knew who this was.

Silvy felt exposed and afraid, stopped on the road as they were. She looked and saw that their guards were stringing arrows to bows. Medor was speaking commands. It was interesting, she had thought earlier, that the queen's men were taking orders from a serjeant of Orane. Instructions had clearly been given before they'd set out. She wasn't thinking about that now. She wasn't really thinking at all. She was staring towards the place Medor had indicated: the woods on their right, north side of the road, up ahead of them.

"Fucker has stopped them too far away," Rogier rasped.

Thierry said nothing. He had no idea what would be a *good* thing here, or how to achieve it even if he knew. The man who'd brought word to the inn said, "We can charge them! We're two to one, at least."

"They have bows and crossbows, you son of a dung heap," Rogier said. He was angry. Then, "All right. We'll go through the woods, get closer, fucking quiet as you can. If we're near enough and not where they expect us, we can be on top of them before they loose their arrows. Let's go."

They went. Again, Thierry did what he could to keep up amid the trees and roots. He stumbled, almost fell. Exhaustion and fear.

"They are here," said Medor.

"How do you know?" one of the queen's men said. "I see nothing."

"We aren't supposed to see them. I can feel it. They'll be moving this way, in the trees. They'll have seen our bows, will want to be closer before they charge. But they will charge, I think." He pointed. "Right about there."

And almost as soon as he spoke the words, the Jacquards burst from the woods, screaming.

From the outlaws' point of view, the problem was that closer was not that much closer, because the forest angled back from the road where Medor had stopped the carriage. So the Jacquards were exposed, running across scrub grass and wildflowers. Some carried swords or axes, some had clubs, Silvy saw.

But they were running into arrows. Readied and aimed, because Medor Colle had told the guards where to look.

Seven outlaws fell. Silvy counted them, including the big man leading the charge, wounded in his thigh. He struggled to his knees as she watched, tried to stand, couldn't. He was shouting something.

Arrows, she thought, made such a difference in a thing like this.

A thing like this.

As if she knew anything! What was a thing like this? It was a feral outlaw band wanting to kill or capture them. There were four women in the carriage, only one of them worth a ransom. She knew what that meant for the rest of them. She slipped her knife from where it hung down inside her clothing. She knew how to use it, a little. Tavern life.

Didn't have to.

Their guards were very good. Medor Colle was more than that, when he drew his blade and advanced. She watched him. Grace, she thought, in the dealing of death. Something bitter about that. Another volley of arrows had taken three more of the outlaws.

Two of the Jacquards, seeing the others fall, turned to flee back to the woods. They, too, were killed by arrows before they got there—or wounded. She didn't know which.

Only one of their own guards was hurt in the hand-to-hand fighting. He was down on the road, clutching at his knee. A blow, it looked like, not a sword wound. Their men were significantly more skilled than the outlaws, she understood. They were trained and chosen for this. *A thing like this.* One of Marina's ladies was whimpering; the other gripped her sun disk as tightly as she could, white-knuckled, but kept quiet.

"We're all right," Marina di Seressa said to them, to Silvy. "We are."

Silvy was still staring out towards the woods. She wondered if there might be more. A second wave? Then . . .

"*Look!*" she shouted. "Medor, look! Don't do anything!"

"I see him," the serjeant said. "*Hold all arrows!*" he cried to the other guards.

Silvy had the carriage door open by then.

She was down and on the road and running as fast as she ever had, racing across the grass towards a man leaning on a staff as she approached. A man she knew very, very well.

She slowed as she came up to him. She wanted to hug him so fiercely, but then she saw how Thierry looked, and instead she enfolded him gently, more so than she ever had in all the time they'd known each other.

"Oh, my friend," she said. "What did they do to you?"

He didn't answer. He was weeping helplessly. She held him, didn't let go.

"You're safe now. We have you. And you are safe."

It was Marina, right behind her. She was looking, Silvy saw, glancing over her shoulder, much less composed than she usually did.

"You will never be safe as long as I live," came a voice she didn't know. It was the big man, the Jacquard leader, on the ground not far away. "You betrayed all these men."

"I didn't," Thierry said, finding his voice. "I—"

"I will kill you, if Jad allows," said the man. "I vow that."

"I'm sure you would. But Jad doesn't allow," said Medor Colle. "I'm afraid he doesn't."

He stepped over that way and he ran the fallen outlaw through the chest with his sword. Neatly, no wasted expenditure of effort, blade in to kill, then out, to be used again now, if required. Calmly he bent and wiped it on the grass. Birds were singing all around them in the springtime countryside, Silvy would remember.

"Medor," said Thierry, so quietly he could barely be heard. "He . . . I don't think he was a bad man." He coughed.

"*What?* You are clever, but a fool in the world beyond Orane," the serjeant said. "A child. What do you think they would have done to the women had we been fewer in number?"

Thierry looked at him, and then down.

Medor turned to the other guards. "Leave two or three alive for questioning. Kill the others right here."

"They won't talk," one of the queen's men said.

Medor laughed briefly. "The big one wouldn't have. Some of these will. They may not know anything, but they'll talk. Almost everyone talks."

"He was going to give me a bedroom and a . . . a bed," Thierry managed, glancing up again. "To sleep. Upstairs. For . . . for sleeping in." He looked like death, sounded like it.

Silvy saw that Marina was weeping now, looking at him. Then she realized that she was too. She was still clutching his hand. She let it go.

"Thierry, it is over," Marina said again. She wiped at her eyes. "You can sleep as long as you need to, then insult anyone you wish!"

"Can't . . . think of anything," Thierry said. "I'm not . . . I am . . ."

Medor caught him as he fell. Cradled him in his arms. A large man holding a smaller, broken one.

Thierry woke in darkness. Had no idea where he was. A hard seizure of panic, that he was in the dungeon still, and . . .

But no. He was in a bed, a soft bed. Someone had taken off his clothes and put him here, under blankets. He had no memory of it happening. He was—

He was not alone. A scent he knew. He turned on his side, coughing. Climbing towards awareness.

"Ah. There you are," said Marina di Seressa, quietly. "Lie easy. We've had a doctor in to salve and bandage you again while you slept. He left something for that cough, too. I have no idea what."

"Why . . . why are you here?" He sounded like a marsh frog.

"It is displeasing?" A hint of amusement.

"My lady . . ."

"I wanted to be. I didn't think you should be alone tonight."

He closed his eyes. Her scent, of course, remained. And now an awareness that she, too, was unclothed.

"I am not . . ."

"Of any use to me? Messire, such a thought!"

He lay there in the darkness. Medor had said he was like a child. He remembered that. He felt like one. He coughed again. He didn't feel equal to this conversation. Said, "Where are we?"

"The inn in the village. The Jacquard's. Our guards killed four other men here. Cleaning it out, they said. Medor also sent for more men, from one of the châteaux nearby. They came at sundown."

"While I slept?"

"While you slept, yes. What would you have done?"

What would he have done? Nothing.

A jagged memory of the man at the table by the wall earlier, the feral expression with which he'd eyed Thierry. The bed was soft. Rogier had said it would be. Rogier was dead, killed by Medor Colle, while threatening Thierry's life. He'd had an arrow in his thigh. He was a murderous outlaw.

The bed was really very soft. And the darkness was . . . different from what it had been for so long.

Marina di Seressa murmured, "Also, I'd never expect a man in your state to be of use to a woman tonight, to address your earlier comment. Your almost comment. I am here, as I said, because I didn't think you should awaken alone in the dark tonight, Thierry Villar. After where you were."

"My lady . . ." he managed.

"If you call me that again, I will be forced to injure you myself," she said.

"I'm sorry," he managed. "I'm . . . Is Silvy . . . is she . . . ?"

"Silvy is asleep in the next room. Would you prefer her to be here?"

"No! No, we aren't . . ."

"I know. She told me. But," said Marina di Seressa, "you and I aren't, either."

He sighed. He truly wasn't equal to this. To anything, really.

She shifted the bedcovers over him better, quite gently, and turned the other way in the bed.

"Sleep, Villar," she said. "It is safe to sleep."

So he did that. He slept. Was dimly aware at one point of her head upon his chest, her hair loose about them both, and a sense of being alive and in an infinitely better world than it had been when he was awakened that same morning in the dungeon of Aurage.

The wheel of fortune. Artists and poets use it as an image. We live upon it, rising and falling through our days.

CHAPTER X

On a bright morning in the late spring of that year, someone loosed an arrow at the provost of Orane as he rode out from his home in the city.

"*Provost! Down!*" one of his serjeants screamed. They'd been on extreme alert all spring. It saved his life.

Robbin de Vaux threw himself forward over his horse's neck, to the right, clinging on. The arrow flew over him. It struck a glancing blow to the horse immediately behind his before falling to the street. Serjeants immediately surrounded the provost, screening him. The man who'd shouted the warning, was pointing across the square at an open window on an upper floor.

The horse ought to have been only slightly injured. It died, foaming white at the mouth.

Poison on the arrowhead.

There was rage among the serjeants, both for the attempted assassination and for the dead animal. They loved their horses as extensions of themselves. Half a dozen men galloped across the square, dismounted, and were surging up the stairs, having banged open the front door of a building with a goldsmith's shop on the ground level and accommodation above.

Two lingered to seize the goldsmith, who shouted an urgent protest that he knew nothing about what had happened. He was arrested and interrogated at the Châtelet. It was fairly quickly decided that he had spoken the truth. He didn't own the building. Hadn't leased space upstairs to anyone. His left hand never worked properly again, unfortunately.

On the third floor the remaining four serjeants burst into a room— and found a man standing by the window.

He had his bow levelled at them, an arrow nocked. "If you kill me," he cried, sweating and fearful, "you will never know anything!"

"Why would we need to kill you right now?" asked Medor Colle, returned to Orane from duties to the west and leading the serjeants again. A brisk nod of his head and two men loosed their own arrows, each into an upper arm of the assassin. They were highly skilled at this. The man cried out, dropped his bow. He turned to leap from the window, but Medor was on him by then and clubbed him to the floor with the hilt of his sword.

The man, they saw, was not especially young, no identifying livery. A good archer; it had been a long arrow across the square.

"Careful of his arrowheads," Medor said. "Gloves on to claim them. Then burn the gloves." He hadn't seen the wounded horse fall and die, they had been galloping this way already, but he had an instinct. A family trait.

They were not gentle in the cellars of the Châtelet that morning. There were those who said you could not trust what a man said under extreme interrogation, but in the Châtelet they acted as if they could, until information suggested otherwise. The archer was unknown to them. The name he surrendered, the man who had hired and paid him, was not.

Aubrey, the other of the two senior serjeants, had already sent word for the city gates to be closed, without exception. It was an extreme measure, would not be popular on a market day with carts and wagons and foot traffic going in and out, but this was an extreme moment.

Once the name was learned—and it didn't take long—the serjeants added to those instructions, advising the guards at the city gates as to what man they were now looking for.

Corbez Barthelmy, whom they'd thought dead at his noble employer's order, being too much of a risk to the Duke de Barratin, was seized while trying to pick the lock of a doorway in the wall by South Gate.

He was distinctive: very tall, tonsured like a cleric, and for some reason (arrogance? folly?) wearing again the red, hooded cloak he'd worn when he'd led the assassination of the Duke de Montereau in the dead of the winter past.

Intelligent caution was not always a trait of dangerous men, the serjeants of Orane had noted many times. And Barthelmy proved to be no master criminal, though he'd accomplished something that had thrown Ferrieres into chaos, and was still doing so. Foolish men could do great damage, the provost had been known to say. You did not pity them their folly, you took advantage of it when you could.

By sundown Barthelmy had confessed to several things, and begged, through broken and missing teeth, for a cleric to help usher his soul to Jad's light and mercy. This was denied him. There was great anger.

He was dead in the Châtelet before the moons rose that night. His disembowelled corpse was carted to Gallows Hill the next day and hanged.

He'd been a soldier. A disreputable, thieving one, though not without courage in battle, apparently. He'd hated the Duke de Montereau for reasons to do with his wife. She'd left him years ago, the interrogators determined, and there were no children.

So no one but the darkly curious went to view his gutted, swinging body on the gallows. The archer from the window, hanging beside him, did have family in Orane. They mourned, weeping, on the bare slope below. He'd been hanged in the normal way, which is to say while alive. The money he'd been paid had been found and seized in their home. They were going to have difficulty surviving. None of the serjeants was sympathetic.

There were, as always, and even more so in turbulent times, messages to be sent about crime and justice.

And at least one more message yet to come, Robbin de Vaux decided, late at night in his own study. He had calmed the fears of his wife and the two older children as best he could. Now there were things to do. Again. He sent men to awaken and bring to him the cleric responsible for the university, who happened to also be the high cleric of Orane.

Hutin Peyre lived now not in the cleric's house on university lands but in the magnificent palace created when the Great Sanctuary on the island was built.

A discussion needed to be had to stave off a conflict in the city, the sort de Vaux had lived through before. He wanted someone arrested, and he wanted the high cleric to agree to it.

It didn't happen. He hadn't really expected it would.

"Understand me, and what you are doing," he said to the golden-robed cleric quivering with fury in front of his desk. "We *will* do this. He *will* be taken and questioned. This is about treason, in winter and now today. We have new information sustaining this allegation. When you object today before the queen and the two dukes, you will be aligning yourself with that treason. No one will be inclined to be indulgent. You have a choice."

"I have none," the high cleric said, bravely enough, though a quaver was in his voice, too. "Clerics and students and teachers of the university are entitled by settled law to our own judicial procedure. One that *you* do not control, provost!"

"Ah. And will you say this, too, about the tonsured murderer who has just confessed to killing the Duke de Montereau in the winter, and buying an archer to kill me in revenge this morning? Are you sure, my lord cleric? Really?"

There was a pause. The high cleric cleared his throat. "We will take counsel as to this man Barthelmy, whom I believe to be no cleric at all. But that is not what you are asking of me."

He was far from a fool, de Vaux thought. He wouldn't be. Even so . . .

"I think you are making a terrible mistake. One that will affect your own status, and perhaps even the freedom of the university.

Take careful thought, high cleric. That is all. You will be guarded here and escorted back to your residence in the morning. After we have made an arrest."

"You are really going to do this?"

"I just told you I was. I brought you here to help me control what will follow. To give you a chance to be praised as a wise man before the queen and the dukes. You have declined. Aubrey, see that the high cleric has whatever he needs for the night."

He waited until Aubrey and the cleric had left the room, then he summoned Medor Colle to go onto the university residence grounds with five men to arrest Denis Cassin, advocate, and take him to the Châtelet.

"A cell for the night," he said. "Food, water, no questioning. I will be there in the morning to do so myself."

Which was extremely unusual. But all of this was. And then . . . and then a message came, very late, and de Vaux changed his plans. If he was summoned to the court, to the queen and the dukes in the dead of night, the cleric and the lawyer were coming too.

In Robbin de Vaux's experience, beautiful women, of any age, rarely desired a room to be brightly lit. The queen of Ferrieres, he had come to realize, was different. Bianca di Rizzetto evidently preferred to observe closely those she was speaking with, and wanted light for that. A shrewd, dangerous woman, he had long since decided. Had to be to survive, with the king so fragile.

The small reception room in the palace was, accordingly, replete with torches and lamps when they assembled to await her arrival, well after midnight, both moons setting. This *could* have happened in the morning. That it did not was telling. Someone had awakened her, and she had taken action.

Queen Bianca entered, sweeping into the chamber with an entourage that included her husband's uncles—the two dukes, who were now, with her, custodians of the realm. Those awaiting them bowed.

Normally, the high cleric of Orane would have been standing with the queen. Instead, he was behind de Vaux, here against his will. So, too, was the lawyer, Cassin, visibly unhappy. With cause, mind you.

It occurred to de Vaux, rather belatedly, that he himself might be at risk now. He had chosen to believe that Barthelmy had fled Orane the night of the assassination, and had most likely been killed by Barratin.

Neither, it seemed, was true.

That was reflected in the queen's first question. The dukes deferred to her, as was likely wise in her current mood.

"This assassin? You have him now?"

"He is dead in the Châtelet, your grace," de Vaux said. "He confessed to what we needed to know, after strict questioning. His body will be on Gallows Hill in the morning. If you approve."

Everyone knew what "strict questioning" meant.

"It took you," said the queen, "a very long time to find him."

What he'd feared. Not how he'd wanted this to begin.

"We were led to believe he'd left Orane and been killed by—"

"Yes. I know. You thought the Duke de Barratin had him killed. You were wrong?"

"We were, your grace. But we found him. And he has talked to us."

"After trying to have you killed, as well?"

"Yes, your grace."

"Why?" She was visibly, vividly angry.

"Because of, it appears, my accusing the duke of being behind the assassination."

"Behind? In front of! Responsible for!"

"Yes, your grace. You are correct."

Her expression changed. There were torches and lamps and lanterns. He could see it. "You are all right, provost?"

"By Jad's grace, and the alertness of my serjeants, the arrow missed. A horse was struck and died."

"They killed a horse?" The queen loved riding and hunting. Always had, from girlhood in Batiara, before she was deemed old enough to be an important piece in the marriage game and was sent away to marry a king in a foreign land.

"It was poisoned, the arrow," said de Vaux. "So were the others in his sheath when the archer was captured."

She nodded. "And he talked to your men?"

"He did. He named Barthelmy. Whom we found trying to escape the city."

"Good," said the queen. "Uncles, have you questions?"

"Not yet," said the Duke de Regnault. He was paying close attention, however. He had risen in stature, was the general view, since the assassination.

Barille, his brother, just shook his head when the queen glanced at him. He was the more reluctant figure here. Would rather have been in his own château, away from Orane, away from all this, attending to pleasures. Everyone knew it. He *was* here, though. Had to give him that.

The queen said, "This filth, Barthelmy, he was a tonsured cleric?"

"Your grace!" exclaimed Hutin Peyre, the high cleric of Orane. "It is our belief that—"

A royal hand was thrust sharply upwards, stopping him mid-speech.

"Your time will come, high cleric," said the queen.

Peyre, a man of the south but long in Orane, was wise enough to fall silent.

De Vaux, with the queen's eyes back on him, said, "He was tonsured, yes. In the winter and now. It may have been a deception."

"You don't think he was a true cleric? Or a student?"

"I don't believe so," said de Vaux.

The queen turned to the man in the yellow robe with the sun disk about his neck. The provost felt a very slight measure of pity for the high cleric. "Now you will speak," Bianca di Rizzetto said.

Peyre swallowed. "We hold no views as to protecting this man.

We never thought he was truly a holy cleric, and he was never a student. He is," he raised his voice, "a murderous traitor in our view!"

"Did you," asked the Duke de Regnault, "say this in the winter? After the king's brother was slain and Barthelmy was identified?"

He knew the answer. The high cleric had not done so. Had opted for silence. And there was silence from him now. Hutin Peyre was learning, de Vaux thought, how dangerous it was to bluster, and that choices had consequences.

"There may be," said the queen, with a deadly calm in her voice, "some reason to reopen discussions with the High Patriarch in Rhodias about how Orane and the court may be best served by our high cleric."

As close to a death sentence, or one of dismissal and exile, as royal words could be, without going straight there, Robbin de Vaux thought.

"I assure you of my undying loyalty to Ferrieres!" exclaimed the high cleric.

"Undying," said the queen, eyebrows raised. "Indeed?"

De Vaux winced on behalf of the other man. A man he intensely disliked, after years of judicial disputes.

Queen Bianca said, "And so we come to the distinguished advocate and orator." Her disdain for Denis Cassin was palpable. "You will defend *him*, high cleric?"

Peyre was not a coward. "It is my duty to do so, your grace. Denis Cassin is a genuine cleric, a teacher, part of the university. Not subject to the provost of Orane's interrogations. This is long-settled law."

"Have *you* interrogated him?" It was Regnault again. And again the high cleric fell silent.

"They have not," de Vaux risked saying. "No one has. To be fair, this has all happened very fast."

"Perhaps we might start right now, then," said the queen, briskly. "Messire Cassin, what have you to say about the confession tonight, that your client and patron did order the killing of the king's brother, an act of treason to Orane?"

Cassin was less visibly brave, de Vaux thought. But he was nimble, effortlessly nimble with words.

The lawyer said, "Your grace, an advocate has a duty to his client. He does not embrace that client's actions or views! The duke had written to admit the actions, had denied legal and ethical *fault.*"

"But *did* you embrace those views?" asked the Duke de Regnault, and for the first time the provost heard anger in his voice, too. "If you were to be formally interrogated now, what would we learn? Are you, for example, still being paid by that client? For support? What would we discover about communications from the Duke de Barratin now?"

And that last, thought de Vaux, was perhaps the key question.

He said, as gravely as he could, "It is the high cleric's position that I am not even permitted to inquire."

"Is that true?" said the queen.

Hutin Peyre, that high cleric, actually took a step backwards. Her voice could make a man do that.

He said, "There are . . . there are . . . legal precedents as to jurisdiction and—"

"*Is it true?*" Queen Bianca asked again, and now her voice put de Vaux in mind of the winter they had endured, and the night Rollin de Montereau died in the street.

No answer from the cleric. Nothing from Cassin. Nothing at all.

It was decided that, because the matter involved treason, the advocate Denis Cassin was properly subject to questioning by the provost of Orane regarding the activities of the Duke de Barratin, both in winter and at the present time. A cleric, if one was requested, could be present to observe. The provost was admonished to use only necessary means of interrogation.

"Necessary" carried all the consent de Vaux required. Nonetheless, the next morning, when he arrived at the Châtelet, after he'd had Cassin locked in a cell overnight, it proved quite easy to induce him to talk.

Cassin did not, in fact, know a great deal, and de Vaux believed this because he had surmised it. The man was too soft for someone as shrewd as Barratin to have confided in him. Cassin confirmed what he'd been paid, which was a great deal but hardly noteworthy. His defence of Barratin in the winter had been constructed around necessity and loyalty to Ferrieres, not, as he'd already noted, denial of the murder. De Vaux had been there, he knew this.

He wanted to know if Cassin was privy to anything happening now, and he satisfied himself the man was not. There *was* a cleric in attendance. He'd have nothing to complain about, other than the very fact of the distinguished academic Denis Cassin being interrogated by the provost. That was a victory of sorts, de Vaux thought.

"Take what you are given, push for more when you need to." Jean Montel, once constable of Ferrieres, his mentor and friend, had told him long ago, about sieges and battlefields. Applied to more than warfare.

He sent Cassin home with an escort, unharmed, if very deeply shaken. And certainly an enemy now.

He was considering his next actions when they received word of an Anglcyn fleet preparing to sail to the conquest of Ferrieres, with King Hardan, fifth of that name, on board the flagship.

He had seen an opportunity in the chaos here, had only waited for spring and safer weather. The long war was not over. It had begun before any of them had been born. It would outlast them all, Robbin de Vaux thought bitterly.

There is general agreement that King Hardan V of Angland, young, bold, fearing no danger—with a rabid beast's thirst for blood (at least as reported by chroniclers in Ferrieres)—left his shores with a quickly assembled fleet in the spring. Quietly, in order to gain the element of surprise when he invaded yet again, aiming this time to reach Orane itself and a final conquest, capturing the mad king and his divided court, in a war that had gone on so long no one remembered peace.

He thought he had planned well.

He had in fact done so. And yet, the wheel of fortune rules us. Chance, happenstance. None of us are gods, even if some of the emperors of the Ancients claimed to be.

Hardan's soothsayers and astrologers, his chiromancers, his land and sea commanders . . . not one of them anticipated or foretold the storm that overtook his fleet, though everyone knew spring storms did come, with shocking speed at times, in the channel between the two countries.

That channel, wild, turbulent, dangerous, had long protected Angland from the continent. That spring it did the opposite: famously, infamously, irrefutably.

The story that spread and became legend was that a young woman, a girl, really, from the village of Broché had made her way to the coast with a number of followers and had knelt in a sanctuary there, or by the sea under the sky, and invoked Jad's mercy on Ferrieres—before anyone even knew there was an invading fleet on the waves.

And the storm came that very evening, out of a suddenly black sky!

She had been saying, this Jeanette, that she heard voices sent by holy Jad. Voices that instructed her to do all that she did, that guided her to the seashore, and afterwards.

Later, of course, it would be alleged by her enemies that what she had heard were demons of darkness from beneath the world, not voices from the god. That she was a heretic, an accursed witch.

The stories told—and heard—are shaped by what we need to, or want to, believe.

But some things are nonetheless agreed upon. There may be worlds where a wild storm did not come boiling up out of the west in the channel, where there were only blue skies and fair winds, where an invading fleet landed on the coast without incident and proceeded inland.

It was not so in this world, under Jad.

King Hardan survived to stumble wearily ashore. Only about half his fleet did so with him, it was determined in the wan morning light. The other half (perhaps a little more) were smashed in their ships and drowned. Famously, infamously?

Who was telling the tale?

He was bold, King Hardan. No one ever disputed that. He refused to huddle on a bleak coastline waiting for the wind to change and allow him to beat his way home in failure and shame, with so many dead—and with rebels all over his court, slavering at the opportunity his failure had given rise to.

He chose to carry on. He might or might not reach Orane now, but he would do damage, as much damage as he could in his rage. Killing, as it happened, came easily to him.

Even so, even with great events occurring, receiving the chroniclers' attention, men and women in all times and places go about their own lives, as best they can.

What else are we to do?

⚜

"Have you heard about the girl?" Marina di Seressa asked.

"What girl?" Silvy said.

They were in the delicately furnished, brightly coloured sitting room of Marina's family château two days north of the Livraise. The glass doors to the garden were open. Sunshine, late day. Drone of bees, scent of flowers from by the windows. Marina's daughter and son were outside with an attendant. They were chasing butterflies, and laughing.

"Jeanette. The Maiden."

"Ah," said Thierry Villar. "The one who prayed for a storm, they say? I overheard the servants talking about her. They were making the sign of the sun disk, over and again."

"We don't know what she prayed for. But yes, her. She is now coming this way, I heard."

"Oh?" said Thierry. He put down his book.

He had largely recovered. Strength, will, a desire for life. Some nights he still woke from very bad dreams, but many people had those, for different reasons. He had let his mother and stepfather know he was all right. He had been advised by the provost that it was wiser to stay away from Orane, still. There were complex events taking place.

Marina's hands were calm in her lap. She had, more than any woman he'd ever known, an ability to *be* calm. And she was calming.

"She's meeting the two dukes at Chervaux," she said.

The dukes were Barille and Regnault, of course, the king's uncles. And there was a sizable enemy force in the land. Again.

"The queen is coming as well," Marina added. "She has asked me to attend upon her. She also wants you, Thierry."

"What?" he said, startled. "Why? And why would the court come meet this girl?"

"I have no idea. As for you, the queen might want an expression of gratitude for your rescue. Or something else. I really don't know. We have been isolated here, haven't we?"

Thierry sighed. "My gratitude is very great. Even if I'm not good at showing it, and I really want to be back in Orane."

"Maybe this will lead you back?"

Silvy said, "It could, you know. Regardless, it is time for *me* to return. Lovely as this has been, I do have a tavern to attend to." She smiled at the other woman, saying it. The two of them had been sharing a bed here.

"You tire of what we have to offer in the countryside?" Marina di Seressa said. But she also smiled.

"Perhaps some of it may be offered, and found, in Orane?" Silvy said, looking demure.

Thierry's turn to laugh. "I suddenly feel as if I should go outside and chase butterflies."

Marina gave him a look. She said, "We will take guidance in

Chervaux. Silvy can go home any time. Easiest and safest from there, with a proper escort. I might be asked to go back with the queen. Thierry is wisest to stay here until we know more."

"Alone? I will go mad," he said.

"Not alone. My mother and children will be here to amuse you," Marina said, placidly.

He didn't answer that.

"And you might write better in solitude," she added. And did not smile. "We'll leave for Chervaux in the morning, with guards. I'm going to ask at the next château for some of theirs. We've done that for each other before. If the Anglcyn have landed again, it is a dangerous time. Silvy will be my attendant, if she's willing."

Silvy allowed herself a half-smile. "You have found me unwilling in anything?"

And was rewarded richly because both the others flushed.

They didn't leave until the day after next. It took time for ten requested guards to arrive, although they did come. Courtesies among the nobility, Silvy thought. This had been a taste of a world she'd never even slightly known.

She had even begun to learn how status worked here. They were two days from the river and the châteaux strung along the Livraise like jewels.

Marina's home was among several owned by distinguished families, but not those of the first order of nobility. Rank in this valley was measured by how close you were to the river. And Chervaux, right beside it, the largest château of all, belonged to the crown.

It was even being expanded, she saw as they rolled up to it. It was already enormous, more a palace than a hunting lodge, though she knew the court would always hunt when it was here.

Thierry was on his horse among the guards, she and Marina in the carriage. Again. With the same two attendants. There had been no incidents on the way south; they were a well-protected party.

They pulled into a vast courtyard—immaculately groomed gravel, flower beds all around—and came to a clattering halt. She and Marina stepped down.

Someone was waiting. Someone in armour, very young. A woman. Short brown hair, plain features, extremely blue eyes.

"They are not here yet," she said gravely. "I am Jeanette. Who are you?"

CHAPTER XI

"I am Marina di Seressa, and these are my friends. Hello, Jeanette. I have heard another name for you."

"The Maiden," the other woman said. She made a face. "I don't like it."

"Why? If I may ask?" Thierry, looking at her, felt uneasy. Her eyes were bluer than any he'd ever seen.

The girl-woman shrugged. "I am a soldier. Whether I am a maiden or not has nothing to do with that. But my army likes the name."

"Your army?" Marina asked.

Jeanette gestured to a meadow past the work being done on a new wing for the château. They looked, and saw the smoke of many fires. "They walked night and day from the sea to come here," she said. "Men and women, both, will fight for Ferrieres with me." She paused. "I have things to tell the court."

Tell the court, Thierry thought.

The girl turned to look north, where the long tree-lined path to the royal hunting lodge came down from the main road. There was nothing to see or hear.

"Ah. They are nearly here," said Jeanette de Broché, matter-of-factly. "And . . . the king is with them. As I asked."

"Dear Jad," said Marina, with a gasp.

The girl looked at her, unsmiling. A round, serious face, smooth skin, lightly freckled, hair cut very short, those blue eyes. She made the sign of the sun disk. "Always," she said.

Silvy had said nothing at all. She was just staring at this girl.

Thierry looked again at the smoke from the campfires, then turned to gaze along the empty, silent path leading here. Not quite silent: there was birdsong. He felt entirely unsettled, and they'd barely exchanged a handful of words.

Then Jeanette lifted her head, as if hearing something none of them could hear, and she walked a few steps north, so that she'd be the first person anyone would see, coming into the courtyard. Thierry became aware she had a sword on her hip. A soldier, she'd called herself.

It was, as best he remembered later, only a matter of moments before he heard the sound of horses and shouted commands. A large number of guards in royal livery came riding down the path. They fanned out to both sides of the courtyard. Then there came eight carriages, and a great many more soldiers and guards. This was royalty, after all. It became noisy, crowded, dusty, chaotic. Marina's guards made way, moving back towards the château.

He and Marina and Silvy also backed up to stand near the steps leading to the hunting lodge, beside the assembled servants and a tall man in blue and gold who was clearly the steward here. And who also looked afraid, Thierry decided.

Memory can be precarious. It might have been more than just moments after the girl had sensed they were coming, but they did come, those soldiers and royal carriages. The court had arrived, with the king. As she'd said they were about to.

Thierry also remembered the wind dying down just then, but that might not have happened.

Jeanette is almost never afraid. Not since the first voices came to her at home. Then, she'd been terrified that these voices were demons, enemies of the god and his mortal children. Because surely Jad of the Sun would not speak in any way to a miller's daughter from the village of Broché in the countryside of Ferrieres, or have . . . something do so on his behalf.

They had summoned her, though, the voices. They had. That had happened. To her. On a winter's night. A summons to go outside. She had done so. She was not able to refuse this. She'd dressed quietly in the room she shared with two of her sisters and had walked out. Everyone else in the house was asleep. It had seemed as if the whole world was. Both moons overhead. The sun, and the god, under the world.

But the voices had only grown clearer, more precise, and, doing what she was told, Jeanette had gone into their tiny village sanctuary. It was unlit (candles were expensive) and very cold and she was alone there as she knelt on the uneven wooden floor before the altar and the sun disk.

And then, after she'd prayed for guidance and for love, one voice in her head had instructed her that she had to leave her home and go north. She had never been outside the bounds of Broché in her life.

She was to gather people to her, and be prepared to fight and die for Ferrieres when the time came. It was, she thought, a command.

And she is. Prepared to do that. Fight and die for Ferrieres. From that time, that frigid, moonlit night in Broché, Jeanette has been ready, and unafraid. Astonishingly unafraid. Everyone died, didn't they?

In the morning her mother had wept. Her father said they were well rid of her—refusing any husband offered in the village, not nearly enough help at the mill to earn her keep. There were five other children to feed. They could have an apprentice or a servant girl take her bed and be of more use, he said. He walked out, didn't say goodbye to her. She thought he was grieving, but wasn't sure.

Two of her brothers came with Jeanette, one older, one younger. She wasn't expecting that. Her father was enraged when he saw the older one preparing to go. They fought, out by the mill. Her brother had a blackened eye at the start of their journey.

They are still with her now, both of them, at this enormous hunting lodge. They are among the army of men and women that has formed around her. That had begun gathering from the time she started north towards the sea, though not going there yet. She isn't supposed to, yet.

In every village and town they passed through, she went into a sanctuary and prayed, with the cleric, or without him, if he deemed her immodest, unwomanly, even heretical, with her talk of hearing voices from the god. Then she would go outside to speak to whoever had come to see this strange girl, and she'd invite them to join her in defending Ferrieres for Jad. At some point, someone had handed one of her brothers a breastplate small enough for her, and a sword for her to carry.

They began calling her the Maiden, and word of her progress started to precede her. There came to be larger crowds awaiting her arrival wherever she went. Most would pray with her, listen to her speak of the need to defend Ferrieres against the enemy she had been told was coming again.

Everyone knew who their enemy was, north across the channel. They had landed before, many times. Taken cities and castles. Many times. The war was very old. It was time, Jeanette said, for it to end.

There was war within the country, too, by then, or the risk of it, but she didn't speak to that. She invited men—and women, if they wanted to, and could—to join her on a march to the coast, because it would soon be time for that, she said.

She is still not afraid. She never does become fearful. Not of dying.

It is springtime by then, and it is a disrupted, uncertain world in which they all live. Many do set aside their lives for a time (as they think) to follow the Maiden. The name stays with her.

And then it seems there are many hundreds of them, and they do turn north, and they come at last to the sea.

A stony strand, east of walled Calienne. Wind and waves, white-caps, seabirds calling. She prays in an abandoned sanctuary near the shoreline. It is so small only a handful can come inside with her, the roof barely there, birds' nests, the wind. All the others kneel outside. And after, she walks down to the water under a morning sun, the god's gift of light, and she kneels again, in her armour, sword at her hip, and she prays again to holy Jad.

The story begins there, from that moment: that she'd invoked the storm that smashed the Anglcyn fleet that was already sailing towards them that day.

Black clouds and drenching rain and shattering waves hit those ships at sea. That storm hurtled in from the west, crashing along the channel, thunder and lightning obliterating what had been a mild blue sky towards a spring day's end. Out of nowhere, men and women later said.

Many died in the wreckage of many ships.

Good men, bad men. The sea does not care.

Jeanette knows she never invoked it. Had only prayed, as always, for respite, safety, protection for Ferrieres and its people. And its king. She always prayed for the king. She would not ask Jad to kill *any* of his mortal children for her, though if battle came she'd take that on herself, as best she could.

She calls herself a soldier but knows nothing of warfare. Not even how to properly use her sword. Her older brother has been learning how to fight, and the younger is unexpectedly good with horses.

She only knows, absolutely, in her soul, that the god is guiding her. She doesn't know why. Why *her*. It is not a question she asks any more. She only hears him, or voices that speak his will. She never doubts that now.

She is told, within, when she stands up on the strand by the sea, the sky still blue in that morning moment, that she must start back south. She is to go to a place called Chervaux, and send word ahead that the court should meet her there. *And the king*, she is told.

"And the king," she says to the riders she sends. They have a few horses now. Her older brother Peire is one of the riders. They have not been apart since leaving Broché. This is new. She will miss him. She is still not afraid.

He rides to Orane, while other riders go ahead of her to this place named Chervaux on the Livraise, wherever that is. She does not know the world, where places are.

Nearly five hundred people are with her now, almost all from the countryside, or villages, walking through Ferrieres. Trusting her. It can be called an army, if someone wants to do that. Their weapons are sticks and staves, pitchforks, rusted family swords, some knives and daggers. They are given food and drink wherever they pass. People kneel before Jeanette now when she goes by. She doesn't like that but cannot stop it from happening.

She does not know how her brother succeeds in getting word to the palace, to the queen.

But by then the tale of the Maiden has spread. Some clerics are deeply suspicious; others choose to see her as a miracle sent by Jad. From the start Jeanette has divided people. This never changes. But Peire is admitted into the palace, to the queen, and he says what his sister has told him to say.

The queen of Ferrieres summons the only adviser she trusts in matters that might touch the half-world. And so Gauvard Colle, brought to her, listens also to Peire de Broché. He looks shaken after (he never looks shaken) and says, quietly, "I think you must do as she requests."

"Including the king?" asks Queen Bianca. "Really?"

"Including the king," he says.

"Will you come?"

"I will do whatever you ask of me," he says. "And I should like to meet this girl."

By that point, word had also come that what is left of Hardan V's wrecked invasion fleet has come ashore—and is not turning back. It is said they are headed southeast from Calienne, burning villages and farms and villagers and farmers as they go. Hardan is a vicious man.

There is great danger, and great opportunity, because of the storm. The world, as men and women have it, can offer these together sometimes.

The king and queen, and the leaders of the court of Ferrieres, set out for Chervaux two mornings after, through the city's walls and west, well-guarded.

Prince Girald, the heir, stays in Orane. Also well-guarded.

It took time, even for the well-trained staff at Chervaux. There were so many people to be assigned rooms, and fed, including those being quartered in the outbuildings, and the Maiden's army sleeping in tents or outside in the meadow.

The king was watched in pity, shuffling in slow, painful-to-see confusion from his coach into the hunting lodge.

But by late afternoon the members of the court had assembled in a very large ground-floor room with four fireplaces, a heavy wooden throne, and heads of animals mounted along the walls.

Chervaux might have been more a palace than a hunting retreat, but it *was* a place for hunting. Once, King Roch had reportedly preferred being here to anywhere in the world.

Now, he did not seem to know where he was, Thierry Villar thought.

The king was neatly barbered and dressed, but his posture was slack. He looked dazed and inattentive. There was an unsettling feeling that he might soil himself, or explode into violent motion at any time. Perhaps it was the two attendants, standing watchfully by him as he sprawled on the heavy chair on its dais. The queen stood a few steps ahead of it, and below.

She was looking at Jeanette de Broché, in front of her, alone.

"We are here," Queen Bianca said calmly. "Why are we here?"

Further along the room—with Silvy and, unexpectedly, Medor Colle, who had come with the court and his uncle—Thierry couldn't see the Maiden's shockingly blue eyes now. She didn't like that name, he reminded himself. It was hard not to use it, though, in one's thoughts. It was hard to call her, or think of her as simply Jeanette, a miller's daughter from Broché. It occurred to him he had no idea where Broché even was.

She was too much outside the world, he thought. Of course she was also in it, of it, shaping it, because—they were all *here*! Because she'd summoned them.

"Why," the queen had just asked.

And was answered, quietly, a country girl's voice, but very clear.

"I am here to awaken the king," Jeanette de Broché said. "And then we must prepare to go fight the invaders and destroy them."

A murmur, oddly like the sound of the sea, in a crowded room. Too crowded, Medor had muttered. His eyes kept scanning the chamber for danger. His uncle was standing alone, not far from the queen, dressed in a sober, dark-blue travelling robe. His face seemed strained, Thierry thought.

Queen Bianca was now looking to Gauvard, as if for help. The two dukes behind the throne were silent. They seemed frightened, almost amusingly uncertain. Except nothing here was amusing, Thierry thought.

Gauvard Colle, with the queen's eyes on him, said to Jeanette, "How will you do that? Awaken him."

"By praying," she said without hesitation. "With Jad's intercession. But not here. We need to be alone in a quiet room."

"You will *not* be alone with the king!" snapped the Duke de Regnault, shaken out of uncertainty. "It is not to be considered!"

"Then the queen can be with us," the small woman in armour said calmly. "She can pray too."

Queen Bianca turned again to Gauvard Colle. He said, "We send two guards with you. She removes her armour and sword and is searched for weapons. There is . . . there is nothing to be lost, your grace. If she fails and you wish to kill her for this disruption of the court, you can do that."

"She summoned the storm that smashed the fleet," the queen said, a quaver in her voice.

"We don't know if—" Gauvard began.

"*I didn't do that!*" said Jeanette de Broché. "I would not do that. I prayed to Jad for shelter for Ferrieres and the king. I always do."

It was so strange, Thierry Villar thought, when a large number of people became entirely still. He could hear birds from the garden.

"Two guards," said the queen. She had taught herself to sound decisive during the king's many periods of incapacity, however she was really feeling. "And you, Messire Colle."

Gauvard Colle, famously, liked gossip, new tidings, being the one to share such things. He didn't keep a wide circle of friends, was too easily irked by people, but he did have intimates, and was known to tell a good story.

He spoke only twice of what happened in that room, and did so cryptically.

The queen never did.

The guards remained at the back of the chamber after searching the girl, and since one of them was Gauvard's nephew and the other was the commander of the royal guard, they remained circumspect all their lives.

Gauvard Colle watched the girl kneel before the chair on which the king had been seated, near the fireplace in this smaller room. No artifice, no adjusting of the room, drawing of curtains. She just knelt down on the floor to pray. Nothing more. It was so . . . ordinary, he thought.

There were tall windows across the room, opposite the door, tall flowers beneath them, then a garden, and then the first beginnings of a vineyard being planted. The river would be past the trees. Trophies of the hunt were on the walls of this smaller chamber, too. Heads of stags and boars.

The king looked as he had in the great room earlier: uneasy, vacant, inattentive, but somehow on the edge of doing something disruptive. His attendants were not with them now. A mistake? Gauvard had heard about incidents. They were why King Roch was kept almost entirely out of sight when unwell. Both of the guards, he saw, including his nephew, were alert. They could cross the room quickly, if needed. The queen stood beside the girl, the Maiden, and a little behind her. Gauvard was nearer the door, where he could watch.

The difficulty was that he suddenly couldn't clearly *see* Jeanette de Broché.

It was the strangest thing. She was right in front of him, kneeling. But as soon as she formed the circle of a sun disk with her hands and closed her eyes to pray she began to shimmer and blur, to vanish and reappear in his sight. He blinked. Rubbed his eyes. No effect. She was there and gone, present and not quite so. He had never experienced anything like this in his life.

He decided she was frightening.

He didn't pray, though he saw that Queen Bianca had also closed her eyes and was murmuring words of a litany. She, too, was holding a sun disk now. Gauvard Colle did not do so. He was not a devout man, wasn't even properly a follower of Jad, though he didn't *disbelieve*: he just saw the sun god of the Jaddites as one among many powers in the world, in the many worlds.

The king of Ferrieres made a sound.

A guttural cough, then another. He was visibly unhappy now. He shifted position, his hands gripping the arms of the chair. Gauvard saw the two guards look at each other. They stayed where they were, though.

The girl opened her eyes at the noise. After a moment she stood up. And Gauvard Colle saw, with deep unease, that she looked . . . *angry*. Her prayers had not worked. She took a step forward. So, now, did the guards. He felt like doing so himself. Held back. Not his role here. At least he could see her properly again. The blurriness had passed when the praying stopped. He didn't know what to make of that.

He had long since accepted that he would never truly understand the half-world, even if he was more a part of it than anyone he knew. The first lesson was the unknowability. You accepted, with both gratitude and apprehension, whatever you were given.

The girl said, in her country accent but with no diffidence at all, "Your grace, you are needed. This must end! Come back to us. Do so now, in the god's holy name."

And after a long moment King Roch looked at her. He *looked* at her.

The sound this time came from the queen. And, Gauvard realized, maybe from himself. The king just looked at the girl steadily. And then . . . he moved. He straightened his back. He lifted his handsome head. His hands left the chair arms and settled in his lap. But . . . that was all.

Again a flash of anger in the blue eyes of the girl. The woman. Jeanette de Broché. And something else. He was in a position, where he stood, to see when pity and sorrow overtook her. Not fear. He never did see fear in her.

She took another step forward. She was extremely close to the king now. Unacceptably so, really. Then she knelt again, right before him. Her hands reached out and took his, shockingly. Gauvard saw the queen clench her own hands into fists. The guards remained frozen.

The girl said, "Whatever has held you from us and from yourself, your grace, in the name of Jad and with all the need of your people I command it to be gone. Come back to us!"

I command, Gauvard Colle thought. He shivered.

There was an aching interval of silence. Then . . .

"Have I been long away this time?" asked King Roch of Ferrieres quietly.

He had a beautiful voice, Gauvard thought.

The queen began to weep.

Gauvard realized that he was doing so as well.

Jeanette de Broché said, also quietly, "Yes, your grace. You have. Too long. Welcome back."

She released his hands. She stood up, took a step backwards. Gauvard saw her sway. He was quicker than the guards, stepped forward, steadied her. Helped her move to the side of the room where he'd been. Kept holding her, an arm about her shoulders. She was shaking. He was certain she would fall if he let her go. He did not let her go.

I do not understand the world, he thought.

But it was all right, he also thought. It was all right.

All his life, and he lived a very long time, and even saw Sarantium again, Gauvard Colle would remember that afternoon, that room. The king's eyes, also blue, registering all of them. And the girl, trembling like an autumn leaf in a wind beside him, held by him.

"Oh, my dear lord," whispered the queen.

The king looked at her. He smiled, very gently. "I left you alone again?" he asked.

She nodded. Tears were streaming down her face. She wiped at her cheeks with the backs of her hands, careful of the rings she wore. He noticed that because he noticed things.

"I don't know what you did," Gauvard Colle said softly to the girl beside him. "But thank you. For all of us."

"I don't know what I did, either," said Jeanette de Broché. She sounded terribly young. He wasn't a compassionate man, but he felt compassion then.

⚜

There are places in the world where important things have happened. Personal ones: births, deaths, childhood discoveries, love found, or lost. Or events impacting the wider world of kings and countries. Sometimes those larger ones happen years, or even centuries apart in the same place, if it survives.

It is not really surprising that a smaller reception chamber in the hunting lodge of Chervaux, built for royalty and loved by generations of it, should be one such place.

Decades after that day, in a time after the world has greatly changed, another king of Ferrieres, the grandson of this one, will receive an emissary from the High Patriarch in Rhodias. The emissary is a military leader, sharing military plans. A woman of no status at all will be present in the room, as she happens to be a part of the emissary's entourage. She will discover, because she is clever and alert, a spy from a hostile country beneath the window, hidden among the flowers.

For reasons of state the spy will not be executed, but he is sent home, expelled from Ferrieres, and his right hand is severed.

On the way, he will die of the wound festering. It was not intended, but it happens.

He is in no way central to the tale of that later time, the conflicts that ensued not long after, but he has a family that mourns him, and his death speaks to a hard truth: you can die at the margins of a story as easily as at the centre of it.

Or just be a glancing comment in another tale.

Thierry could not sleep. He had a room to himself, a genuine luxury. Even with all the guards and courtiers accompanying the royal party, there was room for privacy in Chervaux for someone favoured— however improbably—by the queen. The bed was extremely comfortable, the room was large.

But he lay wide awake. He was thinking about the night his life had changed in the winter now past, when they had gone and seen a dead, butchered body in a street across the river.

Had that not happened . . .

How did you not think about moments like that?

He heard an owl outside. Then a wolf, distantly. Night sounds in the countryside. He really didn't like it. He'd rather hear drunken singing from a street outside. Instead, here, there was also the steady passage of guards below, boots crunching on gravel. All of this registered clearly. He was too far from sleep.

He was adjacent, it seemed, to very great events. Plans were being swiftly made. The king was back among them. A blessing of Jad. Thierry had gone with others to the sundown rites in the sanctuary here. He'd stood with Silvy towards the back, and chanted the responses as a tall cleric led them.

The king had been at the front. Returned to himself, and to them.

Later, he had asked Thierry Villar for a poem.

They'd finished the banquet in the dining hall. It had been the queen who'd summoned Thierry from where he was seated down the long oak table.

He had risen, dry-mouthed, to approach the table at the top of the room, nearest the windows. He had walked past stags on the walls, the one over the fireplace utterly magnificent—so many tines to the horns. He didn't know hunting, or stags. He only knew Orane.

He was presented (*he* was presented!) to the king, sitting amid those of his court who were here. He saw Marina sitting near the queen. She smiled a little, but he could see she was apprehensive. The Maiden, Jeanette, was also at that table, looking lost, he thought.

She'd rather be outside, he was sure, among her own army, in a tent or under stars.

The king of Ferrieres said, "We have been told, Thierry Villar, that you did us loyal service after the foul murder of our brother. We are grateful." He paused, smiled, continued in the beautiful voice, "We had not thought tavern poets could do that."

He *knew* of Thierry?

"Your grace," he stammered, saying the thought aloud, "I am honoured you know who I am. It is far beyond what I deserve."

Another smile. "We are told otherwise. But . . . if we have poets here, they should be put to use, surely, at a banquet. We know that in the taverns the fashion is to improvise verses. We have even heard some of yours, profane as they are."

Thierry winced.

King Roch continued, "So, a poem, if you will, Villar, to celebrate our return. But perhaps . . . not profane this time? We await you."

Dear Jad, Thierry thought.

But he was a poet, and he did do this, had done it so many nights in so many taverns, drunk or sober. This was the same thing, wasn't it?

It wasn't, but he needed to act as if it were.

He cleared his throat. "Your grace, my conceit, often, has been to pretend I am making my bequests as I die. I offer . . . mocking gifts to those I have deemed deserving of mockery. And have sometimes been . . . crude with that. Tonight . . . tonight, your grace, there will be no mockery. I feel grateful beyond anything I can say to see you here. To be here to see it."

He paused, but the words had begun in his head. He was all right. This was what he did. He said:

> To the golden king of Ferrieres,
> What can a tavern poet bequeath?
> A clear blue eye, a sharpened mind,
> A strong arm to defend his people,
> An awareness of how much loved he is.

And it was there for him now, all of it, already. Because sometimes a verse came to you whole, flowing like a river. Even as you began it, you knew where it wanted to go, to carry you, and that was so this night. He felt a different gratitude, a kind of joy—that this was what he did, what he was. He went on:

> And this poet vows that if, before he dies
> And is vouchsafed a glimpse of light,
> Any sword passes through his life,
> It belongs to the king. Whether given to me,
> Or wielded by another. Badly by a tavern poet,
> Or with skill by . . . anyone else
> In the world given to us by Jad!
> My gift, if I have any at all, is only for words,
> But they, too, are yours, your grace,
> To the end of all my days.

A silence. That sometimes happened in a tavern after he was done. This was longer than that, and was different. People were waiting. Of course they were.

The king of Ferrieres, golden-haired, blue-eyed, alert, and *with* them, said, "Oh dear. A sword poem? Very serious, Messire Villar. We were told you were amusing."

But he smiled, saying it. The queen laughed aloud.

"Apologies, your grace," Thierry managed. "I can be earnest at times, I fear. And feel, as I said, grateful tonight. We all do, I will venture to say."

"So do we," the king said to him. "You will be rewarded, Thierry Villar. For this, and for what you evidently did while we were . . . away."

He lifted a hand, in benediction. And with this, there finally came the applause, as if those in the room had needed that gesture to unlock them. It continued. A release throughout the chamber.

Thierry lowered his head. He bowed. He wasn't formally dismissed, but when he straightened he saw Marina make a small gesture with one hand, and he walked back to his seat along the table, past the giant stag head again. He collapsed on the bench, reached for his wine cup, drained it. It was refilled by a servant instantly.

He didn't look at anyone for a few moments. He was thinking of his mother and his stepfather, how they would have felt, seeing this. Overawed, and so proud.

He had never done much to make them proud. It felt strange now, to be thinking that way, but it was true, wasn't it? He wanted to swear, mutter something scurrilous. He didn't. He didn't do either.

Later, remembering, awake in the night, he gave up on sleep. He dressed and went down the wide staircase and outside, under the waxing moons and a clear night of stars. There were guards everywhere but they let him pass. One even held open the heavy door for him. He went down the steps to the gravel drive where they had stood when they'd arrived. There were campfires to his left, where the Maiden's people were. She had evidently gone back to them, refused to stay in the hunting lodge.

He heard the door open and close again, footsteps behind him. He turned to look.

"A sword?" said Medor Colle. "Was I the only one who found that amusing, from you?"

"Only person who knew how ill-suited I am to using one?"

The other man came down the steps and stood behind him.

"Are you following me again?" Thierry asked.

"Assigned to guard, yes. You seem to be my current burden in life, Villar."

"Even in the middle of a night? I'm sorry."

The other man shrugged. "Not my worst-ever task."

Thierry grinned a little. "The provost? He's all right?"

"You didn't hear what happened?"

"No. How would I have?"

"He's not the provost anymore."

"Oh, no," Thierry said. "That's—"

"No. No. De Vaux will be named constable of Ferrieres. Because we're going to war again, and he was a protegé of Jean Montel, who was constable some years back. The king remembered that, apparently."

Thierry thought about it. "And the current constable?"

"Has now been linked to the Duke de Barratin," said Medor.

"Oh."

"He's in the Châtelet."

"Oh," Thierry said again. He thought some more. "You'll . . . go north with de Vaux, to wherever the fighting is?"

Medor shook his head. "No. It seems I've been named provost of Orane for the time being."

"For the time being?"

"That's what they told me."

"Good for you," Thierry said, and meant it. "But that finishes you as my personal guard. Whatever shall I do?"

Medor snorted with amusement. Then, "Stay out of the city for a while yet, please. I'll have enough to worry about."

Thierry sighed. "They told me I'd probably have to do that. Any idea how much I hate it?"

"Some idea," said the other man.

They were silent, looking at the campfires in the middle distance, and the stars.

Eventually Medor said, "We'll have someone keep an eye on you, when you do return. That all right?"

"Does it matter if it is or isn't?" Thierry asked.

"Not really," said Medor Colle. He gestured. "Shall we walk?"

They did a loop around the hunting lodge, passing guards posted along the gravel drive, then going back along the river side. There were paths leading down to the Livraise, Thierry saw.

They kept going, past the construction now, the piles of timber and stone for the new wing, and finally came back up nearer the fires of Jeanette de Broché's army. They didn't approach. They stopped and looked at them.

After a time, Medor said, "They are starting north in the morning. She wouldn't delay. Said she only came for the king, and that now she's done what she had to do."

"What do you make of her?" Thierry asked. He heard the owl again.

"I have no thoughts. My uncle doesn't know, and if anyone would, it would be him."

"Can she survive? Going off to find the Anglcyn before the army even assembles?"

"I have no thoughts," said Medor Colle again. "This is beyond me."

They started walking again. It was a beautiful night. They passed the entrance and kept on going, a second loop around Chervaux in an easy silence. Stopped again, looking at the Maiden's army's fires.

Thierry looked overhead. The moons, and the glittering, impossible profusion of stars at night in the countryside. He could understand the Asharites worshipping these cold, hard watchers. But did they watch? Did they care in any possible way about men and women here?

He said, surprising himself, "I would like to call you a friend. I can use one. I hope that is all right."

Medor stiffened. Was silent a long moment. Thierry thought he knew why. There were so many ways, he thought, for people to be afraid, or lonely, or different.

"I can use one too," the serjeant finally said. Or, rather, the newly appointed provost of Orane said. And added, "Thank you."

They walked back to the entrance and went in and then up the wide stairs. Back in his room, Thierry slept this time.

When he woke in the morning and came down again, he learned that the army of the Maiden had already left, with the rising sun, after prayers.

The king and his court did the same later in the day. Back to Orane. Marina was with them, Silvy was (he hadn't had a chance to say good-bye), Gauvard Colle was. And Medor, of course. Tasks to be taken up.

Thierry Villar? He was escorted north by the same guards who had brought them here. Back to Marina's small, graceful château. Where her mother and children were. Where he was supposed to write better poems in the quiet of the countryside.

At least he could ride better now, he thought. The unexpected pleasure of that. Among the wonders of the time for him, looking back, was that he liked his horse, and riding the springtime roads as summer came.

I did. I really did come to love that horse.

CHAPTER XII

As has been said, it is a source of wonder how differently chroniclers can record the same events.

These variations apply not only to high dramas in the world. The memoirs of two cloth merchants in Batiara, describing a modest transaction, can do so with extreme and sometimes startling differences.

Even in stories told within a family, never written down, only shared around a table or by a fire or in a field working with a horse and plough, dramatically varying recollections are more usual than easy agreement. We regard our own memories as truths, when they are often just the stories we have told ourselves over time. They become the truth we live by, or with. They become our lives.

But when there *are* chronicles to read—when the events are indeed high drama, involving war and fire and many deaths—the discord manifest in words written and preserved can be significant. Not just as to getting at some "real" truth, which is impossible in many cases, but also for observing how history gives rise to legend—to moments at the heart of how a people come to see themselves.

This is the case as to the story of the Maiden's army and the Battle of Azingar, near the northern coast of Ferrieres.

King Hardan of the Anglcyn, for example, was either a monster, savagely killing anyone he encountered, burning because he could, enraged by what the storm had done to him, and fearful of an uprising back home—or he was a fierce and brave military leader, refusing to let misfortune at sea cause him to falter in what he saw as Jad's mission for his country.

King Roch of Ferrieres? He was a madman, briefly emerging at unpredictable intervals from slack-jawed, blank-eyed drooling and clawing at his cheeks and arms—or he was a gallant leader of his people, once afflicted by demons that had been vanquished with Jad's help at that time.

And the Maiden? Jeanette de Broché? Ah, well. The differing views of her are well known. They mark the hopeless entangling of history and story and legend, past the point of ever sorting them out.

In the mornings on first awakening, and at day's end when he had his last meetings with his commanders among the nobility, Robbin de Vaux felt too old for what he'd been asked to do for Ferrieres.

He had pain in both knees after years in the saddle, and marching, and fighting hand to hand, and his bowels were uncertain now. One sword wound, in the thigh, hurt him at night, routinely. It came, like an unwanted guest to a banquet, when he lay down in the dark of a field tent. He was the banquet, he sometimes thought, the wound come to devour him.

But during the day, most of the time, he felt entirely capable. He had lived with his injuries a long time, knew them well, and he had tasks to do, for his country and the god.

He was now in a place he knew from childhood. The de Vaux lands lay not far from where they were, just a little to the east and then north. He could have been at his own castle in a long day's ride. He had thought about sending his wife and children there, but Orane was safer: the Anglcyn were burning where they went.

He even understood about that.

King Hardan, aside from having a lust for blood (which he did), would be terrified right now. Indeed, depending on what happened when the two armies met, if they met, he had made the sort of mistake that could end a reign and a life. He should have sailed home, even in failure, Robbin de Vaux thought, even with a great many dead at sea and ships lost.

But, the constable admitted to himself, he really did not have a clear picture of the Anglcyn court across the channel. There would surely be rivalries and ambitious men, just as there were here. It was possible that Hardan could not safely go home without some sort of victory to claim.

It was Robbin de Vaux's task and intent to ensure that did not happen. Right now, accordingly, he needed to know where Jeanette de Broché and her so-called army were. And he didn't.

He had a better sense now, from his advance riders crossing and recrossing wet and muddy terrain, as to the location of the Anglcyn. Which was more than a little strange, he thought.

There were noblemen in his own army who would not be unhappy if he failed. They could step in, they'd be thinking, even as they nodded sagely during his evening briefings and orders. *They* could save their beloved, beleaguered country after an incompetent constable's disasters: the cavalry of the lords of Ferrieres, glittering and gallant, surging like another storm wave to smash the infantry and archers of the invaders from the sea, winning great glory. Such matter for songs!

Robbin de Vaux would happily have had half of them disembowelled. Ferrieres had been a victim of this preening vanity so many times in this long conflict. War as a game of lords—lordlings!—who viewed it solely in terms of themselves and their advancement. Laurels for the cavalry! And rank! And wealth!

Awareness of past follies, deaths, ruinous ransoms for the captured . . . this did not enter the shallow waters of their minds, he thought bitterly. Even if they failed (heroically!) and were taken to Angland as prisoners to await redeeming in aristocratic comfort, hunting in new forests, banqueting with new friends and among compliant Anglcyn women who found the nobles of Ferrieres worldly and elegant . . . well, there were worse fates!

Disembowelling was on de Vaux's mind too often of late, meeting with these men in the evenings, trying to make them understand and accept his commands. Perhaps, he thought, it was discomfort with his own bowels that made that the currently preferred fantasy for killing the fatuous.

That very evening, having learned from riders just returned that they were genuinely close to Hardan's force, he was told that two of the lords wanted permission to duel each other in the morning. A slight of some sort, deemed irremediable.

It really was too much, the stupidity.

"Permission granted," he'd said crisply to those assembled, including the two at odds with each other. "My only condition is this. You fight to the death. If one of you does not die, you will both be executed for vain folly, and for treachery damaging Ferrieres on the eve of war. I will happily be accountable to the king for this."

He dismissed them all. Men shuffled out, in silence.

De Vaux doubted very much there'd be any duel. Whatever mortal offence had been done by one man to the other . . . it would somehow emerge tonight to be not so mortal, after all.

He had Aubrey stay behind. He'd brought him north, a man he could entirely trust. Medor was now provost in Orane. Arguably unfair to leave him there without the most competent of the other serjeants, but such things happened in a time of war. You did what you could with what you had. Medor, he thought, would manage.

Unless Hardan destroyed their army in battle here, and gained an open path to the capital. The city walls would almost certainly hold, and the Anglcyn would be a long way from the sea and their ships, but there would be panic. And possibly treachery. Always that risk. And hunger, if the invaders managed to besiege Orane.

Best he not be defeated here, in short. He had ideas as to that. Was unsure if the lordlings were sufficiently under control to make them happen. Commanding an army, de Vaux thought, was sometimes about battling your own people before battling the enemy. He wasn't sure if that was his own idea, or if Jean Montel had told him something of the sort long ago, when they and the world were younger.

Aubrey affirmed no new messages from the king.

There had been some sort of evidence the previous constable had been in league with Laurent de Barratin. It might be true, it might not. The man was dead now.

The Duke de Barratin was wildly, murderously ambitious, but he was also shrewd, good in the field, and he commanded a well-trained force from his cities to the east. Robbin de Vaux *really* did not want them to align themselves with the Anglcyn.

It was unlikely, but not impossible.

The Barratin lands owed a preponderance of their considerable wealth to the textile trade, making cloth to sell around the world—and making it from Anglcyn wool. They remained part of Ferrieres, linked to the royal family, their dukes swore allegiance to the crown, but the notion that *they* might be the proper kings of Ferrieres was not a new one. Not even, necessarily, a bad one.

He couldn't afford to dwell on that last right now. His task was immediate, and involved a carefully chosen battlefield.

He really did need to find that girl and the country and village people who were following her banner, carrying spades and pitchforks and wooden clubs. If Hardan found them first and slaughtered them, as he would, the wound to Ferrieres would be very great—because it was the Maiden who had restored the king to them with her piety.

She mattered. She was a symbol of their resistance and of Jad's grace.

Hardan would know it too, de Vaux thought. He might chop her to pieces and bear her head into battle on a pike.

His riders did not find the Maiden's army before the Anglcyn did.

It could be called a failure, but it really wasn't. She could have been anywhere in a wide, empty land, and the villagers and farm people they'd asked had shared nothing. They regarded *everyone* as a threat to her. Jeanette was theirs. Their champion, their voice before Jad. By keeping silent, those who had seen signs of her army were helping her. Or so they thought. So they wanted, urgently, to believe.

It wasn't true, as matters unfolded, but we can ardently believe things that aren't true.

Robbin de Vaux did blame himself for not finding her, however, all his life. Because of what happened. Because of what he believed he might have prevented with more foresight, more skill, more cleverness.

In truth, it would have been luck. Only that. Men and women hate to acknowledge how much of a role fortune plays in our lives.

The Anglcyn, staying in tight formation because their numbers were so reduced, *not* sending out more than a handful of scouts ahead of and beside their path through northern Ferrieres, stumbled upon the peasant army of Jeanette de Broché. An accident. Random. It was as simple and as deadly as that.

They located her followers in a muddy field, as all fields here were after recent rains. The scouts rode back at speed to report. It was not a great distance. It had been twilight by then. King Hardan gave orders that the Maiden's force, if it could be called that, should be trapped in that meadow and engaged at sunrise to be destroyed.

It rained again at sunrise, the land became even more waterlogged, Jeanette's men and women (she had many women with her) moved awkwardly, boots or even bare feet sinking into the mud. The famed Anglcyn longbows killed them with ease. The Maiden's people had nothing with which to reply. It was a slaughter.

The rain stopped, a wan sun broke through clouds.

The killing continued in a sodden meadow, from a distance, arrows and more arrows. There were piteous screams and cries. Some of the Anglcyn archers disliked what they were doing. None stopped doing it.

There was a cluster of people visible in the centre of the dwindling ranks of the Maiden's army. They were trying to protect her, holding up makeshift shields of hide or blocks of wood against the death falling from the sky. Raining down, after the rain.

After quite a short time, as such things are measured—it was still morning, the sun was still rising—the order was given for the Anglcyn infantry to advance. They had to make their way through that muddy, sucking terrain, but there was no opposition at all by then, just that small circle of ragged people around a woman, a girl, who was wearing armour, a helmet, and holding a sword. She could be heard praying, or, the Anglcyn would later say, invoking aid from demons.

They killed the wounded in the meadow as they approached, then they killed those trying to defend her, with only a handful of their soldiers even injured.

They took Jeanette de Broché alive, as ordered. Also, as ordered, no one assaulted her, or offered indignities beyond spitting at her, or gripping her arms more tightly than was needed. She was not resisting them. She was praying.

She did not weep. They noticed that. And it was clear, once they could hear her, that she was indeed invoking Jad. This fact was not shared when they brought her back to their camp and king, so the story of her demons circulated, which was useful for Hardan.

That day, towards sunset (no rain, little wind, a clear sky, both moons rising), she was burned at a stake on a pyre they'd raised near their camp.

It was much larger than it needed to be to kill a small woman, but Hardan wanted it to be seen at a distance. Proclaiming that she was dead here, at his hands, this ignorant peasant girl who was supposed to be some sort of emblem of Ferrieres and Jad's love for it and resistance to him.

She was, he said—watching her burn, black smoke rising into the evening—an emblem of death and folly. Only those things.

The Maiden kept praying to the god for as long as she could. Those closest, tending the pyre with fresh wood, could not help but hear her, until the roar of the flames grew too loud. She was silent by that point, in any case.

The smoke told him exactly where the Anglcyn were. And what they were doing, of course. Not far away, as it happened. De Vaux had his army set out immediately, and he kept them going as darkness fell. They were able to stay on a road for much of the way. It was muddy, but not nearly so bad as the meadows and fields were.

He also knew what he wanted to do when morning came. He felt rage—and guilt, already. He channelled his fury towards his lords and officers in the last evening meeting before battle. He was extremely precise, those present would remember. And not courteous at all.

"If any lord of Ferrieres rides forward with his cavalry before my order tomorrow," the constable said, "my instructions will be that the archers with us are to shoot him dead, and those who follow him. I will defend myself before the king, if we survive. I may or may not succeed in that. But you will be dead if you disobey. Is this understood?"

He looked at each of the noblemen, one by one, these young, proud, arrogant lords of Ferrieres, chasing a dream of glory in their minds, ready to pursue it in battle in the morning, and he made each of them acknowledge what he'd just said.

At sunrise, smoke was still rising from the Maiden's pyre. They picked their way through a stand of trees north of the road and then fanned out to be on two sides of the invading force, make Hardan deal with that.

Jeanette led them to the enemy, men and women would later say. A last service.

King Hardan had deliberately placed his forces in a wide meadow, clogged with muck that would clutch and grab at anyone trying to ride a horse across it. He knew the nobility of Ferrieres, and he knew his longbows: the strength of his army for decades now.

He didn't know the new constable. Or the increasingly well-trained archers of the country they were here again to conquer.

The miracle, Robbin de Vaux would later think, and say to friends after, was that his nobility obeyed him. They outranked him, all of them, at court. Not here, however, not in the field. And he was, evidently, good at making people believe he meant what he'd said. No one wanted to be killed by an arrow from their own archers as they rode boldly forth to fame.

Instead, on orders given, and with the rising sun behind many of them, the archers of Ferrieres began loosing *their* arrows at the Anglcyn infantry and archers in the meadow. No one rode forward. No one.

It was, though the constable could not know it, exactly what Hardan's force had done the day before to the Maiden's army. Irony is for afterwards in war. Killing is the thing of the moment.

The Anglcyn had a tactic, the same one the army of Ferrieres was using now, whereby foot soldiers held up shields to screen themselves and the archers. For de Vaux's force, the trees helped, too; he had most of his bowmen stay at the edges. Hardan had not expected this at all, and it took time, and some difficulty, to realign his forces to offer proper protection to their own bowmen, and many men were, in fact, already dead or wounded by then, both archers and infantry.

The sucking mud of the meadow, chosen to slow and trap the reckless cavalry of Ferrieres, took its toll, instead, on the army of Angland that day.

The sun shone throughout, pale and bright, rising, then overhead. The arrows kept flying, from both armies, but to far, far greater effect against those in the open meadow. Trapped in the trap they'd thought to have laid.

It was named Azingar, that place, after the village just to the west of it, south of the walled city of Calienne. It entered the history and legends of a country. Azingar. It was where the Maiden was foully burned by the Anglcyn, then they themselves, their king mastered by the brilliant new constable of Ferrieres, were destroyed in the cause of freedom. And in vengeance for Jeanette.

The cavalry of Ferrieres advanced, not hurrying, only when the army in the meadow had been so diminished that the assault was almost too easy. Anglcyn archers and infantry threw down their bows and pikes and swords to surrender.

They were not allowed to do that.

They were slain, most of them.

A handful of the Anglcyn lords were permitted to yield. Ransoms were important. Ordinary soldiers—archers and foot soldiers, some of the horsemen—they could be killed, they didn't matter. Dukes and counts did. It was the way of things. The man who captured an important figure could negotiate for and claim his prisoner's ransom for himself. With luck, you could make your fortune.

King Hardan had looked as if he'd wanted to fight to a warrior's death in that churned, trampled meadow. He was not permitted that, either. On the constable's order, he was wounded in the right shoulder by an arrow, not by a nobleman's sword. His own sword fell, then, and was claimed. He himself was seized—by ordinary soldiers. They were not courteous.

The pyre the Anglcyn had lit was still smouldering on the western side of the meadow. Some wanted to build it back up and burn the invaders' king on it. Robbin de Vaux did not consent to this. His control of his army by then was absolute. A victory so complete will do that for a commander.

Only a small number of the army of Angland ever made it home: those left to guard the ships, and the few who'd grasped the disaster unfolding that morning and had fled from the meadow of Azingar, then made their way north to the coast. They had enough mariners to get three ships back to their own coast.

The weather was mild, benign: sunshine, and a good wind for sailing.

Usually there are no headstones for the dead of a battlefield. Sometimes a mound is raised.

What we know, or decide we know, of the past needs to be judiciously weighed and measured. It rarely is. We have our allegiances, even when centuries have gone by, season after season, year after year after year.

In due course, back in Orane, King Hardan was not accorded the customary privileges extended to a royal prisoner. Royal hostages were hardly unusual in those decades of war; the chroniclers had records of many such figures, and their courteous treatment while ransoms were negotiated and eventually paid. It sometimes took years.

There were two circumstances that prevented this from happening in the case of King Hardan. One was the burning of the Maiden of Ferrieres, the one who'd summoned King Roch back to them, who had brought the storm. Who had, in dying, shown the army of Ferrieres exactly where the enemy was—so the great constable, Robbin de Vaux, by then the Duke de Curton, had said.

The other complication was that Angland refused to pay the ransom demanded. King Hardan's brother Jarl was, it appeared, in no great hurry to have his brother back and his own place on the throne surrendered.

King Jarl, as he began, very quickly, to style himself, yielded many castles and tracts of land the Anglcyn held in Ferrieres, including the back-and-forth, taken-and-retaken castle of Curton on the coast, which became de Vaux's seat and reward.

Nor was King Hardan released upon any sworn oath by him, to mingle with the court in Orane. He remained confined on an upper floor of the Châtelet, in perfectly acceptable rooms. He had servants, food and wine, reading material, access to the small sanctuary. But he remained . . . a prisoner. He was never received by the king of Ferrieres. Nor was he ever ransomed by his brother. Ferrieres would have been content to take only a portion of the originally demanded sum and send him home to cause strife and chaos across the channel. It didn't happen.

Instead, on the counsel of the Duke de Regnault, a trusted emissary was sent by King Roch the next spring to Angland. Ostensibly, the task of this man, one of the Regnault family, in fact, was to negotiate newer ransom terms in person. More privately, closeted with young King Jarl and one adviser of his, a different agreement was reached, also involving the transfer of a substantial sum to Ferrieres.

Hardan, once king of Angland, died in the Châtelet of Orane a few months later, after contracting, it was said, a sudden illness the doctors were unable to master.

His body was sent home.

His two young sons also died suddenly, not long after. The usual rumours circulated. Nothing was ever proven, nor was proof assiduously sought. Hardan's wife, once his queen, was sent by King Jarl to a safely remote Daughters of Jad retreat. She didn't appear displeased. She rose, in time, to a position of importance there.

Azingar in the north of Ferrieres became a place of pilgrimage. A handsome sanctuary was built there in the name of Jeanette de Broché, and inns sprang up in and outside the village, which grew into a town—places for people to stay overnight, or drink to ease the dust and fatigue of the roads. Relics of the Maiden were on display in the sanctuary, and some were sold to the credulous in shops in the town and lining the way to the meadow. She was, in time, named a Blessed Victim by the High Patriarch in Rhodias, numbered among the elect of Jad. The meadow where she died, where her spirit was said to linger, was deemed a holy place.

She was not there. She had not died there.

⚜

For those who do not grasp the ways of country folk, of remote villages, it might seem inexplicable that a young woman could give instructions to the king of Ferrieres, command his wits to return to him, and he to his people—and yet obey the directions of her older brother, even if they ran hard against her wish to stay where she was, and serve Jad, and die.

For others, with more knowledge, this will seem evident, obvious, proper.

In the evening, after they had seen, and been seen by, the advance riders of the Anglcyn army, Peire de Broché, his sister Jeanette, and their younger brother Eran rode away in darkness, on two horses, from the meadow where their ragged army was encamped and would soon be killed.

Peire made himself very clear about this. The enemy was here, had found them, and the army of Ferrieres was not yet with them. It had been a mistake, in his view, to come north alone, but he didn't say such things to his sister, whom he adored and worshipped . . . and now wanted alive, for Ferrieres, for Jad, for all of them.

About half their force also left in the night, scattering back to their own lives, carrying and sharing, sometimes into old age, memories of when they'd marched with the Maiden to glory.

Peire also did another thing.

Before leaving, he spoke to a young woman and offered a proposal to her, privately. She accepted, without hesitation. Doing this, she said, would be an act of piety: her own gateway to the god and eternal light.

They gave her the Maiden's armour and helmet and sword. Jeanette objected fiercely. Then, weeping, she yielded to her brother. Her older brother. In the morning, when those remaining in that meadow saw the enemy moving, the young woman pushed the visor of the helmet down to hide her face.

Jeanette and her brothers were a distance west by then.

In the night, riding behind Eran on one of the horses, Jeanette had begun to shout and cry, demanding they return, that she was being false to the god by doing this, betraying the voices she'd heard. Her brothers insisted otherwise: that she had to stay alive, to offer Ferrieres continued guidance by way of the word of Jad. That she was *needed*.

She didn't agree. She continued, under the stars and the risen moons, to wail and weep. She said her destiny lay in Azingar. That she had to be burned. Several times she tried to throw herself off the horse. Once she did do so, and stood up, limping, and started walking back east in the night.

Unhappily, in grief, Eran took out his knife and clubbed her on the head with the haft. He put her back on their horse, held her there. She was unconscious as they rode on.

In the morning, in countryside none of them knew, Jeanette, awake by then, told them she wasn't hearing her voices anymore.

Her brothers looked away from what they saw in her eyes. She had stopped weeping.

She never wept again.

They rode on without clear intent or destination. In time, Peire settled on the western coast of Ferrieres as to where they were going.

They changed their names. Jeanette entered a holy retreat by the sea. She became known over the years for her willingness to tend the sick, other holy women there, or those sent to them for care. She developed great skill in doing so. Gentle hands, a calming, quiet manner. She saved many lives, including women having difficult childbirths, sent because she was there. She was much loved in this new identity.

She almost never spoke, only when it was necessary.

She was known for her eyes, the deep, arresting blue of them, and the compassion there. She had a sweet voice when the morning and evening and festival rites were chanted at the retreat.

Her brothers found work with a miller nearby. They understood the workings of a mill from Broché, from their father. Peire married the miller's daughter, and the two of them inherited the mill and raised a family there. Eran rode off one morning on his horse, and no one knows what happened to him.

Not uncommon. Not all stories have their endings known. Not all people.

Back in the meadow, where so many had died, no one ever betrayed the deception fashioned to save the life of the Maiden. The helmet was removed from the girl wearing it when she was taken, and the armour. She had light-brown hair and blue eyes. The Anglcyn knew that these were the colours of Jeanette's hair and eyes. This woman prayed without stopping from the time the enemy attacked them, and continued when she was seized, and then for as long as she could when she was burned to death on the pyre they raised. No one learned her name.

Her name was Lysbet Guerin, from the hamlet of Cassaude near the Livraise.

Brave beyond any words one might ever offer.

INTERLUDE

Of a morning late that spring, the lady of Château Arceval came riding to the home of her neighbour and occasional friend Marina di Seressa.

Marina was not there. She was with the queen in Orane.

The lady of Arceval had known this. She wanted to see the man, the other poet, in residence there now with only Marina's mother and children, and the servants and guards, with him.

Her own husband was very recently away in the north, at war for Ferrieres, summoned with other noblemen and their forces by the newly named constable. He was old to be doing so but had taken most of their household guards and gone to serve his king, who was—miraculously—returned to them in this time of need.

She had a handful of people riding with her, and she carried her most favoured falcon on her wrist as they went. A woman, a young woman, renowned for her beauty, needed an excuse for a visit such as this one.

She was Alaina d'Arceval, said by some to be a creature of the half-world.

It had long been noted how calm raptors were on her wrist, how swiftly they came to her lifted arm and call, how patiently they took food at her hand. The hunting dogs were the same, and it was rumoured she had tamed a wolf.

Some said her husband liked her to ride with him when he hunted stags in the woods north of them because they were always found when she was with his party. Some also said, if quietly, that he was equally compliant to her needs, himself.

She brought good fortune, the lord of Arceval used to say. She rode exceptionally well. And could handle a bow, like some pagan goddess of the forest.

Sometimes there had come deep, strange, roaring sounds when they were hunting far into the forest. Not a boar. Not a bear. Certainly not a wolf. Those with the lord and lady were often fearful then. The lady did not look afraid at such times, it was noted. She'd smile a private smile, making her even more beautiful.

No one ever saw the creature that roared in the forest, far off among the dense, close shadows of the trees.

Thierry had drinking companions who seemed to remember all their dreams, or many of them. They'd recount these at interminable length and with depressing frequency. Even Eudes, from behind the bar in The Lamb, normally so taciturn, would sometimes share a dream he'd had the night before. Many of his involved boats, for no obvious reason.

But why would dreams be obvious? Wasn't that the point of them? Why people paid Kindath fortune tellers or other dream-readers for explanations?

For his own part, he didn't dream, or remember them very often if he did, except for the recurring one, and he didn't need a Kindath woman to explain it.

He dreamed of Orane. Even within Orane, wherever in the city he was sleeping. He dreamed himself walking his city, different times of day, hearing the sounds—bells, shouts, market cries. The women and men in the streetwalkers' quarters, more discreetly inviting. Yellow-robed clerics intoning in street processions for funerals or festivals, swinging their censers as they went. Crowds in the squares, into the evenings in summer, gathered around a performer, the ever-present pickpockets moving among them. Laughter in such crowds. Or disdain if a musician or juggler was deemed weak.

Orane was—everyone said it—the hardest place for a performer. They had high standards in his city.

He dreamed tastes and smells, too. Meat pies at street stalls, and fish pies and pastries. Pigeon tarts. Lamb chunks roasting, boar meat in winter. Open flasks of wine at a stand. Fresh bread early in the morning, everyone with their favourite baker, every vendor with their own cry.

He'd dream himself walking, and looking about, even if he had just spent half the day walking and looking about! It was as if his love for the city spilled into his nighttime life, the shadow world of sleep. When others imagined strange things, shaped fantasies of power or images of passion, dealt with terrors of one kind or another, Thierry Villar dreamed himself in his city and in love with it.

He was a simple man in that way, he thought. Didn't really want people knowing this about him, it was almost embarrassing. Orane had terrible problems, of crime and filth and poverty—there were maimed beggars and hungry children everywhere. At certain times of day some streets gave off a stench you could apprehend from a distance. The tannery district, the street of the fishmongers. Or just the usual disposing of garbage and human waste from an upper window into the streets and lanes, in the hope that at some point rain would wash it down the central gutter and into the river.

Not all lanes had a central gutter.

Even so. Even so.

You could look up from almost anywhere in Orane and see the golden dome of the Great Sanctuary on its island, lord of all the other sanctuaries. You could see sculptures among the spreading trees in the parks, or glimpse them in the palace courtyard, or those of noble families, looking through the tall iron gates. You could hear music— or poetry!—in the taverns all day and evening long.

That was his world. He would wake in bed in Marina di Seressa's country home—a better bed than any he'd ever had in Orane—and be aware of how distant he was from his city, and how long it might be before it was safe for him to go back. Marina was there now. Silvy was in The Lamb. His parents were in Orane. *Everyone* was there but him. He thought about Silvy, patrolling the floor of the tavern, organizing everyone. Doing it calmly, unruffled by almost anything. He missed her.

He was under orders, just about, from Marina di Seressa to use his time here to write better, do work more ambitious than sardonic poems of mock bequests to people he disliked, however much loved those verses were.

He was trying, with limited success.

He was in the garden now, trying to shape words for a different sort of poem. Something about the Maiden, and Chervaux, about seeing her there. Something, something . . .

But he wrote in taverns amid noise! Or in rooms above them, or walking the city, shaping lines in his head. Here? It was so . . . it was too *calm*. He was realizing that solitude, peace, might not offer his own best access to poetry. He *liked* noise and bustle. Conflict, traded insults, drunken jests, raucous shouts. Unexpected lovemaking. Women laughing! He loved all that. Improvising from a tavern's long bar amid chaos. Memorizing words he'd just devised, until he had a chance to write them down.

He didn't know if Jad cared about poetry, about art, or if some abandoned god of the Ancients did, but he knew that here, with no one around, behind Marina's quiet house, in this wide, grassy space amid flowers, with the forest beyond it, he felt as if there was . . . nowhere to hide.

He hadn't ever thought of himself as hiding.

And of course there *were* hiding places! He could walk into the woods, be lost there for a morning or afternoon. Avoid his desk or a table that way. Perhaps a bear or a wolf would devour him. In which case someone else—Marina!—could write his elegy.

Maybe he'd find Jad there. Or a forest god. Or maybe words, a poem about doing that?

He swore. Declared himself a fool.

But the countryside really was too different, too unsettling to him. He had almost died earlier this spring in the Jad-cursed countryside, in a dungeon not far from here.

He didn't hunt, hadn't any sort of taste for early-morning rides, even if he now liked having a horse.

He could read here, yes, Marina had many books. But he could also fail to find his own words and pin them down.

He was wide open, accordingly, to what happened, like a coastline without a sheltering bay before a storm.

The steward informed him that someone had come riding.

He assumed Marina's mother had a guest, which was not infrequent. It was not so. She herself had gone visiting; he had seen her leave in the carriage. He didn't know where. Why would he? She was distantly polite to her daughter's poet-guest from the city, but no more than that. They hadn't dined together since Marina had gone back to the court from Chervaux.

He didn't think Clare di Seressa approved of him. A tavern poet of dubious reputation? Two young children in the château? The children liked him, as it happened. He told them stories here in the garden each afternoon when the weather allowed, inside if not. He liked them, too. Thierry had no siblings, of course, little experience of children.

Her son—six years old? seven?—had asked him once, at story hour, "Are you a poet like Mama?"

Someone had told them, obviously.

"I am, yes. Not quite the same." Not an important thing to say, he thought, but . . .

"Mama works very hard."

"I'm sure she does."

"All the time!"

He really didn't know children, but the earnestness touched him.

The steward, approaching now across the garden, explained that the lady of Arceval, their visitor, evidently wished to greet him. Should he have her shown out here, bring wine for the stone table?

Thierry, mildly confused but grateful for a diversion of any sort, agreed that this would be the proper thing to do. He was adequately dressed. Had taken to wearing—at Marina's suggestion—some of her late husband's clothing. The servants had altered shirts and tunics and trousers to fit a smaller man. He even had on a well-made dark-brown hat against the afternoon sun just then.

He would later remember he'd been standing beside the table and chairs placed beneath the chestnut tree, looking out at the woods. Had thought he saw a fox at the edge of the trees, but it had disappeared before he could be certain.

He heard voices, the steward escorting a woman across the carefully manicured grass. He turned. And was comprehensively assaulted by desire. It hit him like a blow.

She was slender, tall; a small, neat nose, high, vivid cheekbones, large, very wide-set, very dark eyes in an almost triangular face. Her hair, pinned under a riding hat, with tendrils drifting free, was black. She looked like a forest spirit, he immediately thought, one that had come from the trees beyond the garden, not along the road and through the house, not a noblewoman of Ferrieres.

"So many poets here now," the woman said quietly, smiling. Only that. First words.

She took off her hat and laid it on the stone table. He watched her. She adjusted, slowly, the pins holding her hair. Then took a seat, still smiling at him, looking up, entirely at ease. There was a light breeze, from the direction of the woods.

The steward made the formal presentation, bowed, and withdrew to bring them the promised wine.

"Poets? I am trying to be one here, yes," Thierry said. "Not my world, to be honest. Too much quiet?" He was trying not to stare at her. Was failing. "I'm sorry my lady Clare is not here to greet you. I'm sure she won't be much longer. She returns from her morning visits around this time."

"Returning soon? A pity," said the black-haired woman. Thierry blinked. "I find Clare tedious, but please don't tell Marina I said that! *She's* not tedious at all. Have you bedded each other here yet?"

"What? No!" Thierry exclaimed.

"How can that be? She's so lovely, and you have a pleasing look, though you'd do better with a proper shave. She's unattached, and I am told you are also."

"Marina di Seressa has been gracious enough to allow me to remain here while Orane is judged . . . unsafe for me," Thierry stammered. "After her return to the city. With the queen. I would never presume upon—"

"Presume? That is how you think? How foolish," said this woman, this Alaina d'Arceval.

He was remembering, necessarily now, a night in an inn in a village near the Livraise, when he had awakened in darkness and in pain, and Marina had been lying there, unexpectedly, to reassure him if he woke in the night that he was safe, had not been entirely broken in a dungeon.

"We move," Thierry said, "in different worlds."

"Not necessarily, from what one hears of events in Orane last winter. But that can also be alluring, don't you find?" said the woman. "Different worlds?" He watched her raise her arms to adjust a hairpin again, slowly.

After a silence Thierry said, simply, "Sometimes."

He was having difficulty gathering and holding thoughts. There was a scent she wore that he did not recognize. It had probably been devised for her. He *didn't* move in a world where women created their own perfumes.

"Often, I would say," she murmured.

The steward, blessedly, was coming back across the grass now, leading a servant with a tray. Thierry found he needed time to hunt for composure. He saw wine, two silver cups, a bowl of apricots, another with spring apples. He had no idea how they had apricots so early in the year. The tray was set down. The steward eyed Thierry for permission and poured when he received a nod. Then he withdrew with the servant back into the house. The light breeze continued from the north.

The woman, his guest, selected an apricot and bit into it with small white teeth. Thierry realized that he very much wanted, alarmingly, to bite her lower lip. She looked at him, and he had a sense she *knew* that was his thought.

"There will be," she said, looking past him to the trees, "a fog later. I can feel it in the wind. I shall ask Clare if I and two attendants may stay the night, rather than ride home in mist. I have already sent my hunting party home."

How had she known to do that? Why was she . . .?

"Your room is on the second floor? The west wing? They usually do that."

"It . . . it is, yes," said Thierry Villar. His mouth was dry. He spoke the thought that came to him. He was prone to doing that, for better or worse. "My lady, are you . . . are you linked to the half-world? To know a fog is coming?"

And to look the way you look, he also thought.

She laughed, the perfect white teeth again. "Some do say that is so, I've heard. I find it amusing, even useful. But . . . not really. We just know our weather in the countryside. I disdain certain conventions of the world, and my husband is sadly away at war, and it is very quiet here, as you'll have discovered, however much violence may be happening elsewhere."

"Not really," she'd said. Half-denial of the half-world?

You could use that last phrase, Thierry suddenly thought, in a poem of a certain kind. If your head ever worked properly again.

"Very quiet, er, yes, it is," he said, wincing inwardly at how empty-headed he sounded.

She took another bite of the apricot. She removed a riding glove and used a finger to wipe away some juice on her chin. She licked the finger. Removed the other glove. She had long fingers. He reached, a little desperately, for wine.

And then a fog did come—from the north on a new wind that rose late in the day. It hid the trees at the edge of the forest, and the forest itself, of course. Sounds were muffled. The château became an island in the world. In some world. The servants drew the curtains, lit fires.

Marina's mother had returned by then. She made quick, capable arrangements for a dinner guest, and then did, of necessity, invite their visitor to stay the night. Her guest now. Thierry didn't think she approved of the lady of Arceval, either. She didn't approve of many people, he suspected, but there were *conventions* to be observed.

He did tell the children their story, inside by a fireplace, as it had turned chilly in the garden, and strange. He had no memory at all, after, of what tale he'd invented for them.

Later, they dined, three of them at the long table, with another fire lit and many candles and lamps. Their guest led the conversation, lightly, wittily, speaking both of neighbours and of events in the wider world. Even of the Maiden who had restored the health of the king, Jad be thanked and praised.

She asked Thierry questions about Chervaux, what had happened there, noting how remarkable it was that he had been present, that Marina had been, for such a dramatic moment. Their hostess retired shortly after the meal, as was her habit.

The steward had already made arrangements for their guest and her attendants. The attendants were offered beds downstairs among the household servants. Alaina d'Arceval had said she wouldn't need them for the night, but would be grateful for a night robe to change into, upstairs.

Thierry excused himself and went off to the library, which was also Marina's writing room. He'd been doing that most evenings. She had her books there, including copies of her own writing, bound in leather, on sumptuous paper. Seressa, she had told him earlier, was where such things were done best. She knew who to work with there. He had never lived anywhere with so many books.

He spent an interval in the room. He didn't work. He couldn't. His thoughts were scattered like birds startled from a tree. He was trying to understand what had happened to him. What *was* happening. He was no stranger to desire, or to women. How could he be, in the life he lived? This was . . . different. Was it her scent? The black eyes and hair? The sense of something wild in her? The way she'd bitten into an apricot in the garden? But hadn't he been . . . ensorcelled even before that? Was that the word?

Was it of any importance to decide, at all?

There were lamps lit for him. They knew his habits by now. He read from one of Marina's poems. A retelling of a story by another woman writer from long so. A folk tale of enchantment, in fact. A knight wounded in combat, carried to a ship named *The Reverie*, a boat without any sailors. It carried him magically across the water—it wasn't clear where—to dock itself beside a castle wherein lived a lady imprisoned by her jealous husband. And the lady and her maidens came aboard and found the wounded, unconscious knight and nursed him back to strength, and she kept him with her secretly, and . . .

Marina was skilled, witty, the rhymes elegant. The observations of that world were sharp. Because she was, he thought. She was sharp. It *was* far away from what he knew and wrote, what he wanted to add to the world himself. He wanted to conjure with a different sort of people than those in gardens and castles and bowers of love, with birds flying in and out of windows, caged, then free. But he finished reading her poem with admiration.

She knew her readers, her courts, what she needed to write to keep doing her work, pleasing patrons, maintaining her mother and children here. Living this life. He thought about that. She might have married again. Had chosen this path, instead, offering pleasures and insights into men and women for the men and women of the court. Obligations accepted, as to what they wanted—but done by her own choice.

Men and women, he thought. *Men and men*, and *women and women*, too.

And sometimes solitude.

A light knocking at the door. It opened before he could respond.

She still wore her riding clothes, and her scent. It entered the room with her. She looked at him from just inside the door. She said, thoughtfully, "I think you are a man at ease with women. Used to having them come to you. In the taverns, no? I think you are also unusual for a small man. I think you wait. Most, I have found, try to prove their assertiveness. Well, if you wish to lie with me tonight, Thierry Villar, you will have to come find me. To show me that you do so wish."

She turned, went out, closed the door.

He found he was having difficulty breathing. She would know that, he thought. Of course she would. He set down Marina's book, which he'd still been holding. He stared into the fire. Why was he so overwhelmed? Surely this was just another assignation among many others with women who wanted him, or accepted his coins over a loud room below.

It wasn't, though, was it? He suddenly wished he could ask Gauvard Colle about Alaina d'Arceval. Was she a creature out of faerie? Where terrifying beasts roared in the nights, unseen? Gauvard was the only person he knew, whether man or woman, or changeable, who might have any kind of answer.

The curtains were drawn against the night and the fog. The world was not what it had been this morning.

He stayed there for a time, then he left that room and went slowly up the two flights of stairs to where his bedchamber was. Farther along the empty hallway there was door half open, and a light could be seen within. He kept walking, his steps steady enough. He went there.

She was standing beside the bed. The night robe they had given her—or that she had selected—was white for innocence, and thin, silk, and buttoned only partway to her throat. Her hair was unbound now, for bed. For him.

"Very good," she said. "Though we are wearing too many clothes, don't you think?"

Some time later.

An interval, an interlude in the world, in his life.

"Are you here for my soul?"

She laughed beside him on the bed, a luxurious ripple of sound in darkness. There had been a lamp burning while they made love; she had blown it out, after.

"What use would I have for that?" She squeezed one of his nipples, hard. He winced. She laughed. Said, "You may do the same to me, of course."

"On command?"

"Would that be so very bad?"

His heartbeat, astonishingly, had grown rapid again. "No," he said, "I suppose not." He lowered his mouth to her breast. Began circling with his tongue.

Heard her catch her breath. Was pleased by that. A lessening of control in her. She said, "That is . . . that is very . . ."

"I hope so," he said.

Laughter. "I only wanted your body for tonight. I've never bedded a poet."

He lifted his head. "Oh? Are we different?"

She smiled again, that very private look. "Possibly? As I said, you are unusual. Most men are anxious just to find release. You are . . . patient?"

His turn to be amused. "I'm not, really. But . . . maybe poets learn to be patient waiting for the right words?"

"Or woman? You have really never slept with Marina?"

"No," he said again. That night at the inn didn't count. "You imagine my life to be more exciting than it is," he said.

"I do!" She turned on her side and lowered her mouth to bite his neck, and then an earlobe, hard. Earlier he had, yes, bitten her lower lip, as he'd wanted to do since the garden. "I imagine so much about the taverns of Orane," she said.

"To be honest," Thierry said, "you are the most exciting thing that has happened to me in this way in a long time."

"Only in a long time?" said Alaina d'Arceval. "Not . . . ever? I am disappointed."

Thierry laughed softly. "It might be ever, yes."

"Good," she said. "That's better."

And it seemed talk of excitement had him excited again. She seemed to sense it. She reached down and discovered that this was so.

"How pleasing," said the lady of Arceval. "You make me happy the fog came in, so unexpectedly, and forced me to stay the night."

He still half believed she was a faerie from the forest, a wild creature. From a world farther from his own than courts could ever be.

Are you here for my soul?

Later, another owl outside, in what might or might not now be mist and fog. Still in her bed, still entangled, both of them damp with sweat.

Later yet, in darkness, he dressed and went back to his own chamber. She'd kissed him from the bed, quite gently, after not having been gentle at all. He felt unsteady on his feet, drained. He felt as if he'd taken a journey. *A boat without sailors*, he thought.

In the morning when he went downstairs he was informed that their guest had already gone.

Later that week, unable to stop himself, he went riding one morning to Arceval.

He went through the open gates and across the courtyard. He was watched by two guards, then greeted, courteously, at the doors. He was informed that the lady had gone to stay with her family during the time of the lord's absence at war. Thierry was offered food, a refreshment. He declined, rode back.

He never saw her again.

I only wanted your body for tonight.

He dreamed of her, and those dreams he remembered. They woke him, in fact, many times.

He wrote, while still at that château, and in that solitude, a sequence of poems through the late spring and into summer that were different from anything he'd ever done before. Often late at night, in his chamber. Written by a candle's light. Then he'd blow the candle out and sleep. Darkness, light, darkness. The way the bird of legend was said to fly, from the night through a lighted hall and back into the night.

Those poems marked a demarcation, it would afterwards be said, in what Thierry Villar had to say with and through his work. And perhaps also in who he was.

Marina di Seressa, when she read them after his eventual return to Orane, said, eyes bright, looking up after she was done, "Ah. Oh my. I see Alaina visited you." And laughed at how vividly he flushed.

It seems to me that most moments in a life can be called interludes: following something, preceding something. Carrying us forward, with our needs and nature and desires, as we move through our time. It also seems to me that it is foolish to try to comprehend all that happens to us, let alone understand the world.

PART III

CHAPTER XIII

There were many people he wanted dead. Some more urgently than others. Laurent, Duke de Barratin, had a long memory, back to childhood slights and indignities from his cousins. King Roch and his brother had been beautiful when young, too. He never had been. Such things could matter in a life.

His immediate ambitions were not diminished, even if circumstances had changed.

The greatest change being, of course, the king's return to health.

It had happened before. Roch could come back to his right mind, then slide again into reclusive, frightened madness, throwing Ferrieres into chaos again. They had watched it happen many times.

The chaos of the king's madness last winter was what the duke had hoped to use to claim the power he felt should have been properly his, not residing in greedy, cruel, elegant Montereau.

Elegant Montereau was, at least, dead. In an icy street near the home of the cold bitch queen—who had then arranged for an investigation and hearing that had undone his own plans comprehensively.

He didn't underestimate the queen. But he hadn't expected her to proceed so decisively. Burkard van Aribert, the only one of his courtiers he really trusted, had warned him about her. Had to give the man that.

Barratin had been forced to leave home when the snows melted in the lowest mountain passes to the south. He made the demanded pilgrimage to Rhodias. Had had no choice, really. He'd knelt before the fat High Patriarch, Tessio, with his narrow, watery eyes, paid the fat bribes expected, kissed his ring and foot, expressed his contrition in the throne room and then again in the glittering sanctuary, before Jad's altar.

A hugely expensive, time-consuming journey.

He was very much aware of time passing.

And while he was away south . . . some peasant girl no one had ever heard of (how could they have heard of her?) had somehow brought the king back, at Chervaux.

Demons surely controlled her, Barratin believed (he believed in demons, everyone did)—because it *could* not be the will of Jad. The god using a vessel like that? An ignorant, unwashed girl?

She had been burned as a heretic, quite properly, by the Anglcyn.

But *then* . . . then the army of Ferrieres under Robbin de Vaux, another man he hated, had defeated and captured the king of the Anglcyn. And Hardan was still imprisoned in the Châtelet of Orane, shockingly (no ransom!), against all norms, and so . . .

And so the shrewd, bitter, ambitious Duke de Barratin was agonizingly suspended between the too-swift running of time and the terrible thought that he might not actually have any good choices now.

He rejected that second thought, that dagger. He had to, it was his nature. There were, he had always believed, ways to proceed. You thought things through, you forced a passage. Especially if you knew what you wanted and devised well. He was good at thinking and devising.

Better than his cousins. He *would* be a better king for Ferrieres, ruling it with Barratin. He lived in that belief—and many shared the thought.

Still, it was challenging. Roch might recede into spittle-flecked, straggle-haired madness again, but right now, *now*, he was on the throne and giving commands. And he was loved, loved as Laurent de Barratin had never been, loved because he had returned. Because of the Maiden. The fucking Maiden.

As if the whore would have been a maiden, thought Laurent de Barratin.

And meanwhile, the prince, the heir, the older son, once frail and wan, was reputedly less so now. He was coming of age. Month by month. Day by day!

Windows and doors closing.

He still wanted Robbin de Vaux dead, though it was harder to have him killed now, for many reasons, including the fact that the man was an exalted hero of Ferrieres, elevated to the nobility.

Also, he hated the scrawny, scruffy, inexplicable poet who had somehow stood up in winter and balked the process for which Cassin—that fraud, that poseur, that *failure*, Denis Cassin!—had been paid a fortune to ensure that the murder of the Duke de Montereau would set the stage for Barratin's emergence as the saviour of Ferrieres. The resister of tyranny. The voice of the people!

It hadn't played out that way. Who could have known that the foul-mouthed gutter poet was an advocate? Trained by Cassin, even! Bitterest irony. In certain moods he could appreciate irony. Not in this matter.

So he had been sent into exile. On holy pilgrimage through the mountains to this gross, greedy High Patriarch and the grasping clerics surrounding him, standing in a row with their hands extended. They hadn't been subtle in their demands.

It offended him. You could be greedy and ambitious but keep it decently cloaked, couldn't you? Were *they* what Rhodias was today? He would swear before Jad he was a more decent man than any of them.

He was wealthy, he could pay them. He did pay. He had travelled with chests of money and many guards. But he kept a ledger in his mind with the names of those who had crossed him.

And he'd bought a palazzo here. A statement made with that. Had hired one of his own northern artists—van Leyland, working just then in Rhodias—to paint him frescoes there, and had his people choose an architect to renovate the place. There were advantages to being seen as a player in the politics of clerics and High Patriarchs.

Also, he liked the art he saw everywhere in Rhodias. He had never been beautiful like his cousins, but he had taste, and could let these people know it. They had made him endow a sanctuary, as well. Of course they had. Van Leyland would decorate that, too.

But as to the Barratin wealth . . . the great victory over Angland's vicious king (he had admired King Hardan, kings *needed* to be ruthless in the world as it was) . . . well, that complicated affairs back home, too.

Laurent de Barratin, with his palace in high-walled Berga and his busy ports on the sea, depended so much on wool from the north coming steadily across the channel to work with and send on as finished goods. His stature, his ability to pay his army, defend his cities and his family, came from the textile trade. They exported fabrics everywhere—through Batiara, yes, and all the way to Sarantium, bringing back silver and gold, jewels and spices, artists and stone carvers and philosophers, and so much else.

Almost enough money to have led him to the throne in Orane.

It still might, if all went as it yet could.

It might be a more delicate dance now. Steps to be determined, music not yet clearly heard. He could not easily rebel against King Roch. Things were not the same as they were in the iron cold of winter. Then there had been room for him to move. To step forward. Vanquisher of a tax-crazed tyrant. Hero of the people.

Not now.

A different dance, undeniably, but Laurent de Barratin could almost hear a new music playing, almost see what he needed to do.

But then there came events in Rhodias, Jad curse it, and curse all clerics living in and around the Patriarchal Palace, grotesque with avarice and lust. Events no one could possibly have predicted or controlled. It was, he would think furiously, *unfair*. Why were things never fair for him, from childhood on?

No one in Rhodias liked the axe-faced Duke de Barratin. Cold-looking northern features, narrow nose, hard eyes, hard voice, even when apologizing on orders from Ferrieres, and agreeing to build a new sanctuary here.

The problem, it was agreed, was that he might be an ugly, unpleasant man, but he was powerful and important. And shrewd. Also, there was the fact that the Council of Twelve in Seressa had made it clear that Barratin needed placating because a great deal of money flowed from his lands in trade.

The Patriarchal Palace was sensitive to situations where a great deal of money flowed.

The difficulty, the High Patriarch agreed, glumly, was that the man was fabulously wealthy—and might yet become king of Ferrieres! There were too many murky details as to King Roch's miraculous recovery. Some girl, hearing the voice of Jad? Really?

So this northern duke could not be dismissed or disdained. Even if he'd admitted to the murder of another duke, and one they did like.

The Duke de Montereau had visited here years before, seeking a patriarchal blessing—and buying art. The Patriarch remembered it well. He'd been younger himself then, not plagued as he was now by gout. A handsome, quite appealing man, Montereau, although it had become clear, quickly, that he wanted only women in his bed, more's the pity. Sophisticated, amusing, an obvious taste for good things and good wine. Engaging company. They'd arranged for the women, of course.

Dead now. Murdered by his axe-faced cousin.

The Patriarch and clerics of Rhodias were not averse to a murder when necessary, but some actions did cross a line, surely. Butchered in a city street? His head severed? It was . . . vulgar.

"The problem," Viotti di Virenza had said sententiously, when the five most senior clerics met with the Patriarch, "is that Barratin's an important man. We know it. And we know that where there is power, the precepts of holy Jad cannot always . . ."

The problem. The problem.

The problem with Viotti di Virenza, thought High Patriarch Tessio, behind the slits of his watchful eyes, was that, aside from being nakedly ambitious himself, the man was . . . he was *oily*. Slippery. He never finished his sentences! Left them suspended for others to complete, whereupon he could always deny any untoward meaning! Make *you* guilty of a dark thought.

Here, the unspoken was simple: if power did not protect someone from the justice of man and the god, what did that mean for those in the room just then, including the High Patriarch? It was obvious: but di Virenza hadn't said it aloud.

Devious, Jad-cursed fucker of children. And probably sheep! Tessio hated him. He would be cursed to darkness before he let Viotti di Virenza succeed him on the Patriarchal throne.

But the fucker was right. They did need to keep Barratin cordial, lest he come to the throne in Orane as an enemy. You needed to guard against the future, always. And there were so many possible futures to guard against! They could extract payments from him, he'd expect that, but they could not offend the man, whatever they felt.

He looked, in truth, like a man quick to take offence.

Tessio had been startled to see the warmth displayed by the artist, van Leyland, when he'd been summoned and had encountered the duke here. They'd actually embraced—chastely, two men from the north greeting each other with obvious pleasure. The Patriarch took note of the warmth. It meant that there was more to Barratin than they'd thought. Also that the artist would now likely start working for him right away, and Tessio couldn't even protest, since they'd just compelled the duke to build and decorate a sanctuary!

His mood was, accordingly, foul when he went to sleep, after inadequate assuaging by both his preferred young bed partners. Some nights, especially latterly, they just could not accomplish that for him. Pain and rage undermined. The world intervened.

And so, in the middle of a night, High Patriarch Tessio lay awake and pondered something. He was old now, and Viotti di Virenza was not, and the other man was deeply cunning, had tentacles like an octopus, and he *would* very likely succeed to the throne of Jad.

It was not to be allowed, the High Patriarch decided, propping himself up on pillows and drinking from one more glass of wine in his canopied bed.

He died that night.

When he was discovered in the morning, there were no signs of foul play to be seen. The most-preferred bed partner had, as it happened, removed the Patriarch's last glass of wine and poured it out into the slop bucket. Then he'd wiped the crystal glass clean, as instructed.

The young man, who had relied on his beauty and a belief in his own cleverness, also died, a few days later. Also with no clear evidence of how or why, though his youth and vigour suggested it might have been untoward. He didn't matter much by then. No one investigated.

Chaos in Rhodias followed, and in the whole of the western Jaddite world. An assembly of high clerics was summoned, as was usual, to choose a new Patriarch, with all the extreme, frequently deadly turmoil of that.

Laurent de Barratin went home.

He was not about to linger in the cesspool of Rhodias while the clerics schemed a successor. He had received his attestations of pilgrimage, of an endowed sanctuary, and of Patriarchal forgiveness. Those came from the throne, the office, not the pig-eyed man now dead. He could go home carrying his formal exculpation for murder. Why he had come.

The successor, his people told him, would almost certainly be Viotti di Virenza. Barratin had no views on this. He did offer di Virenza a prudent gift before he left, an enormous golden ewer for serving wine at a banquet. Cost him a stupid amount of money.

As events unfolded, however, it was not di Virenza who was chosen. The Council of Twelve in Seressa and the Duke of Macera both opposed him, and made it known, and when they acted together it was almost overwhelming, because they rarely did.

Di Virenza snarled and raged. He scattered unfinished thoughts and imprecations; he offered both cities money on a staggering scale from the coffers of Rhodias. Without success.

He wasn't killed. It wasn't necessary, because he dwindled into insignificance in a remarkably short time. It was pleasing for many to see it play out. If you aim for a throne and miss, that can happen.

The new High Patriarch was from Varena. A compromise choice, a deeply pious man.

No one really liked a pious man in Rhodias. He didn't live long either. There was too much power residing in that throne and around it to have it wasted on someone virtuous. He might . . . he might even initiate reforms!

In the east, the star-worshipping Asharites took note of these events, and in those days the first stirrings of an intent, not just an aspiration, to conquer the golden city of Sarantium emerged. It would take time, but it would happen.

In Rhodias, the artist van Leyland worked on two new commissions. He had been told by his duke to do the palazzo first, and patiently. Barratin (a man he liked, their natures meshed well) wanted it to be a statement of northern taste and wealth in a city of wealth and some taste. The sanctuary, when it came to be built, could be decorated at speed. Not carelessly, of course, but . . .

There are ironies embedded in art and time. The work in the palazzo was carefully planned and achieved. Skilful, but ultimately unexciting. Blessed Victims in procession in the banquet room was the main work. Blues and golds, mostly. Expensive colours.

The quickly done frescoes in the Barratin sanctuary in Rhodias, on the dome and on the wall behind the altar, became the signature works of Claus van Leyland, forever. They were what he was best remembered for, long after.

The wall fresco behind the altar, especially, was a thing of extreme, risk-taking genius. It was a painting of the fall of Heladikos, but *without* the god's son shown, no chariot of Jad, no falling boy-man seen. Heladikos wasn't there; there was no heresy to attach to the work.

It was simply a land-and-seascape off some coastline, women and men living their lives, the god's golden sun rising, like hope. The piety was in how beautifully it illuminated life: ships on a calm sea, farmers in their fields, horses and cows and dogs. A distant stag at the edge of a forest. A cart laden with firewood on a winding road. Shepherds and their flocks on a rising slope. A plump, golden-haired milkmaid with her swain. Weavers in cottage doorways. Fields ripe with yellow grain, like the sun.

No one could say there was a son of the god in it. There was not. But everyone looking at that work, if they were minded to, could imagine, privately, the splash of a body into the sea, then disappearing there. The terrifying glory of flight, and the terrifying fall.

So much uncertainty lies in art, and what endures. Where and when the lightning flash of brilliance will strike. What is valued in a given time, or over time. And what is lost, forgotten.

It is the same, writ large, when we consider actual events in our lives: faith, doubt, war, peace. Famine, abundance. Storms at sea, or sweeping across the land, bending or breaking trees. Rain or drought. Winter's ice. Ice in the heart. Afternoon sunlight for the autumn's harvest. Health, sickness. Desire. Calamitous misfortune. Friendship. Love.

Silvy always thought that her having part ownership of The Lamb was an indicator of how generous a man Eudes was. He declared that it was simply a measure of her skill at running a tavern.

It was a good partnership.

Some years ago he had been forced to leave Orane in haste, to return to the the southwest where his family lived and owned land. His father was ill, likely dying. Silvy hadn't known where Eudes was from, or about the land, and neither had Anni. People tended not to ask questions about origins in Orane, and perhaps particularly not of an extremely large man. Eudes happened to be one of the gentlest people on earth, but he didn't like people knowing that. Wasn't useful in a tavern for keeping order.

He was away for months, in the event, and Silvy's period of dealing with affairs in The Lamb, intended to be brief, lasted through that time. It seemed there were matters to address back home after Eudes's father did die and was buried.

He told her a little about this when he came back. He had not sold the family property. Had arranged to divide the farm, and to assign the mill to someone for an annual fee. He had leased the land, half each, to two cousins who hated each other. His mother would have the farmhouse for as long as she lived, and a share of the profit and produce. He'd advised each cousin to keep an eye on the other, made both responsible for his mother. Told them he would return and kill them if they cheated him. He *looked* like a frightening man.

He'd also retained a third relative—a man who didn't like either of the other two (they were a fractious family, Silvy came to understand)—to monitor both, and send him notice if he saw anything untoward. He paid this man a fee to do that. According to Eudes, the affairs of the family land had been calm ever since.

He was extremely clever. Silvy and Anni had both known that all along. Anni had wondered whether she should marry him.

"He has *land*!" she said.

"Has he suggested marriage to you?" Silvy inquired.

"No, but I could ask him?" Anni said, a little doubtfully.

They both knew Eudes was not really the marrying kind. Wasn't even really the lovemaking kind, either. His bed with Anni was quiet. Silvy had spent enough nights upstairs with the two of them to know. Anni knew it better, of course, but Silvy did know. You could sometimes tell, with a man. Or a woman.

Still, the sweetest person they knew. And after he'd returned from that journey home, he'd signed over a small but real share in The Lamb to Silvy. She'd run the tavern extremely well in his absence. He'd looked at the records, heard from regular patrons. And Silvy was a woman, didn't have the advantage of bulk and strength in keeping order. Things which always helped.

She had cleverness instead, a head for figures, and a sharp tongue. And the men who worked for them, making food or behind the bar or in the stable, pretty much adored her, and were always ready to deal as needed with anyone unruly.

So she was a person who owned property now. A share of a successful tavern in the city.

It was, and she knew it, a kind of miracle. A gift of the god. And of Eudes. And, indirectly, of Anni, who truly showed no envy or resentment. Anni shared his bed. Silvy was usually in her own, downstairs, except on the coldest winter nights, or when Anni really wanted her, and made it clear.

Marina di Seressa had invited her to stay in the palace when they'd returned with the king and queen from Chervaux: she was a lady-in-waiting to Queen Bianca now, formally. But Silvy knew it was an invitation born of courtesy, that their time as lovers had been an . . . interlude.

She'd learned that word from Thierry. It meant, he'd said, a time in between. In a life, or in a poem. After one thing, before the next. Sometimes a bridge, sometimes a break, he'd said. A pause. Interludes could operate differently in life, in writing. She hadn't paid a lot of attention to the writing part. Thierry was the poet. She was his friend, but didn't care about writing craft, and he could go on about it, if she was honest. He liked to explain things. She humoured him, some of the time.

But she'd remembered the word, and that was what her springtime in Marina's bed in the countryside felt to have been. For both of them, she thought. Besides—and this is what she told the other woman—she had a tavern to attend to. It was her present and her future.

"You will visit me here?" Marina had asked.

"You need only invite me," Silvy had said. "And you also know where The Lamb is."

But they hadn't seen each other since returning to Orane. It was all right. Interludes were what they were, Silvy thought. Sometimes you just needed to understand that.

On a night in summer, Jolis de Charette came into the tavern with a small cluster of people. Two other women, one man, the women wide-eyed; they'd never been here before, clearly. A different world for them.

Silvy, seeing her enter, bristled like a cat, knowing what had happened to her friend because of this woman.

Anni hated Jolis, too. Same reaction visible from her by the table she was just then dealing with. They'd have gladly thrown her out, in her showy burgundy gown. A burgundy gown and gold jewellery in a tavern? It was absurd.

Eudes, being Eudes, kept calm. This was a well-off woman bringing her patronage and friends, and—who knew?—perhaps sharing word of The Lamb with other well-off people looking to spend time among the so-amusing common folk of Orane. It was business, wasn't it?

Silvy was behind the bar just then. Busy, but not busy enough, unfortunately. There was no poetry or singing yet, though the usual aspirants were clearly waiting for the right moment.

"Hello, Sylvia," Jolis said, walking over.

Silvy didn't bother correcting her. Or replying. She kept pouring flasks of wine that had been ordered by a table near the door.

After a pause, Jolis added, casually, "Has Thierry been in?" She had a high-pitched, irritating voice. Or, more likely, Silvy hated her enough to *find* her voice annoying.

But asking after Thierry? That was too much.

"Really?" Silvy said, staring hard at the other woman now. "*Really?*"

A wince, which was a reward of sorts.

"I just wanted to tell him something," Jolis de Charette said, all gold and burgundy and scent and silk. She'd had her companions find a table; they hadn't followed her to the bar.

Silvy said nothing. Waited.

And Jolis, as beautiful as ever, perhaps even more so, in truth, said, "I'm getting married! I wanted him to know."

Silvy blinked. Said, coldly, "Why?"

Jolis de Charette shrugged. There were diamonds at her ears, they glittered with the movement. "Just did."

"I see. If I remember, I'll tell him. If he can ever come back to Orane, after two attempts to kill him. One was yours, wasn't it?"

She hadn't had to say that last, but she'd wanted to.

"It *wasn't*!" Jolis said. "I knew nothing—"

"I wish you a dozen children in as many years," Silvy said crisply. And walked away with wine flasks for the table that wanted them. Proper patrons. Regularly here. Not vicious people. Not excited by murder. She'd let Eudes take care of Jolis's party.

She'd have happily poisoned them all, she told Anni later.

"Should have!" Anni said loyally.

She was a sweet girl.

Jolis didn't stay long, once aware Thierry wasn't expected. She called a goodbye to Eudes when they left; he nodded courteously back at her. Silvy glared at him after the door closed. He didn't pay any attention. He was good at that.

Three nights later, another thing happened. It brought excitement, fear, fragility, disruption. The awareness of how life and the world can wound us. The terrifying glory of flying. And the likelihood of a fall.

The messengers saying he could return came from Medor Colle at the end of summer. Thierry went with them the very next day. Didn't linger. He'd been writing, yes. New work he thought might be good. He was less unsettled by the countryside and its strange silences—and noises—by now. He liked Marina's children.

But he still didn't want to be here. And to be told he could go back to Orane, well, it was like being freed from another imprisonment, wrong as that association surely was.

It was *his* association. He was allowed it, he told himself.

He rode back one more time to Arceval very early the next morning, but he could see, from the top of the drive, by the locked iron gates, that no one was home. They left for Orane right after that.

Medor's message had been carried by four serjeants, so he had an escort for the ride. Excessive, Thierry thought, but he really had no way of knowing, did he?

Long, bright, late-summer days, not quite harvest time. They rode through wine country and past wheatfields tall with grain. Stick figures stuffed with straw to scare off crows. The tracks of boars at the edges. One very large one seen in the mist one morning, grey, scarred, colossally tusked. They didn't get close to it.

They rode into Orane on an afternoon of brilliant sunshine and he heard the bells of his city again from all the sanctuaries, the great domed one on the island and the smaller ones. Almost but not quite in unison.

There were crowds in the streets, he heard cries, laughter, shouts of anger. Salespeople were hawking whatever it was they were trying to sell. The city smelled as any large city did; it would probably take him time to readjust to that, he thought.

That was all right. He was home.

He went to his mother's house before anywhere else. Two of the serjeants went to the Châtelet to report their arrival, two stayed with him. He was going to protest that they need not, but he didn't. Medor would have given them orders.

They would have to talk soon, he thought.

He went inside that small, comfort-rich house. They were both there, by good fortune. His mother was preparing the evening meal early. Ambroise was sitting at the table, leaning on an elbow, and they were talking quietly, easily. He paused in the doorway a moment, taking that in. The pleasure it gave. Then his mother saw him, and cried out, and he became . . . he became a part of the pleasure as they embraced.

He cried. He mocked himself for doing so, but he wept, holding them.

Eventually they released him and stepped back. Ambroise went across the way—he was moving well enough, Thierry thought, watching him—and returned with a flask of the pale golden wine used for the rites. Thierry raised an eyebrow, and his stepfather laughed. His mother set out three cups. They toasted his return.

"Orane is safe for you now?" Ambroise asked.

"I think it must be. The new provost would not have sent me word if he didn't think it was."

"You trust him?" his mother asked.

"I do. He's a friend."

Medor was. He really was. Thierry was looking forward to seeing him. Likely in the morning.

Over the chicken and the beans he asked the question he needed to. "Did you receive an offer?" He was looking at Ambroise, who flushed crimson, amusingly.

"The . . . new post? That ridiculous thing? Oh, Jad, Thierry. You knew about that?"

"I did. Didn't seem ridiculous to me," he said.

"Nor to me," his mother said, very seriously.

"High cleric of Orane? *Please!*"

"You said no?"

"Of course I did! Me? In the Great Sanctuary? At this stage of my life? The managing of everyone there? Of . . . of everything? Please!" Ambroise said again. "I am an old man and I like where I am."

"You are not an old man," Adelie said.

Ambroise sighed. "But I do like where I am. Allow me that?"

"Did they not also offer you high cleric of the university?"

Ambroise glared at him, trying for outrage and failing. "You seem very well informed about this, for a man who has been hiding in the countryside."

Thierry grinned.

His stepfather's expression changed. "Wait! Did . . . did *you* suggest it? Thierry!"

"I might have taken note that, with what happened to Hutin Peyre, there were two positions that needed filling, not one, and they didn't have to be merged as they'd been with him."

"And you . . . proposed this to . . . ?"

Thierry cleared his throat. "A woman of the court who has the ear of the queen, who had already decided Peyre was too obviously a servant of the Barratins to remain. Ambroise, you wouldn't even have to change sanctuaries, yours is part of the university. And the students *need* a man like you."

"A man like me." Ambroise tried to make a jest of it. "And what is that?"

"Decent. Honourable. Wise. For starters."

"Dear Jad, what *happened* to you in the country?" his mother asked, in a voice so startled that both men laughed.

"Did you say no to that one?" Thierry asked his stepfather.

Ambroise Villar flushed again. "Not yet. I promised I'd consider it. I have until harvest rites to decide."

"Not far off," Thierry said.

And was shocked to hear his stepfather swear. A thing that never happened.

He laughed again. Then his mood changed, looking at the two of them. Something came to him, a thing he should have said and done long ago, he thought.

"I would like," he said, "with your permission, to call you Father from now on. You *are* my father, you always have been. You have given me a life, in so many ways. I will honour Rochon Larraigne all my days, but . . . you're my father. May I call you that?"

And was touched, and even shaken, to see the other man begin to cry. Then he realized he was doing the same, again, and his mother was.

Through her tears, Adelie said, again, "Dear Jad, what *happened* to you in the country?"

He could have tried to explain, but he didn't.

—

Small things can matter so much in our lives, along with moments that aren't so small.

It was still light when he went out. Summertime. He told his mother he'd come home to sleep.

The serjeants had stabled the three horses somewhere, probably back at the barracks, he thought. Two different men were outside now, waiting for him. They walked to The Lamb through busy evening streets. Someone was singing a ballad at the edge of a square. He stopped to listen for a bit. Another part of home.

He was smiling in anticipation, heard welcoming voices as he went through the doors of The Lamb.

And there was Silvy. By the bar, seeing him almost immediately. She walked straight over, full of fierce intent, and punched him, hard, on the shoulder.

Had to have hurt her hand, he thought. Which didn't help him much. There was a bench behind him. He sank into it, rubbing at his shoulder. She didn't shake her own hand, or rub it with the other. Or anything.

"So good to be welcomed back," he managed. "Is there wine for a poet?"

"Fuck you, Thierry," Silvy said.

CHAPTER XIV

Claquin Guiene, who had come to the city ignorant and awkward, and had been accepted into the guards of the Duke de Montereau, and had seen him murdered in the street last winter, was in The Lamb that evening.

He was a serjeant now. Had accepted an offer to join their ranks shortly after that terrible night. Seems someone had noticed and respected how he'd handled himself. That was the phrase the provost's man had used when Claquin had attended at the Châtelet to receive this proposal.

He could have stayed with the Montereau family, as a guard for the widow, serving the angry son who was nearly of age now and hated the Barratins with the proper fury of someone whose father had been murdered (and whose own future had been placed very much at risk).

He'd done it, though: become a serjeant. Wasn't entirely sure why, he wasn't good at reasoning through why he did things. The woman who lived with him and who he (mostly) loved and who (probably) loved him said it was a flaw. She had identified many flaws in him over the years.

But being a serjeant was a good position, and it ensured, pretty much, that he'd stay in Orane, and he liked it in Orane. The Montereau family went back and forth between the city and their château. Many of their guards, also, had found themselves headed north to war in the spring. Some glory for those who were there for the defeat of the Anglcyn, but Claquin noted (and pointed out to his woman) that none of them received promotions, or ransoms for prisoners taken, or anything at all. Just risk on a battlefield, or on the way to and from.

Glory doesn't feed you, he'd said. She hadn't argued with him that time, as he recalled. They had a child on the way, due at autumn's end.

Right now, in the tavern, he was, as often, not certain what to do.

He'd been posted as one of the guards tonight for the poet who had returned to the city. Guiene had been assigned to him when Thierry Villar arrived inside the walls, escorted. Seemed the poet was a friend of sorts to the new provost. Guiene wasn't sure yet what he thought of Medor Colle, but the others seemed to like him well enough.

The poet was actually someone he remembered. From that winter night. The murder. The *murders* he reminded himself. Two of their men had died with the duke.

Could have been him. Maybe that's why he thought about it so often.

Right now, in The Lamb—a good tavern, in his view—he was unsure how to react to the fact that the poet had just been assaulted by one of the women who worked here. It was a serious punch, he thought, directed at a man they were here to guard, but also . . . it was a woman! And just to the shoulder. But not . . . playful?

He stayed where he was, uneasily, sitting at a table by the wall, but he leaned forward a little, to see better. The poet seemed surprised more than anything, he decided. That made sense. Claquin was very surprised! Then he realized that people were laughing, amid shouted greetings to Villar. It didn't seem cause for alarm, then. Some were demanding the man give them a poem.

Claquin didn't understand poetry at all.

"Fuck you, Thierry," she had just said, surprising herself.

Silvy rarely swore in the tavern. She'd never punched anyone here. Or in her life, really. Maybe in childhood, she didn't remember.

People seemed highly amused by what she'd done. Thierry didn't. He looked aggrieved. Bastard.

"Why?" he had the effrontery to ask her.

"*Why?* Are you serious? You are allegedly a man with writing skills. Access to paper? To couriers, maybe? You sent us nothing! Nothing! No word you were coming back! That it was safe to do so."

She was glad she'd said *us*, not *me*, actually.

"Oh," Thierry said.

"Oh," Silvy repeated, mockingly.

He was still rubbing his shoulder. Such a heroic man! She hoped it had really hurt. Her hand did. She wouldn't give him the satisfaction of showing that. She made the mistake of glancing over at the bar and saw Eudes. He raised one eyebrow, a trick he had. *Jad curse you, too,* Silvy thought. She really was angry.

Probably everyone in The Lamb knew that by now, she thought ruefully.

She looked at Thierry. He hadn't changed. Skin darkened a little. His brown hair lighter, longer, and his beard. But . . . but why was she so *angry* seeing him now? What was that? Was it just the unexpectedness?

"I went to my mother and father's," Thierry said, as if that excused something.

"Very dutiful of you," Silvy said.

"Then I came here."

"Very dutiful."

He was *still* rubbing his shoulder. "Silvy, I should have written. I wanted to surprise everyone. I didn't even write my mother. Childish, I concede it. I'm sorry. Are you well? Is everyone here well?"

She glared at him. "My hand hurts," she said.

"Good," said Thierry. "I'm glad. Will you hug me?"

"Not a chance," she said. "Go get some wine and say hello to Eudes. He isn't furious with you."

"I'll do that. And then we can . . ." He trailed off because his eyes had gone past her to the door, which had just opened. She could hear when the front door opened, even if the room was crowded.

"Jad's blood," said Thierry.

Silvy turned to look.

"Jad's blood," she said.

Jolis de Charette came in. Again. Entering with a tall man, almost as well dressed as she was, and she was very well dressed.

"I am not talking to her," Thierry said.

"I'd stab you if you did."

She would remember having said that, after.

"She was here before," she said. "Asked for you. Said she wanted to tell you she's getting married."

"What? Why? Why in the god's name would she think I—"

"I have no idea," Silvy said. "Quick, go get your drink."

It was too late, though. She thought about that, too, after. If they hadn't kept on talking, if he'd just gone to Eudes when she'd said to . . .

Life was full of such moments, she decided later. And held to that thought for the rest of her life.

Jolis called out Thierry's name, and came straight over to the two of them, long legs, long-striding, bejewelled again, the tall man trailing her. Thierry turned his back. He didn't go to the bar, that would have looked too much like flight. And Jolis would have followed him anyhow, Silvy realized.

Of course she would have.

She faced the other woman. Who was always so unfairly beautiful, almost stupidly desirable. "You are not welcome here. You know that. Please take your pretty man and go."

"I just want to—"

"Tell Thierry you are marrying. Yes. We know. I assume this is him, the pretty man. Have you started on your twelve children yet?"

"Silvy, why do you hate me so much?"

Silvy saw, out of the corner of her eye, that Eudes had come out from behind the bar now. He stopped a short distance away.

"Fuck yourself," she said to Jolis de Charette. "You know why." Swearing again!

The tall man glowered at her. "That is no way to speak to your betters! Apologize!"

"No," Silvy said. "We were ready to throw her out before. We can do it tonight instead." Wasn't *quite* true, as to before, but she didn't care.

Jolis went to one side of Silvy and reached out a hand towards Thierry, rings and perfect fingernails. He still had his back to them.

Jolis closed her fingers on his shoulder.

Silvy, watching, saw him flinch. So she did it again. She punched someone. Second time in her whole life, that she could remember, now twice in moments. She hit Jolis de Charette with all her strength on the side of her head, the cheekbone. Might have heard a crack. The other woman shrieked. The tall man moved quickly, held her upright as she staggered.

"*You bitch!*" he exclaimed at Silvy. "Do you know what you have done?"

"Hurt my hand again?" said Silvy, which was silly but satisfying. Also true.

"We'll get this tavern shut down!" he snarled.

Thierry turned around at that.

"I doubt it," he said gravely, "whoever you think you are, and whatever power you think you have. This woman is not welcome here. You just heard it from one of the owners. Jolis de Charette gets people killed. Likely she'll do it for you, if you last long enough. I'd be careful. Take her away now, with some dignity, before they have to throw you out into the dog shit and mud."

"You," said the man, "need a lesson."

"I've had a few in my day," Thierry said. "Go. I mean it. It really is wiser."

"I think not," said the other man grimly.

Jolis was holding her cheek with both hands, moaning. Silvy hoped she'd broken a bone. Was also, she'd later recall, slightly afraid she'd done that. This was not an inconsequential woman.

Then she saw the tall man draw his sword.

"*No!* None of that!" Eudes snapped, stepping to them now, bulky and calm, but forceful.

"I've no quarrel with you!" the tall man said, eyeing a very big person.

"In my tavern? Drawing a blade? Yes you do. You very surely do. Ythier, outside and call for the watch. Now!"

"No need for that," the man said quickly. "This is between me and the rude little fool here. Turning his back on a well-born lady? Talking of throwing us out? Needs manners taught."

"By you?" Thierry said, with what actually sounded to Silvy like a genuine laugh. "Here? In The Lamb? Oh, you're exactly enough of a fool to suit her. Are you at least rich? Do you have a title?"

"That'll do," the tall man said. And assumed a fighting stance.

"Stop it!" Eudes roared. "Now!"

There came a sound from behind the man with the sword. Someone clearing his throat. He was actually skilled with a blade, had been to war in the spring with the king's army. He spun, very quickly.

Claquin Guiene had learned some skills with weapons in his time as a guardsman. He hadn't been with the serjeants long enough to improve further, but he was undeniably capable now.

Didn't matter. Didn't help. He'd been too conflicted, approaching, torn between his assigned task to guard the poet and an awareness that the man in front of him was—clearly!—significant. He'd hoped, even as he came over to them, that the tavernkeeper could resolve this; he'd already sent someone for the guards.

But Guiene did go over that way. He was on duty here. Ought to have declared himself a serjeant as he approached, called it out loudly. Made it clear before he arrived at a quarrel. People were given pause by serjeants of Orane. Even, he supposed, important people. He hadn't fully sorted through his new status yet, in truth.

Never did. You need time sometimes, and time was taken from him.

First thing was surprise. The blade in his chest. Then pain. An astonishing degree of pain. He'd never been badly injured in his life, remarkably.

It seemed so unfair, Claquin Guiene thought, so *wrong*.

Then he died.

There was silence for a heartbeat, then an uproar engulfed The Lamb. The man with the sword, Jolis's affianced, tried to step backwards and away, but there was, very quickly, nowhere for him to step. He was surrounded by enraged, shouting people. He was the only one with a sword, but there were several knives out, and men and women were cursing him to darkness in the god's name.

The poet and the tavernkeeper both knelt by the man he'd stabbed.

"He's dead," said Thierry, sounding deeply shaken. He looked up. "You're going to hang for this."

"He was . . . he was attacking me!" the tall man exclaimed. His name was de Mardol. "I feared for my—"

"Where is his sword?" Villar said, standing up.

The dead man's sword was, unfortunately for the dead man and for the man who'd killed him, still sheathed.

"He's a serjeant of the provost of Orane, you stupid, murderous fucker," the poet snarled. "They *will* hang you for this. You'll be two more deaths for this abomination of a woman."

"I did nothing!" Jolis cried, but you could hear her fear.

"Fuck you," said Silvy again. "They should hang you, too."

Sounds from the door. Another of the serjeants entering. There had been two to guard him, Thierry knew. One inside, one at the doors. And behind this man, close behind, came two of the night guards.

"There has been a murder," said Eudes. "We all saw it, and he's holding a bloodied sword. Arrest him. Get him out of my tavern. And her! Get her out!"

He rarely sounded angry, Thierry thought. But it was rare for a man to die in here.

"I am the Vicomte Fermin de Mardol," the tall man said, a little shakily, to the three men now approaching. "My family are—"

"Drop the blade and come with us," said the other serjeant. "Now." His own sword was out. He was white-faced with fury, seeing a dead colleague on the tavern floor. "It will please me to kill you if you resist. I'm sure there are enough good people here who will help. Sword to the floor. Now."

De Mardol hesitated, then he sheathed his sword instead of dropping it, but he did comply that far. The serjeant nodded at the city guards and they each seized one of the man's arms, not gently.

"The Châtelet?" one of the guards asked.

"Oh, yes," said the serjeant. He looked at Eudes. "May I ask you to have my friend carried there?"

Eudes nodded. He was breathing deeply, Thierry saw, working to control himself. The serjeant and the guards and their prisoner left.

Looking down, Thierry suddenly realized he knew the dead man. Hadn't recognized him before. He was one of those they'd encountered the night Rollin de Montereau was murdered. For some reason that made this even worse.

He looked at Jolis, who was still standing there. "You love men dying for you, don't you?" he said.

"I don't!" she exclaimed, a hand still to her swollen cheek.

"Just bad luck?" he asked bitterly.

She didn't answer. She never did answer that.

She left, instead. Demanded an escort. Eudes sent two men with her. It was the right thing to do, in the night streets. Always important to do the right thing, Thierry thought bitterly.

Eudes made arrangements for the dead serjeant to be taken to the Châtelet. They needed a cart. He seemed calm again. Thierry didn't feel so. He remembered he'd promised his mother he'd sleep at home tonight. He said that to Silvy.

The look on her face froze him.

"You are not allowed to be a fool right now, Thierry," she said. "You had two guards. They are both gone. One is dead. You are *not* leaving here."

"They said I wasn't in danger," he said. "That I could come back."

"And a man drew a sword on you, and a man was killed!"

"That . . . this was different. This was just Jolis!"

"Ah. Just Jolis. I see. And the man with the sword, the *vicomte* with a sword, has no friends in Orane? If you go to the door I'll stab you myself, Thierry."

He looked at her. She was rigid with tension. "Violent tonight?" he managed to say.

Silvy shook her head. "Don't even try to be amusing. If you don't want to stay down here, head up to my room. But you aren't going into the streets. I will send a message to your mother that you'll be home in the morning. Some of us know about sending messages."

"Now you're the one being amusing," he said.

"Not really," she said coldly.

He looked down again at the dead man.

"Very well," he said.

She gave him the room key. He was deeply shaken. He watched the men Eudes had called in as they wrapped the body in linens and carried it out to a waiting cart. He could send a message with them to the Châtelet, he belatedly realized, and have another escort come take him home.

He let things be. For Silvy, he told himself.

He lingered in The Lamb for a time, talked to a few people he knew when they came over. Everyone was quiet, subdued. He drank some wine but not very much. The crowd slowly thinned out. Not a tavern people wanted to be in just now. Eventually, he went through the inner doorway and up the narrow stairway to the room where, really, everything about his present life seemed to have begun, in the dark of winter.

He used a taper he lit at a lamp in the hallway to light the one in Silvy's room. It was a warm, late-summer night. He opened the window and the shutters. Needed air, even if he couldn't go outside. Her orders. She had *punched* him. Then Jolis. Did he even know this woman? he thought.

Actually, yes, he did. He did know her.

Stood by the window thinking about that. Confusing thoughts, chasing each other. Looking down, he watched people leave the tavern, talking loudly once outside, excited. Two dogs began fighting in the street, just out of sight, then they stopped. He looked at the blue moon, risen over the rooftops.

The street grew quiet. He heard the sound of Eudes or Silvy locking the main door. Everyone had gone, then. He heard the sanctuary bells ringing. Orane. Its bells. He was back in Orane.

There was silence again.

This had not been the return to his city he'd expected. When did things go as you expected? he thought. He was thinking that when Silvy entered the room.

"I thought you'd be asleep," she said.

He shrugged. "Thought I'd wait for you."

It was true, he realized. He *had* been waiting. And that came with a different kind of awareness.

She crossed to the lamp by the bed. She said, a little awkwardly, "I'm sorry I hit you."

"No you aren't," he said.

She shook her head. "I really am." A half-smile that he knew. "Not sorry about Jolis. Think I broke her cheekbone?"

"Might have."

"Good," Silvy said.

"Could make for trouble."

Her turn to shrug. "I doubt it. Her man killed a serjeant tonight."

Which was true, of course. He looked at her across the room: slim, light-brown hair, brown eyes (he knew they were, couldn't see it in the lamplight). And brave. His friend. His friend.

He drew a breath. He said, his voice a little shaky, "Silvy, I . . . has something happened here?"

"Happened?" A silence. "You mean . . . us? Here?" Hard to tell but he thought she looked pale now.

He nodded. It had become difficult to speak.

"You mean," she said bravely (she was always brave), "should we become lovers, finally?"

All he could do, he found, was nod again.

He saw her also nod her head, down and up, just the once. "I think . . . I think it might be time?" she said.

And with those words, he was suddenly so aroused, so much desiring her. And . . . and more than that. He didn't move yet.

He said, from by the window, "If I walk towards you, it feels like so much changes. Not just tonight."

"Is that bad?" Silvy asked. And he caught the shift in her voice.

And suddenly he was not uncertain anymore, not afraid. He said, "It isn't bad at all for me, my dear." If she could be brave, so could he, he thought.

He saw her smile. There seemed to be tears on her face. "In that case, my dear, start walking," she said. "My bed is here. And . . . and so am I. We aren't far from you."

He crossed the room.

It is possible to love someone, even for years, and not know it. Or to hide from it, in denial, and then in a moment . . . know it, and not be afraid.

Their first lovemaking, lit by the lamp, with the blue moon in the window, was more tender than either had words for (and he was a poet). The second, later that same night, was . . . less gentle. And both were very deeply pleasing for both of them. Almost shockingly so.

Afterwards, lying awake, he said, very softly, "I don't feel I deserve this much kindness from life?"

"Kindness?" She laughed. Almost luxuriously, he thought. "Oh, Thierry. And besides, if you don't, I do. I deserve it!"

He laughed too. Then they were quiet together, entwined, in a room that seemed to contain more of light than a lamp and the blue moon still in the window ought to have been able to offer them. To allow.

"I'm sorry I punched you," she said again, much later, lazily, drifting, almost asleep, the moon gone.

"I'm not," he replied, feeling her head against his shoulder. But she *was* asleep by then.

Didn't matter. She knew. And he really didn't mind at all that she had hit him, before. It had led him to realize a thing about her, and then about himself, and how the two of them might fit together, going forward in the world.

Despite urgent attempts at intervention by his family, the young Vicomte de Mardol was hanged three days later on Gallows Hill.

It was a serjeant he'd slain, in a public place, and one not even wielding a blade. You couldn't do that in Orane. And de Mardol had already drawn his own sword against a man protected by the provost. Known to the king and queen. There were many witnesses, and much anger.

You could think of it as sad. Fermin de Mardol had never been known as a violent or a troublesome man. Innocuous, had been the general view. He'd served honourably in the spring campaign. A skilled rider. Good swordsman.

In thrall to a woman, it was said. Not the first such man for that particular woman. She was exceptionally beautiful, it was widely reported.

I made a point of reminding myself of the serjeant's name in the morning. Claquin Guiene. Newly among them, recruited by de Vaux after the night of the assassination, in fact. I went to the Châtelet very early. Offered to help his family, if he had one. I didn't know.

Medor told me the provost's office would look after that. He seemed angry I'd even raised the matter. We had much to discuss, but we didn't talk any more that day. Entirely the wrong time. First death under his command, it appeared. And Medor had also been present that winter night when we'd encountered Guiene in the street.

He sent me home with a new escort. I didn't argue, I remember.

I did light a candle later that morning, and asked my father to name the dead man in the rites. Not much. Nothing at all, really. He'd been alive, young, living—for good or ill, knowing happiness or not. Then he was dead in a tavern on a summer night. The night my own life altered again and love came in, as through an open window. A gift. A blessing of the god.

What are we to make of such things overlapping, coinciding, in our days?

CHAPTER XV

All wars bring suffering with them, but the worst are civil wars.

Someone wrote this down first, of course, someone always does. But it can seem, if you read the works of chroniclers, that every writer of the history of his time, or an earlier one, knows the phrase, believes it, uses it himself.

It isn't even subject to the usual issue of which side of a conflict the writer takes as his own. Civil wars mean father against son, brother against brother, villages divided, a country in chaos.

But . . . the observation is only sometimes true, one might better say, and some have. Not *always*. "Always" is a dangerous word. But consider an invading force: coming through mountain passes when the snow has melted enough, pouring in numbers down valleys and their rivers, to conquer. Rape and murder, fire and atrocity, bodies chopped to pieces in villages and towns, children spitted upon pikes, the ruthless theft of everything that isn't buried in woods or fields or hidden some other way. Gold and goods looted from holy sanctuaries, country estates, homes, farmhouses, artisans' shops. Men and women tortured to reveal hiding places, killed if there are none. Famine, with food stolen everywhere, because armies need to eat.

These horrors come more often with an army from away—and they do come. They are part of the dance of War with Death. It has been painted. Leaders of armies know what they must offer to keep the loyalty of their soldiers while many of those are dying themselves one way or another, mostly of disease, some on battlefields. And commanders *must* feed their men, far from home.

Nonetheless, it is still proper to write that civil wars bring their own kind of grief. They can leave a land depleted, broken—*and* vulnerable to invasion. The one war begetting the other. Few things happening in any country on such a scale are not noticed elsewhere, and can be seen as an opportunity.

The fates of kings, princes, dukes, courts, all are interwoven with each other, and with the lives of those they govern, well or badly.

⚜

He'd had no reply from the king in Orane. None. It was a shaming outrage. He flushed just thinking on it. He had written twice, was not going to disgrace himself and his lineage by doing so a third time.

Laurent de Barratin had many defining traits, but foremost among them, perhaps, was pride.

The king of Ferrieres was his cousin, just as the man he'd slain had been his cousin. That might, he conceded, as his thoughts chased themselves around, be argued in different ways. (He did prefer the word "slain" to "murdered." "Slain" spoke of old tales and heroic poems.)

But he'd gone to Rhodias, exactly as had been demanded of him. He'd knelt before the pig-eyed Patriarch and kissed his foot and his ring. And spent a great deal of money there.

Was there any point to that abasement if no forgiveness resulted in Ferrieres? He didn't really like that word, either. Forgiveness. In his own view, his cousin Rollin had been squeezing him mercilessly for years, as if by the throat. One cousin, one duke, had to emerge triumphant. There was no real way the two of them could continue on either side of the young Prince Girald, with the father, the king, drooling mad.

Of course the father was no longer so. And Hardan of the Anglcyn was locked in the Châtelet of Orane, and was not, it was increasingly evident, ever going to be ransomed. More likely, Barratin thought, Hardan would be killed for his brother back home. For a price. It was what he'd do, were he the brother in Angland. They didn't want their king back, was what his spies there told him.

Treachery, he thought, in his garden in Berga on a summer's evening, could come from anywhere. He ought to have killed Corbez Barthelmy the night of the assassination, for example. The red-cloaked man (stupidly so, it marked him too much) had been an obvious source of danger after organizing and leading the attack. Burkard van Aribert, whom he trusted, had urged it from the start.

But the man Barthelmy had proved more cunning than expected. He'd written two letters with full confessions detailing what they had done, and by whose orders and payment, to be revealed if he were suddenly to die, or even disappear. And he'd informed the duke of this by way of another letter. Wouldn't surprise Barratin if there were *three* letters. One sent to some place of holy men. He'd have done that, too.

So, yes, he ought to have killed the man, but he couldn't! And then Barthelmy had been taken in Orane. An idiot. Idiots could be cunning sometimes. They were still fools. But dangerous ones. Barthelmy was dead now, and would have told them everything they wanted to know in the Châtelet.

It began to rain in the garden. Stubbornly, he stayed outside.

It felt as if too many things had turned against him, the duke thought. And he wasn't a man to accept that passively. To just sheathe his ambition, accept the wealth of his dukedom, his wine, his mines to the east, the vastly profitable cloth trade.

He had, and he knew it, too much anger in him. Was too easily provoked.

Yes, he had a very good life here. He still wanted more. For himself, for his heirs. What was a man if not what he left behind?

Someone more detached might have noted that his analysis of events might overlook how much envy he'd always felt for his golden cousin, from childhood. He himself had been the clever, ill-favoured one. Rollin? Rollin was the clever, beautiful one. It was, it always had been, unfair.

He didn't believe, at all, that his own cool, haughty wife had been seduced by Montereau. That her portrait, unclothed, was on a wall in some secret chamber in his city palace or the château to the west of Orane. But it burned him like a brand that many people did think so.

It had been one more mark against the ledger of his cousin. Enough of them, over time, to have been worth a murder, he had finally decided. Accepting an ordered pilgrimage to Rhodias. And after returning to Berga sending letters of ingratiating entreaty to Orane that he be allowed back at court to take his proper place on the royal council.

In reply? Nothing. Nothing at all.

And you could not, you could *not*, even if you were the miraculously returned-to-health king of Ferrieres, ignore Laurent de Barratin. It was—it was really not permitted.

He'd been on the very edge of claiming that throne, ruling Barratin *and* Ferrieres. Even uniting them! He might be so again. If the world as Jad had made it would not give you the things you deserved, you needed to find ways to take them. That was the lesson. And in doing so burn away, as with a purging fire, some of the memories of childhood and his cousins.

Marina wasn't certain, but she mostly believed the queen kept her close by because they were both from Batiara, and there was a trust in that. Odd, by some measures, as their city-states were rivals back home, but here in Ferrieres, that could be seen to be less important? Home was a long way off in time and over mountains or the sea, and both their lives were here now. Irreversibly, really, from when they were young.

She wanted to be home, in fact, but *home* was her château to the west, not the city in another land where she was born and raised, and from where she'd come north to be married. It had been—and she knew this was rare—a good marriage. Her husband's death had been a wound, and not just for the financial disaster that had ensued for her and the children.

It had made her a poet, though. There was that.

The current problem was that it was intensely difficult to find time and quiet to write, and she *needed* to write. She had commissions for long poems. Paying ones, from nobility who saw a work by her as adding to their own stature. And the queen, who wanted her by her side, did not actually *pay* for her company. Marina had a pleasant suite of rooms in the palace, ate with Queen Bianca most nights, had the drama of being close to great events, but . . .

But none of that paid for her château, or anything else. Nor was the queen the sort to take it well if asked for money. If Marina wrote a poem-cycle for her, it would be expected to be a gift. The queen was profoundly resistant to paying anyone for anything. It was well known. They were like that in Macera, she thought. Could not help but think. A deep city-state rivalry.

So she snatched, as a thief might, whatever time she could to work in her rooms. She had promised the Duke de Varelle an epic verse on his ancestors' heroism by autumn. It was late summer now and she had a long way to go.

Accordingly, when her maid knocked and reported visitors, she was not pleased.

"Who?" she asked shortly. You were permitted to decline visitors here. Or make them wait.

Names were given. She smiled, stood up from her desk. "Show them in," she said.

There were some people she did like. Not many, but there were.

Marina kissed them both, Silvy first, as was to be expected, really. But she also drew Thierry into an embrace and kissed him on both cheeks. She had ink on her hand. He liked seeing that. Said as much.

"I am taking what chances I can find," Marina said ruefully. "I have a poem due too soon." She glanced at what he was holding. "You have brought me something to read?"

"What I wrote in your château. For the use of which I will always be grateful."

Marina smiled. "I learn from the children that they loved having you."

"I told them stories in the garden."

"No one else does," she said. "They'll remember." She tilted her head. "I should like to be told a story."

Silvy grinned. "Don't get him started!" she said.

Marina looked at her a moment, then back at Thierry, and then she smiled again.

"Oh, good!" she said. "You two have finally figured out what was obvious to everyone else." And laughed to see them both react.

She gestured them to chairs. Sat at the writing desk again, as if proximity might produce words, somehow, even while they talked.

"Obvious?" Silvy said. "Really?"

"To anyone paying attention," Marina said.

"Why would anyone pay attention?" Thierry asked.

Marina made a face. "I did."

"An entirely different thing," Silvy declared.

Marina smiled again. "Are you going to be one of those unpleasant couples who join together against everyone?"

"Possibly." Silvy laughed. "Will you ask us to leave?"

"I will not." She rang a bell and ordered wine to be brought.

After a time, wherein most of the talk was of the court and unsettling rumours about the Duke de Barratin, Silvy excused herself. She had duties at The Lamb, she said. This visit was an escape, and she'd promised to keep it brief.

"May I come see you there? I do mean to."

"Eudes is uneasy now when elegant visitors come," Silvy said. "Better I come to you?"

"Then do that."

After Silvy left, Marina turned to Thierry.

"You've done well there," she said. "Took long enough, but you have."

He looked down.

"I may be slow in some ways," he said eventually.

"Or well-defended. As a city against a siege."

"Maybe. Maybe that. I don't know."

"Defending your freedom to work?"

"This from the woman lamenting she has no time to write?"

She grinned. "I believe I have missed you, too, Thierry Villar. Now let me read what you brought. Drink your wine in silence, please."

He did. Was extremely anxious.

When she was done she looked at him, eyes bright, teased him about Alaina d'Arceval. Was pleased to get the reaction she did. But then . . .

"These are something new."

He nodded. "I think I learned that . . . that there might be more I have to say than the quick and angry. Mocking?"

"And that is unsettling you," she said. Didn't make it a question.

"It is. Yes."

She nodded briskly. "Good. We are permitted to change, Thierry. That," she added, "might be my own difficulty. Patrons know what they want from me. Even more than those in a tavern know what they expect from you. I need to deliver that, to be paid. And acquire new commissions. It becomes a constraint."

He looked at her in silence. "You know you are extraordinary, don't you?" he said finally.

She smiled again. "You aren't going to talk yourself into my bed," she said. "Appealing as you sometimes can be."

He smiled back. "I am, as you seem to have noted, in love. And I wouldn't deserve your bed, anyhow, Marina."

A private smile as she glanced downward. "You have another copy of these poems?"

He nodded.

"Leave this one with me. I know some people who ought to see them. If that is all right?"

He nodded again. Hesitated. "You can't go home, to do your own work?"

"Not yet. The times are . . . too challenging. Too dangerous, I should say. And the queen trusts me."

"That remains your real problem," he said. "I think everyone does."

"My problem," she repeated thoughtfully. "I see. Perhaps I should become untrustworthy."

When he left, she embraced him again.

He walked back towards The Lamb. Had two escorts waiting at the palace gates. They were intensely vigilant as they walked the streets. He hated needing guards, didn't think he still did. Had lost that argument to Silvy and then with Medor Colle.

Though he had barely seen Medor since returning to Orane. It disturbed him.

One encounter at the Châtelet among several of the serjeants. Not private. The new provost, a man he'd really begun to think of as a friend, had been brisk, cool, distant.

"I came back only when you sent word it was safe," Thierry had pointed out, making his case.

"Might have been a mistake on my part," Medor said.

"What happened in The Lamb had *nothing* to do with—"

"Villar, we are not going through this. You'll have a guard until it feels to me that matters have changed enough."

Villar. Not Thierry.

That had been a week ago.

On impulse, Thierry changed his route. He told the two serjeants. They needed to be alerted. They were men following orders, and one of their own had died doing that.

A large number of the serjeants of Orane had escorted the wagon bearing Fermin de Mardol to Gallows Hill. And had stayed to watch him hang.

Thierry hadn't gone. Neither, unsurprisingly, had Jolis.

He gave the serjeants their new destination. It was a neighbourhood with a mixed reputation. Good homes among some . . . rather less so. A hint of the disreputable, in various ways. They moved closer to him, one before, one behind.

It was daytime in Orane. Sunlight, white clouds, a breeze. They heard sanctuary bells mark another hour as they went, and then the songbirds came again, after. There were trees in summer leaf in gardens behind walls, and in public squares.

There was still danger in Orane, even in daylight. It was, he knew, part of his city. It held, Thierry thought, so much of life, the variety, the richness, the hazards of it.

You could fear that, or love it.

They came to the door he remembered, and he knocked. Brass knocker, shape of an owl. A servant answered this time. He announced himself. After a moment the servant came back and escorted him to a room he also remembered.

"You took Jad's own time getting here," said Gauvard Colle.

"I wasn't aware I was awaited."

"From when you came back to the city. And you should have been aware."

"How? Really?"

"Because you know me and have been here before."

"That makes," Thierry said, irritated, "no sense at all."

"Some people are far too concerned with things making sense."

Gauvard smiled his annoying smile and ordered a servant to bring wine. The wine would be good, at least. Thierry felt he needed it. Gauvard Colle induced that feeling. He wore a woman's robe today, and a silver necklace with a lapis lazuli stone. Two windows were open; the scent of flowers in the back garden came into the room.

"You have questions?"

The wine came. Thierry waited until it was poured. He took a long sip of his. It was, yes, very good. He saw Colle smile again.

"From Barratin," the other man said. "They make excellent wines, as you likely know."

He did know. Everyone did. He shook his head. From Barratin? Now? Everything Gauvard Colle did seemed intended to unsettle.

"Do you know," he said, "I think you play with people a little bit the same way Jolis de Charette does."

Gauvard looked affronted. "Not a kind thing to say!"

"Perhaps. But even so. And when I knew her she was a girl trying to test and learn her power. You're not that."

"Makes it worse?"

Thierry hesitated. "It would, if it weren't done with wit."

"Ah! So I'm all right?" Eyebrows arched. "Because I amuse?"

Thierry nodded. "Though you mostly want to amuse yourself, I think."

"Well, if anyone else would bother . . . !"

Thierry laughed. Had to laugh.

Gauvard Colle smiled, then pursed his lips. "Ask your questions, pretty man."

He said, "Do you believe in faeries, or . . . spirits in the forests?"

"Yes."

Only that. But a direct gaze now.

"You have encountered them?"

"Not in any way you'd understand. But only a fool believes the world holds only what he has seen. I try not to be a fool. Are you?"

Thierry looked at his wine cup. "I also try not to be," he said. "I'm sure I fail sometimes."

"We all do. There's wisdom in knowing it. You bedded a woman who made you think these things?"

Again he hesitated, to frame his answer. "She . . . bedded me, I think."

"How pleasant for both of you," said Gauvard Colle. "Why does this matter?"

And so . . .

"I am also trying to understand why your nephew is angry with me."

"Ask him." The answer was very quick.

"I would, if he gave me a chance."

And this time the hesitation was in the woman or the man—or someone who was both—in the chair opposite.

"Be careful with Medor," Gauvard said finally. "For him."

"What? He's the provost of Orane, it isn't my—"

"That's not how things are in these matters. You know it, Thierry Villar."

And he did know, suddenly. With those words spoken.

He took a breath. He said, quietly, "I see. I . . . really didn't realize. I miss too much, it seems. I will try to be careful." And then, "Thank you."

Gauvard, no hint of anything but gravity, said, "He will be all right. Always has been. Just don't cause . . . unnecessary pain?"

And Thierry said, "You have experienced this, yourself? Unnecessary pain?"

Gauvard Colle stiffened. He said, "Not an unreasonable question, but I am not inclined to answer it."

Thierry nodded. "Should I go, then?"

"Unless you have more you need from me."

Thierry shook his head.

Gauvard said, "There is danger coming. And," he added, "do not be clever and say there always is."

Thierry *had* been about to say that.

"Find the constable," Colle said. "De Vaux will know what needs doing, if anyone does."

"Me? Why do *I* have to find someone?"

Again a hesitation. "Not sure," said Gauvard Colle. "That is often the way with me. But it feels a true thought."

"From the half-world?"

"From somewhere. You should do it. Find him."

Colle walked him to the door. Before opening it, he said, "Come see me again, if you have the chance. Bring my nephew, if he'll come."

It was still light outside. It felt as if it ought to be nighttime now, Thierry thought, stars and the moons.

In the palace, Marina di Seressa was summoned to the queen at almost exactly the same time this conversation was happening. She'd been re-reading Villar's new poems, and feeling something unusual for her: envy.

Not of the work, though she admired it greatly. No, she was envious of how life or whatever else (Alaina d'Arceval? Delicious, really!) had allowed him to grow into these words.

She had told him, earlier, that people were permitted to change. But she also hadn't lied when she said that her patrons knew what they wanted from her.

And she, in turn, knew what she needed from them. She was maintaining a château, retainers and guards and those who managed her tenants to the east and south on the estate. She *had* an estate. The great good fortune of that. Her husband's, but preserved now by her, with her writing. An amazing thing. For anyone, not just a woman. But . . . more so for a woman?

She imagined a time when she was older, less a part of this world, of the court, when she might live there in quiet. Her children grown, settled, well married. She could do work that did not have to please someone commissioning it.

Was that greedy? Demanding?

Probably, she thought. She should accept the gifts she'd been given. The fact that her work was in demand.

Or, she could take a wealthy man as a lover. Or marry again.

She didn't want to do either of those. Easier, on the whole, to invite women to her bed to address those needs that did still occupy her. And keep the freedom she'd come to value so much. She had time yet, Marina thought. Maybe. You could only say *maybe* in the world Jad had given them. You might die of a fever tomorrow. Or a war could come.

She changed into clothing suitable for the queen and went down the corridor with an attendant. It wasn't far.

The concern, it emerged, with no preamble, had to do, again, with the Duke de Barratin. Her view was solicited. She framed her reply as a question, always wisest with Queen Bianca.

"Should the king have replied to Barratin's plea to be allowed back?" Marina asked. They were alone.

"It wasn't a plea, his majesty told me."

Something in the tone of that.

"You . . . haven't read the letter?"

"There have been two, I am informed. No."

Terse. It was clearly a troublesome point. The queen was standing by a tall window, her back to the room and to Marina. She had been reading a friend's poetry earlier, and now there was . . . this. It would be a lie to say it was not exciting.

Women, she thought, needed always to fight for any impact they might want to have. In the world. In their own lives. Even a queen who had led in governing the country while the king was mad. And now the king was not mad, for which they all gave thanks, but . . .

But she had not been shown the letters.

There was something else. She was going to have to ask, Marina realized. She had been part of the queen's circle long enough to know. And to know there were risks.

Life was a risk.

She said, "What else, your grace? What is troubling you?"

Queen Bianca turned. Looked at her. Even before she spoke, Marina felt a tremor of apprehension.

"We have received word. Barratin is moving this way with an army. Not just his guards."

Life, Marina thought again, was a risk. It was laden with them.

She said, quietly, "That doesn't sound like a man pleading to be admitted to court."

"No," said the queen. "It does not."

"What . . . what does the king intend to do?" She was frightened now.

"Raise the army. He has little choice. He's summoned the constable and the dukes. I think they'll plan to meet Barratin east of here."

"Civil war, then?"

"Yes." One word.

Marina said, cautiously, "Do you want to summon Gauvard Colle?"

The queen had a way of glancing up to one side when she was thinking. She did so now. Then she looked back at Marina and shook her head. "I need to know more first. But I am not sure I am going to be told more." A pause. "The king would never do it, I don't think. Nor Robbin de Vaux. Codes of honour. But . . ."

Another pause. This one inviting her.

You had no choice, with such an invitation.

"But?" said Marina di Seressa.

Queen Bianca looked at her. A cold glance. Her father in Macera was said to be a cold, hard man. "But," said the queen of Ferrieres, "I think the Duke de Barratin needs to be killed."

Could poetry, could any writing, matter in the face of this? Marina thought. Was there even room for it?

Two windows were open to the afternoon. You could imagine, if you were so inclined, a wind of the wider world sweeping into the room. She had an image of the Dance of Death, a thing she wanted to write about, if her life ever allowed her to choose her own subjects.

Merchant and lord and lady, farmer and artisan and craftswoman, soldier and courtesan, and a child.

Dancing with the skeleton, hand in hand in hand.

Thierry was in the antechamber of Robbin de Vaux's home in the city. A room he knew well. Just beyond was the chamber where de Vaux worked from home. There were a handful of soldiers and four serjeants here, half outside the room, half in the courtyard. The serjeants had surprised him. Then he'd realized that Medor, now provost, would feel a responsibility for the constable when he was in Orane.

De Vaux was not here, was evidently at the court with the king. No one knew how long he'd be, or what was happening. Rumours were like flies in the summer air. Thierry settled in to wait, and think. He didn't know why Gauvard Colle had told him to find the constable, what possible role he had to play. But he—trusted wasn't quite the right word, but it was close—he *understood* that Colle knew things most people did not. Because of what he was. What she was.

"You can still ignore it," Silvy had said in their bed last night. "He doesn't control you."

He could do that. Could ignore all this. He'd said, fumbling for clarity, "It is because something communicates with Colle. I have seen it. Experienced it."

"So?" asked the woman he had finally realized he loved. And who appeared to love him. "That's Colle's life, not yours, Thierry."

"I'll at least talk to de Vaux," he said. "I owe him that much."

She wasn't satisfied, but she'd let the matter drop.

And so he was here now, waiting.

De Vaux came back towards sunset. He looked tired, but he nodded courteously at Thierry and ushered him in to the private room. He'd have much to do now, Thierry was certain. This was graciousness.

"Thank you," he said.

"What do you need of me, Villar?" De Vaux took his seat behind his desk, as always. He gestured and Thierry sat opposite. They were alone.

"I don't know," he said. "Maybe—I don't know why—you need me?"

De Vaux raised his eyebrows. A moment passed. The bells began outside, all over Orane.

"You've been to see Gauvard Colle?" asked the constable of Ferrieres.

He had always been so quick, Thierry thought. He nodded. "Yes."

"He told you to come here?"

"Yesterday afternoon."

De Vaux sighed. "I have no idea what to do with that man."

"Well, if *you* don't, I certainly don't."

A snort of laughter.

Thierry took a chance. "What has happened?"

With almost no hesitation, de Vaux said, "Barratin has raised an army. He is about ten days from here, maybe a little more."

Thierry swallowed hard. It took him time to form words. The bells were silent. Had done their task, marking the hour. He stammered, "What . . . what does he want?"

"He may want the throne," de Vaux said, calmly enough. "It seems King Roch elected to ignore his letters demanding he be restored to the royal council."

"Demanding?"

The constable nodded, as if Thierry had asked the right question.

"I saw both letters today. I'd not have called them a demand myself, but I'd also say they weren't far from that. And the king saw them that way."

Thierry sighed. "This isn't going to end, is it?"

The constable looked at him, and shook his head. "Maybe. It can. But I don't know how."

CHAPTER XVI

He didn't really want to kill the king.

Another assassination might be too much for Ferrieres and the wider world, let alone for Jad and his own soul. There was much to think about.

Because, on the other hand, could it not be argued that doing so, then moving swiftly to claim power and ensure peace, would save many lives, leave a country to carry on . . . villages unharmed, men and women not slaughtered, fields and vineyards intact, to be harvested soon? People *grateful* to him for this mercy?

The Duke de Barratin, normally sure of his judgments, swift with them, was still uncertain as he assembled his army outside his city of Berga.

Then they started west. Towards Orane.

Their route was a series of roads and towns he knew well. He'd done this journey so many times. He prayed as they went, morning rites and sundown rites, holding a new golden sun disk, and he stopped at many sanctuaries. He didn't normally do that. Was he getting older? Some men began to think about their souls more as they aged, it was known.

But he held to his earlier thought through the long summer days: you could not ignore courteous letters. Not from him, not even if you were the king of Ferrieres. The dukes of Barratin were too long-established, had too much power, and he was *family*.

And he'd been courteous! Had only petitioned to be allowed back among the king's advisers, among his own uncles and cousins. It wasn't as if Laurent was the only man ever to have killed a rival for power! (He didn't say that.)

His army was in his own lands for much of the progress west, and the men responsible for provisions had arranged for food and drink. But even when he crossed out of Barratin lands—ten or twelve days still from Orane, with so many on foot—he refrained from attacks on the villages they passed and the two walled towns. These were people he might govern, one way or another, in the days and years to come. And claim taxes from. Money shaped the world. His father, he remembered, had called it the sinew and purpose of war.

He had food purchased. They didn't steal it. That might have to happen later, but not yet. This campaign could drive him deeply into debt if it went on too long, because you *had* to pay your soldiers or they left you. Or killed you. Or abandoned you to be killed. He knew the stories. Every commander did.

But if he could merge Ferrieres with Barratin—if he could do that for himself, for his sons and his grandsons after—there would be no throne more powerful in the world, and it would be theirs. A truth worth fighting to make it happen.

Or, if the chance arose, worth arranging another assassination?

Which was not nearly as costly, and might save many lives.

He had his younger son with him. Perhaps a mistake. Guiart was only fourteen, but it was past time for the boy to start learning of warfare and armies. They'd be part of his life. And if his older brother died, he'd be the duke of Barratin one day. And perhaps king of Ferrieres. Besides which, Laurent de Barratin was discovering he enjoyed seeing the boy, being with him. A late realization, but a true one.

The older brother was in Berga, safely (more or less) behind its walls. Arnoul would govern there with his father away. He wasn't happy about this, and he wasn't quite ready for the role, either, but one needed to learn some things by doing them, and there were advisers with him at home. Loyal ones. Or, more precisely, Barratin hoped they were loyal. He had them watching each other. The world was too uncertain for more than hope. And sometimes, he thought, hope was foolishness.

He found himself thinking of his sons a great deal these days. And, yes, his soul, and Jad.

Another modest sanctuary dome appeared along the horizon ahead, pale gold in the afternoon light. He remembered it. Once, headed for Orane, he'd become ill, had thought he might die. They'd brought him there. Sickness could happen to anyone at any time. And if you died of it, the god would judge your deeds, and your soul as it was then, and offer you light, or darkness. You lived in the knowledge—and the fear—of that judgment. He was hardly old, but he wasn't a young man anymore. He had a grown son back in Berga, and a younger one with him now.

He ordered a halt and dismounted outside the sanctuary. He went inside with Guiart and his senior officers to pray. The clerics who greeted them were deferential, visibly afraid of him. Both things were proper, he thought.

It was when they were leaving that the incident occurred.

He had noticed the new cleric leading the rites up by the altar and the worn, faded sun disk. The man was still young-looking, but with a dramatic head of silver hair. Vivid blue eyes, the duke saw, when the cleric came up to him on the portico as he stood looking at a suddenly arriving rain shower before going out into it to ride on.

"Thank you, good cleric," Barratin said graciously. "It is always proper to seek Jad's blessing on the road."

"We would never deny prayer and repentance to any traveller," the cleric said. A deep, clear voice. This one didn't seem, the duke thought, deferential or afraid.

"Of course," he said, turning to go.

"But you would be wrong if you think you have the god's blessing just now."

Barratin stopped. He turned back. He felt as if he'd been slapped.

"What did you just say?"

"You heard what I just said, my lord duke. We may be somewhat isolated here, but we are not without access to tidings, or to seeing what goes past us." The man drew a breath, then said, shockingly, "Between a confessed murder in winter and now a march with an army towards Orane and your anointed king, you delude yourself as to what awaits you from Jad."

"How dare you!" rasped Burkard van Aribert. Two of the duke's officers came nearer, hands on swords.

"I dare because I must speak the truth of the god or I fail in my office," said the cleric. He wasn't especially tall but he stood very straight. "A quick prayer on the road is nothing, a matter of moments, but the darkness that lies in wait is eternal. Go home, my lord duke. It is not too late! Pray there, and properly repent. Money spent in Rhodias is not enough."

Really, thought Laurent de Barratin, *how does he dare?* He felt rage coming over him in dizzying waves. He worked to control it. Rage was often his undoing.

"I will let the High Patriarch be the judge of that," he said.

"Of course you will," said this astonishing cleric of a roadside sanctuary. "Very well. On your way, then. You will die one day, soon or late, and Jad is waiting. There is no bribing your way past the god."

"You should be killed for this effrontery," said Barratin. "There are men here who will gladly do it for me right now. But I am not the evil person you deem me to be. I will leave you to your ignorance. Good day, cleric."

He went out into the rain, fury consuming him.

Which became the problem. As it had been before in his life. Even after mounting up and starting west again he could not calm himself, or think clearly. His breathing had become shallow, his mind jumbled with rage.

And so.

And so, a little distance along the road, as that summertime shower ended, he called van Aribert to ride beside him and ordered that someone be assigned to go back and end the life of the cleric with silver hair. He felt he would choke if he did not order this.

He added, "It is to be arranged as a loyal soldier doing this of his own will after hearing of what happened there, the insult of it. *Not* by my orders. Do you understand?"

"I do," said Burkard van Aribert.

"Then have that soldier killed, quietly, after we stop for the night. And take his body away. Bury it or throw it in a pond."

He still remembered Corbez Barthelmy, who had known too much and could not be killed, because he had sent letters.

Alas, the events of that day did not unfold as he'd commanded.

The soldier chosen to commit the murder of a cleric (and then be killed) was a young man named Pons van Cové. Originally just Pons Cové, it later emerged, but his father had changed the family name to sound more northern when he moved them from the village of Broché to Berga on the sea, in search of a better life in the cloth trade there.

Which he had found, being intelligent and industrious and pious. And for which he gave continual thanks to holy Jad, and raised his three children to do the same. And yes, Broché had been the village of the Maiden. It was even determined afterwards that the two fathers had known each other.

The world can be vast, or very small.

As it happened, under the late-day sun that came out after the rain, Pons van Cové refused to kill the silver-haired cleric at that sanctuary when he rode back to it.

He was also clever, like his father, and surmised he'd be killed himself, afterwards. He knelt before the cleric and he told of the order he had been given. The cleric, who was much more than clever, immediately set about preparing his own letters.

Two went that same evening to Orane, one to the Great Sanctuary there, and another to the court. A good horse and a good rider could greatly outstrip an army with foot soldiers. Those letters reached Orane in days.

The cleric also sent another letter, which would take longer to arrive, to the High Patriarch in Rhodias, detailing what van Cové had been ordered to do by a man rejecting the demands of decency, faith, and the god. He invited the Patriarch to send someone to take testimony. He left out, unsurprisingly, his own remarks on the portico about bribery in Rhodias.

Then he summoned one of his senior clerics to act as a notary, and he had Pons van Cové dictate his story, and sign it, and the cleric affixed the sanctuary's seal, and they did this three times, and hid these documents.

Then they settled in to wait, and pray. The cleric did anticipate his own death now, along with that of the soldier. He hoped it would do some good in the world Jad had given his children.

Those deaths did not happen.

The Duke de Barratin, when the soldier sent to do his will did not return, drew certain conclusions, and decided that for now he had larger matters to address than an arrogant cleric in the countryside. The cleric—and the soldier—could be dealt with later. And would be. He was still angry, but he had taken control of his rage.

Back in the roadside sanctuary, Pons van Cové had not stood up after kneeling to reveal the instructions he'd been given. Instead, kneeling still, he'd beseeched that he might be permitted to remain there, take vows, enter the sanctuary as an acolyte, with a view to being initiated in due course as a true cleric of Jad.

He was accepted in this request.

He ended up having a different sort of life, however. Who can know where and when storms will crash upon us, or what slanting sunbeams, as at summer twilight, might illuminate our lives?

Pons van Cové and his beloved were eventually to become the subject of a famous poem by the celebrated Marina di Seressa. The poem that marked a divide in her body of work and how the world understood her.

It was largely invented, that long poem. Poets do that, tellers of tales do. But the foundation was real. Van Cové had indeed met Célia Maronniel when he was sent in early autumn with firewood and wine to the retreat of the Daughters of Jad that lay not far from the sanctuary. She, too, was an acolyte, seeking a life with the god.

The poet had them falling instantly in love, deeply and entirely, at their first meeting. It might have been so. No one knows. It *is* known that they left together not long after, and made their way south.

They were not betraying anything when they did this. The point of being an acolyte is to assess and be assessed as to the truth of one's vocation among the servants of Jad.

They were given food and drink and blessings, and a mule to carry their goods, and they . . . disappeared down a path to the south, and from the sight and knowledge of men and women forever.

But not from legend, because of the poet.

It was not an immediately successful work for Marina di Seressa. It really did mark too great a change from what she'd written before. No enchanted ships, no maidens imprisoned in richly described gardens, no courtly settings at all. But it endured, and over time its reputation grew. And as a consequence, the names of Célia Maronniel and Pons van Cové also endured. Surviving through time is a victory for art.

She had them journey through many perils—parted, reuniting—all the way to the sea in the south. In one passage, Pons is abducted by three brigands who believe he might be worth a ransom. Célia enlists a dozen stout clerics from a nearby sanctuary to her aid, and they rescue her beloved.

Originally, the poet confided to a few, it had been Célia captured and Pons saving her, but in the middle of a restless, windy night on her estate the thought came to her that she could write it differently, and she did. Because she could. It was her poem. No one had commissioned this work. No one had a right to any expectations of it. All they could do, really, was read it or not read it.

In the poem, the lovers finally settle in a town near Massilia on the southern coast. They live long lives together, and they die at very nearly the same time, days apart, not to be separated in life or death. They are buried beside each other by their children. The poem ends with a description of their shared grave by the sea, with waves and a sunset.

That poem was Marina di Seressa's truth superimposed on the absence of knowing what had happened. Or, more properly, it was her invented tale. Not quite the same thing.

Not quite. But near enough to make such stories one of the things we use to carry us through the uncertainty of our own days.

She sent it, anxiously, to a few trusted people when she thought it was done. She received a reply by courier quite soon from one of them.

"There you are at last," wrote her friend Thierry Villar.

Only that. But it said so much.

On the bottom of the page he had drawn a symbol, an elaborate arrow, in fact, inviting her to turn it over. On the other side he'd written, "Oh my. I see Alaina visited you."

She laughed so long and so loudly it disturbed the servants.

Ambroise Villar had finally accepted the post of senior cleric for the sanctuaries and the two holy retreats on the grounds of the University of Orane. He declined to be named a high cleric with this, as the previous one had insisted upon. An affectation, some said, a showy demonstration of how humble he was. He still had the power to assign and dismiss those beneath him, didn't he? Did the title matter?

Some of those saying this might have killed for the position, of course. But Ambroise Villar wasn't making a show of humility; it was genuine, and most knew that, because he'd been observed in his own sanctuary over many years. Envy has little to grasp hold of with some people, even if it tries.

Because he'd declined the also offered, hugely exalted position of high cleric of Orane, including leading the rites in the Great Sanctuary on the island, with a handsome residence adjoining, there was an ongoing issue as to who should be appointed there. Both the king and the High Patriarch in Rhodias had thoughts concerning this appointment. It was a position of power, deeply entangled in politics, not just faith. Which is why there was an issue.

Also why Ambroise had declined, and his son knew it.

But what this meant was that for the current period, until the matter was resolved, Ambroise Villar had agreed to supervise some matters related to the Great Sanctuary, and lead the principal recurring rites there, although not the daily ones. Those he continued to perform in his own small, long-time sanctuary, and he still resided in his modest quarters there.

But he also now received, by messenger twice a day, all communications sent to the attention of the high cleric of Orane—since there was none.

One of these messages, a few days after an incident to the east at a roadside sanctuary, caused him to send a note to his son requesting Thierry's presence.

He was forced to pay attention to several university sanctuaries now, moving among them through the day, but he was in his own (it was vanity to call it his, he knew, but after so many years . . .) when his son arrived.

Ambroise showed him the communication from the east. The one that had been sent to the high cleric of Orane, who did not currently exist. It mentioned that the same letter had also been sent to the court. And a third copy to Rhodias.

Thierry, who had changed greatly since the winter, was decisive. He was also trained in the law, Ambroise knew—at this university.

His son said, "This matters. Someone has to take the statement of this man, van Cové, before he is killed. Have I your permission to talk to people about it?"

It was an astonishment, really, that his son was now someone who could say a thing like this and mean *important* people.

"Are we doing right?" Ambroise asked. "Do we have a side in this? Would Laurent de Barratin be worse, governing Ferrieres?"

His son raised an eyebrow. "Are you asking that to test me?"

"Perhaps," Ambroise said.

"Well. Well, then. The Duke de Barratin murdered his cousin. And that same day he attempted to have your presumably beloved son killed in an icy winter street because he grew suspicious of me after a visit to his home. So, yes, I think our family has a side here, beyond everything else."

Ambroise smiled at him. "If I hadn't known you were a poet, now I would."

"What? Why?" Thierry had not expected that.

"Really? What normal person would say 'icy winter street' there when 'street' was all that was needed?"

Thierry laughed. "So now you know," he said. "Finally! It . . . sounded better?"

His father's smile deepened. "Exactly what I mean." Then, "Thierry, you need me to wait? Not do anything?"

"Is there anything you *can* do?"

Ambroise shook his head. "Not really. He's written to Rhodias. That will take time, and would supersede anything any high cleric here could do, and I'm not—"

"You're not the high cleric, I know. I wish you were."

"You just want to ring the bells in the Great Sanctuary," Ambroise said.

"Can I? Please? Can you make that happen?"

"No," said his father. "Besides which, you'd have no notion how. Will you be with us for the evening rites and a meal? Shall I tell your mother?"

"Not tonight. There are people I must see now, quickly."

"You'll tell me what happens?"

"You know I will."

They kissed and he left.

He went to Medor first. Someone at the court would have received this same letter, but Medor might not yet know of it. It wasn't certain he *needed* to know, as provost—this was not a matter for Orane in particular—but Thierry had been looking for another chance to see him.

On reflection, on his way through the noise of the city, he sent one of his two escorts to Robbin de Vaux's home, to tell him where

Thierry was going, and that it was important. If the constable was available, it made sense for him to be present for this. Probably should have done it the other way around, he thought. Gone to de Vaux and sent a note to Medor. Too late now. He wasn't very good at this.

Unsurprising. The thought came, and not for the first time, how strange it was that he—and his father now, because of him—seemed to be involved in these events. He was just a tavern poet.

Which made him smile to himself as he walked. *Icy winter street*, indeed. But the words one chose were a way of seeing, of understanding the world. And the sound of them mattered. It did!

At the gates of the Châtelet he said that the matter was urgent. After a brief interval he was escorted to the room Medor was using. Thierry gestured, and the other man dismissed the serjeants attending on him. Medor was still reserved, even chilly in manner. It didn't matter. Not for this.

Thierry said, "A letter was sent to the Great Sanctuary. It made its way to my father. He called me to see it. He agreed I could bring it here to you." He was trying for a brisk tone himself.

The provost took the letter, read it through quickly, and then again. He looked up. "This isn't really for me, is it?"

"Might be. They are headed for Orane, no? Your uncle sensed it."

"You went to Gauvard?"

Thierry nodded.

Medor nodded. "We have word of that army. The constable has summoned the king's forces to assemble. He will ride now with those who can get here quickest, others will follow."

"That's war, provost." He kept it formal.

"Well, yes. An army is coming. Did you hear me?"

"I did. But this letter may give us another way. With the clerics of Jad now involved."

Medor's slow, almost reluctant smile. "You're a lawyer. One could forget."

"I prefer that being forgotten, usually. I did also send a note to the constable at his home. I don't know when—"

A knock at the door. Medor called for it to be opened.

Robbin de Vaux entered. "Medor, we have something to discuss." He stopped, registering Thierry's presence.

"You received my message?" Thierry asked.

De Vaux shook his head.

"You just came here yourself?"

"From the court. A letter has been received. What is it you need? Why are you here?"

Sometimes the sheer randomness of life could astonish you. How could you ever invent a story, Thierry thought, that was more strange than what really happened? Easier to stick to poems of mock bequests!

"Same letter, I suspect," Medor said, holding it up. "It also went to the Great Sanctuary."

De Vaux was the quickest thinker Thierry knew. "And so to Ambroise Villar?"

Both of the younger men nodded.

Medor said, "Thierry thinks there may be a way to use this, bring in the clerics, perhaps forestall a war?" He said *Thierry* this time. That was good.

De Vaux nodded. "I had the same thought. That soldier from Barratin needs to give a sworn statement."

"Before he's killed?" Thierry said.

"Before he's killed, yes."

"Perhaps they've arranged for it already," Medor said. "Giving a statement."

"Perhaps. The cleric who wrote this letter seems an intelligent man. But we're sending someone to take the details for us. I still have to leave with the army. And Medor, you'll need to order the city into full defence. Have it proclaimed."

"I know," said Medor. "What else?"

"In Orane? I'll leave that to you." He paused. "I'll set out in the morning. We'll want to pick our battlefield."

And with that, Thierry abruptly had another thought. A dark one. Although almost, he thought, poetic.

"I have an idea," he said. "If I may?" The two men looked at him, waiting. Waiting for *him*.

He cleared his throat and told them.

There was a silence.

"I admit I'm surprised, Villar," said Robbin de Vaux, finally.

"A battle is better? War is?" Thierry asked. But he felt deeply uneasy with what he'd just said.

"Not really. Perhaps not at all. Very well. Medor, set this in motion, too. Just in case. Use fast riders and horses. Choose a good place. Keep me posted."

He left them. To ready an army.

Thierry looked at Medor Colle. He felt shaken now. The presence of darkness, a shadow crossing the sun. "You all right?"

Medor nodded. "I'm less surprised than he was, Thierry." Using his name again. "It is a shrewd thought."

"That's the word we're using? Shrewd?" He really was unsettled, he realized. Who was he to be suggesting such things?

"May save many lives."

"Or none."

"We are supposed to know? Shall we ask my uncle? He won't know either. He'll say as much."

Thierry looked away and then back. "What should I do now?"

"Be where I can find you. I think . . . I haven't really had time to think, but if we do this, it may make sense for you to be there."

"Me?" He hadn't expected that.

"Yes. Work it through. When you have time. If any of us have enough time."

A dismissal, but not a cold one. But at the door Thierry took a breath and turned back.

"I need to say another thing," he said. Medor's expression from behind the desk quickly became remote, unreadable. Such a defended man, Thierry thought.

Another deep breath. This was difficult. He said, "Medor, whatever you do or are, I don't care. You are my friend. I said that at Chervaux."

A pause so long he thought there would be no answer. That he would walk out having ended any illusion of friendship.

Then, "That's the trouble, perhaps? That you don't care." Medor cleared his throat. "We should both attend to . . . I need to do many things right now."

Thierry turned again to go, then turned back a second time. He had begun this.

"I need to know. Or to ask. Can you still *accept* me as a friend? I will be loyal until death. I think . . . I think you know it."

Medor stared at him, unblinking. Then, after what seemed another terrifying interval, his slow smile returned.

"I can still use one of those," he said.

Thierry found himself able to breathe again.

"Good," he said. "Thank you."

"Can *you*?" asked the other man. "Can you still use a friend loyal until death?"

"Oh, Jad, yes!" said Thierry.

"Good," said Medor. "That's good. Now go. We will drink together when it is allowed. If we live."

But then he added one more thing, himself.

Fear and happiness could coexist in the world, Thierry thought, outside. However strange a truth that was.

"I think we might also want your father for this," the other man had said. "Please advise him. If this idea of yours comes to pass, it may also be about clerics and the god."

Bright sun above Orane as he walked, a beautiful late-summer's day, for all those living in that time and in that place.

CHAPTER XVII

"Have you been *ordered* to do this? Or are you choosing to, Thierry?"

Silvy's face. Fear, fury, some potent mixture of the two.

He said, "Love, I doubt they'd punish me if I said no. But I don't believe Medor would have asked if he didn't think there was cause."

"If he didn't think there was cause," Silvy mimicked. An attempt to sound sardonic. It fell flat; she was too distressed. "You *want* to be there, at whatever risk. You are . . . you are drunk on being so close to great events! Even if it kills you. And your father!"

He looked at her. At the woman he knew he loved and would always love now.

"Please don't say that. I don't think it's true. Silvy, if you ask me to decline, I will. I cannot speak for my father."

"Don't put this on me!"

They had quarrelled before, over the years, as friends do. This was different. They were more than friends. That enormous change in the world.

"You are right. I won't. I'm sorry." He meant it. But . . . Medor had suggested he *work this through*, and by now he had.

They were in the small garden at the back of The Lamb. He wondered if anyone could hear them. Hoped not.

He said, "It is not on you. It is me. I need to see through what began that night in winter. And then later, when Barratin tried to kill me."

"Ah! Give him another chance, you mean?"

"Silvy."

"Don't you *dare* say my name that way! Don't you dare!"

She had tears in her eyes. Of rage.

"Again, you are right. But I played a role at the start, and there maybe one for me now because of that. Or not at all. It may come to nothing, and I'll ride back here with my father while armies shape our lives with a war. This is . . . about trying to stop that."

"And Thierry Villar is *so* important in this!"

He almost said her name again, the same way as before, but did not.

He just said, "I don't think I'm important at all, but I have been asked to be there. I will not refuse. There is too much in this moment."

She opened her mouth for another sharp retort, and stopped.

She was thinking, *I may lose him. I may never see him again.*

There was an actual pain in her chest. She thought about how women saw their husbands, fathers, sons, grandsons go off to war, to fight and die, all the time. All the time. Without the faintest illusion they were important in events.

Her turn to draw a slow breath.

She said, "Go with Jad, then, my love. Come home to me."

He stepped forward to kiss her on the mouth and she kissed him back. There was salt. Her tears.

He went from her. A stop in their chamber to collect some gear, including his knife. His fearsome knife! Bold Thierry Villar, he thought, riding to war! His horse was in the stable of The Lamb. It was saddled and ready, he'd asked on the way. He mounted up. It would be a lie to say he was not afraid, and another to say it was not exciting. He didn't know how to sort those feelings out.

Silvy was completely unable to attend to her tasks in the morning. Eudes saw it. Told her she should go off for a bit. To a sanctuary, or anywhere else, he said. She looked at him, about to refuse, then had a thought. She asked him if he knew where a certain person lived. Eudes did. He knew a great deal about Orane.

She walked there. A fair distance, but she needed to be moving now.

"Ah," said Gauvard Colle when she was ushered into his sitting room. "I had a feeling someone would come. Was not sure who it might be. You are the woman from The Lamb. You were at Chervaux, as well."

"Yes," she said. She felt uneasy and defiant. They often went together for her. She added, "You know what is happening?"

"I know the army is moving out, and people we know are with them. What *will* happen, I do not know. But . . ."

Colle was such a strangely alluring figure, she thought. So hard to define or pin down. Tall, slender, long grey hair, delicate features, beautiful fingers.

"You are expected to say 'But what?' now." He smiled.

She shrugged. "I'm waiting," she said.

The smile deepened. It seemed a cold smile, but not a malicious one, she thought. But then, what did she know?

Gauvard said, "I have been asked by the queen to go east as well. Sometimes if I am physically near to people and events I can see them better. And . . . I *do* sometimes see your friend, the poet. Villar."

"Thierry? What? Why?"

"I don't know. We don't always know. I like him. He's a pretty man."

She had no idea how to respond to that.

Gauvard's expression grew serious. "They will be at risk. All of them. I can seldom do anything, but . . . Tell me, do you care for him?"

Silvy stared at him. "I do," she said. "Very much." Her voice was steady, she was glad of that.

"And I love my nephew. Do you want to come with me? I am being offered a carriage. There will be room. I likely have no role, *they* likely have no role, except for my nephew if there is war, but that will be back here in Orane."

"So why bring me?" Silvy said.

"I like you," said Gauvard Colle. And smiled.

They left that afternoon.

They were behind the army, but caught up to it and passed it in their carriage, taking a side road around marching soldiers, and then another that led through vineyards in the sun back to the main road, ahead of the army and the dust of it.

His father was in one of the carriages behind the king's. Thierry rode beside it. Medor Colle was up front with de Vaux and the other leaders. Medor wasn't formally one of those, but de Vaux had appointed him a military officer before they set out.

Knowing who you could trust mattered, Thierry thought.

His principal feeling now was fear for his father. Ambroise was not really old, but his health was not strong, and he had not left Orane in years. Journeys in the heat of summer were not good for anyone.

And he was only with them because his adopted son had offered his name as someone who could replace Hutin Peyre when the high cleric was disgraced and exiled. If anything now happened to him, for any reason, it could properly be judged Thierry's fault, and he'd never forgive himself.

The possibility terrified him. Especially because it had *also* been his suggestion, to the constable and the provost, that they might try a certain thing to avoid this war. That was also why he was here himself, without any clear role—except that Medor had had a thought of his own.

Thierry reminded himself that the alternative—their likely future—was war. His absurd suggestion was better, wasn't it? *Wasn't it?*

Had to be, he told himself again, but with bone-deep uncertainty.

The Duke de Barratin was brought word from his advance scouts that two riders were approaching from the west in the livery of the royal family and carrying a banner of parley.

They had been riding hard, a scout added. Their horses were exhausted, and the riders were sweat-stained and weary. It was late afternoon, another hot day, near to the time he'd call a halt. Barratin did so. Told them to have Roch's envoys given food and drink before they were brought before him.

There were courtesies to be observed, even if you were headed towards war, with an intent to kill a king.

They were presented to him in due course. With proper deference, they knelt.

"Speak," he said. "What are you charged to say?"

They told him.

He hadn't expected this, but it wasn't a complete surprise. No military leader, no duke, no king *wanted* a battle. You could win, lose, or win at such a cost it amounted to losing—and so many different things went into which it was.

Even the *weather* could destroy you. Or save you. Better, if there were any pathways, to find a way around a looming battlefield. If there were not . . . well, he would fight, and expect to win.

"Where?" he said. Giving nothing away. He was good at that, when not provoked to rage.

They told him, and how they proposed the location be prepared. The place was a few days ahead for an army marching, rather less for men on horseback or with carts. The envoys suggested how matters might be arranged, handed van Aribert an envelope under royal seal.

"It is in writing here," one of them said. He looked respectful, but not as afraid to be here as Barratin would have liked.

It seemed proper to him, this proposal of a parley. He'd have to decide, as he headed towards it, what he'd do if the king *did*— however belatedly—welcome him back to the council.

"I agree," he said finally.

He could have consulted with his courtiers, but other than Burkard van Aribert's there were no opinions he genuinely valued. Not a good thing for a leader, but it was a truth. A thing he'd need to address when time allowed, he thought.

"Wait," he added. "I assume the king will be there? Not just a representative?"

"Yes, my lord," one of the envoys said. "That is his desire and intent."

"Good," said Laurent de Barratin.

It *was* good. He wanted to see his cousin Roch in this alleged recovery from madness. Assessing that mattered.

"We will be there in three days, perhaps four. We will send the proper people ahead, to help prepare this meeting place. You may tell the king. You will be given food and drink and fresh horses. May Jad," he added, "be with us all, and Ferrieres."

"Yes, my lord," the lead envoy said, and made the sign of the sun disk.

Laurent de Barratin did the same. He ought to have done it first, he thought.

The two men were escorted away. They would not linger. Time mattered now.

This proposal was a new thing, Barratin thought again, but it might work very well for him.

He looked over at van Aribert, who nodded briskly. "I will arrange the necessary craftsmen and supplies, and an escort for them," he said.

"Yes. And select good men to be part of the ten we'll bring in. You, me, my son, seven others.

A sudden notion, about bringing the boy, but it felt a good thought. Guiart had much to learn, and the presence of his son would show good faith. Roch, who was clever, might even intend to bring the prince. Both of them in the one place? A temptation.

He teased the matter in his mind through the evening, working out, as over a game board, what he most wanted, what might be next best, what he would accept if offered. He watched the two moons rise, waxing towards full, and the progression of his thoughts seemed good to him.

They continued west in the morning. The supplies and craftsmen had gone ahead, with wagons, before sunrise and the morning rites.

—

Every army travels with a substantial supply of wood. You couldn't always find enough for what you needed, depending on where you were. It was needed for cooking fires, and for warmth in evenings if a campaign extended into autumn. Cut planks were for scaffolds if formal executions were required, or for a burning you wanted people to see, as it had served for this Maiden who had somehow restored the king. Planks were required to help carts, wagons, carriages through muddy or sodden roads, or rivulets, for bracing or repairing siege engines or towers. And you needed carpenters and woodcutters to handle all this, and more.

He had the wood, and the carpenters. He'd never marched along this road leading an army against Orane before, but he'd campaigned often, with his father at first (as Guiart was doing now), and then against insurrections within his own cities, and dangerously ambitious forces to the south and east.

You learned in the field, and you kept people around you who knew what was necessary. Sometimes you learned because of the *absence* of what you needed, and those lessons, if they didn't kill you, never went away.

The meeting that took place at the ancient river crossing, an arched stone bridge along a road that had been used for well past a thousand years, became known as the Encounter at the Aven.

The bridge had seen much, the river even more, of course. This became another moment among many. Time can stretch back a long way in some places, and much is lost, forgotten.

Wait long enough, most things are.

Carpenters for both sides had indeed arrived ahead, greeted each other, consulted, and accomplished their assigned tasks. Each end of the bridge now had a wooden barricade, almost twice the height of a man, closing it in. A canopy had been contrived overhead, using cloth from tents, affixed to the barriers at each end and to poles lashed to the bridge at intervals. It was summer and very hot, the shade would help. They had decided, after discussions, not to affix barriers along the sides of the bridge. That would enclose the space too much and make it unbearably warm within, it had been judged by the craftsmen. Also, it would have been difficult to do.

The constable of Ferrieres and Count Burkard van Aribert, who occupied that same office for the duke, were advised by their carpenters, when they approached, that they should ensure no one was on the river or along its banks in arrow range. It would be a challenging bowshot, but they deemed it important (for their own well-being, in part) to let people of rank know it might be tried.

This advice was noted, but even with the two armies agreeing to stay well back, it would be difficult to enforce. Archers assigned to guard against an assassin could also *be* assassins, after all. A risk embedded in what was happening.

There were many.

It was, people would remember after, a very bright morning when two groups of men approached the bridge from opposite ends. It was not yet as hot as it would be later. It was windy, which served as a defence of sorts against bowmen, along with the close proximity of all those who would assemble on the bridge.

The Aven was narrow here. It flowed swiftly northeast, a long way yet from the sea. It would widen and slow as it went. It was bright-blue now in the early sun, with flashes of white. Quite beautiful, in fact.

Ten men were in each party, by agreement.

The king of Ferrieres would not—would *never*—not carry his royal sword at such a time as this, so the duke of Barratin was permitted to carry his as well. Those with them were to be unarmed. This agreement was not, in the event, entirely acceded to. Fear can lead to that. So can other things.

Beside the bridge, looking down into the river in the sunlight, young Guiart de Barratin cried out in delight, and to the duke his father he said, "There are pike in the water! I see one! Can we fish for them after?"

"Unlikely," the duke said. "We don't have equipment, in any case."

His son looked bemused. "I know how to fashion a fishing pole, Father! It isn't hard."

Laurent de Barratin thought: *I really don't know this boy.* Life hadn't allowed him many chances. Or he hadn't chosen to take them. He resolved, again, to remedy this. He had memories, some of them affectionate, of his own father from when he was young.

"Unlikely," he repeated. "But with Jad's grace, we will find a time and place for you to fish back home this autumn, and I will join you. Now come. The bridge is waiting. Watch everything. Listen to everything."

Both parties approached, and then waited. The new wooden gates, hinges expertly placed by skilled men, were opened at each end. Twenty men, or rather nineteen men and a fourteen-year-old boy, passed through. The gates were closed. The Encounter at the Aven began, though some might say it had begun long ago.

A distance off, beyond bowshot, but with a clear view along the river of the bridge and those walking onto it, Gauvard Colle and Silvy Gautier stood by their carriage, alongside a dirt road that had led them, again, through vineyards.

"Dear Jad," one of them said softly, seeing the wooden gates close.

It was Colle who had invoked the god, unusual for him. The woman was silent. And then she saw Thierry and knew him (she thought, *I will always know him*) among those entering with the king and now standing behind him.

He can die here, she thought. It was strange, how you could become aware of the beating of your heart.

Those on the bridge were now sequestered inside. They were covered by the tent cloths overhead, artfully achieved, though they flapped a little in the breeze. There was a silence among those gathered. The king spoke first, as was proper.

"My constable is armed, cousin. I see one of your own company is, as well."

"I assumed the constable would be, and van Aribert is simply balancing that scale," said the duke.

"Balancing," the king murmured.

If you wanted to, you could hear a sardonic note in his voice. He was tall and fair-haired and composed.

The wind whipped at the cloths above them, they could feel it on their faces, from the north.

"Why are we here, Roch?" said Laurent de Barratin. Only the king's name. No salutation. The absence of one could not be missed. He stood, rigid and attentive. He was thinking: *He is not mad. He is as I remember him.* It was unsettling.

Everyone was so motionless, Thierry Villar thought. It was as if they were already figures in some future painting. He was terrified, trying not to show it. Probably failing in that. He had caused this gathering to happen. He stole a quick glance at his father. Ambroise stood tall and expressionless. Waiting.

"You have not knelt, cousin," said the king of Ferrieres, quietly. "Is there a reason for this discourtesy?"

Thierry swallowed hard. It had begun.

The duke's head snapped back briefly as if a blow had landed. He recovered quickly. He said, "Discourtesy, you say? You did not even reply to my entreaties. Was there a reason for that, cousin?"

Thierry couldn't see the king's face from where he stood, but his bearing did not change. Gravely, King Roch said, "They were not entreaties, Laurent. They were demands. We do not reply to demands. You do not make requests very well, you know, let alone entreaties, to use your word. Never have. From childhood. It is a flaw."

"*That* is how you choose to explain your conduct?"

A quick response. Perhaps too quick.

Another silence. Then the king again, "We will also explain not replying because you killed our brother, Laurent. Your cousin. Are you forgetting this? Somehow?"

The duke, narrow-faced, deep-set eyes, said, "I went to Rhodias. As requested. I did exactly what was asked of me, and received absolution there."

"Yes, there," said King Roch. "Does that mean forgiveness in Orane? In Ferrieres? In our family? We expect you to kneel and beg for that forgiveness, Laurent, before anything else can happen here."

The duke had reddened, Thierry saw. His face was not unreadable anymore.

"I have an army," he said.

"This has been noted, yes," said the king. "So do we. But there is still a murder to address."

And then.

And then the king of Ferrieres glanced over his shoulder at Thierry Villar. And by some process—to do with the king, or himself, or something he could not name—Thierry suddenly grasped why he was here. His task. He didn't know what Medor had sensed back in Orane, but . . . he had told Thierry he should come, and he had. He was on this bridge.

"Something is about to happen," Gauvard Colle said to Silvy, to himself, to the morning wind in a summer vineyard.

"Will he die now?" Silvy asked, and never knew why she'd said that, other than that it was her heart's fear, and sometimes you needed to speak that aloud.

Thierry stepped forward. And as he did so, he realized he wasn't afraid anymore. That he could do what needed to be done. And done by him *because* he was so inconsequential—and that, in itself, would be a provocation.

"You really do need to kneel before your king," he said, lifting his voice. His very good speaking voice. "And beg royal forgiveness for murdering his brother. Don't you understand why that is so? Rhodias has nothing to do with it."

He used no honorific. He had something to achieve here. A task.

There was a shocked silence. Then:

"And who the *fuck*, in the holy name of Jad, are you?" demanded the duke of Barratin.

"I'm a poet," Thierry said calmly. "We've met. In your palace in Orane. Then you sent men to kill me, too, remember? But you needn't kneel for that. I'm not important enough."

He saw recognition dawn, with memory.

"*Did* you do that, cousin?" asked the king. "Did you also try to kill this man?"

"He did, your grace," said Thierry Villar. "On the same day the duke of Montereau was chopped down in the street."

"I . . . This man invaded my home!" the duke exclaimed.

A mistake.

"Invaded?" said Thierry. "I did that? Was I very fearsome?" His tone offered mockery. He knew how to do that.

And . . . the king of Ferrieres laughed aloud. He laughed. That, Thierry thought, would lacerate the other man more than anything else. Which was the point now. Though he himself could die.

"I request permission to have this presumptuous fool executed," said Duke Laurent, proving that last thought true.

King Roch said, "Denied. We take this matter seriously, cousin. Among other things, this is also the man who destroyed your advocate's lies at the trial proceeding. You are . . . you are partial to murder, aren't you?"

It could be seen in Barratin's face, the rage rising in him.

"It seems to us," added the king, as if an amusing idea had just come to him, "that if we have a poet here, it would be shameful not to have a poem before we commence whatever formal discussion we are to have. After you kneel, of course. A verse to honour this encounter. Don't you think, cousin?" He turned to Thierry again. "You have improvised for us before, Thierry Villar. Pleasingly. Will you be good enough to do so again?"

"Oh, dear Jad. Right now!" said Gauvard Colle. "Send him all your strength. Do it now!"

"*What?*" said Silvy. "What do you mean? How do I do that?"

"You can see him. They are all right there. Do it, woman!"

"You bastard!" Silvy cried. "I have no idea—"

"You love him, and he needs whatever you have. Use it. Send it! It is why you are here!"

And so, understanding nothing at all, Silvy tried. She did try.

His death, Thierry thought, would be worthwhile if it somehow resolved this without a war, wouldn't it? Maybe the king had decided he was expendable? He could be given to Barratin, after whatever words he offered? Another . . . balancing?

He thought of Silvy. She was in his head. Always, but fiercely now. In the midst of this moment. He knew she loved him. He knew what she was. He knew he wanted to live with her, lie beside her through all the nights, all seasons, all years. Draw upon her strength. Share his. Be worthy of her. But also, also . . . be worthy of what the king now needed from him.

His father was just behind him. Thierry didn't look back.

It was as if, he thought, someone was scripting all their lines, writing them down, assigning them roles. He pictured a man, bearded, blue-eyed, no longer young, evoking them all, guiding what they were to say, and do. Shaping and telling their stories, perhaps with compassion, perhaps even with love.

A folly, a fancy. No time for such things now. If ever.

"As you wish, your grace," Thierry Villar said. "I have been known for improvising bequest poems. In taverns, mostly. But not only. Here is one for you."

He paused, for effect as much as for words, because he knew how this should begin, and what it needed to do. His task.

And looking straight at the duke, on that ancient bridge across the Aven River, he said, feeling strangely, unexpectedly strong:

> And for the Duke de Barratin in all his power
> What can a poet bequeath that he has not?
> Perhaps love and affection, for distaste and contempt?
> The affection he has never had? So let him be given
> A ring, dazzling, a splendid ruby, red as shed blood
> On snow, on moonlit ice in a wintry night.
> That all who see it can admire, and so, perhaps,
> Admire the man wearing it. Let him seek
> A reflected glory in that gift. But let him also know
> It is all the glory he will ever have: that blood red stone,
> Red as the heart's blood of the winter's dead.

Silence on the bridge after that. What could there be but silence? Thierry Villar thought. There wasn't going to be applause. The sound of his voice faded away. They could hear the wind, the murmur of the river rushing past below, the tent flaps above them, birdsong overhead.

"Roch," Duke Laurent said softly to his cousin the king, "whatever else, Roch, you must now let me kill him. This is too profound an insult. You know it. It cannot be endured."

And that was when the cleric Ambroise Villar, with immense dignity, stepped forward to stand beside his son. He said, "You do like killing people, do you not, my lord? As his grace the king said. You also sent a man to kill the senior cleric of a sanctuary east of here, didn't you? A holy cleric, my lord duke."

"I did not!" Barratin exclaimed, too loudly. "I just wanted him to be—"

"You wanted him dead," said Ambroise Villar, implacably. "You sent a soldier to do it. I can tell you we have sworn documents from the cleric and the soldier, both. These have also gone to Rhodias. But this is a matter, as well, for the clerics of Ferrieres."

"What? I am to endure this from a wrinkled fool in a yellow robe?"

"No," said King Roch. "From the man acting as high cleric of Orane, cousin. And we have seen the letters ourself. From the cleric you wanted to kill, and from the man you ordered to do it. You have just lied to us."

The king looked at Thierry. Again.

And so . . .

"Shall I offer another verse for you, my lord duke? About this? The attempt and then a coward's lie? What gift is worthy of such a nobleman? Give me but a moment, though, and I believe I can—"

He stopped. Because the duke of Barratin had drawn his sword and taken two steps towards him.

Two steps.

Three, and Thierry Villar would have been been dead on that bridge. The third step never happened. What takes place, what does not: so many forks and branches along the twisting roads of time, so many wheels of fate turning, turning, lifting and lowering, one person, another, into light, into darkness.

The dagger that struck Duke Laurent de Barratin in the eye—a dagger in a place where no such weapons were to be—was thrown, with considerable skill, by the provost of Orane, Medor Colle, stepping up beside the poet, beside his friend, the man he had said might need to be on the bridge.

But his was not the only forbidden blade there.

"*No!*" cried Gauvard Colle from down along the riverbank. "*Medor!*"

Silvy looked at him, a hand to her mouth. His delicate features seemed suddenly gaunt, ravaged. He shouted, "Make it not so!"

She saw him close his eyes. His hands clenched at his sides. He fell to his knees, facing the bridge downstream. Facing it blindly, she thought, with his eyes shut. But . . . perhaps not so. Perhaps another way of seeing?

She didn't know. She knew nothing. But she knelt on the summer earth beside him and placed an arm around his shoulders, holding him close to her. She heard him speak words. They were clear, but she did not understand them.

There was movement on the bridge. Shouting reached them, even as far away as they were.

It was not Burkard van Aribert who threw the blade at Medor Colle. It was another officer of the duke's army, stepping up. And he, too, was skilled. His own illicit knife was perfectly thrown to strike the provost in the heart and kill him there.

And yet it did not.

It should have. It was about to. Instead, it hit him in the left shoulder. It . . . it veered to the side in flight.

It did that. No man there could ever assert this for certain, but several thought it, thought so against their will. That they saw this happen, this impossibility. Never said so. Not one of them. Even Thierry, who was right there, and watched the dagger thrown, and who had perhaps the best view of it, never spoke a word about this.

On the bridge, the duke of Barratin was still upright, somehow. Was not yet dead, even with a knife in his eye.

"*Father!*" his son cried.

Barratin lifted his head. He swayed. "Do not kill the boy, cousin," he managed to say. "Do not do that, Roch!"

Before he was stabbed by a sword. From behind.

And this blow . . . this blow was inflicted by Count Burkard van Aribert, who thereby killed his lord, who had always trusted him.

Van Aribert immediately dropped his sword, bloodied as it was. The duke lay on the stones of the bridge, lifeless now. Medor Colle was on his knees not far away from him, a hand at the shoulder wherein another blade lay buried.

The king of Ferrieres, surrounded now by his officers, encircled by them, appeared to Thierry to be astonishingly at ease. How was that possible? he thought. Golden, preternaturally poised, King Roch said to Burkard van Aribert, "You did this why, my lord count?"

Van Aribert knelt before him. "Because there is no need for war now, your grace. There is no one to want it. And this killing can go against my name, no one else's."

Barratin's son, Thierry saw, was also kneeling now, beside his father's body, in the spreading of blood across the ancient stones. He had spoken of *blood red* in his poem a moment ago, he thought.

This was what had been intended, he knew. He *knew*. The king calling on him, twice. Provoking the duke to break the truce in his rage, his pride. A commoner addressing him with such contempt. They had—*he* had—acted to drive Barratin to a point where he could not kneel before the king and offer contrition. Could not. And so he had drawn his sword.

Lives saved, Thierry urgently told himself. So many lives might now be saved.

"You have not answered our question," said the king to the man who'd just killed Laurent de Barratin. A boy was beside his father, weeping as if he would never stop.

"He . . . he should not have ordered the cleric slain," said van Aribert. "And he did also direct that the soldier be killed, to hide it. It . . . was wrong."

"Ah. And killing his cousin? My brother? In the winter?"

"I was not there, your grace. The two of them were enemies from long before. And they . . . they were equals? That, I could leave to Jad."

"Not this?"

"Not this, your grace."

The king said, almost in sorrow, Thierry thought, "No one will ever trust you again, van Aribert. Your name will be accursed. Though you might have helped avert a war."

"I know this, your grace. I accept that fate. I would ask, if you are not now to execute me, that I be permitted to withdraw to a sanctuary of the god and take an oath of holy office among the clerics there."

"Where?" asked King Roch.

But they knew, they all knew. It was only a few days east of them, along this same road. A quiet, holy place.

Medor was all right. He could even ride. There were doctors with the army (more or less capable, but the best they had). They started back towards Orane that same day. There were hours of sunlight left.

They kept van Aribert with them, for his own safety. It was a certainty he'd be killed by someone in the Barratin army for what he'd done. He could find his sanctuary and a religious life later, King Roch decreed. And indeed, he did live, and he did do so, passing the rest of his days in piety, and contrition. This is also a thing that happens.

The boy travelled with them as well, Barratin's son. A hostage, but he was also a cousin, family. He was kindly treated. And there was also a likelihood, de Vaux told Thierry on the road, that he'd be safer in Orane than with his older brother who was now, as of this day, the duke of Barratin.

Thierry didn't know how that worked. It was a world that was alien to him.

Both armies had agreed to withdraw, west, east.

It was over, de Vaux said. For now, he said.

"You always have to say *for now*," the constable added. They were drinking wine at sunset where they had stopped for the night. "It is the way of Jad's world."

Thierry went to the tent where Medor was.

His friend (his friend) smiled. "I couldn't let him kill you," he said. "You were only on that bridge because of me."

"And everyone was on that bridge—"

"Because of you. I know. Aren't we powerful men?"

"Mighty in our strength," Thierry said. "But that makes it twice you have saved my life now."

"At least twice," Medor said. "You are a burdensome friend, it seems."

Thierry smiled at that. So did the other man.

"I . . . didn't know you had a knife on the bridge."

"And why would you know what weapons I carry?"

Thierry sighed. "Are you allowed wine?"

"I believe I am, and would like some urgently, even if not."

They drank together, saying little, saying much thereby.

Earlier, south of the bridge in the vineyard, kneeling near the river-bank, Silvy Gautier felt Gauvard Colle trembling, and she heard him weep, fighting for breath and control.

"What . . . what were the words you said?" she asked. "I heard them, but I didn't understand."

"I don't know," he said, a hollow whisper. "I don't remember any words. What did I say?"

"You said *Weaver at the Loom*," Silvy told him.

"I don't even know what that means!" Gauvard said. "Is he . . . did you see . . . is he all right?"

"He walked off the bridge with the others," Silvy said. "I saw it. I did. Truly."

She felt like weeping as well.

"I . . . don't know what that means," Gauvard Colle repeated. "Those words."

She held him for a long time, tenderly. Not knowing that tenderness wasn't a thing he'd experienced very much in his days, or not for a long time. Later, they also started back west, for Orane. For home.

The sun moved through that long, late-summer day, rising, setting. Wind, high clouds. The carpenters were the last to leave the river. They took down the barriers and the poles and the tent cloth covering they'd contrived. Then they also went back, with their carts and wood, the way they'd come, east or west, to rejoin their armies. They bade farewell to each other courteously, the shared respect of craftsmen who knew they'd done a job well.

And then there was no one left on that bridge, or beside it, and the body of the dead man was being carried home. There was still blood on the ancient stones. Rain would wash it away in due course. It had done that before. The moons, rising, shone down upon the arched bridge and the river, and the stars did. In the teachings of that time and place, Jad of the sun was in the darkness below, battling demons to protect his children, as he did every night since the world had been made, and remade, and remade.

EPILOGUE

A number of years after the events here recounted, when some of those present in this story were dead, some diminished, some exalted, but with most simply going about their lives, far from any importance or illusions of it, a ship approached the celebrated harbour of Sarantium, among a number of others doing so at the same time, as was almost always the case.

It had sailed from Seressa, that immensely wealthy city-state in Batiara, flourishing in part because of its trade to the east. Escorted by two war galleys down to the end of what was increasingly being named the Seressini Sea (which they liked and encouraged) against a growing threat of pirates, including those from a small, well-guarded city across the way in Sauradia, the merchant ship, laden with goods, had proceeded out into the Great Sea and then east, without incident, to the City of Cities.

Sarantium had borne that name for past a thousand years.

On board, standing at the prow, were four people who had paid for passage, sailing to Sarantium at the behest of the oldest of them, who had lived there when much younger, and had lately wished to see it again, ardently, and wanted them with him.

He did not say *before I die*, but the others knew he carried that thought, and it was present for each of them in their decision to join him for this journey.

The years had deepened affection among them, and permitted love.

Gauvard was weeping now, Silvy saw. He had become increasingly emotional from the time they'd come to stand here in the wind, before sunrise, waiting for the city to come into view. And now it had, with the light.

"*We cannot forget that beauty,*" Gauvard Colle whispered.

Thierry looked at him, then back at the glory growing nearer, brighter, with the god's sun behind all its domes, the water sparkling as with diamonds upon blue. The phrase was a quotation, he knew, from the older man's tone. He would ask about it later. He put a hand on his friend's shoulder, and simply looked and breathed. Salt air and glory. He thought he saw dolphins. He never had, before.

Orane was his love, always would be, but this . . . this was splendour and richness, gold and silver, and awareness of time and loss. Another half a dozen passengers had by now come to the prow. The four of them stayed close to each other.

"You did not lie, uncle," said Medor.

"We are not even there yet," Gauvard said softly, scarcely audible in the sea wind. "And you must try to imagine it a thousand years ago in its majesty, the Great Sanctuary newly risen, the Hippodrome we can see beside it flourishing, not a ruin. Imagine . . . picture in your mind fifty thousand people, and the emperor, cheering for the chariots."

"I can't," Silvy said. "It is beyond me."

"This city is beyond all of us," Gauvard said. He wiped at his eyes. "I cannot say how happy I am to be back."

This was not a person, whether man or woman, who spoke of happiness, Silvy thought. They had grown close, beginning with a moment by a riverbank years ago. She laid her head against Gauvard's shoulder and watched Sarantium come to them.

There were, even after decades, people who remembered Gauvard Colle. Some knew him as a person who could access the half-world, and that was important here, Thierry came to realize. Others recalled him in different ways: sensuous, adventurous. Gauvard had had lovers here, men and women, and some who slipped between the two, as he did. One, who had been more than merely a lover, was recently dead, they learned.

It had been a long time since he'd been here. People leave us. We leave them. Thierry's mother and father had died two years before, within months of each other. He would not have come east had they still been alive.

People Gauvard knew gladly helped them find a house in a district not far from the imperial palaces. Not the best neighbourhood, not the worst. You could, Thierry learned, buy many different things here, including varieties of love, if desired.

His friend Medor, who had taken leave from his position as provost of Orane, handing that role to Aubrey, was hesitant at first to explore the city and its people. He was by far the most anxious of the four of them here. But one night, over a dinner of lampreys and fresh-caught fish on the terrace of a tavern by the port, he stood abruptly when the meal was done and walked out with another customer who had been looking at him—a tall man, younger than Medor, but not so much younger—and his life changed.

He was freed in that city to be what he could not be in Orane. And that tall man, a merchant from Batiara, Tazio di Cenna, became the partner, the companion, Medor Colle had never had in his life—and remained so. Remained. We can be given such gifts sometimes, if we are deeply fortunate.

Thierry Villar wrote there, from the start, steadily. Many of the poems were about Orane. They became, for a number of readers (and scholars, afterwards) his defining works, those poems from his Sarantium years. This happens often in art: being away from a loved place brings it more vividly to us. The need to evoke, recapture—images, feelings, memories. He flourished in Sarantium, remembering home.

Silvy Gautier, walking alone one morning, stopped by the open doorway of a small workshop and stepped inside to see what was happening there. They were crafting mosaics.

They greeted her courteously (not always a thing that happened in a city notorious for arrogance). They let her observe quietly and then, as she kept coming back, they undertook to teach her some of their craft. She became an apprentice, initially cleaning and sweeping and sorting tesserae, but, after an interval, she was allowed to handle and place background stones herself, for pieces that would go into the homes of the wealthy.

Most of these would be destroyed when the city fell.

She came to know the pleasure of *making*, day after day, adding that to the joy of being with her love, and being loved.

They never had a child, she and Thierry. Physicians consulted (another reason they had come east) included a grave Kindath with a long grey beard. Remedies were proposed and tried.

They never had a child. Sorrow will be present among joys. Our lives are made that way.

They had intended to come for a visit and sail home. They stayed for years, all four of them. Gauvard Colle died peacefully there— friends by his deathbed, not only the three of them. He went to whatever he believed in, content with his life, at ease with mystery. He was laid to rest, by virtue of the intercession of a friend of rank at court, in a corner of Valerius's Great Sanctuary of Jad's Holy Wisdom, under one of the smaller domes.

Silvy, still young, died only a year after that.

A fever took her, seemingly out of nowhere. No plague was in the city, but her fever did not abate and she was gone the third night, like a tide receding before morning came.

Thierry was lost, broken, a shadow, alive but moving unseeing through whatever light there was for others in the world. Medor spoke to his uncle's friend at court, and for love of Gauvard, and memory of him, Silvy Gautier of Ferrieres was buried beside him. They had come to love each other, after the riverbank.

Only their names were on their grave markers, set flat in the marble floor. They are still there, despite all the changes in the world.

Thierry stopped writing in that time. He felt emptied out, owned by sorrow. Aware of the good fortune that had been his life, but unable to reclaim a sense of that.

One day, making himself walk abroad, as another spring came to the City of Cities, he decided to do what Silvy had done, because she had done it. He went to the artisans' quarter and stood in different doorways, watching craftsmen at work. He *had* a craft, he was a poet, but he couldn't yet access that again.

Instead, he took employment at a shop that made toys for children. Small birds, of different metals and wood and leather. Their heads moved, and with some their wings also did, wonderfully. They were painstakingly made, objects of beauty and craft, much loved by the children of the city.

Thierry was told that in legend there had been a sorcerer, or more than one, who had been able to capture souls in birds like this, and that they could speak. He didn't believe that, but he liked the idea of souls in mechanical birds, and he had been close enough to the half-world because of Gauvard to know that things were possible that one might never credit.

He did, once, on a summer night, see one of the blue fires moving—dancing—in a laneway near the Great Sanctuary. The city had been known for these long ago. They'd become rarer and rarer, he'd been told. But he saw one. He was allowed that.

He made the decision to go home the next morning. It felt, finally, to be time. He told Medor that same day.

So Thierry Villar left Sarantium some years before it fell, though the first hints of danger had begun arriving. He had dreamed of Orane many nights, in a city that instilled a habit of dreaming in people living among ruins of greatness. He began to remember his dreams. You could, some said, dream away your life here. He went to where Silvy was buried, and Gauvard, and he wept for what was lost, as we do. As we must, if we have loved. Then he left.

Medor Colle remained in Sarantium, in the east, building a life there, allowing himself, belatedly, joy. Much later, at a great age, but still strikingly vigorous, he died on the walls beside the last emperor, wielding a sword for Jad and the City of Cities, fighting at the end next to two other men, both from Batiara, a soldier and a cleric. Fighting for the golden city, where he had found acceptance for what he was, and acceptance of himself thereby.

Thierry left his ship at Seressa, and stayed for an interval there this time. He had nothing, he realized, to hurry back towards. He travelled to cities and towns nearby, including a visit to Varena and the mosaics there, because Silvy had told him her family was from that place, and she had come to love mosaics, and because Gauvard had wanted him to see these. They moved him, unexpectedly, to tears.

He dearly wished he knew the name of the artist who had made the two facing-each-other images of Sarantine courts a thousand years ago. The faces and the craftsmanship haunted him. He stood there and looked, and felt he couldn't leave, couldn't stop looking. No one would ever know who made them, he thought. It was a grief. But they were here, he told himself. They could still be seen. There was that.

Eventually, when the weather allowed, he joined a party and went overland through the mountain passes back to Orane, the city he had never stopped loving all his days.

And there he remained, with only short journeys two or three times a year to the country château of his last dear friend, also a poet, where she mostly lived, some days' ride west of the city, north of the Livraise River.

He had a son who had grown up very near there, on one of the closest estates, in fact, but he never knew that. What we know, what we don't know. The stories we tell, the stories we cannot.

And so, finally, at this leaving and this end, is truth, among all the interwoven tales: I knew love, had true friends, may have done good in the world in a time that threatened war. And I wrote some poems. I did that. I did that.

ACKNOWLEDGEMENTS

Poetry guided me towards a book once before, the great Tang Dynasty poets leading to *Under Heaven* years ago. So it isn't a new thing for me that François Villon is a major part of the origin story here. And his most celebrated line, "*Ou sont les neiges d'antan,*" is likely embedded in my instinctively starting in the depths of a winter. The snows of yesteryear, indeed. Villon's tendency to write mocking bequests in verse is also here, of course. Writing is not usually "fun" for me, but riffing on those poems was. Two of the books that offered renderings of the poems and helped unpack the (scanty) information we have about his life were *Danse Macabre* by Aubrey Burl and *Poems: François Villon* by David Georgi. There are others, but the details of his life remain sketchy.

And, yes, there's an echo of Christine de Pizan in this novel, too. Poets, what can I say?

Another part of the inception here was reading *Blood Royal*, by Eric Jager: a recounting of the assassination of the Duc d'Orléans in Paris—and the chasing down of who was behind it, amid the chaos of the Hundred Years' War. The book is a *bit* of a bait and switch, as it needed to segue from that investigation to a more general history of the time, but was of real use and inspiration.

I never knew it, but it seems I might have had a desire to "save" Joan of Arc, though those who have read me before know how much the notion that doing so might exact a price (on someone else, often) is a part of how I think and write. I also took the opportunity afforded to reverse the victory of Henry V at Agincourt. I hope I am forgiven, perhaps even indulged.

On Burgundy and the Burgundian dukes—especially, of course, John the Fearless, who inspired my Laurent de Barratin—I was very much taken by Bart van Loo's *The Burgundians*. It is (and he notes it himself a few times) a very much "on their side" book, written with flair and wit. Alternative takes and readings of people and events can be found elsewhere, easily.

I recommend (if you have a birthday coming up?) the newest edition of Johan Huizinga's masterwork, which I reread for this novel. This version uses *Autumntide of the Middle Ages* as its translation of the title. It is a sumptuously presented and illustrated rendering of a classic. I also reread the relevant volume of *A History of Private Life*, edited by the great Georges Duby, and a few works I admire on daily life at the time. Chiara Frugoni's books on this, for example, are useful and entertaining, both.

Turning from books to people, I actually regard it as a good, reassuring thing that many of my own "usual suspects" remain in my life to sustain and support me, along with a few new people. Lara Hinchberger and Jessica Wade were quick and thoughtful in their notes and attention to detail. Catherine Marjoribanks, our copy editor, informed me that this was our *eleventh* time working together, and copy editors know these things. That tells its tale of affinity, and my appreciation. My agents, John Silbersack and Jonny Geller, in New York and London, are trusted friends as well as professional associates, in both cases for many years now. This has been reassuring and rewarding, both.

I cannot here name and salute all the editors who have acquired and then shepherded my work into their languages but it feels past time to now express how much I value their doing so, and how much pleasure I take from seeing my books well presented in other countries and cultures. It remains one of the pleasures and rewards of what seems to have become a long career. If I single out Apriori, my Ukrainian house, and their gorgeously, bravely done editions in the midst of war, I hope it will be understood.

The internet and how people get their information has changed greatly but www.brightweavings.com remains my authorized site, with a great deal of information on it (some of it funny). It exists because of the initiative of Deborah Meghnagi twenty-five years ago, as I type these words, and it has been sustained by the attentiveness and the care of Alec Lynch. My appreciation for both is ongoing. Martin Springett has again done a map for one of my books. His art and his friendship, both, remain vivid for me.

Is it strange to thank one's readers around the world? It doesn't feel so. I have had a more-than-forty-years career of shaping novels. I have been *allowed* to do this, been able to take time in doing each one—a rare, even an astonishing gift in today's book world—because people keep finding them, and urging them on others. Calling it a gift feels right.

My brother Rex is always my first reader, bringing focused intelligence to that, and a generous understanding of what I try to do in my work (in the books as a whole, and in each one individually). He knows my appreciation.

This will be the first of my novels that my mother doesn't read. I feel that deeply. My parents—lovers of books, bonding over them on their first date, even—are remembered, always, with my love and gratitude, and now with a redoubled sense of loss and absence.

My wife and my sons carry the dedication to *Written on the Dark*. I have named them before in dedicating novels. It feels entirely right to do so again.